Full Moon Friday

To Bethany!
Enjoy!
Sue Merrell

SUE MERRELL

Jordan Daily News Mysteries:
Great News Town (2011)
One Shoe Off (2012)
Full Moon Friday (2014)

Also by Sue Merrell:
Laughing for a Living (2010)

http://suemerrellbooks.com

DEDICATION

For "All the lonely people.
Where do they all come from?"

— *From "Eleanor Rigby" by The Beatles*

ACKNOWLEDGMENTS

Although *Full Moon Friday* is a work of fiction, many of the incidents in this book were inspired by the experiences of journalists, nurses, cops, and other professionals. I'd like to recognize the contributions of Terry DeBoer , Teri Holtslander, Timothy Otterbein, Roderick Kelly, Tom Rademacher, Kym Reinstadler, Mary Kay Williams, and Sue Willison

I'd also like to thank the talented team that worked with me on *Full Moon Friday* including my editor Jane Haradine, my graphic designer Ryan Wallace, my writing coaches Roe Van Fossen and Martha Robach, and all my first readers at Peninsula Writers.

I'm sure there are many others I have failed to mention who suggested full moon tales or creative curse words. My apologies. Blame it on the moon.

Jordan Daily News Staff

Becky Judd, 31 —tall, thin black reporter with a passion for justice
Dick Stone—Sports editor
Donna— intern
Duke (Ormand Dukakis), 44—reporter, columnist, and recovering alcoholic
Hammond Reginald— managing editor
Helen—the receptionist
William "Hoss" Peyton, 52—hefty copy desk chief
Josie Braun, 38—petite city editor nicknamed Peter Pan
Mack Stanton, 65—distinguished perfectionist photographer
Nick, 30—baseball loving, heart-breakingly handsome assistant city editor
Page (Stanley Pageniewski)—the quiet, giant photographer
Phil—copy editor
Rudy Randolph—education reporter, former day-care director
Sis—Librarian

Rest of the characters

Amy Stillman—emergency room charge nurse
Andy Barton—principal at Westside Elementary
Bill—Zach's assistant
Brad Snyder—executive director of the A-Lab
Brittany Davidson—Nick's wife and emergency nurse
Carolyn Cantrell—Tom's mother, junior college theater director
Chet Sanders—Cade County Deputy
Claude Dixon—apparent shooting victim at Holiday Quad
Cord McCoy—bodyguard for Dee Licious
Don Miller—Cade County Chief Deputy
Dee Licious—Rock star with movie role
Fred Wheeler—Justice Department agent
Gail Bulosi – school secretary
Greg Garrett –husband of Polly, Josie's neighbor
Henri Baptista—A-Lab scientist from Samoa
Jennifer Dukakis, 18—daughter of Duke and Sharon
Kevin Walsh, 10— son of Josie Braun and Kurt Walsh
Kurt Walsh—Josie's ex-husband, head of Downtown Development Board
Linda Cantrell—Tom's sister who has Down Syndrome
Margaret Hinkle—senile elderly woman
Michele Ames – shooting victim at Holiday Quad
Neal Taylor, 67—former WWII prisoner of war who's having flashbacks

Peter Hampton —pick-pocket with blood phobia
Petra Oligivich—Russian scientist at A-Lab
Polly Garrett—Josie's neighbor, mother of Timmy
Reuben Jetter —community crackpot known for Elvis sightings
Samuel Gilbert —A-Lab scientist from New Zealand
Samuel Kent – federal agent
Sharon Dukakis—Duke's wife
Stan Barrows—bridge tender who loves musicals
Theodore Sanders—Cade County deputy
Timmy Garrett—Kevin's best friend
Tom Cantrell—homicide detective for Jordan City Police
Zach Teasdale, Cade County Coroner and wealthy businessman

Friday
February 13
1987

12:07 AM

Bridge bells began clanging a few minutes after midnight. Traffic was light in downtown Jordan at that hour, but one by one the red-and-white striped gates came down on the five streets that crossed the Illinois Waterway: Cole, Rose, Jackson, Pike, and Emerson. The drawbridges were Jordan's trademark, saluting river barges day and night.

Bridge tender Stan Barrows was perched on a stool at the controls of the Rose Street Bridge, singing along with the insistent bell.

"Clang, clang, clang went the trolley. Ding, ding, ding went the bell. Zing, zing, zing went my heartstrings ..."

A beefy black man with a barrel chest, Stan bellowed the words in a deep baritone that shook the windows. He added broad, dramatic gestures, as if he were performing in a musical about a lonely bridge tender. But there was no one to see his performance. His control room was a narrow second-story room. Windows wrapped around the river side of the building, giving him a good view up and down the Des Plaines River. His control panel was underneath the windows, looking much more high tech than the clunky blue-painted steel of the fifty-year-old bridge.

He looked down as the gate slowly moved into place. Two cars were stopped on the bridge approach. Rose was a one-way westbound street, so no cars were coming from the other side of the river. Stan watched as the gate swung down on the other side. The bridge wouldn't move until both gates were all the way down.

He glanced upriver to the Cole Street Bridge. It was starting to open. The moon was full, and a ribbon of white danced on the water as if the river were electrified. He paused to admire the sight. That must have been when the kids ran out onto his bridge.

"Come on, it will be fun," Eric Thomas said, grabbing the girl's hand.

"It sounds dangerous," Jennifer Dukakis replied, pulling her hand away.

She was smiling, so Eric repeated his invitation. "Come on. I've ridden the bridge lots of times. It's easy. I'll show you."

Jennifer hesitated only a second and then allowed herself to be pulled past the gate. She was eighteen now. Breaking a few rules seemed like a good way to exert her independence. Grab the gusto in life.

The pedestrian concrete sidewalk became a wooden plank path on the metal bridge. The deck of the bridge was made of open steel grating. Heavy

1

girders lined either side of the roadway, keeping cars and trucks from the pedestrians. An ornate metal fence, painted the same light blue as the bridge, ran along the outer edge. The dual railings turned the walkway into a walled corridor, partially hidden from the bridge tender.

To avoid detection, Jennifer followed Eric's example and ducked her head as they ran out onto the bridge. The wood echoed a hollow slapping sound as they ran down the walkway, but it could barely be heard over the insistent clanging of the bell.

"Stop here and hold on," Eric said, falling to his knees before they got halfway across. "Get down so they don't see you."

Jennifer dropped beside him and looked through the diamond design of the ironwork at the river below. A large white moon shone right down on the river route.

"It's beautiful," she said.

"You just wait," Eric said. Tilting his head toward her, he was about to give her a kiss when the wooden floor they were sitting on jerked. The bridge was opening.

"Oh, my God," Jennifer said, ducking her head into Eric's shoulder. Her pretty pink ski jacket already had a smear of road grime from the bridge floor, but she ignored it. Her long blond-streaked hair furled across her collar and onto the navy blue of Eric's wool coat. Grinning, he put his arm around her and grabbed onto the railing just beyond her, locking them in place.

"Hold on," he said, clutching the crossbar in front of them with his other hand. Jennifer mirrored his hand holds as the angle of the floor beneath them became steeper.

"I'm slipping!" she screamed.

"Plant your feet against the rail like this," Eric said.

The bridge was almost vertical when it stopped. The teens had wedged their bodies between the railings, their young muscles holding firm.

"Oh, the river is fabulous from up here," Jennifer said. "And the moon is like right there!"

"I told you it was worth it," Eric said, beaming.

With the bridge in the up position, the riders were now visible to Stan.

How the hell did they get up there? he wondered. He looked upriver. A tug was pushing four barges of coal and iron through the Cole Street Bridge. There wasn't time to bring the Rose Street Bridge down and nab the riders. They'd probably run off on the other side anyway.

"This isn't some stupid carnival ride!" Stan yelled, though he knew the trespassers couldn't hear anything over the bell. The tug with its train of barges was coming closer at about eight miles an hour. The riders were going to get pretty tired of holding on. *Serves them right*, Stan thought. *Full moon brings out the crazies.*

2

As he watched, he figured out the young people were a couple, a boy and a girl, hugging and kissing while holding on to dirty, cold steel high over the river.

"You're some kinda Romeo, buddy boy," Stan mumbled. "What's wrong with parked cars? Ya gotta spice up your love life by hanging off a bridge? Well, this is the last time you'll ride my bridge, I can tell you that!"

Stan dialed the police station, which was just around the corner.

"A couple of high school kids snuck through the gate and went up with the Rose Street Bridge."

"East bank or west bank?" the dispatcher asked.

"East now, but when the bridge comes down, they could run the other way."

"Hold the traffic after you're down. I'll send a car to the west end," the dispatcher promised.

Stan stood up and looked down. Four cars waiting. The barges were moving under the bridge now. The moon was so bright he could pick out the tugboat captain and his crew, waving as they moved through. When the tug and barges were well past, he squeezed the lever to lower the bridge. The old steel framework groaned and jerked, dropped a few feet, then stopped. Red lights were flashing on the control panel.

"Dang it," Stan said. He opened the door under the panel, checked the connections, moved a couple of levers. The bridge didn't budge. He called the police number again.

"I'm the one who called about the kids on the bridge."

"Are they okay?" the dispatcher asked.

"I think so. But the bridge isn't. Big blue monster is stuck. Brake relay switch, I think. Won't get fixed 'til morning. Might need some help getting the riders down."

"On the way."

Stan ran down the stairs to the street level. He yelled at the four drivers and waved them toward the Cole Street Bridge. Then he went around the huge concrete counterweight that balanced the bridge. Street lights illuminated the pavement, but the raised portion was dark except for a few red hazard lights. He shined his flashlight up the walkway.

"You done it now, you loony lovers!" Stan yelled. "You broke my bridge! It won't budge!"

The bridge had started down a little. The wooden walkway was still at about a sixty-degree angle, like a bizarre slide from a Jules Verne playground. Stan figured the riders could slide down the walkway fairly safely, but the slide ended about six feet off the ground. Below was a gap big enough for a person to fall right through into the river.

"Just hold on! Help is coming!" Stan yelled up the walkway. "Stupid kids," he mumbled as he ran back into the control house. He returned with a

3

big black safety net they used under workmen. In his other hand he had a long grappling hook. A police car pulled up to the gate and two officers joined Stan and looked up the walkway.

"Holy hell," one of the officers said. "They sure picked the wrong night to go bridge riding."

"And the wrong bridge," Stan said as he connected the net across the end of the raised walkway. After a few maneuvers the S-hook slipped into place, and Stan started working on the remaining loose corner. They could hear the girl crying now and the boy trying to comfort her.

"Just hang in there," Stan called up. "We'll get you down."

"I'm slipping! I'm slipping!" the girl wailed.

"Is there another way up there?" the policeman asked, looking around the massive steel girders lined with rivets.

"Yeah, I can go out on the catwalk, but I need to secure the net first in case they slip," Stan said.

A scream and clatter above snatched everyone's attention. The girl lost her hold and slipped down a few feet. Stan and the officers could see shadowy movement. Something whooshed down the walkway and struck the corner of the net Stan was trying to secure.

"Damn," Stan exclaimed as a large leather purse pulled the net off the grappling hook, bounced off the concrete, and fell into the river below with an almost soundless *plunk*.

The girl was still wailing.

"I got her!" the boy yelled. "We're OK."

"Stupid kids," Stan mumbled as he reached the grappling hook over his head and tried to snag the corner of the net that was flapping in the dark. "Shine that flashlight over here," he told the policeman. "I want these kids arrested. Call their parents. This is dangerous shit. Somebody's going to get hurt."

Once the net was in place, Stan told the officers he could climb up the girders to rescue them, but the riders should be able to slowly work their way down the walkway. "You can slide on your butts!" Stan shouted. "You'll get dirty as a chimney sweep, but you'll survive."

"Just hold onto the railing and go slow," one of the policemen said.

Stan scurried up a ladder to a catwalk. The narrow metal walkway was intended to provide maintenance access, but it ended close enough to the raised section of bridge that a person could step across. "You want me to come up there?"

"No, we're coming," the boy said.

The two scooted along the rough wooden walkway toboggan-style, holding onto the banister supports to slow their descent. When they neared the catwalk, Stan reached for the sobbing girl. She grabbed his arms and

4

leaped across the space. Her sudden movement caught the boy off guard. He slid down the walkway and fell into the net.

By the time Stan had guided Jennifer along the catwalk and down the ladder to the pavement, the police officers had pulled Eric down from the net.

☼

The phone awakened Ormand "Duke" Dukakis at a quarter to one in the morning. An investigative reporter for the *Jordan Daily News*, he was accustomed to getting tips from helpful police officers in the middle of the night.

"Yeah," he barked groggily into the receiver.

"Hey, I know your daughter's eighteen now, and I shouldn't be calling you, but if it was my daughter, I would want to know."

Duke bolted upright.

"Where is she? Is she OK?"

As the policeman explained the situation, Duke's wife, Sharon, awakened enough to suspect the call was about their daughter.

"What is it? Tell me."

Duke waved a silencing hand to his wife.

"OK, I'll be right down."

Duke slipped out of bed and headed to the bathroom.

"What is it?" Sharon asked, following behind him.

"Crazy crapachinos," Duke called over his shoulder. "Where was our darling daughter supposed to be tonight?"

"Play practice at the college. They open tomorrow night."

"Do you know some guy named Eric? Eric Thomas?"

"He's in the play too. I think Jen is kind of sweet on him. What happened? Were they in an accident? Is she OK?"

"She's OK, but this wasn't any accident," Duke said, returning to the bedroom. "Jennifer's been arrested for bridge riding."

"Arrested?" Sharon's hand automatically covered her mouth. "What do you mean bridge riding?"

"Sneaking out after the gate went down just for the thrill."

"Sneaking out! On foot? Oh, my God, they could have been killed."

A junior high English teacher, Sharon was used to the bad choices young people make. She just wasn't used to her daughter being so foolish. Sharon wore a flimsy pink nightgown, her normally neat hairstyle sticking out in odd clumps like a punk rocker. In twenty years of marriage, Duke and Sharon had learned to overlook bed hair the same way they ignored the few extra pounds they each carried.

"She's going to wish she was killed when I get through with her," Duke said, zipping up his jeans. He didn't bother to run a comb through his wavy brown hair. He kept it short. A comb didn't make much difference. He pulled on his brown leather bomber jacket over the white T-shirt he'd worn to bed. No need to dress up for this errand.

"They're going to release her into my custody, but we'll have to make an appearance in court in a few hours. This is the real thing. She's gotta take responsibility. She's an adult now. Stupid kids."

Duke kissed his wife on the forehead. "I'll be back."

Duke knew the Jordan police station as well as he knew his own home. He had spent hundreds of hours in this lobby going through routine reports. He had ascended the elevator countless times to the second floor offices to talk with detectives about a case. He'd even gone beyond the lobby's steel door into the secure area—interview rooms, booking and the jail beyond. But tonight the desk sergeant asked him to wait in the lobby while an officer retrieved "the subject" from a holding cell.

He chatted with the sergeant, looked through the paperwork, and signed a form promising Jennifer would appear in court at eight o'clock. Then he paced. Why was it taking so long? Suddenly the heavy steel door opened. The police officer who had called Duke emerged. The men shook hands and exchanged friendly greetings. Then the officer stepped aside as Jennifer ran into her father's arms. She was filthy black, her face, hands, and coat covered with greasy road dirt.

"Oh, Daddy, I'm sorry," she whispered.

He hugged her tightly. "I know," he said. "But not half as sorry as you're gonna be."

After thanking his buddy, Duke ushered his daughter out into the cold February night and headed for the car.

"Don't start," Jennifer said, pulling away from him. "I know you're not supposed to go out there when the gate is down. But sometimes you gotta break the rules, Dad. You gotta try things out, experience life. You can't keep me in a box like a china doll. I'm eighteen now. I'm an adult."

"Then act like it," Duke said quietly. He kept walking toward his car. He wasn't going to get into a shouting match in front of the police station. Not with this irrational, hormonal female. What happened to his daughter, the sweet, smart little girl who would do anything to please her Daddy? Where was she?

Waiting behind the wheel of his old turquoise Pontiac, Duke smoothed his bushy mustache with his hand and then looked up into the rearview mirror as he ran a finger over each heavy brow. Even in the garish glow of the car's overhead light he could see the white hairs were starting to outnumber the brown in his mustache and brows. Tonight would probably make them even whiter. Jennifer was taking a long time to join him in the car. He was beginning to think she had stalked off somewhere when she opened the door and sat next to him. He didn't say anything, but he didn't start the car either.

Finally Jennifer spoke. "Did we really break the bridge?"

"What? No, I don't think so."

"I mean a bridge like that must cost a fortune. As much as four years of college, I'll bet. I don't know where I would get the money to repair the bridge."

"Peacock piddle! Who told you that?"

"The tender. He said we broke the bridge."

Duke shook his head. "He was pulling your leg. I saw the police report. There's nothing about damage to property, just trespassing. Those big blue battle-axes are fifty years old and kinda cranky. They break all the time. But you could have broken your neck, and that's no joke. Daughters are way more expensive than college. I don't have enough money to get a new one."

Jennifer smiled.

"It's not really that dangerous," she said. "If the bridge hadn't gotten stuck, we could have ridden up and down, no problem. And there's a beautiful view from up there. Have you ever done it?"

"No, can't say that I have."

"Well, maybe you should before you go telling other people what to do."

"Other people?" Duke snorted. He turned the key in the ignition and pulled out of the parking lot. "Do you know what would happen if somebody fell off that bridge when it was up? Anybody?"

Jennifer could tell her father's question wasn't meant for her to answer.

"I'll tell you. If some idiot got himself killed on that bridge, they'd close the whole system for an investigation. None of the drivers could get from one side of town to the other for days, weeks, while they looked into 'procedures' and 'problems' and 'possibilities.' People would have to drive an extra half hour to get to work downtown. Restaurants wouldn't have any customers. And if they decided the drawbridges were too dangerous to operate anymore, they'd all have to be replaced with taller stationary bridges like the one in Lockwood. And they'd have to tear down all the old historic buildings in Jordan to make room for the new bridges. And it would cost a lot of money, enough to send the whole town to college. And we'd all have to pay for it in higher taxes for the rest of our lives. Just because some numbskull ignored the gate and got himself killed!"

By the time Duke finished, his voice had risen to a fever pitch. Jennifer waited for a minute to see if there would be any more.

"Gee, Dad, you think you got a little carried away maybe?"

"I don't give a shitake mushroom," Duke said with a little less volume, but still forcefully. "You're an adult now. You need to realize the full consequences of your actions. When somebody does something stupid, he puts more than himself at risk. He disrupts the whole system."

"OK, OK," Jennifer said, shaking her head. "I got it."

They were silent the rest of the way home. When Duke pulled into the driveway, a light in the living room went on.

"Oh, jeez, Mom's on the rampage too," Jennifer said.

They sat another minute, neither quite ready to face Sharon. Finally Duke said, "You remember that little terrier we used to have? Spicy?"

"Sure, I remember Spicy. He was my favorite dog."

"I know you loved him. But you remember how he used to squeeze out of the front door whenever it was open? That dog would knock you down trying to get out of the door."

"Dad, I don't want to talk about Spicy."

"You used to yell at him all the time. We all did. You were just a little kid, and you'd shake your finger and say, 'No, no, no.' But still he would get out of the door and chase cars."

"Dad, please."

"Until one day he runs into the street and gets hit by a car."

"Dad!"

"Well, that's how it is being a parent, Jenny. You love your kids so much, and you keep telling them not to do things that are dangerous. And they are just like that crazy terrier. Full of energy, trying out everything new."

Jennifer looked down and didn't say a word.

Duke threw an arm around her shoulders and pulled her close. "Come on. Let's go talk to your mom."

1:32 AM

Josie Braun was tossing and turning at one thirty in the morning. As city editor of the *Jordan Daily News*, she needed to be running a newsroom in a few hours. Five and a half hours to be exact. And if she wanted to make it to the gym for thirty minutes of weights before work, then she'd have to get up in less than four hours.

But Rudy's call kept running through her mind.

"Would you like to go out to dinner Saturday night for Valentine's Day?"

It was the last phrase that set off alarm bells. Valentine's Day. He wasn't suggesting a casual dinner between friends. He was asking her out on a date. Rudy, the newest reporter on the staff, was asking her out. She had laughed at him. Actually laughed. The conversation had gone downhill from there.

Josie threw off the covers. She went to the window and pulled back the drapes to look out into the yard, as if she might find the answer there. All she saw was a remnant of snow with grass poking through. The moon was so bright even the dirty old snow glistened.

A full moon, Josie thought. In the newsroom, reporters often blamed the full moon for the unusual phone calls they received. But the moon wouldn't cause a perfectly sane reporter to make an insane call, would it?

Josie liked Rudy Randolph. She really did. He had an offbeat sense of humor, but he was never crude or offensive. Unlike most of the reporters, his degree wasn't in English or journalism. He had a master's in child development. He had run the child care center where Josie had taken her son, Kevin, ever since he was a toddler. Two years ago, Rudy was falsely accused of abusing a child in his care. Although a blood test proved his innocence and charges were dropped, the mere suggestion of impropriety had destroyed Rudy's credibility and his business.

That's when Josie got the idea to hire Rudy as a reporter to cover schools and education. She'd been delighted with his work. Still was. Why couldn't he understand that the city editor couldn't date one of the reporters she supervised? It would be a disaster.

She was unsure about the exact wording of the company policy on dating, but she knew there was a statement. Rudy promptly questioned this policy. Josie's ex-husband had worked at the paper until their divorce. The sports editor, Dick Stone, was married to a copy editor. Josie explained that in both cases they had been hired as married couples.

Rudy: So it's OK to be married to a coworker, but you can't date a coworker.

9

Josie: Yes. A marriage is more stable, not as volatile as dating.

Rudy: I don't think we would be volatile. Like you say, we've been friends a long time. We haven't exploded yet.

Josie: Exactly. No sparks.

God, had she actually said that? And then laughed at her own joke? If he was seriously asking her out, that was unforgivably cruel.

Josie padded across the hall to Kevin's room. Her son was ten and seemed to be growing right in front of her eyes. He was sprawled face down on his bed, his arms stretched out in opposite directions and his legs apart. One leg was dangling off the bed, his toes touching the carpet. Josie gently lifted the foot and tucked it back under the blanket.

What was it Rudy had said about Kevin?

I was going to wait to discuss this with you over dinner. But I've been thinking that Kevin needs a male role model. A father figure.

Why would he say something like that? Kevin had a father. True, Josie and Kurt were divorced, and Kurt didn't have much time for his son. But Kevin adored him. Kevin didn't want another father. And for Rudy to imply that maybe he ... It was just too ridiculous to fathom. Where did he get the idea that she needed his help?

Josie ran a hand through her short blond pixie haircut. Why was she allowing this crazy call to upset her? Chippie, their golden retriever mix, raised his head from the plaid dog bed in the corner of Kevin's room. When she walked out, he followed her down to the kitchen.

Josie lived in a split level. The kitchen was only a half flight down. A second short set of stairs led from the kitchen down to the family room.

Josie yanked open the door of the refrigerator. The appliance provided a small pool of illumination in the dark room. It was enough for Josie to see up into a neighboring cabinet to retrieve a white ceramic mug. She snagged a half gallon of skim milk, twisted off the pink cap, and poured a few inches into the mug. She set the mug into the microwave and pushed the power for one minute. Warm milk sounded awful, but it always helped to put her to sleep. Chippie whined by the back door, and Josie let him out into the fenced yard.

While the microwave counted down the seconds, Josie's thoughts returned to the phone call. It wasn't unusual for reporters to call her at home, so she hadn't been surprised by Rudy's call. They had chatted about something unrelated at first. What was it? Running? Yes. Rudy had mentioned that with the snow melting, they should be able to run outside on Friday.

Nick Davidson, Josie's right-hand man and assistant city editor, had suggested the running club two summers ago, right after Rudy joined the staff. The Write Stuff Running Club. They had T-shirts made that first summer. Almost all of the reporters participated, running around the outdoor track at the YMCA during lunch hours. They competed in the five-kilometer race during Jordan's end-of-summer Harvest Festival.

But when winter came, the club fell apart. Only Josie, Nick, and Rudy continued running on treadmills during lunch hour. The second summer, Nick's fiancé, Brittany Miller, joined them for jogs through Murray Park.

Was that it? Was it the four of them running together that had misled Rudy? Nick and Brittany ended up getting married. Did that lead Rudy to believe that he and Josie were a couple? But he'd never indicated any interest. Never reached for her hand or tried to kiss her. Josie had never noticed Rudy looking at her "that way." Nothing!

The microwave beeped and Josie retrieved her mug of warm milk. Sipping it, she wandered across the dark kitchen toward the sliding-glass door in the dining room. She looked up at the big round moon. Shadows marking facial features in the moon were very pronounced tonight. The moon was laughing at her.

Josie shook her head. It was a joke. Rudy was playing a trick on her. Men had such a strange sense of humor. Josie could never understand how men could call each other terrible names with a straight face, and it would be accepted as a form of affection. Rudy had been known to play elaborate practical jokes. Like the time he arranged for a pregnant woman to show up at Nick and Brittany's wedding reception. She created an awkward scene claiming Nick was the father. Then Rudy announced the charade was all part of his "toast" to the bride and groom.

And how about the life-size cutout of reporter Duke Dukakis? The cardboard statue, with the cartoon blurb "Gotcha covered," was left over from some long-forgotten advertising campaign. Duke had kept the likeness right behind his desk for years without much notice. Since Rudy had been on staff, however, the statue had become a source of surprises. When Duke and Sharon went on vacation to Hawaii, the cardboard cutout was dressed in a bikini with an inflated inner tube around its neck. It often sported a hat of some sort—a baseball cap for the start of the season, a knit cap and muffler when it snowed, a cowboy hat or bandana just for fun. Josie was pretty sure Rudy was responsible for adding a handlebar curl to the mustache on the cardboard reporter's smiling face.

Tomorrow morning the statue might be dressed like Cupid with a bow and arrow. Perhaps Rudy was trying to make fun of the pitiful lack of romance in her life. She'd been divorced almost four years and had no love life to speak of. Oh, yes, there had been that brief affair with Duke three years ago, an ill-advised week of passion that clearly violated company policy. It could have destroyed his marriage and their friendship. But he was back with his wife now. Josie rarely thought of him as anything other than an excellent reporter. She had dated the coroner, Zach Teasdale, but that too was better off forgotten. Just thinking about it made her feel stupid.

11

Josie was happy with her life just the way it was. She loved her job at the paper and felt confident and at ease with its demands. Although she was just a tiny slip of a thing—five-foot-two and a hundred and ten pounds—she had no problem taking charge. Some of the staff made fun of her boyish looks by calling her Peter Pan, but there was no question she was the boss of Neverland. Good management was a two-way street. She listened to her reporters and photographers. When they turned to her for guidance, she was quick to set priorities. She didn't need to dominate them.

Chippie jumped up against the slider, leaving a muddy smear on the glass. Josie sighed and shook her head. She left the moonlit dining room, walked back through the dark kitchen and set her empty mug in the sink. Then she opened the back door. Chippie came running.

"You're a muddy mess," she said, wiping Chippie's paws with a rag she kept by the door. "That's what we get when the snow melts."

He followed her when she walked up the stairs. As Josie slipped beneath the covers, she remembered how lonesome the double bed had seemed after Kurt left. Now she was used to having it all to herself. Perhaps that was what had frightened her most about Rudy's call. He hadn't just asked her out. He had actually proposed.

Well, if it's against the rules for us to date, maybe we should get married.

He had said it just like that. A man she had never dated acted like getting married was as routine as choosing what show to watch on television. And she had made the situation worse by treating it as a laughable joke.

Josie: You don't have to get down on one knee, but I think a couple is required to have kissed or at least held hands before the relationship qualifies for a proposal.

Rudy: Half the world would disagree. Marriages are arranged in many cultures based on family status, similar interests. It makes more sense than choosing a mate based on some irrational feeling in the pit of your stomach.

Josie: Sorry, but I'm holding out for love.

Rudy: You mean you're waiting for Cupid to shoot you with an arrow?

Josie: Something like that.

Now, several hours later, she still didn't know if Rudy was kidding around or being serious. If this was Rudy's idea of a joke, then her laughing was appropriate. The whole thing would be forgotten. If he was serious, then she needed to act like the wise boss and good friend she was and kindly decline.

But her anger baffled her. Why was she reacting this way? Could it be that Rudy's proposal implied that this was the best either of them could expect from life? A marriage of convenience. Passion was a pipe dream.

Josie reached for the clock. It was almost two in the morning. She adjusted the alarm to six fifteen. She would need the extra sleep. She didn't want to go to the gym and lift weights with Rudy. She might have to see him at work, but she would avoid him as much as possible. He was a crazy person. Crazy. Josie closed her eyes as the warm milk worked its magic.

1:58 AM

Jordan homicide detective Tom Cantrell reached for the brown slacks folded neatly over the back of a chair. It was almost two in the morning. He had fallen asleep again in Becky's bed. But he had to get home. He slipped on the pants and pulled his soft cashmere sweater over his head. He sat in the chair to put on his socks and tie his shoes.

He looked back at the bed. Becky, naked, was curled like a black kitten on top of the white sheets. Moonlight poured in the tall window behind the bed. It was all like a wonderful fantasy. Becky Judd was the woman of his dreams. Exotic. Willowy thin. And passionate. Not just about making love, but passionate about everything in life. Passionate about her job as a reporter for the *Daily News*. Passionate for the people she wrote about. Passionate about justice. She was like him. She wanted to make the world a better place. No, she was making the world a better place.

Tom's throat was dry from the way the old furnace parched the air. He went into the kitchen, picked up one of the wine glasses overturned in the sink, and filled it with cool water from the tap. The smell of sulfur hit his nose before the first sip.

We'll need a water softener and a humidifier, Tom thought, taking a drink. *We*. Already he was thinking that someday this would be his home with Becky. He looked out of the kitchen window, beyond the fence, onto the snow-swept landscape. It was peaceful out here on the farm. So different from his place in town. Not as convenient, but nice.

His father, Jordan's first black cop, had been born on a farm in Mississippi. Tom had visited his great grandmother there once. They were so poor. Barefoot poor. Rotten teeth poor. It made Tom shiver to remember that place. He grew up thinking farmers were second class. Something he had never wanted to be.

But Becky's house had the elegance of age. Fat oak molding around the doors and windows. Wavy glass in the window that made the landscape look like a watercolor. Some old white dude left the farm to Becky when he died. His will said he wanted to show her "the other side." Now a black woman owned the land and rented it to white farmers. Was that what he had meant by the other side? Or did he simply mean living on the other side of the interstate that seemed to divide the Chicago suburbs from the cornfields of northern Illinois?

14

Tom carefully rinsed the glass and placed it in the drainer. He had a unique perspective on race relations. He was "of mixed parentage," which explained Tom's café au lait skin color and his narrow pointed nose. His parents had taught him that race wasn't about skin color. It was about attitude. His father's father and his mother's father worked together at the tractor plant. His parents had both attended the junior college. His parents had been very similar in attitude despite the difference in their skin tones.

Tom glanced into the bedroom. Becky was awake now, kneeling in the center of the bed, watching him. The way the moonlight shone behind her, she looked like a stone carving of an Egyptian goddess.

"Come back to bed, baby," she called.

"You know I've got to go," Tom replied. He turned his back to her. He knew if he watched her there, the urge would rise in him again. He wouldn't be able to leave.

"I need you, sweet thing," she said. "Don't go."

Tom looked over his shoulder. She was in the doorway now, hugging the doorframe and pressing against it. He imagined her pressing against him like that, and he could feel himself becoming aroused again.

"I have to go. It's late." He headed for the back door, reaching for his leather coat hanging on a hook by the door. "I'll see you tomorrow."

He pulled the coat on quickly, like armor to protect him from her allure.

"Go ahead then. Go back to her," Becky snapped.

"Don't be like that, honey," Tom said, crossing toward Becky in three quick strides. It was hard enough to resist her raw sexiness, but the slightest glimmer of her reproach melted him like butter. "You say that like I've got another woman. Like I'm cheating on you."

"Well?" Becky was standing in the bedroom doorway, naked and unashamed. Her breasts stood up firm, the hard nipples like soldiers at attention. She had her hands on her hips, and her eyes were flashing.

God, she was beautiful.

"She's my mother, for Pete's sake," Tom pleaded. "She worries about me."

"And that's the worst kind of 'other woman,'" Becky said, jutting out her chin. "How can I compete with that? Everything she does is right. I want to grow our relationship, to consider living together, and maybe even more commitment. But how can we if you're always running home to her?"

At six-foot-two Tom was only an inch or so taller than Becky. She stepped in closer, accenting her words by reaching inside his jacket to rub his soft sweater.

"She depends on me," Tom whispered in a vain attempt to counter Becky's argument.

"Oh, yes, that too," she said, pulling herself inside his jacket and rubbing against his chest.

15

Tom offered little objection to her overtures. "I've been the man of the house since my father died."

"I know, killed in the line of duty," Becky added, running a hand up his chest, over the side of his face and into his short military haircut.

"Yes, in the line of duty. She's the widow of a cop. That's why she worries about me."

"I know," Becky said, kissing Tom's cheek and neck. "I imagine losing you every time we're apart. But right now I'm imagining gobbling you up whole."

She ran a finger over the thin mustache on Tom's upper lip. He pushed her away.

"No, I can't. I've got to get home."

"You don't gotta do nothin' but make me scream for mercy," Becky said, pulling in close again.

"Stop, please. I really must go."

Becky stiffened. "You started this. You're the one who chased me. I wanted to keep a professional distance. You're the cop. I'm the reporter. Hands off."

"I kept my distance for the better part of a year."

"When I gave in, I told you I expect more than sex. I expect complete devotion. I don't want just any slap-dash love affair."

"Slap-dash? We're together almost every evening. I haven't looked at another woman in two years."

"Except your mother and your sister."

"You can't really be jealous of Mom and Linda."

"I'm not jealous. I'm angry that you allow your responsibility for them to get in the way of growing our relationship. I told you I don't want a shallow sometimes love. If you want me, you get my whole heart. I'm not going to do this halfway."

Becky reached her hands around Tom's neck. They kissed, her frail nakedness seeming so small and vulnerable in comparison to his armor of clothes and stiff leather jacket. He longed to be naked too, to hold her skin against his. To be one. But he had responsibilities. It was part of being a man.

"See how it is with these clothes between us?" Becky said, as if she was reading Tom's mind. "It's not close enough. And that's how it is if you keep putting your mother between us. We both lose some of the connection we need."

"I wish I could stay, but I can't. I really can't."

"Have it your way," she said and turned, stalking off into the bedroom.

He rushed toward the back door, grabbing his holster and gun that were still on the hook. He picked up his car keys from the counter. He wanted to get out of the house before she called him back again. As Tom opened the door, he heard Becky say, "Hi, Carolyn. Sorry to call so late, but Tommy said you would be awake worrying about him."

Tom whipped around and saw the silhouette of Becky standing in front of the light coming in the bedroom window, phone in hand.

"Well, that's why I'm calling. I didn't want you to worry. Tommy fell asleep on my sofa again. Usually I wake him up and send him home because I know you worry. But tonight he's sleeping so soundly. He's been so tired lately. I just can't bear to send him out into the cold."

Shuddering in anger and disbelief, Tom stormed across the kitchen and flicked on the bedroom light so Becky would have no trouble reading his gesture to "cut it."

Becky smiled at him. "I know, dear. We both want what's best for Tommy. If it's all right with you, I'll let him sleep tonight. He worries about you and Linda being alone at night." Becky paused to listen to Carolyn's response. "Oh, I know you're perfectly safe, but try telling that to a man. They want to be so protective. And it is sweet, isn't it?"

Giving up, Tom headed back into the kitchen. He hung his holster on the hook by the back door, slipped off his leather jacket, and hung it on top of the holster. When he turned around, Becky was vamping against the doorframe again.

"See how easy that was?" she purred. "Now you're free to spend the night. Tonight. Tomorrow night. Every night."

"You shouldn't have done that."

"You're right. ... You should have done it…a long time ago."

They each took a couple of steps and embraced in the middle of the kitchen. Their kisses were passionate, hungry, greedy. After a few minutes, Becky took Tom's hand and pulled him toward the bedroom.

"Expect a call from your mama later today," she said. "You're in a heap of trouble, boy, not for sleeping at my place, but for making your mama seem weak and clingy. Women don't like to be treated like they can't take care of themselves."

Tom smiled and shook his head. "Well, you sure take care of yourself. You're going to get your way, one way or another."

"My way? It's not for me. It's for us. I want us to be so close that we think the same thoughts," Becky said, slipping her hands under his sweater and pulling it over his head.

A month or two ago, Becky would have thrown the sweater on the floor in her hurry to answer passion's call. But as Tom sat down and untied his shoes, he noticed that Becky folded the sweater the way he liked it and carefully laid it on the dresser. They were changing each other, weren't they? Maybe he could consider moving in. Maybe his mother would be OK on her own.

"I want us to trust each other completely," Becky said.

17

"I trust you." Tom pulled his slacks off, folded them so the creases were sharp and laid them over the back of the chair.

"No, I mean complete trust. I want to see what you see, think what you think," Becky said, wrapping her arms around him and nuzzling into his chest. "It takes time to develop that kind of trust. It may take years. But that's the kind of love I want. Total. Can you do that?"

Becky put both hands inside Tom's wine-colored jockey shorts and pulled them down over his thighs. He grasped her head and pulled her lips to his. He stepped out of his shorts as they kissed. Becky wrapped one leg around his waist, clamping their bodies together. Their kisses were deep, mouth open, uninhibited. Tom grabbed her butt in one hand, lifting her slightly. She wrapped her other leg around him. They stood there kissing, a tangle of limbs, lips, and passionate sighs.

"Oh, Tommy," Becky whispered. "You make me tremble."

Tom took one step to the bed and laid her down. "Somebody has to crack that hard shell of yours."

"Oh, you do, you do," she moaned. As Tom moved on top of her, the moan grew into a deep, guttural roar that shook the window and melted into the night.

3:02 AM

By three in the morning, clouds masked the full moon. An inky blackness descended like a deathly shroud over the rural roads surrounding Jordan.

Deputy Theodore Edwards liked the peaceful quiet, but he didn't trust the dark. From the patrol car, he kept scanning the shadows, looking for movement, for burglars or vandals, for evil sneaking up on unsuspecting citizens. His partner, Chet Sanders, was just the opposite. As Sanders drove the vehicle, he dispelled the quiet with incessant chatter. What was it tonight? Something about a massacre in the Philippines. A military coup. Political unrest in the tropical paradise of Fiji. Halfway around the globe. Places neither of them would ever see. Who cared?

"Time for a break," Sanders announced as they approached the Pilot gas station. It was their usual stop in the middle of their shift. There were so many bright lights around the property that the station glowed like a ship from outer space. Rock music blared from huge overhead speakers, interrupted by the disembodied voice of a folksy announcer hawking tires and batteries. The Pilot station was an oasis of downtown daytime in the middle of rural night.

When he got out of the car, Deputy Edwards donned the dark brown Stetson of the Cade County Sheriff's Department. It was too big for his narrow face, swallowing half his head and riding just above his eyes. But Edwards liked the extra height it gave him, and it covered up the bald spot he despised.

A rusted green pickup was at the pump. Edwards walked around it, making note of the license plate. You could never be too careful. He also noted the license number of a black Ford Escort parked near the building. Before he went inside, Edwards walked around the back of the building. Just the old station wagon that belonged to Lizzie, the clerk who worked the night shift. He liked to be sure. As he started to enter the front door, a lanky teen buzzed past him on his way out.

"Oh, excuse me, sir," the boy said, his eyes flashing alarm when he realized he'd almost knocked over a sheriff's deputy.

"Where you headed in such a hurry?" Edwards said, walking around the boy and sniffing the air for alcohol or marijuana.

"Jus' home," the boy said, standing at attention.

19

Edwards looked into his eyes. He saw fear, but they didn't appear glazed by drugs.

"You're out awfully late."

"I was studying at my girlfriend's," the teen stammered.

"Drive carefully," Edwards said and walked into the building. He checked over his shoulder to make sure all the truck's lights came on and the kid used his turn signal pulling out of the station. Edwards then looked around inside. His partner was standing at the counter chatting with Lizzie. Edwards clucked to himself. Sanders wasn't wearing his hat. It was just as well. His partner treated his hat like a Frisbee, tossing it in the car. The top had been crushed more than once, and the brim had a permanent crease on one side.

Still, it meant Sanders was out of uniform. His brown jacket was unzipped, revealing a wrinkled beige shirt with some sort of red stain. Edwards shook his head. How were they supposed to maintain the respect of the community when Sanders looked like one of the local farmhands?

"Oh, yeah, it's a full moon Friday, all right," Sanders was saying as he leaned casually against the counter. He held out a couple of bills to pay for his usual, a tall cup of coffee and a bag of miniature powdered sugar donuts. "We got a call about a body alongside the road tonight, over by the A-Lab."

"National Atomic Particle Accelerator Laboratory," Edwards explained as he approached the counter. He nodded toward the clerk. "Evenin', Lizzie. Been quiet?"

"Oh, just the usual. Steady flow all night. Wouldn't want it too quiet."

Edwards walked away. He prowled every aisle, up and down, and back by the coolers in the corner. Checked the restrooms, including the ladies room. He didn't want any surprises. Lizzie finished ringing up the only other customer and turned her attention back to Sanders.

"Like I was saying," he said as if there had been no interruption, "some motorist reports seeing a body alongside the road out by the A-Lab, so we go investigate. Whadda ya think we find?"

"It was one hundred and eight feet off the pavement, not exactly alongside the road," Edwards said as he walked by on his survey of the store.

"Yeah, it was sorta behind the sign, inside the fence, so we didn't see it at first," Sanders continued. "But there's this pile of snow, you see, and it's melting down. This big monster thing covered in brown curly hair is poking out, like a gigantic werewolf."

"No kidding! You found a werewolf?" Lizzie exclaimed.

"It wasn't a werewolf," Edwards called out as he checked behind the potato-chip display.

"Oh, that's what you say now," Sanders said with a chuckle. "But you should have seen him out there tonight. We were walking along Clark Road with our flashlights, and he finds it behind the sign. 'My God, it's a werewolf,' he says. Isn't that what you said, Teddy? You were the one who said it was a werewolf."

Edwards was at the soda machine now. He pushed his cup under the ice dispenser and waited until the cup was almost full. Then he moved to the Dr. Pepper dispenser. Sanders and Lizzie were looking at him when he turned around with his full cup.

"I think I might have said, 'It looks like a werewolf.' 'Looks like' is a descriptive term. I never intended to imply that I actually thought we had discovered a mythical monster. There's no such thing as a werewolf."

"How do you know?" Lizzie asked. "There could be. Just waiting for some sheriff's deputy to discover it. So if it wasn't a werewolf, what was it?"

"One of them buffalos they got out there at the A-Lab," Sanders said, tearing open a packet of sugar and pouring it into his coffee. "Frozen solid."

"Bison," Edwards said, approaching the counter with his giant soft drink and two long ropes of beef jerky.

"A dead buffalo? That's not good," Lizzie said.

"What do you mean?" Sanders asked as he dumped two more packets of sugar into the coffee.

"Well, you know what they say about the buffalo," Lizzie said. "They're like the canaries in the coal mine. The A-Lab has them out there as an early-warning sign if the radiation gets too high."

"Radiation?" Edwards repeated.

"Yeah, if the buffalo start dying, it means the radiation is too high. We could be next," Lizzie explained.

"It was just one old buffalo," Sanders said, pouring in the fourth and fifth envelopes of sugar. "Gotta be rough trying to graze in the winter. It was his time."

"Wait a minute," Edwards said, pulling out his pad. "Tell me what you know about this radiation business. Where'd you get that information?"

"Oh, it's just what I hear," Lizzie said with a shrug. "Ever since they opened that lab ten years ago, people been saying they have buffalo grazing out there as a safety check on radiation from the accelerator."

"I read the accelerator emits very little radiation. Like an X-ray. It's safe," Sanders said, sweetening his coffee with a final packet of sugar and giving it a stir.

"Maybe so, maybe not," Edwards said. "They get those atomic particles zipping around that great big underground racetrack, it creates an electromagnetic field. Interferes with the normal operation of electronic equipment. Like the clock in your car. It will stop it cold if you happen to be driving by when the accelerator is running. Might even make it run backwards. I've seen the traffic reports."

"No kidding," Lizzie said. "I've had customers come in, and their credit cards didn't work. I always figured it had something to do with that magnetic field from the accelerator."

"Could be. Very well could be," Edwards said, tapping his pencil on his pad. "Go on. How many bison you think are out there?"

"Oh, I don't know," Lizzie said. "I think I read something in the paper about twenty-five, but that was back when it opened. I don't know now."

"We'll check it out. See if any more have been dying," Edwards said, making a note. "We'll get an autopsy on this one for sure. See if it died of radiation poisoning."

"The popscicle?" Sanders asked. "You'll have to wait until he thaws out."

Lizzie laughed. "It's just so funny thinking of a frozen buffalo with all that hair. Ewww."

Sanders laughed too. "Beats the hell out of the human torch," he said. "That's how this crazy Friday the 13th started. We were driving down County Road 7, way south of here where there ain't nothin' but barren cornfields. And all of a sudden ol' Eagle Eyes here says he sees a fire. Way off on the horizon. Just a little glow."

"Experience," Edwards said, puffing out his chest. "A fire has a certain flicker. You get to recognize it after you've spotted as many as I have."

"Well, I could hardly see it," Sanders said. "Must have been a couple miles away. So we drove over that way. Once we could see the location better, we called for a fire engine. But it was too late. The farmhouse was fully engulfed."

"Oh, too bad. Was anyone killed?" Lizzie asked.

"The human torch," Sanders said. "Stupid guy was on oxygen for his emphysema or something. Looks like he lit up a cigarette anyway. Blew himself up. People are crazy."

"Oh, that's terrible." Lizzie shook her head. "Maybe he committed suicide on purpose."

"Yeah, the way some people live is suicide," Sanders said, grabbing his bag of donuts and coffee. "All we need to make the night complete is a UFO sighting."

"Nah, too cloudy and cold," Edwards said as he paid for his Dr. Pepper and jerky. "Eighty-three percent of sightings of Unidentified Flying Objects are on clear nights, when it's at least fifty degrees."

Sanders shook his head. "Yeah, guess those little green men don't want to get a chill."

4:07 AM

William "Hoss" Peyton wasn't scheduled to arrive at the *Daily News* until five in the morning, but as usual he showed up an hour early. There was plenty to do before the others arrived. Hundreds of wire stories had moved overnight. It was his job as news editor to select the best for the small international news hole in the *Daily News*.

The rotund copy desk chief enjoyed arriving at the newsroom when it was quiet and empty. He flicked on lights and absent-mindedly straightened up as he entered the room. The sports department, which was usually the last department to close for the night, was closest to the back door. Invariably the large staff of sports freelancers left chairs out of place, half-eaten pizzas, overflowing waste cans. Before he sat down or turned on his computer, Hoss would roll misplaced chairs back to their desks and carry trash back to the dumpster. Only then was he ready for another day.

Hoss was an orderly, logical man. He had to be. It was his job to fit together all the puzzle pieces of a daily newspaper. Every story had to fit to the letter. And the pages had to be approved on schedule. To the minute. He had no time for nonsense.

But experience told Hoss that this day was going to be more challenging than most. The monthly full moon always brought strange phone calls to the newsroom as well as more auto accidents and petty crimes to cover. But this full moon coincided with Friday the 13th. A double whammy. It wasn't superstition. He didn't believe in some mystical bad luck. But he believed in human nature, and he suspected folks were going to screw things up a little more than usual today.

Hoss also was a bit of a statistician. He knew Friday the 13th didn't coincide with full moons very often, only eight times in the twentieth century. The last time the full moon fell on Friday the 13th was less than three years before, July 13, 1984—a day no one in Jordan would ever forget. That summer Jordan was terrorized by a serial killer. The peak event of that murder spree happened on July 13. That night resulted in five deaths. Hoss had decided to keep that little bit of statistical knowledge to himself. No sense bringing up the horrors of that summer again or suggesting anything that horrible would happen today. But Hoss wanted to be prepared for whatever this day would deliver.

He was sitting in his extra-large burnt-orange chair, coding some sports scores that had moved on the wire after the sports writers had left. His chair rolled between three desks, two with computers and one strewn with dummies. On these white sheets he pencil-sketched layouts, telling the paste-up crew in the back shop where to place the stories as they came out of the typesetting machine.

A trio of bells dinged from the wire room right behind him, like a phone signal from another world. Hoss knew three bells meant a news advisory. No hurry. It was just an advisory. The actual story wouldn't move for several minutes. But Hoss, who was as hefty as his *Bonanza* namesake, was curious. He wondered what had happened in the world. He liked being among the first to know.

He finished up the sports scores, pushed the button that would send the copy to the back shop, and wandered into the wire room. The old teletype machines were so noisy that he kept the door closed, but he actually liked the sound they made. The disembodied "clack, clack, clack" paused every now and then, as if the unseen typist was thinking.

Along one wall were three machines: Associated Press, United Press International, and Copley News Service. At the end of the room was an AP photo machine. In addition to typing copy on endless rolls of cheap rag paper, two of the teletype machines also spewed yellow ribbons of punched paper tape that could be fed directly into the typesetting machine.

Hoss knew that the new computer system would soon make the wire room unnecessary. In a few weeks, they would be able to receive wire stories directly into their computers. A new editing program would make it possible to trim the stories, write the headlines, and send both to computerized typesetters in the back shop without pneumatic tubes or piles of paper. He wasn't sure he trusted that the wire stories would just magically appear in his computer. He preferred hard copy he could hold in his hand.

Suddenly the Associated Press machine sprang to life. Its black metal armor shuddered and vibrated as the keys clacked against the paper. The page lurched forward automatically as Hoss read the faint words through a clear plastic shield:

AUCKLAND, NEW ZEALAND—An underwater nuclear explosion was reported early Friday morning, in the open water west of Samoa. Sources say no nuclear testing was scheduled. The United States and the United Kingdom have tested in the area in the past, but representatives of both countries deny any knowledge of today's explosion.

"Nobody knows nuthin,'" Hoss mumbled, accenting the double negative with the reckless abandon of one who knows better.

When the machine stopped typing, he pulled a long, slender pica pole out of his back pocket and laid it across the paper. He ripped the sheet against the straight edge. The black and silver ruler was a copy editor's right hand. Dual markings in picas and inches measured everything from column widths to photos. But the strong metal edge also was handy for drawing precise dummies, ripping wire copy, and swatting dense reporters who forgot good grammar.

More than a hundred stories had moved on the AP machine overnight, the paper spewing out and folding back and forth into a neat stack below the machine. The adjoining yellow punch tape wasn't neat. The paper snakes had fallen into an unruly haystack as big as the machine itself. Hoss chose a random spot in the middle of the coil, looking for a break in the punch code that marked the end of a story. When he spotted a space, he ripped the tape at that point and carried an armload of yellow tape back to his desk with the sheaf of typed copy.

For the better part of the next hour, Hoss sorted copy and tape, spotting the letter/number code in the punch tape and matching it to the same code on the printed copy. He wrapped a coil of yellow tape into a neat circle around his hand and attached it with a big paperclip to its printed version. Then reading the first paragraph of each story, he selected the most important ones for that day's paper.

A little after five, Hoss was back in the wire room gathering another armload of yellow punch tape when he heard a phone ringing in the newsroom. It wasn't his phone, he was quite certain. No one from the outside world ever called his phone. He used it only to communicate with the back shop, and no one would be there yet. Hoss walked to the doorway of the wire room with his armload of yellow tape. He looked out at the newsroom. The phone rang again. It was coming from the center of the room, either the desk of city editor Josie Braun or reporter Duke Dukakis. It could be a news source calling in a tip. But a good source would call a home number or leave a message on the machine. Hoss waited and let the call ring five more times times. Then it stopped.

He returned to his station of desks. He worked fast now, sketching layouts, attaching copy and photos to pages, stacking the page packets in the basket for copy editors to work on when they arrived. In a few minutes the phone rang again. Hoss suspected it was a crank call. Best to ignore it. But on the third ring, curiosity got the best of him. He punched the pickup code.

"Newsroom."

"Mr. Dukakis? You've got to help me. The dogs are howling again, and I can't sleep."

"Dogs? That sounds like a problem for the police or the sheriff. Where do you live?"

"Oh, they won't do anything. They never do anything. Maybe if you did a story."

Hoss laughed. "We don't have room for stories about all the barking dogs in town. Why don't you give me your name and address. I'll call the right police agency and have them drive by and check it out."

"I told you, they don't care about me. Nobody cares about me."

"I'm sure that isn't true. You live alone?"

"I've been alone since Daddy died five years ago. I miss Daddy. He was a cranky old man, but I would rather hear him yelling at me than be alone day after day."

The story was beginning to sound familiar. This was the lady the reporters called Deluded Debbie. She never gave her last name or her address, but she was a frequent caller to the *Daily News*. In the past year, she had probably called fifty times. It had been a year or more since Hoss had picked up one of her calls, but he heard the reporters talking about her. Sometimes she would complain about a story or photo in the newspaper, but most of the time she was complaining about something she saw on television. She didn't seem to be able to distinguish between the newspaper, television news, or television dramas. Sometimes she was upset about the weather or dogs barking. It didn't seem to matter what her problem was. She just wanted to talk to someone.

Hoss listened patiently for a minute, the phone receiver wedged between his shoulder and his ear so he could listen while he worked. When she paused her story, he snatched the chance to talk.

"Is this Debbie? I think we've talked before. You know that problem with the dogs? It's probably because of the full moon. Dogs like to howl at the moon."

"Yes ... yes, that's probably it," the woman said. "I remember Daddy used to say the same thing. The dogs are barking at the moon."

"And the good news is it's almost morning. The moon will disappear. The dogs will stop barking. Everything will be fine."

"Oh, OK," Debbie said. She was quiet for a few seconds. "I think they've stopped barking already. I'm going to try to go to sleep now. Thanks a lot."

She hung up without saying goodbye. Hoss smiled and paper clipped another yellow tape to its printed version.

5:05 AM

Nick and Brittany Davidson were sound asleep when the bedside phone rang a little after five. The alarm had been set for six, since they both started work at seven.

"We need you to get here as soon as possible," the emergency room nurse told Brittany. "We've got a backup of patients already, and it's only going to get worse."

Brittany sat up and turned on the light. "What happened? Were there a lot of traffic accidents overnight?"

"Traffic accidents, poisonings, flu, you name it," the nurse said. "We've got people in the waiting room who can't even explain where it hurts. This is what happens when there's a full moon. Throw in Friday the 13th, and it's bedlam. Get here as soon as you can."

Brittany sprang out of the bed and scurried to the bathroom.

"What is it?" Nick called after her.

Brittany showed up in the bathroom doorway trying to talk with a toothbrush in her mouth.

"Lots of emergencies," she slobbered through the foaming toothpaste. "We need to go in right away."

They were economizing with one car, trying to save up for a house. If Brittany needed to go in early, Nick would arrive at the *Daily News* a little early too.

"Come back to bed for five minutes," he said, extending his arms.

"We've got to go right away."

"Three minutes," Nick begged, his arms still upraised. He knew his broad grin created deep dimples in his cheeks that Brittany couldn't resist. It had been that way all his life. From his mother to his high school teachers, to grocery clerks, and even his boss, Josie Braun. No woman could resist Nick's dimples. He always got what he wanted when he grinned. And more than anything, he wanted Brittany.

At first glance she was the same perky cheerleader-type he had always dated. Delicate oval face. Shoulder-length blond hair. Big blue eyes. But Nick also loved the Brittany who wasn't so obvious. She was smart, caring, and kind of pushy. He liked that. She wasn't afraid to speak her mind even when she disagreed with him.

That's when he turned on the dimples. Worked every time.

FULL MOON FRIDAY

Brittany hesitated. Her husband was dangerously good looking. Like chocolate cake with chocolate icing. His thick brown hair was so perfectly cut that even first thing in the morning, it draped fetchingly across his brow. What she wouldn't give to have that much body in her hair. And his physique! He had eight-pack abs—a six-pack with a bonus of well-defined pects. His chest was streaked with kitten-soft brown hair that made him extra snuggly. And to top it off—dimples. She smiled and fell into bed next to him.

"Pretty," Nick said, hugging her close.

"Yep," Brittany replied.

Without preamble, they had begun their snuggle game: carrying on a conversation of responses beginning with the last letter of the previous word.

"Perfect."

"Together."

"Reclining."

"Giggling."

"Gasping."

"Grasping."

"Guessing."

Nick laughed at their "G" word predicament. "Goofing," he said finally.

"Going," Brittany said, sitting up.

"Gone."

"Early."

"Yes."

"Sad."

"Don't."

"Tonight."

"Tonight."

They kissed and hugged briefly before Brittany pulled away and began getting dressed. Nick headed for the bathroom. He returned, wiping a smear of toothpaste off his mouth with his hand, and started pulling on his clothes.

"Did the hospital say what happened to cause the overload? Is it a flu epidemic?"

"No, something about it being a full moon and Friday the 13th," Brittany responded. "Sounds like a silly excuse to me. I don't believe in Friday the 13th superstitions. Do you?"

"Oh, no," Nick said, pausing. He remembered the last time there was a full moon on Friday the 13th. The night Scotty was killed two and a half years ago. Scotty. His best friend and Brittany's first husband. Scotty and Brittany had been married only three weeks when Scotty was shot while investigating one of that summer's many murders. Horrible. But if Scotty hadn't been killed, Nick and Brittany never would have gotten together.

Nick watched as Brittany stood in front of the mirror brushing her hair, twisting it into a knot on the back of her head and securing it with a huge

28

tortoise shell clamp. She hadn't made the connection between today's date, February 13, and Scotty's death on July 13. She might have realized he was killed on Friday the 13th, but Nick had never heard her blame superstition or bad luck. To do so would have trivialized the sacrifice of the young cop. She probably didn't realize it was a full moon Friday the 13th when Scotty was killed. Nick hadn't realized it was happening again, or he would have been worried. He hadn't been paying any attention to the phases of the moon. He was much too busy paying attention to his new bride. Just as Scotty had been, no doubt.

Nick shuddered off the uneasiness and hugged his wife.

"I love you," he said. "I really love you."

She seemed flattered. "I love you too, silly. Let's go."

☼

Deputies Sanders and Edwards drove down the narrow side road to a trashy, rusted trailer.

"Is this the right address?" Sanders asked. "It looks deserted."

"Yep, this is the number," Edwards replied without checking the pad where he had noted the address the dispatcher had given them. "Homeowner said somebody was trying to break in."

"Break in? The thing looks like it's made out of tissue paper. If somebody wanted to break in, it wouldn't be difficult." Sanders turned on the car's flashing lights. "I don't want the homeowner to think we're trying to break in. He might shoot us."

"Caller was a female. Margaret Hinkle."

"Well, let's pay Mrs. Hinkle a visit."

The two deputies walked up to the door of the trailer. Both men wore their hats and zipped jackets, according to protocol, even though Sanders' hat was rather lopsided. The steps were blocked by a grocery cart filled with an assortment of cans, bags, and street refuse.

"Looks like a homeless person," Edwards said.

Sanders moved the cart to one side, went up to the door, and pounded on it.

"Sheriff's Department, Mrs Hinkle. Open up."

There was no exterior lighting and not even a glimmer of light in a window. It seemed unlikely that anyone would come to the door. Both men were surprised when the door suddenly opened wide.

"Officers, come in. I made some coffee," the woman said. In the dark, it was hard to tell at first that she was nude. Edwards turned his flashlight on her and quickly turned it away. She was withered and wrinkly, at least 80 years old.

"Ma'am, it's pretty cold tonight. Don't you want to put your robe on?" Sanders asked.

"I know it's chilly. The furnace hasn't been working for a while. I guess I got behind in the bills. But come in. I have a kerosene stove."

Edwards and Sanders exchanged glances.

"You don't have heat, ma'am, or electricity?" Sanders asked.

"I've got some banana nut muffins to go with the coffee," the woman said. "They're only a few days old. No mold on them, I promise."

Edwards shined his light around the crowded room. A silver tea set sat on the table. The woman poured some dark liquid out of a very tarnished pot into a chipped china cup. She held the saucer and cup out for Sanders. He took it and set it back on the table.

"Here, let me get you a coat or something to wear," he said, placing a hand on the back of the woman's head. "Are your clothes in the bedroom? Let's go get you something to wear." Sanders whispered to his partner. "Call for an ambulance. She can't stay here."

Sanders steered the woman down the hall toward the back of the trailer, where he expected to find the bedroom. He pushed open a closed door and couldn't believe his eyes. His flashlight scanned charred walls. There had been a fire some time ago. The ceiling was gone. The bed, piled high with blankets and clothes, was under the stars.

"It's a very comfortable bed," the woman said, sidling up to Sanders. "I could keep you warm."

Sanders smiled. "I'm sure you could, ma'am." Sanders picked up a couple of pieces of clothing. He put a flannel shirt on her and then a sweater. He threw a blanket over her shoulders. "I know a place in town where they have plenty of heat and lights. You can get coffee too. And muffins."

"Banana nut?"

"I think so," Sanders said as he steered the woman back to the living room. Edwards had put some light on the subject. He'd turned on the squad car's headlights to light the exterior of the trailer and pointed the squad's spotlight at the front door so the kitchen was illuminated. He turned off the kerosene heater and set about securing the rest of the area like a crime scene.

Sanders asked the woman about her prowler, but the story soon fell apart.

"Do you have any relatives we could call?" Sanders asked.

"Just Herman."

"Great," Sanders said, reaching for his pad. "What's Herman's last name?"

"Hinkle. Herman Hinkle. He's my husband."

"Oh, where's he live?" Sanders asked, already suspecting the answer.

Margaret looked at him blankly. "Where?" She looked down at the floor. "Herman's gone."

"Did Mr. Hinkle die?"

"Die? No, gone. Herman's gone. He went to heaven."

"OK," Sanders said. "And how about children? Did you and Herman have any children?"

"Just the dogs. And they're gone too."

When the ambulance arrived, Margaret didn't want to let the paramedics in.

"That's the men who took Herman. I won't let them take me."

One of the paramedics was a woman. She asked through the door if she could come in. Margaret said she could.

"I just want to take your temperature and blood pressure to see if you are sick," the paramedic said.

Margaret offered her arm hesitantly. While the paramedic soothed Margaret, her partner moved in a folded gurney. When Margaret saw it, she started kicking and screaming.

"We're going to take you to a safe place," Sanders said.

"This is a safe place!" Margaret squealed. "I lied about the face at the window. I lied!"

The paramedics wanted to give her a sedative, but she was fighting them too hard.

"I got an idea," Sanders whispered to Edwards. "I'm going to go outside. Try to get her into the kitchen so she can see me."

Edwards spoke to the woman in a soft, caring voice. "OK, if you don't want to go, that's fine with us. But we're going to leave. Why don't you come over to the kitchen door and tell us goodbye?"

The woman held back suspiciously as Edwards indicated for the paramedics to go outside. Edwards stood in the doorway.

"Come say goodbye."

Margaret went slowly toward the kitchen and reached out her hand to shake Edwards' outstretched hand. In the glow of the squad's headlights, Margaret saw Sanders wheeling her cart away.

"Hey, that's mine!" Margaret screamed. "Bring my treasures back!"

"We're taking this stuff to town," Sanders said. "If you want your things, you'll have to climb aboard."

Margaret stepped out of the trailer. She looked at the paramedics, and then looked at Sanders and her cart of finds. She took a few steps down the stairs.

"That's my pencil sharpener," she said. "And I want my bowling ball."

"Of course," Sanders said, pushing the cart up to the back door of the ambulance. Soon Margaret was standing beside him, picking out the best of her collection. They loaded several pieces into the back of the ambulance. Margaret crawled inside.

Just before the paramedics closed the door, Sanders patted her hand. "Don't worry. I'll make sure the rest of your stuff is locked up inside the trailer."

"There are no locks," the woman said. "I don't have any keys."

6:02 AM

By six in the morning, a heavy fog had settled over Cade County. Nick dropped Brittany at the hospital and continued to the *Jordan Daily News*. The fog was so heavy he could barely see the building from the parking lot. It looked like a mystical fantasy world. He imagined a castle with a dragon hiding in the mist.

"You're here early," Hoss said when Nick walked into the newsroom.

"I think it's going to be one of those days that can get ahead of you," the assistant city editor responded. A couple of the copy editors had arrived, but Nick was the first to turn on a computer in the reporter section of the newsroom. While the computer booted up, Nick headed to the copy desk.

"Anything big on the news wires or the police scanner?" he asked Hoss.

"Nothing much," Hoss replied. "There was just something on the scanner about an elderly woman being transported to St. Mary's. Didn't sound newsworthy. Just a transport. But I got a call from that woman the reporters call Deluded Debbie."

"Of course." Nick chuckled. "Right on schedule. She doesn't even need a full moon to set her off. Once she gets on a kick, she can call three or four times in a day."

"Do we have an address on her? She sounds like she needs social services or something."

"She never gives her last name. Daddy Dearest must have told her not to give her name and address to strangers."

"I wish he'd told her not to call strangers at five in the morning. I think she was calling for Duke. Something about dogs barking."

"That's our Debbie."

☼

Kevin was surprised to wake up and find his mother at home. "I thought you said you were going to the gym today," he said as he walked into the kitchen.

"Changed my mind," Josie said. "Think I'll stick around until you get on the school bus."

33

"I can get ready myself," Kevin said. "I've been doing a good job. I haven't missed the bus one time since you said I could be in charge on the mornings you went to the gym."

"I know," she said, ruffling his blond curls. "But I thought it would be fun to see you off today."

Kevin pulled a box of cereal out of the kitchen cabinet. He grabbed a handful of sugary multi-colored pieces and stuffed them into his mouth.

"Don't you want a bowl and some milk?" Josie offered.

"Nope, I like mine straight," Kevin said, clicking on the small television on the kitchen counter.

Josie was holding a half gallon of milk in one hand, a bowl in the other. She watched as her son stuffed another handful of cereal into his mouth. If she was going to let him manage his own mornings, get ready for school, and catch the bus on his own, she was going to have to accept the way he had adapted the morning routine to his liking. She poured two glasses of orange juice and set one beside him as she headed upstairs to finish dressing.

She chose camel wool trousers with deep cuffs and a rust-colored silk shirt. Earth tones. Her whole wardrobe was earth tones. It was one of the reasons Hoss liked to call her Peter Pan.

In an instant, it seemed, Kevin was calling up the stairs. "I'm going out to wait for the bus."

"Did you put Chippie in the yard?"

"Done."

Josie ran down the stairs. It was thirty-five minutes after six. The bus was scheduled at forty-five minutes after. Josie hated that his bus came so early. The new route meant the bus went through their subdivision first, then went farther out to the rural stops. It meant Kevin was on the bus almost an hour every morning. Too long for kids to be on a bus. But that's what happened when school districts tried to cut costs.

Kevin was heading out the door, dragging his backpack.

"Zip up your coat," Josie said. "It's cold out there. And where's your hood?"

Kevin paused and zipped his coat. "I took the hood off. It makes me look like a girl."

"Oh, silly, lots of boys have hoods on their coats."

"Uh-uh," Kevin said, pushing open the storm door into the fog.

"Oh, my gosh. The fog is terrible. You can't go out there."

"It's just across the street," Kevin said, disappearing down the sidewalk.

"Wait!" Josie yelled. "I'll walk with you."

Josie didn't have her coat on, but the February morning seemed warmer than usual. That's probably why the fog had settled in.

"It's just across the street," Kevin repeated when she caught up to him.

"Exactly," Josie said, reaching for her son's shoulder. "How can you see to cross the street?"

"Mom, I am ten years old. I know how to cross the street."

When they reached the edge of the driveway, they both paused. The fog was as dense as a curtain. The streetlights only made it worse. They could see right in front of them. The street was clear. But the edges faded away quickly.

"Isn't this cool?" one of the kids called from the bus stop across the street.

Josie could see the kids gathering there, but the fog made them look like a picture that is out of focus.

"Bye, Mom," Kevin said.

Before Josie could stop him, he ran across the span of the street they could see under the streetlight. Polly, a next-door neighbor, appeared suddenly next to her and watched as her son Timmy ran across the street following Kevin.

"This is crazy," Polly said. "How will the bus driver see where he's going? They should have delayed the start of school."

Josie had wondered the same thing. "The fog will burn off."

"Not until the sun comes up. They'll be halfway to school by then."

The lights of the approaching school bus pierced the fog like the eyes of some eerie monster. Josie watched as the kids piled into the bus. As the last one approached the door, Josie ran across the street. She climbed the steps right behind the last student. She wanted to talk to the driver, but she didn't want to yell at him and alarm the children.

"Are you OK with this fog?" she asked the driver in a lowered voice.

"Oh, don't worry, ma'am," the driver said with the enthusiastic smile of someone who had been awake for hours. "The fog is patchy. It's worse here in town near the river. When I turn west up at the corner and head out into the country, we'll drive right out of it."

Josie didn't know the bus driver personally, although she recognized him as the same man who had been driving her son's bus for years. She knew the kids called him Mr. Joe. She noticed he was wearing the same lightweight gray polished cotton jacket that he wore in the spring and fall. A heavy winter coat hung on a hook behind his seat. Underneath she noticed something that looked like a toolbox and a pair of fur-lined snow boots. Mr. Joe looked like a man who was prepared for anything, so Josie trusted that he was right about the fog.

She glanced at the children in the bus. Most of the seats were empty since this was the beginning of the route. Kevin was about halfway back, sharing a seat with Timmy. Both had their heads down, probably playing the handheld auto-racing game Kurt had given Kevin for Christmas.

Josie stood on the sidewalk and watched the taillights disappear into the fog. She silently asked the Lord to watch over them. Sending kids into the world never gets easier.

☼

S t. Mary's emergency room was crowded and noisy when Brittany arrived.

"They used the trauma room so much last night I'm sure it's running low on supplies," the charge nurse, Amy Stillman, said as soon as she saw Brittany. "They never had a chance to resupply, so you should take care of that when you get a chance. But first, I need you to get vitals on the guy in Exam Room 1. He says his wife is poisoning him. Then get some juice for the lady in Exam Room 2. The ambulance brought her in. She's homeless, signs of exposure, dehydration. The guy in Room 3 is so drunk we're not sure of his ailment. If you put him off a little while, he'll probably pass out."

Brittany took the rooms in order, armed with a big smile and a cheery attitude.

"So, Mr. Taylor, Neal. It says here you were born in 1920. That would make you 67. Are you retired?"

"Yes, he's retired," answered the woman by his side. "He's in my hair full time."

Mr. Taylor flashed an angry look at the woman.

"She's poisoning me, I tell you," the man said. "She puts radioactive powder in my coffee. Do you have one of those Geiger counter things? Use that if you don't believe me. It will go off the charts."

The woman rolled her eyes.

"Mrs. Taylor, why don't you wait in the lobby. You'll probably be more comfortable there."

"You don't believe him, do you? This is ridiculous," she said gathering her purse, coat, and her husband's jacket. "Can't you see the old coot is crazy?"

After the woman left, Brittany placed a blood pressure cuff on Taylor, pushing up the sleeve of his red sweater.

"I know she's one of them," he said in a guarded whisper. "Feeding me that yellow powder. It glows. She thinks I don't know. She says it's my medicine. But I know."

Brittany tried to smile politely as she wrote the numbers on the chart and then placed a thermometer under his tongue. When she retrieved the thermometer a minute later, he suddenly lunged his face next to hers, eyes wide.

"Can you see it in my eyes? Look, they're turning yellow, don't you think?"

"Your eyes look fine, Mr. Taylor. Just lie back and rest now. The doctor will be right in."

As she left the examining room, Brittany saw his wife standing right outside the door.

"He's crazy," Kitty Taylor said. "Absolutely crazy. He was a prisoner of war during World War II. Sometimes I think he's back there, fighting for his life. He hides under the bed. Or out in the garage. I've been giving him fiber to keep him regular, but tonight he woke up spitting up blood. They tell me he has a bleeding ulcer and needs his medicine three times a day. I can't even find him half of the time. How can they expect me to take care of him? I don't know what to do."

"The doctor will be right in," Brittany assured the wife. "You can wait in the lobby if you would be more comfortable."

Margaret Hinkle, the woman in the next room, appeared to be in her eighties. Tests had shown she was dehydrated with dangerously low blood sugar. She sat on a chair in the corner of the examination room wearing a flannel shirt and little else. She hugged a huge black bowling bag in her lap.

"The doctor wanted you to have something sweet to drink to lift your blood sugar," Bittany said, handing the woman an apple juice box.

"Do you have any muffins?" she asked in a faint voice.

"I'll see if I can find something." Brittany patted her arm.

In the next room she was greeted by the bare bottom of a young man pulling his pants down.

"You got a bathroom?" he slurred as he wobbled over a chair. "I need a bathroom."

"It's down the hall," Brittany said, reaching out a hand to steady the staggering man. "Pull your pants up, and I'll take you there."

"I need a toilet," the man repeated and proceeded to poop in the chair.

"You can't do that," Brittany said, grabbing a bed pan from the cabinet and trying to put it under the teetering man who was twice her size. His excrement smeared on her arms. "Get up. Get up," she wailed.

"I need a toilet," he repeated, grabbing a handful of excrement and wiping it on the front of her flowered smock.

"Stop that. Hold still," Brittany wailed as the drunk swayed and smeared, leaving putrid brown streaks on the table, the wall and even Brittany's hair. "You're so drunk you can't even shit straight."

Her wails brought laughing spectators. A male nurse, chuckling to himself, pulled up the drunk's trousers and pushed him down the hall to a shower. Mumbling curse words, Brittany quickly cleaned up the exam table and chair as a custodian wheeled in a mop and bucket.

Even after a quick shower and change of clothes, Brittany wasn't ready to return to the madness of the emergency room. She told the head nurse she would restock the trauma room. The room serves the needs of all the major injuries that come into the emergency room: auto accidents, gunshot wounds, stabbings. Lots of people died there, often mean, angry people. The hospital staff joked that the room was haunted by the spirits of some of the ugliest souls in town. It was not a place anyone wanted to enter alone. But after the first half hour of her shift, Brittany was eager for alone time, even in a haunted trauma room. She didn't believe in rumors of ghosts and weird happenings. She wheeled a supply cart into the brightly lit room, counting and replacing sponges and disposable drapes, shiny forceps and scalpels, swabs and gauze. Suddenly, all the lights went off.

Someone must have turned off the lights, thinking the room was empty. "Hey, I'm in here," she shouted. Then Brittany realized that more than the overhead lights were off. Even the little red light on the defibrillator was out. If it was a power outage, the generator would kick in. She waited a few seconds, maybe a minute. The darkness was so deep, so dark, she couldn't move.

She put her hands on her hips and an angry expression on her face. "All right, Mr. Ghost or whoever you are, I don't have time for playing hide-and-seek. It's Friday the 13th, and it's a full moon, or haven't you heard?"

As suddenly as they had gone out, the lights came on. Brittany was a little embarrassed to realize she was actually panting. *Not a good time to take my blood pressure*, she thought. She looked around the room. Everything seemed to be undisturbed, exactly as it was before the lights went out. The clock on the wall read 6:36, the same as her watch. It was as if the power had never been interrupted. As if Brittany had imagined the blackout.

She sighed. *It's going to be a long day.*

☼

Deputies Sanders and Edwards were headed to the sheriff's station. They were nearing the end of their shift. Edwards had his head down and was going through his notes. He filed the reports for their car, and it took quite a bit of time to fill out the paperwork. He thought it helped to have everything in order, all the names and times and interviews at hand.

"Looks like there are patches of fog up ahead," Sanders said. "It's a good thing there isn't much traffic this early, or we'd be getting called to one accident after another."

Edwards looked up. The fog was spooky. The lights of Jordan on the horizon were swallowed up in a soupy haze. Edwards looked to his left, north of town, and then scanned the horizon to the south. Suddenly he saw that unmistakable flicker.

"Fire!" Edwards exclaimed, pointing out the passenger window. "It's the State Forest Preserve. See the glow? That's a fire! A big fire!"

Sanders leaned forward and looked around his partner. "I don't see it."

"Over there. Turn right."

Sanders turned at the next road. Now they could see the glow getting bigger, more pronounced. The clump of hardwoods along the Jordan River stood out on the prairie landscape. An iridescent orange glow peeked through the vertical stripes of black trunks and branches. Atop the stand of trees was a large puff of white smoke.

"Wow!" Sanders said.

Edwards was on the radio, reporting the blaze.

Back in the newsroom, Nick heard the chatter on the police radio behind Josie's desk. He went over and turned the radio up. Sounded like a major fire at the Forest Preserve. Mack Stanton, one of their photographers, lived out that way. He probably was on the way in.

Nick keyed the microphone to the radio the photographers carried.

"Hey, Mack. Come in, Mack. Are you in your car?"

"Mack here. I'm ahead of you, Nick. I heard the chatter on the police radio. I should be there in ten."

En route to the Forest Preserve, Deputy Edwards realized his mistake.

At first the orange glow kept getting bigger and bolder, as a fire would. But the white cloud of smoke hanging over the forest didn't grow big and black. It seemed to be getting smaller. Suddenly the remaining wisps of white just floated away. The closer they got, the more sure Edwards was that the forest was not on fire. But he didn't say anything. What could he do? Ask the dispatcher for a do over?"

"Where'd the smoke go?" Sanders asked.

Edwards looked at his partner with a horrified expression. They had been working together three years. They were good partners, but they weren't good friends. At some basic level they didn't like each other. But when Sanders saw the fear and shame in Edwards' eyes, nothing more needed to be said.

"Damn," Sanders muttered.

They turned onto Illinois Route 53 right behind one fire engine and in front of another. Half a dozen volunteer firemen in private vehicles with makeshift red lights on top were coming from all directions. As the sky began to lighten with the approaching dawn, the orange glow disappeared. Emergency vehicles poured into the preserve's parking lot, but there was no sign of fire. Not even the scent of smoke.

"Where exactly was this fire supposed to be?" the fire chief shouted as he stepped to the ground from one of the fire engines. "Does anyone have coordinates? The preserve is a big place."

Sanders stepped forward, trying to straighten his hat and look official. "You're right, Chief. It's a big place. My partner and I will drive the unpaved road that loops through the grounds and radio if we spot anything. Maybe some of the volunteer firefighters could drive around the perimeter and do the same."

"Sounds like a false alarm," one of the volunteers suggested. "The fog can play tricks on the eyes. I saw a glow, but it didn't look like a fire. It looked like those fancy new vapor lights with a cloud of fog floating around them. Eerie. But not a fire."

"You mean some numbskull can't tell the difference between vapor lights and a forest fire?" the chief bellowed. "I'm going to talk to that dispatcher. There's no excuse."

Sanders and Edwards got back into their squad car and drove the loop, hoping the crowd would be gone by the time they returned.

6:54 AM

Josie pulled into the parking lot at the *Daily News* a few minutes before seven. Duke's turquoise Pontiac pulled in next to her. The fog had lifted and daylight was just beginning to lighten the sky.

"What? No weight training this morning?" Duke called out over the hood of his car.

"No, I didn't go to the gym today. How can you tell?" Josie said, pausing at the back of her red Ford Escort.

"I'm a trained observer," Duke said as he ruffled Josie's short blond hair. "Your hair is always wet when you come from the gym because you're fresh out of the shower. Why don't you give up all the weight-lifting nonsense? Just get a gun and be done with it."

"A gun? What are you talking about?"

"All this fitness training, trying to turn yourself into superwoman. It's just because you're afraid. You've had some close calls. You should get a gun. Then you won't be afraid."

"Afraid? I'm not afraid," Josie said, heading toward the back door of the building.

"Sure you are," Duke said, following close behind. "That's what this is all about. Don't tell anybody, but I keep a gun in my car. Under the seat. I go into some bad neighborhoods."

"And you think I'm afraid? You're the one who's afraid."

"Not since I got a gun."

"Don't you see, the fact that you have a gun proves that you're afraid. I'm not lifting weights because I'm afraid. Just the opposite. I love life. I want to be at my best. Improving myself makes me feel good. Carrying a gun would make me feel paranoid. I'd have to keep looking around for some reason to use it. I don't want to live like that."

"It doesn't make me—"

Duke stopped midsentence as he and Josie reached the back door. A ladder was leaning against the building, right over the entrance. One of the custodians was working on something.

"What's going on?" Josie called up at the man.

"Ice jam," the custodian called down. "The snow is melting off the roof faster than the ice is melting in the gutter. Water is going to get between the walls if I don't bust up this ice jam."

41

Josie and Duke stood there. They couldn't get in the back door without walking right under the ladder. As they waited, Rudy walked up from the parking lot.. Josie bit her lip. She was glad Duke was there so she didn't have to deal with Rudy alone first thing.

"What's up?" Rudy asked.

"Ice jam," Duke said. "The only way to go in is to walk under a ladder."

"On Friday the 13th," Josie added.

"You're kidding me," Rudy said. "You don't really believe in superstitions like ladders and Friday the 13th, do you?"

Josie and Duke exchanged glances.

"I'm not superstitious," Duke said. "But it doesn't look real safe to walk under a ladder."

Rudy giggled and started skipping around them, chanting in an Irish brogue. "Well, I'm a wee leprechaun, you see, and I think this ladder is an enchanted entrance."

Although Rudy was almost six-foot tall, Josie thought he did resemble a wee leprechaun. He had dark auburn hair, twinkling green eyes, and so many freckles his skin glowed.

Rudy danced under the ladder, brandishing his magnetic entry key. "I just take this magic key, slip it into this wee slot, and poof, the door opens."

Rudy giggled delightedly and danced his way through the door.

"I don't believe in leprechauns either," Duke said, grabbing the open door before it closed. He slipped under the ladder and followed Rudy inside. Josie hesitated.

From inside the building, Duke pushed the door open with one arm. "You coming?"

Josie looked up at the workman, hesitated another second, and then rushed under the ladder. Just as she reached the door, the gutter came loose and ice water poured down on her head.

Duke doubled over with laughter. "Puppy puddles. Just because you didn't shower at the gym doesn't mean you should take one at the door," he said between laughs. "You look like a drowned cat."

Josie appeared pitifully small and was shivering as Duke ushered her into the newsroom, announcing her brush with the ladder. Reporters and copy editors gathered around, laughing as she removed her soaked winter coat.

The custodian appeared in the doorway. "I'm sorry, Ms. Braun. It just busted loose. I didn't mean to get you wet."

"Don't worry about it, Mike," Josie called back with a weak wave. "Nothing like a cold splash to start the day."

Rudy pushed through the laughing reporters and held out a fluffy white terry towel. "I always keep one in the bottom drawer for emergencies." He draped it over Josie's head and began drying her hair.

Josie backed away from his touch. She accepted the towel and dabbed at her wet hair. "Thanks."

Becky gave her a hot pink cardigan that was much too big and clashed with Josie's rust-colored silk shirt. But it felt good and warm against Josie's chilled skin.

"Well, we got our Friday the 13th mishap out of the way first thing," Josie said, heading to her desk. "Now we can get down to work."

There wasn't time for joking. Josie needed to check messages and gather information for the news meeting that launched every day at seven-fifteen. Duke stopped her as she was heading to the office of managing editor, Hammond Reginald.

"I gotta run downtown," he said. "Got a court hearing at eight. And the Rose Street Bridge is broken. Thought I'd stop by and see how long it's going to be out. I should be back well before deadline at ten."

Duke was careful to leave the impression he was covering something in the courthouse rather than admit his only daughter was appearing before the judge. Josie scratched the word "bridge" with a question mark on her story list and rushed into the meeting.

"Today's big news is the fire that never was," Nick said, when all the editors had gathered at the round table in Hammond's office. "The call came in about six-thirty that the Forest Preserve was on fire. All these fire engines and volunteers showed up, but it was false alarm."

"A false alarm? What's the story in that?" Hammond asked.

"Mack got a picture of the fire," Nick said, beaming.

"A picture of the fire that never was?" Hammond asked.

"Yep. It was some sort of optical illusion caused by the fog and those new vapor lights along Illinois 53. Evidently, lots of people saw it. Police and fire got a bunch of calls. Some people thought it was a UFO. One guy even thought it was the second coming. Becky's gathering quotes. If we run the picture in color, Mack says it looks pretty eerie."

"And we have full color available?" Hammond asked.

"Yes, sir," Josie said. "I requested color for Dee Licious."

"What's delicious? Some food fair?" Hoss asked.

"Sounds like a porn star," Hammond said.

"Are you kidding me?" exclaimed Nick. "You guys haven't heard of Dee Licious? She's a rocker. Lead singer for Death Metal, one of the hottest new bands."

"Did you say Deaf Metal?" asked the lifestyle editor, Dottie Carson.

"Ought to be as loud as some of these bands play," mumbled Dick Stone, the sports editor.

Josie smiled. "Dee is going to be visiting the Holiday Quad movie theater at ten this morning for the opening of *Dieday the 13th*. It's a spoof of all the *Friday the 13th* slasher movies. They've been coming out with sequels every year since 1980. But there was some sort of delay this year. *Friday the 13th: Part VII* isn't coming out until next year. An independent filmmaker decided to take advantage of all those slasher fans thirsting for new blood and is coming out with this *Dieday* spoof."

"From what I've read, Dee gets ripped to smithereens in the opening scene," Nick said, swishing an imaginary sword through the air. "She isn't in the movie for long, but Death Metal plays on the sound track. The band isn't coming to Jordan. Just Dee, cutting a ribbon or something and posing for pictures. I'm betting horror movie fans and heavy metal freaks will be packing the theater lobby. It should be totally creepy."

"Creepy, huh," Hammond said, rubbing his chin. "Not my idea of big news. What else you got?"

Everyone looked toward Josie. Hammond was often a hard sell. Josie was used to stacking the deck.

"Rudy is working on a piece about the school tax referendum next month. He's got some good examples of what will be cut if the referendum fails. I was planning it for Sunday. It's an important issue, but a little dull for the top story."

"Sex it up a bit," Hammond said, slamming the table. "That's big bucks. Money and murder, the only two topics worth the top spot. What's our investigative genius Duke up to?"

"He's checking into a broken bridge this morning," Josie said.

"Dang bridges are always breaking," Hammond mumbled. "So what's happening in the world, Hoss?"

"If you're looking for big money, Congress is still talking about Reagan's trillion-dollar budget." Hoss rifled through a stack of wire copy. "I'm watching the Dow Jones average to see if it closes above 2,200 again. It's been a good week on the stock market. We've also got plenty of murder over in the Philippines. Troops massacred seventeen civilians in a protest there."

Hoss looked around at the faces at the table.

"There's something else. It may be nothing. We had a story yesterday about the US doing nuclear tests in Nevada. Today one of our satellites recorded a nuclear test clear on the other side of the world, out in the middle of the Pacific. Nobody's claiming it. I'm just thinking with all that political unrest in the Philippines, and Reagan pulling out of the SALT II treaty last year, this could turn into something big."

"Good one," Hammond said, pointing a finger at Hoss. "Josie, work with Hoss to find a local angle. What's up in sports, Dick?"

One by one the editors reported on stories in progress. Suddenly Hammond stood up. "Thanks, everyone." The meeting was over. Little was decided. News is too fluid. A lot would change before the first front page

44

came together at ten, with room for more changes before the final edition at noon.

"So are we just going to forget all about Dee Licious and *Dieday the 13th*?" Nick asked when they were a safe distance from the managing editor's office.

Josie smiled. "Haven't you learned yet? Ham wins in the meeting; I win on the page. We will send Becky to cover the movie event exactly as we planned. She'll come back with a fantastic story. Page will shoot great pictures and, voila, page 1. The problem is timing. Dee is supposed to do her thing at ten, and it should all be over by eleven when the movie is scheduled to begin. If everything goes according to schedule, I think we can get pictures and story in time for the final edition. But if Cutie Pie is late, then we'll just have some sort of inside piece about the fans waiting for her. Dee will be just as luscious on Saturday's front page. News is always slow on Saturdays."

Josie stopped by Rudy's desk. He was down on his knees entertaining a small boy while the lad's mother talked to Dottie about an upcoming social event. Kids were Rudy's passion. He could get children to talk to him when most reporters couldn't. His natural sense of humor made even the dullest school board meeting worth reading.

Rudy's auburn hair was a little shaggy, brushing his ears and curling over the collar of his green turtleneck sweater. The casually irreverent look reminded Josie of a college professor. Not as anti-establishment as a long-haired hippie, but definitely a free thinker.

"Got a new fan, I see," Josie said to announce her presence.

Rudy stood. "Colin here is going to be an astronaut. He wants to go to the moon. I told him to pay close attention when he goes to bed tonight because the moon should be nice and big."

"It's snowing on the moon," Colin said.

"No, not exactly," Rudy said, bending down to Colin's level. "I said when there's a full moon in February, it's called the Snow Moon. But it doesn't snow on the moon. At least I don't think so. You'll have to take a picture when you go there and let me know."

After the boy left with his mother, Josie explained Hammond's directive to "sex up" the school referendum story.

"Sex it up?" Rudy exclaimed.

"Oh, don't worry. That's just journalism talk," Josie said, shaking her head. "It means make the story more appealing to the reader, more fun."

"I thought about that," Rudy said. "I went over and talked to some kids yesterday. I asked what they would do with $1.8 million. I got some pretty wild answers. One boy wants to build a bridge across Lake Michigan so it won't take so long to drive to his grandmother's house in Grand Rapids. A girl said she would build a giant cat house for all the stray kitties. I got Mack to shoot some mug shots of the kids, so we can put their quotes under their pictures. Should make a fun element on the page."

"Rudy, you're a genius. I should have known you would have it under control," Josie said with a conciliatory smile. "Pull it together in case we decide to run it in today's paper instead of Sunday."

"Oh, I need to stop by the school and double check the photo identifications."

"Good. You can run over to the school office now. I'll read your story so we can decide placement."

Josie started walking away when Rudy added, "I ... ah ... wanted to talk to you about last night."

"We can talk after deadline," Josie said, not even slowing down.

When Brittany returned to Neal Taylor's cubicle to administer the dose of antacid the doctor had prescribed, she was surprised to find the cubicle empty. A quick check at the desk confirmed he had not been released or sent for another test. He was missing. He wasn't in the restroom. His wife in the lobby hadn't seen him. Brittany checked the neighboring cubicle where Margaret Hinkle was still clutching her bowling bag.

"Did a man come in here?" Brittany asked "He's sixty-ish, balding, wearing a red sweater."

Margaret just looked at her wide-eyed. Brittany glanced around and didn't see anything out of place in the cubicle. "Someone from social services will be in to see you in a minute," she said and pulled the curtain closed as she left.

When she had walked away, Neal Taylor stepped out from behind the cabinet where he had been hiding. "Thanks, honey," Taylor said. He held Margaret's hand. "You've been a big help. I won't forget this."

He parted the curtain just enough to see a doctor and nurse conversing outside. He held a finger to his lips, and Margaret pulled her bowling ball a little closer.

"There he is. I see his shoes," Kitty Taylor said.

Brittany threw back the curtain as Neal stumbled across the cubicle to return to his hiding spot behind the cabinet.

"Come on, Neal, you're being ridiculous," Kitty said. She reached for her husband's arm and Brittany took his other arm.

"Come on, Mr. Taylor," Brittany said soothingly, "this medicine will make you feel better."

"You won't take me alive! You'll never take me alive!" Neal Taylor bellowed, throwing punches at them.

46

"Good grief, Mr. Taylor, it's just a little Maalox. It will help settle your stomach," Brittany said, grabbing a firmer hold.

A male nurse stepped in, and the three of them managed to escort Neal back to his cubicle. Margaret wiggled the fingers of one hand in a tiny wave goodbye.

☼

At the sheriff's station, deputies Sanders and Edwards filed the necessary reports to end their shift. While Edwards filed a request for an autopsy on the frozen bison, Sanders called the hospital to check on Margaret Hinkle. After they finished the paperwork, Sheriff Walt Coleman summoned them into his office.

"I'm trying to understand what happened this morning at the forest preserve." Coleman said. "The dispatcher said Edwards made the original call."

"That's right, sir," Edwards said. "I saw a glow among the trees and something I took to be smoke above. And there was a flicker consistent with a conflagration."

"Don't try to impress me with big words," Coleman said. "You screwed up, didn't ya? Do you have any idea what a false alarm costs the county?"

"I'm sorry, sir. It was my best judgment at the time."

"Well, I expect better judgment from now on."

"We both saw it, and it did look like a fire," Sanders said, jumping into the conversation. "We aren't the only ones who saw it. I heard several in the squad room talking about the unusual visual phenomenon created by the lights and the fog."

"Yeah, but no one else called in a false fire alarm, am I right?" Coleman said. "Evidently they can tell the difference between a visual phenomenon and a forest fire."

"Sir, Deputy Edwards has an excellent record for spotting fires," Sanders continued. "Just last night he spotted a fire in Cole Township. A farmhouse, one fatality. But if he hadn't spotted the fire so quickly, additional farm buildings would have burned, and it might have been a threat to neighboring property."

Coleman seemed to consider Sanders' defense of his partner.

"OK." He leaned back in his chair. "I'll let this morning's incident slide. But I want your car to report in early tonight. Instead of starting your shift at eleven, start at seven and plan to work twelve straight. This full moon is bringing out the crazies. I suspect we'll need extra men on tonight."

"Sir, that's less than twelve hours from now," Edwards said.

47

"Yeah, I know." The sheriff smiled. "You can file a complaint with the union if you want, but if you do, I'll file a complaint about this morning's misdirection. Do I make myself clear?"

"Sure. We'll be ready to roll at seven," Sanders said.

8:10 AM

When Rudy arrived at Westside Elementary, two fifth-grade boys were outside raising the flag. He loved the way the boys took the job so seriously, carefully unfolding the precious flag, struggling to compress the spring hooks and fit one inside each grommet without dropping the flag on the ground. Then one boy pulled the rope while the other corralled the tail of the flag until it was safely over his head. They both pulled it up as the wind whipped the fabric around and the pulley clanged against the pole.

"Good job," Rudy said as he passed the boys.

The day had barely begun, but the school office was filled with kids. One girl was sitting in a chair with her legs drawn up to her chest. She was rocking back and forth, sobbing quietly. Two boys were trying to explain what had caused a playground altercation. They kept talking over each other as Gail, the secretary, tried to decipher their tale. A little girl with pigtails tired of waiting to get Gail's attention. She pulled a chair up to the counter and climbed up on it. She helped herself to a pencil from a mug on the desk behind the counter.

"What are you doing?" Gail said, reaching for the mug.

"I left my pencil box at home, and I don't have a pencil," the girl said. "Miss Engles will give me a demerit."

The secretary handed a pencil to the girl.

"You ask. You don't climb," she said. "Now put the chair back and get to class, or you'll have two demerits."

She motioned the boys to sit down as well.

"What can I do for you this morning, Rudy?"

"Oh, I just want to confirm a couple of photo identifications, check the name spellings and make sure you have releases for the kids in the pictures."

"Just that, huh?" Gail smiled as the phone rang.

"Go ahead. I'm not in a hurry," Rudy said, gesturing toward the ringing phone.

He took a seat next to the sobbing girl. Once Gail was busy on the phone, Rudy started his monkey impersonation. He scratched his side and made an "*eeee eee*" noise. When the girl looked at him, he stopped. When she looked away, he repeated the sound. Soon the two squabbling boys were out of their chairs, laughing at Rudy.

"Do it again. Do it again," one of the boys said.

"What?" Rudy looked around innocently. "I don't know what you're talking about. You boys better go back to your chairs before Miss Bulosi gets off the phone."

The boys obeyed, but kept an eye on Rudy. The girl stopped her sobbing and rocking. She stole a glance at Rudy. He gave a quick underarm scratch and a trill of "*eee eee*." The boys squealed and the girl smiled. Rudy placed a finger to his lips and shook his head. Gail was still on the phone. Rudy looked around and gave another quick monkey impersonation. The girl giggled, and one of the boys shushed her with a finger to his lips.

Gail hung up the phone and looked over the counter. "Did I miss something?"

"Oh, no," Rudy said. "We've just been waiting quietly, haven't we, kids?"

The boys agreed loudly. The girl just smiled. Rudy walked up to the counter and laid out the six photos he wanted to check.

The phone rang again.

"I'm sorry," Gail said. "We have a bus that's running late."

Rudy waved a hand to assure Gail it was OK, but he remained at the counter as she took the call.

"I tried to call you," Rudy heard her say. "Your bus had some problems with its route this morning. Transportation is sending another bus to pick up the remaining children. It should be there in about thirty minutes. Let me double-check your address and normal pickup time."

Rudy pretended to be busy with the photographs so he wouldn't appear to be eavesdropping. Gail hung up and rejoined him at the counter. She quickly identified the children in the photos and consulted a class roster to check spelling and whether parents had filed a form to allow photos to be published.

"So, what happened? One of the buses break down?" Rudy asked as Gail was finishing the final name check.

"We don't know for sure. It's just a little late. Is that everything?"

Rudy thanked Gail and asked to see the principal, Andy Barton.

"He's pretty tied up this morning with the bus snafu," Gail said. She leaned over the counter. "Why don't you kids go back to class. Mr. Barton is busy. I think your problems can wait until lunch break, don't you?"

Rudy headed back to the *Daily News*. Josie was talking to Becky, so he stopped by Nick's desk and told him he had confirmed the children's photo identifications and releases.

"Good, that will give us a backup story in case Dee Licious falls through," Nick said.

"One more thing," Rudy added. "One of the buses is late, and evidently they haven't heard from the driver. Sounds like a breakdown or an accident.

You didn't get any police reports about an accident involving a school bus did you?"

"School bus? No. But if the driver hasn't called in, that sounds serious."

"Or maybe his radio is out."

"Could be. Sounds like a Friday the 13th kind of problem."

Becky was standing at Josie's desk flipping the pages of her reporter's notebook and giving her editor an animated account of her morning's phone interviews. Josie was only half listening while she scanned the page proofs on her desk, marking errors with a red pen.

"I got all kinds of great comments from people who saw the glowing forest this morning," Becky said. "I think I'll throw in some stuff about the full moon."

"Is that related?" Josie asked.

"Not really. The weather service blames the fog and the vapor lights for the unusual visual effect. But I thought since it's so eerie, and full moons are a little eerie, that it fits together. Did you know they did a study at the university and found that 95 percent of menstruating women start their period within two weeks of a full moon? Isn't that something?"

Josie looked up at Becky and shook her head. "What happened to the other 5 percent?"

"Huh?"

"Becky, think. There's a full moon every four weeks, so two weeks before or after the full moon covers the whole month."

"Oh," Becky said, looking a little confused.

"So what happens to the other 5 percent?"

A slow smile came to Becky's face. "Oh, I see what you mean. I don't know. Dumb study, huh?"

"Anything else on the cop beat this morning?"

"Guy died in a house fire in Cole Township. He was on oxygen for his emphysema. They think a cigarette caught the oxygen tank on fire. Last night some motorist reported a body along Clark Road, but it turned out to be a dead buffalo from the A-Lab."

"Oh, interesting," Josie said, initialing a page proof. "When Duke gets back from downtown, I'm going to have him go out to the A-Lab to get a comment from one of the scientists about some strange nuclear explosion in the Pacific. I'll have him ask about the bison while he's there. I didn't realize they were out grazing in the winter."

"What did you think? They flew to Florida?"

"Sounds better than pawing through a foot of snow looking for something to eat. Anything else?"

Becky looked around to see if anyone was close enough to overhear.

"I got a strange call from the DEA," she whispered. "They asked if I knew anything about Teasdale being involved with drugs."

"The coroner?"

"Yeah. Isn't that something? They're calling me to see what I know."

"Well, Teasdale always seems a little suspicious, but drugs?"

"The source said he flies his private plane into Colombia all the time. They think maybe he's shipping drugs back to the States. But in order to get a warrant to search his warehouse, they've got to have some other connection to drugs. They were asking me if I had heard anything about wild parties at his compound."

Josie shook her head. "The DEA is asking the newspaper to do its investigation? Now I've heard everything. So what did you tell him?"

"I said I'd ask around. Can't hurt to have a friend in the DEA."

"True. Are you ready for Dee Licious?"

Becky beamed. "Can't wait. Really. I'm going to head over there as soon as I finish the cop stuff. I'm anxious to talk to the people in the crowd."

"Good. Call me with some quotes." Josie stood up to hand a corrected proof to Nick. "We'll use it as a holder story. I'm going to have Mack shoot some early pictures of the crowd. We can use that in the first run. Then I'll send Page over to get pictures after Dee arrives, and we'll have that for the final. I need you back here by eleven to write the story."

Nick was on the phone with Deluded Debbie. She was sobbing uncontrollably.

"I swallowed the moon," she kept saying over and over. "It was a little bitty new moon, just a sliver. And now it has grown into a full moon. And I swallowed it. The full moon is in my stomach!"

"I don't think you can swallow a moon, Debbie. Even a little sliver of a moon."

"And when I took my bath this morning, all of my DNA went down the drain. What am I going to do? My DNA is gone. My man in the moon won't have any DNA."

Nick chuckled. "I think the man in the moon is made of green cheese, not DNA."

"Green cheese? I didn't eat any cheese. I don't like cheese."

"Debbie, you're sounding a little better. Do you have a neighbor or somebody who can come over and help you when you get scared? I can't really help you over the phone."

"No, nobody," Debbie said and started to cry again. "What will I do without my DNA? I pulled the plug, and the water drained out. All of my DNA is gone. What will I do?"

Nick shook his head. "Don't worry, Debbie. Just drink a big glass of water, and your DNA will come back."

"It will?"
"Sure."

☼

Duke ignored the closed sign and pulled up in front of Rose Street Bridge. A man in a heavy Carhart jacket approached before Duke could get out of his car.

"Can't you read? The bridge is closed for repairs."

Duke handed the man his business card. "I'm from the *Daily News*. Thought I'd do a little story about the closing. What's wrong with the bridge? How long will it be down? I mean up," Duke said, gesturing toward the blue steel monstrosity sticking up from the pavement.

"Should be working before noon. A relay switch needs replacing. But nothing's ever easy on these things. You can't get a screw to turn 'cause it's rusted. Or a bolt breaks, and it's an odd size. Nothing fits like it should."

"Good, if the bridge is back in operation today, there's no need to do a story. Say, you wouldn't happen to be the tender who was working last night, would you?"

"Nah, I'm the day supervisor. Why?"

Duke pointed to Jennifer in the front seat.

"My daughter would like to thank your bridge tender for saving her life," Duke said. "She and one of her friends rode the bridge last night."

The bridge supervisor raised his eyebrows. "I heard."

"She did a stupid thing, and she knows that now. She made her appearance in court this morning and accepted responsibility for her actions. She'll be paying a hundred-dollar fine out of her savings. She'll be on probation for six months, so I'm pretty sure she won't even be jaywalking."

Duke and the bridge supervisor shared a chuckle, and Duke continued his explanation.

"I just thought maybe if she went inside the control house, saw how the bridge operates, talked to the man, maybe she'd have a little more respect. It's easy to think of the bridge as an inanimate object. She didn't think about how she was affecting somebody else, causing him trouble. She needs to apologize."

"Well, man's name is Stan Barrows," the supervisor said. "His shift doesn't start until eleven tonight. I can give you two a tour of the bridge control shed, if you think that will impress her."

Duke motioned for Jennifer to join them, and she reluctantly stepped out of the car.

"Want to see what makes the bridge work?" the supervisor asked.

Jennifer looked to her father and then back to the bridge supervisor. She shrugged. "Yeah, sure, I guess."

Inside the small frame building next to the bridge, the three of them clanged up a flight of metal stairs. On the second floor was a large room that didn't look that different from a pilothouse on a tug. Windows wrapped around three sides on the west end of the room facing the river. A countertop full of controls ran under the windows. The doors under the counter were open, and a workman was adjusting something with a screwdriver. Duke heard the familiar chatter of a police radio and spotted one on a shelf.

"Yeah, all the bridge control rooms have a police radio. We're part of the traffic system. We have to know what's going on," the supervisor said. "We're not cops, but the tenders use a radio channel to communicate with each other and listen for any ambulances or fire engines headed this way. We try to keep things running smoothly when we can."

"That's it," the workman said, rising to his feet. "The bridge ought to work now."

"Young lady, would you like to make the bridge move?" the supervisor asked.

Jennifer looked to her father and the bridge supervisor. "Yeah, sure," she said, showing a bit more enthusiasm than before.

The supervisor indicated which lever to squeeze. He explained it was a "dead man" switch. She had to squeeze for the bridge to move. If she let go, the bridge would stop. The supervisor turned on the clanging bridge bells and gave Jennifer the signal to lower the bridge. She squeezed. The heavy bridge shuddered and started to move. Jennifer's smile became larger and brighter as the two halves of the bridge came together.

"We'll run a checklist and then reopen the bridge," the supervisor said. "And it's not even nine yet. It's gonna be a good day."

"Thanks for the tour," Duke said and escorted Jennifer toward the stairs.

"You know, it's a shame you didn't get to meet Stan under better circumstances," the supervisor said. "He really likes young people. Raised six kids of his own. Now he's a volunteer band director for the after-school program at the community center. Has those tough kids marching in time all summer. You know, you could stop by the community center if you want to meet him. He has band practice weekdays at four."

Duke looked to Jennifer. "Yeah, that sounds good," she said. "I can stop by after class. Thanks for the tour. I'm very sorry for the trouble I caused last night. Do you like musical theater? I'm a student at the community college, and we're doing *Kiss Me, Kate*, a musical comedy based on Shakespeare's *The Taming of the Shrew*. I'd be glad to give you a couple of tickets."

Jennifer held out two strips of pink construction paper.

"These are for tonight at eight, but you could probably exchange them for tickets for tomorrow for Valentine's Day. It's a big auditorium. I don't think it's going to sell out. We have a show Sunday afternoon too."

The bridge supervisor accepted the tickets and nodded slowly. "Yeah, well, the wife might like that. OK. Sure. I'll go to the play if you promise to stay off bridges."

"Oh, don't worry, sir. I'm cured."

A buzzer grabbed the supervisor's attention.

"Well, look at that. We got the bridge down just in time to put it up again. It's going to be a heavy day on the waterway. The river never freezes over, but during a cold spell it gets clogged with ice around the edges, especially the pockets where the barges dock. When you get a couple of warmer days like this, the ice melts. Everyone wants to move to the next stop before it gets cold and icy again."

Duke and his daughter headed down the stairs. A breeze was blowing down the river valley, making them hurry back to their car. Upriver the Cole Street Bridge was opening. Bells clanged on the Rose Street Bridge, and they watched as the majestic monster slowly rose in front of them.

"The bridges are neat, aren't they?" Jennifer said.

"Yeah, if you're not trying to get to work on time," Duke replied.

☼

Across the river, Carolyn Cantrell watched the same bridge ballet, one bridge after another. When the barge had passed and the Jackson Street Bridge lowered, she drove her white Taurus over the noisy metal deck. Just a block into town, she turned into the municipal lot at the police station. All these years later, whenever she visited the station, she always thought of her husband.

The low dark-brick police station, attached to the even older white-stone city hall, was brand-new in the sixties. It was everything modern and promising, just like her marriage to the city's first black policeman. Oh, they were the perfect modern couple then. She was the blonde flower child with straight hair down to her waist and a skirt that brushed her ankles. He was the beefy black man who trimmed off his gorgeous Afro so he could join the police force. Although he had been gone for eighteen years, she was still in love with that man.

She walked into the station and recognized a familiar figure standing at the front desk. He was a little heavier and grayer, but Carolyn smiled to think that Reuben Jetter still was bugging the Jordan police. Reuben was what her husband used to call "a regular." He was constantly reporting unidentified flying objects or faces he recognized from the "Wanted" posters in the post office. A few years back, a new police chief banned him from the building. Reuben responded by filling out magazine subscription cards with the chief's name. Suddenly the office was inundated with *Playboy*, *Hustler*, *Field and Stream*, *Guns and Ammo*, and dozens of other publications. A few weeks later, the bills arrived. Afraid he wouldn't get credit for his juvenile prank, Reuben called the chief to ask if he was enjoying the magazines. Reuben had even gotten himself arrested a few times for disturbing the peace or damaging public property with graffiti. Once he ran for a city council opening, claiming the arrests had been on purpose as his "undercover" inspection of the city jails.

"But I tell you, I saw Elvis," Reuben was saying to the desk sergeant. "It was him. I got some photographs. Just develop this film, and you can see for yourself."

"Yeah, I know, Reuben. Where was he this time? Burger King?" The sergeant chuckled as he rolled the film canister around in his hand.

"No, actually he was at Denny's eating a fried-egg sandwich with ketchup. It's one of his favorites. That's how I knew it was him. He was in a disguise. He was wearing a flannel shirt. And his hair is gray and thinning now. But you can tell it's him. Just look at the pictures on this film."

The sergeant handed the canister back across the counter.

"You keep 'em, Reuben," he said. "They might be worth something."

"You don't believe me." Reuben turned around to Carolyn. "You believe me, don't you, lady? Elvis Presley is alive."

Carolyn laughed. "Well, I guess it's possible."

"See, she believes me," Reuben said, turning back to the desk sergeant. "He's in town to see his daughter."

"Lisa Presley is in town?" Carolyn asked.

"Oh, no. Not that daughter," Reuben said, spinning back and forth between the sergeant and Carolyn as he talked. "The King had lots of ladies and lots of illegitimate children. But you can tell them by the eyes. Those pale blue eyes. And the black hair. And the talent. They can sing like him. He's the secret father of Dee Licious. She's coming to the movie theater today. That's why he's here, to hook up with her."

"Uh-huh," the desk sergeant said. "Well, you'd better hurry over there and get some more pictures of the two of them together, don't you think?"

"I plan to," Reuben said. "They'll be worth hundreds of dollars. Thousands even. All the magazines will want them."

He was still chattering about his latest scheme as he headed out the door. Carolyn and the desk sergeant exchanged smiles that grew into laughter after the door closed and Reuben was safely outside.

"To think our days are wasted on such as these," the sergeant said. "It happens every time there's a full moon. I got a call this morning from a guy who said aliens were getting into his house through the electrical outlets. They sounded like your typical little green men except they were electric. They glowed like little Christmas bulbs. They were under the furniture and behind the refrigerator and all over the house, he said. They were trying to hide from him, but he knew they were there because of the glow."

"Oh, my," Carolyn said.

"Yeah, I listened to this man go on and on for several minutes. Then it hit me. I says, 'Wait a minute. You say they come in through the light sockets?' 'Yeah,' the man says, real serious like. 'Well, then that's your interstate commerce,' I says to him. 'You gotta call the feds. It's outta the city's jurisdiction.' So I gave him the number for the FBI. I shouldn't have all the fun." The desk sergeant laughed heartily at his brilliant ruse.

Carolyn took the elevator to the second floor. She walked back into the investigations office, greeting one officer after another by first name. These were members of the family. Old friends who knew her husband. New friends of her son. People who had sat at her Sunday dinner table. Carolyn enjoyed seeing them again. She should stop by the office more often. Yet when she caught her son's eye across the room, she knew he wasn't glad to see her. She was intruding where mothers aren't welcome. But she would say her piece. He would hear her out.

"Hi, Mom," Tom said, placing his hands on his mother's shoulders and kissing her cheek politely. "What are you doing here?"

"I don't get to see much of you at the house these days," Carolyn said, taking the chair next to Tom's desk. He sat down and pulled his chair close to hers so they could talk softly.

"I'll be home tonight," he said. "And I'm off this weekend. We'll talk then."

"I suspect Becky will have something to say about that."

"Listen, Mom. I'm sorry Becky called you last night. She shouldn't have done that."

"I'm glad she did," Carolyn said, smoothing her skirt self-consciously. "I know she doesn't like me."

"Oh, Mom, that's not true. Becky is fond of you and Linda."

"Linda perhaps, but she doesn't like me because I'm white."

"Mom, that's ridiculous. Becky's not a bigot."

"Prejudice comes in all colors, son. I saw the startled look on her face the first time we met. Nobody warned her that your mother was white. And no matter how much she smiles and tries to treat me nice, I can see that she doesn't really trust me."

"Mom, that's nonsense. We'll talk about this tonight. This isn't the place—"

"Oh, but this is a perfect place. A place where our words will remain civil because they must. A place where you won't storm away in a huff if you don't like what you hear."

"Mom."

"You have a temper, Tom. And I tend to tiptoe around your temper. That's why we never talk about these issues. About the perceptions people have about me being white and you being black. How they see us differently. People do, you know."

"Mom, I've got work to do. We'll talk this weekend."

"No, we can't solve all the issues of race, I know. But I want you to hear me on this one. When Becky called me last night, it was a huge breakthrough. She wasn't playing nicey nice anymore. She was calling me woman to woman. Not black woman to white woman, not girlfriend to mother, but woman to woman. Equals. She was asking me to understand her feelings. She was trusting that I would, and I do. I don't want to come between you and your woman. I'm not an invalid, you know. I raised you kids. I'm a capable person. And I won't have a son of mine using me as an excuse not to commit to the woman in his life."

"Mom, my relationship with Becky isn't any of your business."

"You made it my business every time you used me as a crutch to fend off any permanent commitment. I don't want you living at home anymore, Thomas. You are a grown man. You shouldn't have your mother doing your laundry and fixing your breakfast."

"Mom, I had no idea you felt like this."

"I didn't either. But I remember how it was with your dad and me. Both of our parents were opposed to the match, naturally. But your father wouldn't let it go. He worked hard to win my father's respect because he knew I didn't want to disappoint my dad. Eventually I realized I was leaning on my dad, letting his prejudices keep me from confronting my own fears. I had to let go and commit to your father, or our relationship would have withered away. If you love Becky, I don't want you to lose her because you're leaning on me. Love is scary. Commitment is even scarier. But unless you grab it with both hands, it will slip away."

Tom sat in stunned silence. Carolyn stood up abruptly.

"There, I've said it. It's up to you what you do with it. I know you're going to have a busy day, what with the full moon and all. I'll understand if you don't make it to my show tonight."

"Show?"

"I knew you would forget. *Kiss Me, Kate*. It's the musical I'm directing for the college this semester. I gave you some tickets for opening night."

"Oh, yeah, I remember those. That's tonight? We'll be there. Me and Becky."

Carolyn smiled. "Good."

☼

Neal Taylor needed to escape, but there were too many people outside his cubicle. All those men and women talking about him. There was only one other choice. He slipped under the white sheet wall into the next space. Margaret Hinkle still was sitting in the same chair with the bowling ball bag in her lap.

58

Neal held a finger to his lips. Margaret responded with a finger to her lips. Neal headed across her cubicle to the other side, away from the main corridor. He pulled the curtain just an inch or two and spied the dark hall and double doors beyond.

"Take me with you," Margaret said in a meek voice.

"I can't. It's too dangerous," Neal said, looking at her over his shoulder.

"But I'm afraid," Margaret said. "I don't trust them."

"You'll be OK," Neal said with a smile. "No one would hurt a beautiful woman like you."

He blew her a kiss and slipped out the back of the cubicle. He pressed his back along the wall and slithered toward the double doors. Through the window in the door he saw the lobby beyond. Rows of people sitting in chairs waiting. And her. The woman who had tried to poison him. He pressed his back against the wall again, hoping she hadn't seen him. At the other end of the hall he saw a man in a light blue uniform with no insignia. He'd noticed the uniforms in this country were devoid of buttons and ribbons. The officers wore plain white coats, but the soldiers were dressed in green or blue or magenta, with no insignia. Just a name tag clipped to the pocket.

Communism, Neal thought. *It was so plain. No individual distinction.*

The soldier in blue was pushing one of those gurneys. Another fallen soldier, no doubt. At the far end of the hall, the soldier slammed a button on the wall. A pair of doors opened and he pushed the gurney through. That was the trick. Those doors.

Neal looked down at his clothes. He was wearing the jeans and red sweater she had given him this morning. He stood out among the more spartan soldiers. Wedged along the wall behind the cubicle was a cart. Neal lifted the lid. Laundry. It was the ideal place to hide. But as he looked inside, he spotted one of the plain light blue uniforms, just like the man he had seen at the end of the hall. He snagged the uniform, tucked it under his arm and slipped back into the cubicle with the beautiful woman waiting.

"You're back," Margaret said. "I thought I'd lost you forever."

Neal pressed a finger to his lips. He laid down the blue uniform and began ripping off his sweater and jeans.

"Oh, my," Margaret said, smiling shyly.

"Get on the gurney," Neal whispered, pointing to the bed in the center of the room. "I've got an idea."

As Neal put on the blue uniform, tying it tight around his waist, Margaret carried her bowling bag over to the gurney. With some difficulty, she climbed aboard.

"We'll have to leave this behind," Neal said, reaching for the bowling bag.

"Oh, no," Margaret said and tightened her grip on it.

"This is going to be a difficult trip," Neal whispered, looking deep into Margaret's eyes. "We don't have time for suitcases or sentimentality."

"Oh." Margaret whimpered a bit, then released her grip.

"Now lay back and I'll cover you up with this sheet," Neal said.

Margaret did as he requested. He pulled back the curtained wall and wheeled the gurney down the hall. As he neared the double doors, he stopped and slapped the button on the wall as he had seen the other soldier do. The doors opened. Neal wheeled the gurney ahead with a brisk, confident walk, as if he knew exactly where he was going.

☼

A few minutes before nine, Rudy called Westside Elementary and asked to speak to Andy Barton.

"I'm sorry, the principal is not available," Gail said.

"I'm just checking on that bus," Rudy said. "Has it shown up? Is everyone OK?"

Gail hesitated. "I don't know," she stammered. "You'll have to talk to Mr. Barton."

Rudy chuckled. "Now, Gail, I figure you know just about everything that happens at Westside. I bet you know exactly how many freckles are on Mary McGregor's nose, don't you?"

Gail smiled. "Lots."

"So when you tell me you don't know something, it means you do know, but you can't tell me."

"I really don't know," Gail said.

"If the bus had turned up, and the kids were at school, you would tell me. And if there had been a terrible accident, and the kids were injured, you'd be calling parents right now. And you would tell me."

"It's not my place."

"So, if you're not telling me what happened to the bus, that means we're in that dangerous area someplace between routine and disaster, am I right?"

Gail sighed. "Mr. Barton just hung up. I'll connect you now."

After a quick hello and identifying himself, Rudy blurted out his question. "Has the missing school bus been located?"

"I wouldn't say it's missing," the principal said. "It's just delayed."

"But it's almost nine. The bus is more than an hour late. At what point do you declare it missing and notify the police and the parents?"

"Rudy, you've run a day care center. You know you don't jump to conclusions and alarm the parents. We have three cars running the route the bus would have taken. It's a long rural route. I am confident the bus will be located any minute."

"But if the driver hasn't called in, that pretty much means he can't call. He's injured."

"We're not making any assumptions at this point. It takes a while to look over the possibilities."

"By now you know which child he picked up last, and which kids he didn't pick up, so that leaves a relatively small area where the bus disappeared. Either it's there or it's not."

"OK. My clock says it is now nine o'clock. I notified the sheriff's office at eight thirty, and we agreed to wait until nine to start notifying parents. The sheriff's department has two squad cars out there patrolling the area where the bus was last seen, in addition to one car from the district's transportation department. Now that the appointed hour has arrived, Gail and I will be calling parents and inviting them to come to the school. We are turning the library into an information center and lounge for the parents, so the sheriff's department will have easy access to them. You're welcome to join us. And you might as well know. I'll be calling your editor in a minute or two. Her son, Kevin Walsh, is one of the students on the missing bus."

9:03 AM

Rudy volunteered to break the news to Josie, and Andy Barton didn't disagree. Informing parents wasn't a task the principal coveted. Josie was giving Becky last-minute tips for her story on Dee Licious. Becky was to call in some fan comments and scene descriptions by ten, call when the star arrived so Josie would know if everything was going according to schedule, and return to the office by eleven to write a story for the final edition.

Rudy wanted to give Josie a chance to hear the news in private. He had known her as a mother much longer than he had known her as a boss. She would always be a mother first in his mind. He stopped by Nick's desk.

"I'm going to need you to help me get Josie into the conference room," he whispered.

"What's up?" Nick asked, looking over his computer. "It's not a good day for one of your jokes."

"I've got some bad news. She's going to want to hear it in private."

When Becky headed out the door, Rudy moved to Josie's desk.

"I need to talk to you in the conference room for a second," he said in a voice he hoped sounded serious and sincere.

"Not now, Rudy. We're juggling a breaking story. Maybe after deadline."

"I really need to talk to you now."

"Come on, Peter Pan. let's see what Rudy has to report," Nick said, approaching behind Josie's desk. "You're gonna want to hear this."

Josie looked up at the two men, glancing from one to the other. Something odd was going on.

"I want to get my work done, and you should too," Josie said. "Is the referendum story ready to roll if Dee Licious falls through? And what about that other story you mentioned this morning, Rudy? Something about a late bus, I think."

The men exchanged glances.

"Is this about the bus?" Josie asked, looking from one serious face to the other. She remembered the way Kevin's school bus had looked that morning. More than half empty. Kevin and Timmy sitting in the middle playing their game. Mr. Joe bubbling with early-morning enthusiasm. The kids chattering.

"Is this about Kevin's bus?" Josie said, standing up. "Is it his bus that's late?"

62

"I'm afraid so," Rudy replied.

Josie's eyes grew wide as she realized something horrible had happened.

"Conference room," she said, pointing across the busy office. She broke away from the two men at her desk and hurried toward the small glassed-in room. She had to do something, move in a forward direction. Think. She could handle just about any development on the news front, but not something that would affect her son. She needed air. She needed answers. She needed time. Precious time.

She plopped down in a chair. Rudy pulled out the one next to her. Nick closed the door and remained standing.

"So what happened to this bus?" Josie asked.

"They don't know," Rudy said. "They've been looking for it for more than an hour. It just disappeared."

"School buses are big and yellow. They're kinda hard to overlook."

"It picked up twenty-three kids, that is if no one was sick. They're still checking with parents to be sure that all the kids were at the appointed stops. The last kid was picked up about seven. The bus didn't make its normal pickup at seven-ten or any of the stops after that."

"The bus hasn't been heard from since seven?" Nick asked. "Don't they have radio communication or something with the driver?"

"Nada," Rudy said, shaking his head. "The bus is equipped with a radio, but the driver is not responding."

"I'm assuming the sheriff's department is involved, checking all the ditches," Josie said, nervously tapping her pen on the table. "I mean it had to go off the road somewhere."

"Mostly flat corn country," Rudy said. "Nothing much in the way of dangerous curves or hills. Not even many railroad tracks."

"It has to be somewhere," Josie exclaimed. "I put Kevin on that bus at six forty-five. How could he just disappear in fifteen minutes?" Josie's voice cracked. Nick put a hand on her shoulder.

"They are turning the school library into information central," Rudy said. "They want all the parents to go there so they can keep them informed as soon as something breaks."

"You go on. I can handle things here," Nick said softly, patting her shoulder again.

Josie took a deep breath. "I should call Kurt."

She paused only a beat or two before reverting to editor in charge.

"Nick, let Hoss know about the story. Tell Sis to pull a morgue file photo of a school bus, color if we've got it. And I'm putting you in complete charge of the Dee Licious story. You'll have to decide whether to move it inside depending what happens with the—" Josie couldn't finish her thought. If something terrible had happened to a bus full of school children, it would push all other stories off page 1. She took a breath. "Rudy, find out as much as you can about the driver. His name is Joe. The kids call him Mr. Joe. He's a forty-ish guy. Stocky. Seemed cheery this morning. Get a picture of him."

"I'll call the transportation office," Rudy said, getting up. "I can run over there and pick up a mug."

All three headed out of the conference room, their direction set.

"And the kids, we'll need photographs of all the kids," Josie added.

"That'll be a little harder," Rudy said.

Josie paused. "Maybe we can get some from the parents that come to this gathering at the school. I'll call Kurt and head over there."

"I'll go with you as soon as I finish this story," Rudy said. "You shouldn't be alone."

"I'm used to it. I'll be OK."

Kurt, Josie's ex-husband, was a former reporter for the *Daily News*. Now he worked as director at Downtown Development. Money was not the root of evil in Kurt's world, but the ultimate solution to whatever went wrong.

"How about helicopters? Have they been looking for the bus with helicopters?" Kurt asked as soon as Josie apprised him of the situation.

"I don't know. The sheriff's department has some cars patrolling the rural area."

"They need helicopters. They need to get the state police involved. The FBI. This is a kidnapping. They need the FBI."

"I think it's a little early to be calling it a kidnapping. It's probably an accident. There was so much fog this morning. He went off the road someplace they haven't looked."

"Pollyanna, Pollyanna," Kurt said in a sing-song voice. "Face the facts, babe. There's something else going on here. I'll call the mayor's office and representative Curtis. We've got to call in the big guns. I should never have let you put Kevin on the bus in the first place. Why don't you take him to school? You never know about these pervert bus drivers."

"I talked to the driver just this morning. He seemed nice."

"Perverts seem nice too. Why don't you just drive the kid to school?"

"Because I need to be here by seven, and school doesn't start until eight. The kids aren't supposed to arrive at the school until seven forty at the earliest."

"So hire a sitter, one of the other parents. You don't stick a kid on a public school bus. That's one of the worst places in the world. All the riffraff. Drugs. Fights. He's exposed to everything on a bus."

"Well, if you are so concerned about school buses, why didn't you offer to take your son to school every morning? I can't imagine you're in your office before eight or nine."

"I have breakfast meetings occasionally. Besides, this isn't about me. This is about you. You're the one who put our son on the bus."

"Kurt, something terrible has happened to Kevin. Don't blame … Oh, why do I bother?"

As soon as Josie was able to get control of her voice, she told Kurt about the parents gathering at the school library and hung up. She wouldn't subject herself to Kurt's blame-everyone-else tirades.

She stopped by Rudy's desk.

"I'm going to head over to the school now. I'll call you if they report anything new."

"Wait up. I'm almost finished with the story. I'll take you over."

"Don't worry about me. I just happened to think about my neighbor Polly. Her son Timmy is on the bus too. And she's in the middle of a terrible divorce. Her husband is a real scumbag. We'll support each other."

Josie looked around for her coat. It wasn't on the hall tree behind her desk. Hammond tapped her shoulder.

"Nick just told me. You get out of here. Go be with your family. I'll handle things here."

"I think Nick's got it under control."

"Who's localizing the wire story about the nuclear explosion in the Pacific?"

Josie sighed. She'd forgotten all about that.

"Duke," she said. "He's still downtown checking on a broken bridge. I figured to send him out to the A-Lab when he gets back. They've got scientists from all over the world."

"Good idea. I'll take care of that. I'll call the PR office out there and grease the wheels. I play golf with Snyder, the executive director. You get going now. This is a time to be with family, not work."

Family, Josie thought as she looked around frantically for her dark green coat. *What is family? Kevin is my only relative within two hundred miles.*

She spotted the coat stretched over the radiator. It was still damp from the overflowing gutter. She draped it over her shoulders and headed out.

This is my family, my home. This office, these people. If something has happened to Kevin—

No, she couldn't even imagine it. Nothing could happen to him. It just couldn't. She should call her parents. They lived four hours away. They deserved to know. What would she tell them? What could she say? Maybe she should wait.

In the parking lot, she ran into Duke heading into the office.

"Jordan is the only place I know where 'bridge up' is an acceptable excuse for being late to work," he said, chuckling. "Kinda early for you to head to the gym, isn't it?"

"I'm not—" Suddenly, she completely lost it, dropping her purse onto the sloppy asphalt wet with melting snow. Sobbing, her head fell into her hands. Duke was the one person in the office who knew her naked. He was the only one she could show her pain to.

"Bouncing buffalo chips! What happened in there? You and Hammond have a fight?"

"It's not Hammond," Josie cried as Duke draped an arm around her. "It's Kevin."

"Oh, no! Something at school?"

"He's not there. He's not at school. His bus never showed up."

"A school bus is missing? Mushy monkey mounds, that's huge!"

"I know. I can't decide whether I'm worrying about accident injuries or some whacko pedophile. Should I be thinking like a mom or like an editor? All those kids. All those poor kids."

"You be the mom, we'll be the reporters. We've got it covered. Is Rudy on the story?"

"Yeah. I'm headed to the school," Josie said, blotting her eyes with a green suede glove. "They've asked the parents to assemble there."

"Good. I'll head out with the police patrol. We'll find them. Don't worry."

"I appreciate your offer, but I'm afraid Ham has other ideas. He wants someone to localize a wire story about a nuclear explosion on the other side of the world. He's calling the A-Lab to set up an interview for you with one of the scientists. Do it. It's not worth fighting him. You'll be finished by noon. Hopefully the bus will be found by then."

"But if it's not found?"

Josie smiled as much as she could. "Then it will be Dukey Boy to the rescue, just like old times. I've gotta get to the school. Sorry to slobber all over you."

"Anytime."

☼

Peter Hampton loved winter coats. They were a pick-pocket's playground. As he stood in line at the Holiday Quad Theater, he watched one man after another reach under his coat or jacket to retrieve a wallet in a back pocket. But after the ticket was purchased, the wallet was deposited in a handy coat pocket, where it would be ready for the popcorn and soda purchase. A generous, loose pocket in a bulky coat. Piece of cake.

Many women skipped purses entirely in the winter, using those big coat pockets for keys, wallet, and lipstick.

Theater lobbies were always prime picking locations, crowded with fans waiting for a movie to open, talking to friends, unconcerned about a stranger shuffling by. A special movie opening like this one was a gold mine. Trusting young people, crowding in together, waiting to catch a glimpse of a movie star. Pete squeezed in between them, apologizing quietly as he bumped a shoulder or hip.

Pete was a non-descript scrawny guy with light brown hair and tiny hazel eyes that faded into his face. He wasn't tall or short. He was practically invisible. Even if someone spotted him, they always had trouble describing him to the police. Blending in was his gift. That and being ambidextrous. He'd always been just as good with his left hand as he was with his right. His fingers were nimble, his grip sure, on either hand. Of course, it didn't make up for his flaw.

Vasovagal syncope. A fancy name for a stupid flaw. He fainted. A drop of blood, a cut finger, a bloody nose and he was out cold. "Blood injury phobia," the doctor called it, a condition that affects about 15 percent of all people. It wasn't a matter of fear. No amount of psyching himself up could overcome the problem. It was something in his genes left over from the cavemen, the doctor said. It caused his blood pressure to drop—quickly followed by the rest of his body. There was nothing he could do to prevent it.

And it didn't have to be his own blood. He fainted the first time when he was three and his brother got a bloody nose.

"Sissy," his father said. But Dad was a drunk and did a lot of falling down on his own, so Pete never put much stock is his father's opinion.

"Just stay away from blood," his mother said.

Pete didn't watch football or wrestling or horror movies. Even in this theater lobby, Pete didn't look at the movie posters. As long as he was careful, it wasn't an issue. Picking pockets wasn't a blood sport. He slipped his hand into a few pockets, lifted a few wallets. And he brought home enough money so he didn't need to turn to more confrontational crimes.

On a big haul like this one, he needed to work in stages. After he snagged a wallet, he would wander over to a dark corner, put the cash in a pocket in his shirt, and dump the wallet in a trash can. He didn't want to fill his pockets with fat leather wallets bulging with photos. The bulk would get in his way. He wasn't into credit card fraud. Cash was quick and clean. If a cop stopped him, he wouldn't have half a dozen wallets with different IDs. Just a healthy wad of dollar bills.

Up ahead Pete spotted a young woman with dyed black hair and too much makeup. She paid for her extra-large Coke and dropped her wallet into the yawning pocket of her billowy black coat. It was an invitation. Pete kept an eye on her as he moved in closer. Just as he was about to reach a hand into her coat, a voice behind him said, "Excuse me."

His other hand automatically closed over the pistol in his jacket. He didn't like the thought of violence, couldn't imagine shooting someone. Wouldn't shoot. But in a pinch, just showing the gun might buy him enough time to run.

"Hi, I'm Becky Judd from the *Daily News*," a tall black woman said with way too much enthusiasm. "If you don't mind me saying so, you look a lot like Dee Licious. I bet you get that all the time."

The overly made-up girl giggled. "It's my eyes. People say we've got the same eyes."

"Do you mind if I ask you a few questions for a story I'm doing?"

Pete moved on. The reporter didn't even see him. Of course she wouldn't. He didn't look like a movie star. He didn't even look like a movie patron. Then he saw a man dropping a nice little trifold wallet into his coat pocket. He would do just as well.

☼

The Death Metal tour bus was stuck in a traffic jam about ten miles east of Jordan. The exterior was covered with gigantic caricatures of purple and black spiders. Two spiders playing guitars, another one playing drums. Romancing a microphone was a sexy black widow—at least as sexy as a spider wearing four high heels can be. Spiders were the band mascots. "Creepy crawly" was the phrase they used to describe themselves.

The spider theme continued inside the bus with gauzy strands of spiderwebs hung from the built-in overhead cabinets, draped in the corners, stretched across the window. It looked like Halloween decorations, but Dee Licious thought it was trendy décor. She was seated at a table on the bus, brushing the long silky mane of Spritzer, her four-pound, tan and silver blue teacup Yorkshire terrier. Cord McCoy, her bodyguard, ambled down the aisle and plopped down on the purple sofa near the driver. He was too big for everything on the bus. Too tall for the ceiling, too wide for the aisles, too long-legged for the couch.

"We're never going to get there at this rate," Cord moaned.

"You in a hurry to mix it up with the horror movie crowd?" asked Jim, the driver.

"I'm in a hurry to get out of this bus. It cramps my style," Cord said lying back on the sofa with his legs trailing down the aisle.

"Don't rush it," Dee said, brushing the tiny dog who sat quietly on the table. "Fame is fleeting enough. I want to enjoy every day of it."

"Yeah, what do they say? Fame lasts fifteen minutes," Cord said, pulling his white Stetson over his eyes.

"More like forty-six seconds," Dee said. She tied a purple ribbon around a tiny tuft of the dog's hair. "I got up at five a.m. three days in a row to go to that studio. Put on makeup, take off makeup, scream and sit and scream and sit. For three days. And all they used is forty-six seconds. Not counting the blood pooling under the legs because those weren't my legs, you know. Those

68

were some stupid stand-in. A leg model. As if these legs weren't good enough," Dee said, thrusting a booted foot into the aisle.

Cord wished he had thought to put in his earplugs. The ones he wore whenever Dee sang. Whenever the band played. How had he gotten himself into this mess? Why couldn't he be protecting somebody important like President Reagan? Granted, somebody with Cord's arrest record could never get hired by the Secret Service. But it was just a few drunken brawls. Nothing serious. The least he could do was find a country music singer to guard. Some nice little lady he wouldn't mind risking his life for. But not this tramp. Not this ear-splitting noise they called music.

"What did they pay you, $100,000 for forty-six seconds?" Cord drawled from beneath the hat. "What's that figure? A thousand a blink?"

"Oh, they got their money's worth all right," Dee said, adding another bow over one of Spritzer's ears. "How many faces you think would have the instant recognition they needed for such a quick shot? And I have the fan base. That's what they were paying for. Oh, they got their money's worth all right. That's why they have me at these premieres. Cashing in on my face."

"It's not exactly a premiere," Cord mumbled. "The movie is opening everywhere today."

"And I'll be visiting eight Chicago-area theaters for the opening-day performance. They invited me to promote their movie."

"If this traffic keeps up, you'll be lucky to make three out of the eight shows."

Dee tossed the dog's brush at Cord's hat.

"What are you doing wearing that hokey thing? Makes you look like a stupid cowboy. What did you do with the black fedora I gave you?"

"Listen, I don't tell you how to dress, though you could use a few pointers."

"Why you smug bastard!" Dee stepped across the aisle to stand over Cord. "You work for me, buster. You'll wear what I tell you."

"The black hat makes me look like a goon," Cord said, adjusting his white Stetson to block his view of Dee.

"It goes with your sidearm," she said, tapping his underarm holster. "That cowboy hat looks like you should have a pair of six-shooters strapped to your hip."

"I could do that," Cord offered.

"You know what would be cool," Dee said, tossing Cord's Stetson on the floor of the bus so she could see his face. "We could get you one of those little berets and a band of ammunition to wear across your chest. And you could carry an Uzi."

Dee gestured dramatically as she spoke, the little dog held in her outstretched hand. Suddenly the dog relieved himself all over Cord.

"What the—" Cord sprang to his feet so fast his head hit the overhead cabinet. When he automatically touched a hand to the bump, it snagged the grauzy web decoration. He flailed his arms trying to untangle himself.

"That mutt peed on me!" he exclaimed.

"Oh, it's just a little tinkle water," Dee said, giggling. "Don't be such a baby."

"You ought to potty train that little cretin. I can't believe you carry him around in your purse, and he's not even housebroken."

Dee hugged the dog. "Spritzer would never wet in the purse. That's his nest. Doggies never wet the nest."

"Well, you ought to get him broke or get rid of him."

"Maybe he is broke. Maybe he pees on command, just when I want him to. Maybe that's why I call him Spritzer."

Cord growled and reached for Dee. She scampered away, trouncing all over the Stetson on the floor.

"Uh-oh. Guess you'll have to wear another hat," she said, stomping on the flattened chapeau once more for good measure.

9:45 AM

When Josie arrived at Westside Elementary, the parking lot was full. She went to the back of the lot where snowplows had piled the scrapings of the entire parking lot for more than a month. It looked like a miniature mountain range. The piles were top heavy instead of neatly shaped, with huge icy chunks teetering on top of each other. Josie's Ford Escort was small, so she backed into the edge of a snow mound, hoping she was out of the roadway. She paused a moment to pray.

"Oh, Lord, be with Kevin and the other kids. Protect them. Bring them home to us. Help the police as they search. And the parents. Give us strength, Lord. Help us to understand. I just don't understand what has happened."

Josie coped the way she always did: She found a job to do. First she located Polly. She hugged her neighbor, and they sniffled a little. When she looked at Polly, she saw herself looking back. Polly's son, Timmy, was sitting right next to Kevin. Whatever happened to one had undoubtedly happened to the other. They bid their kids goodbye together this morning. Their fates were hand in hand.

Josie knew many of the other parents too. As they exchanged greetings and words of concern, Josie asked for wallet photos. They all knew she worked at the newspaper. If anyone thought her request was cold and callous, no one said so. Josie knew these parents loved their kids, and they all wanted to see them again. Healthy. Laughing. The way they were in the wallet photos. Word that Josie was looking for pictures spread through the room. Soon parents she didn't know were coming forward to offer photos of their children as well. If they could amass the twenty-three photos, maybe the spell would be broken. Maybe if their pictures were all together, the children would reappear.

Josie had collected eighteen photos by a little before ten when Chief Deputy Don Miller walked into the library to address the group. Josie felt a sense of connection that Miller was the one to bring the news. Three years before, Miller's son Scotty had been killed while investigating a murder. Miller was a hard-nosed cop, but he was also a father who had been hurt. He didn't smile much. It wasn't his way. But he would tell it straight.

"It's been three hours since Bus 62 was last seen. We have patrolled the route that the bus would have traveled, as well as alternate routes, and we feel quite certain the bus has not broken down or gone into a ditch. Helicopters from the State Highway Patrol have joined in the search, so we can cover a wider area. There are many barns in the county where a bus could be hidden. All of those will be systematically searched. Roadblocks have been set up along the major highways leading out of the county. The Illinois Highway Patrol is on the alert for any suspicious school bus anywhere in the state.

"How about the bus driver? What do we know about him?" one of the fathers shouted.

"Joseph Wilson has been a school transportation employee for four years. There have been no complaints against him. He has no criminal record. He is single, forty-two. A check of his apartment found nothing unusual. But we are tracking down family and neighbors. I will be coming back and reporting to you as often as we have any developments. In the meantime, I will have two deputies here running interviews with parents. Perhaps one of you saw something. Or perhaps there's a situation in one of the families, an ex-spouse perhaps, who is unhappy about custody arrangements. If anyone has received a threat or a ransom demand, that's something we need to know."

Josie looked around. The parents were eyeing each other. Polly was crying.

"What is it?" Josie whispered.

"Do you think Greg would do something like this?"

"No, of course not," Josie said, giving her friend a reassuring hug. Polly's former husband was a cheating scoundrel who had hit her. But a kidnapper? Surely not.

"He was awfully mad that the judge gave me custody."

"You'll have to tell the deputy," Josie whispered. "But it's probably nothing."

After Miller left the room, Josie and Polly agreed that Polly should talk with one of the deputies as soon as possible. Josie went with her. The deputy called one of the other officers over, and he escorted Polly to an interview room. Josie was watching her walk down the hall when Rudy came up beside her.

"How you holding up?"

"Huh?" Josie said, noticing her reporter for the first time. "Oh, I'm doing fine. You just missed Chief Deputy Miller."

"I caught him outside."

"Oh, what did he have to say?"

"Probably the same thing he told you parents."

"I don't know," Josie said, shaking her head and looking around to see who might overhear. She motioned Rudy to follow her across the room. She took one of the child-size chairs at a round library table. Rudy joined her at a matching chair. "I think we are just being placated. I don't think they are telling us everything that's going on."

72

Rudy sighed. His eyes had lost their usual playful twinkle. "I don't think the parents are being placated. I suspect you're here to be probed."

"Probed? Miller thinks one of the parents did this?"

"Cops follow procedures. Procedures say to look for motive. The motive has to have something to do with an individual child on that bus. A disgruntled spouse. An enemy of one of the parents. Someone extorting money from one of the families."

"Money? If a parent could afford to pay ransom, do you think his kid would ride a public bus to a public school?"

Rudy shrugged. "Probably not." He reached for the photos in Josie's hand. "You get all the photographs?"

"I have eighteen. Maybe the office can fill in some of the others. A couple of the parents didn't have any with them, and I didn't find a couple of the parents."

Rudy scratched a note at the top of his pad. "I'll ask if there are any parents who have not been contacted or who haven't responded to the request to come to the school. I'm sure the sheriff's department would consider that suspicious."

"There are lots of parents who aren't here," Josie said. "Look around. There are only a few obvious couples sitting together, comforting each other. In most cases it seems to be one spouse per family."

"That's a shame. This is when a couple need to support each other."

"You have an idealized view of marriage," she said, shaking her head. "Life intervenes. Maybe one of the spouses couldn't get off work or is working out of town. Maybe a spouse is staying home with younger kids."

"How about Kevin's dad?"

"Oh, you know Kurt's ego. He can't be expected to sit around and wait for updates like ordinary people. He's got to go out and shake the bushes. He's probably taking credit for calling in the state highway patrol and the helicopters. He's talking to the state representatives, making political hay."

"He's doing what he does best," Rudy said.

"I guess." Josie responded with a heavy sigh. She looked around the room. One of the women was sobbing. Some mothers were tending younger children. Most of the men were gathered in a circle exchanging ideas. "You know, he didn't even have a decent breakfast before he left this morning."

"Don't start blaming yourself."

"Why not? You told me you blamed yourself when your wife and daughter were killed when you lived in Vermont."

"I was driving the car."

"Was the accident your fault? Did you get a ticket?"

"No, some drunk went through a red light. Hit us broadside."

"See."

73

Rudy shook his head. His normally twinkling eyes were a dark, dull gray-green, like murky water. Without his usual bright smile, his face seemed drawn and ordinary. "I understand why you feel like blaming yourself," he said, looking down. "I'm just saying it wasn't your fault."

"The missing bus may not be my fault, but I could have sent him off with a good breakfast. He just had a couple handfuls of dry cereal. I should have made him sit down and put it in a bowl with milk."

"Why? Because that's got the Good Housekeeping seal of approval? Energetic boys like Kevin hate to sit down. They like to move around while they eat."

Josie was surprised that Rudy was disagreeing with her. "Are you saying Kevin is ADD?"

"I don't like labels," Rudy said. "It's more natural to eat standing up. Man is a hunter-gatherer. A natural breakfast would be nuts and berries, walking around from bush to bush. In a natural environment, standing while eating would be a survival instinct. Don't fault a kid for living by his instincts just because society wants him to sit in a chair with both feet flat on the floor and a napkin in his lap."

Josie stared at Rudy. His eyes had a faint glisten and his cheeks were getting more rosy. "You're always on the kid's side aren't you?"

Rudy smiled. "Yep, guess I am."

"Well, I'm not like you. I'm not parent of the year. On those days when I go to the gym before work, I leave Kevin on his own to get dressed and get his breakfast and catch the bus. All alone. What if I had done that today? What if I hadn't been there to put him on that bus?"

"Then you'd just be blaming yourself all the more."

"I certainly would."

"And it wouldn't have changed what happened."

"What did happen, Rudy? What has happened to our kids?"

Rudy looked around the room. "I like the theory that one of these parents knows."

"You're kidding me! They're talking to my neighbor Polly because she and her husband just split. But I can't imagine he would kidnap a busload of kids. Remember that Mark Twain story about "The Ransom of Red Chief?" Only an idiot would try to kidnap a busload of wild Indians."

"Maybe. But what if a disgruntled dad, like Polly's ex, wanted to get custody of his son? He gets on the bus after he knows his son is on board. He knocks out the driver and ties him up. Drives the bus into some abandoned barn out in the country. Rips out the radio so they can't call for help, disables the engine, and drives away with his son in a car he had waiting for him in the barn. He'd be on a plane at O'Hare before the bus was reported missing."

"Is that what Miller told you? Is that what he thinks?"

"Well, he didn't get into that much detail, but more or less, that's what he said. And it makes sense. There has to be a motive that makes sense."

"It does make sense. And it would mean it's possible the kids are OK."

"The driver is probably trying to get the bus running right now. He may be afraid to leave the kids alone and walk down a dirt road looking for a farmhouse. There are some pretty desolate areas in the county."

Rudy knew this was only one of the possible scenarios, but it was possible. It offered a good prognosis for the passengers, so it was the only theory he dared to share with Josie.

"And maybe the kids are OK," she repeated. "A little scared and cold, but OK."

"Yeah," Rudy said, patting Josie's hand. "They're OK."

☼

Back at the *Daily News* office, Duke, Nick, and Hammond were gathered around Hoss's desk reading the latest wire bulletins from the South Pacific. Tall, thin, and white-haired, Hammond didn't usually get involved in the day-to-day decisions. Once he claimed a story, however, he wanted to orchestrate every word from the headline to the interview questions.

"The real coup is to talk to the scientist from Auckland, New Zealand," Hammond said, as if Duke and the others might not know where Auckland was. "They've got a ban in New Zealand against nuclear arms. Won't even let American ships dock in their ports if they are carrying missiles. And then to have this explosion a few hundred miles away—"

"Thousand," Hoss said quietly. "The explosion was more than a thousand miles away from Auckland. A few hundred miles west of the Republic of Samoa."

"Oh? Yes, well, there's a scientist from Samoa too. Though I'm sure the New Zealander would be the better spokesperson on the issue of nuclear arms."

"Do we know yet who caused the explosion?" Duke asked.

"Reagan is blaming the Soviets, the Soviets are blaming the Americans. The usual," Hoss said, tossing two wire printouts to Duke.

"Could it be Fiji?" Nick asked. "We've been having stories about a military takeover there."

"I don't think they're into nukes yet," Hoss replied. "They're just outgrowing monarchy. At least I haven't seen any wire stories blaming any of the South Pacific nations. Now, it could be France. They have holdings in the area, and they've got nuclear capabilities. But what we think doesn't matter. All we can do is try to keep up with the international blame game."

"Ask the scientist to explain this double flash," Hammond said, circling a line in the wire copy. "That's how the satellite recognized it as a nuclear explosion. On a photograph from outer space. Amazing. Find out what that double flash means."

Helen, the receptionist, approached the cluster of men. "Excuse me. Which of you is the 'nice doctor guy' who spoke to Deluded Debbie this morning about her DNA?"

"Oh, gee, that would be me," Nick said. "Is she on the phone again?"

"Who or what is Deluded Debbie?" Hammond asked.

"Oh, just one of the kooks who calls once in a while," Nick explained.

"Especially when there's a full moon," Hoss added. "I talked to her earlier today about a barking dog."

"Tell her this is a news office, and we don't have time for such nonsense," Hammond said brusquely, waving Helen away.

"I'm worried about her," Nick said. "I wish she would give her full name or address so we could ask a policeman or ambulance to check on her."

Chuckling, Duke tucked one of the wire stories inside his reporter's notebook. "You take care of the kooks, I'll go chase the nukes." He pulled on his dark brown leather bomber jacket. "I'll call in a couple of comments in time for the final edition."

Rudy was coming in the back door when Duke was leaving.

"How's Josie holding up? Any news on the bus?" Duke asked.

"Nothing new," Rudy said. "They're interviewing the parents trying to find somebody with a motive."

"One of the parents?" Duke exclaimed. "Yellow yak yuck. That's hard to believe. How's Josie taking that?"

"She's hanging in there, holding other people together. You know Josie."

"Yeah, she'll hang tough. Well, I've gotta go make sense of some mystery explosion in the South Pacific. I'll be back by lunch. If they haven't found the bus by then, maybe we can work on it together this afternoon."

"Sounds good."

Rudy went to Nick's desk to deliver the twenty-three photographs. He was able to add to the eighteen photos Josie had collected with a few photos from the school office. The missing school bus had become the top story on the front page. Nick figured once the television and radio stations picked it up, media would descend from all over the Chicago area. The *Daily News* had to have the most complete story possible before all the facts and faces were on the five o'clock news.

Becky had called in a good story about the horror fans waiting for Dee Licious, and Mack had supplied great photographs of young people dressed in their horror best. Many wore the hockey goalie mask of Jason in the *Friday the 13th* movies. Some had striped shirts and sporty hats like Freddy Krueger in

Nightmare on Elm Street. But mostly they wore gothic black, a sea of dyed hair, heavily made-up eyes, and black clothes. The package of photos and comments had moved to page 3 where it could comfortably accommodate the star—if she arrived in time for the final edition—or survive without the star if she was too late.

Mack's eerie morning shot of the forest glowing in the fog was the main photo in the center of page 1 with the forest fire fiasco story below. A wire story about the South Pacific explosion ran down one side where it could easily accommodate any local additions Duke called in.

It was almost ten thirty and Nick hadn't even thought about taking his normal ten o'clock break. It was one of those days that wouldn't slow down. Rudy was talking about Miller's disgruntled parent theory when Nick heard a snippet on the police scanner that got his attention.

"Did they say dive team?" Nick asked, heading behind Josie's desk to turn up the radio. "That's all we need. Some vehicle driving into the river."

Almost as fast as the words came out of his mouth, Nick and Rudy caught each other's eyes and thought the same thought out loud. "The bus?"

As the men listened to the police scanner, it became apparent the sheriff's deputies were investigating a spot called Bartlett Bridge Road where a rural gravel road ended in the Jordan River.

"Where is this place?" Rudy asked. "Is this anywhere near a school bus route?"

"I think I know where they are talking about," Nick said, leading the way toward the county map on the wall. "There used to be an old wooden bridge there years ago, but it washed away in a flood. Since then the road has been just for local access for a couple of farmers. Can't imagine it would be on a bus route. But if the bus got on that road by mistake, it could have run right into the river."

"I'm on my way," Rudy said, grabbing his corduroy coat.

"Take Mack with you. He knows those dirt roads better than anyone."

☼

As Duke drove through the gates of the National Atomic Particle Accelerator Laboratory about ten miles north of Jordan, he felt as if he were stepping back in time rather than leaping into the future. Flat fields stretched out along both sides of the gently winding road. Clumps of uncut prairie grass pierced the remnants of snow. Huge wooly-brown buffalo nibbled in scattered groups. When the 7,000-acre research center opened a decade earlier, natural prairie grasses were planted. A herd of twenty bison was set to grazing in the fenced property, symbolizing the state's western frontier history, as well as the new frontiers the lab was exploring.

Most of the lab's research took place underground. The accelerator featured a huge circular tunnel four miles around. Beams of minute subatomic particles raced around this high-tech track at almost the speed of light.

Beyond the fields and buffalo, Duke could see the sixteen-story A-frame headquarters. A semicircle of flagpoles wrapped around one end of the building, with colorful flags from the two dozen countries represented in the staff of scientists.

Duke pulled into the visitors' lot and walked across the concrete bridge that spanned the frozen moat around the building. He paused at the center of the little bridge, listening to the army of flags whipping in the stiff February breeze and the metal pulleys clanging against the poles. That's when he noticed the noisy tractor. Behind the building, a yellow front-end loader was grunting the way the big tractors do. He watched as the tractor lowered its scoop and edged forward into a mound of dark brown dirt. No, the mound moved as one when the forks of the scoop struck it. A boulder? No, it was a buffalo. A dead buffalo.

He watched as the huge yellow machine lifted the carcass, moved forward a few feet, and then dumped it into the bed of a dump truck. A worker lifted up the tailgate and secured it. The truck headed down a service road with the yellow tractor following behind. Duke had read Josie's email about a sheriff's department report on a dead buffalo the night before. But that was supposed to be near the road. This must be a second buffalo. Two dead buffalo?

Duke headed for the front door that opened to the airy lobby of the modern structure. Two office towers were joined by the windowed lobby that soared up the full height of the building. Shiny open stairs and walkways crisscrossed the space at various levels. A rounded see-through elevator was descending in the middle. It looked like a fancy hotel in Disney's Tomorrow Land.

The public relations office was close to the front door so media weren't wandering all over the place unescorted. Communications director Leslie Gray met him in the doorway.

"There you are," she said with her hand outstretched. "I haven't seen you since, what was it? The transportation story?"

"Yeah, your guys tried to convince me some high-speed electromagnetic floating railroad was just around the bend," Duke said, shaking Leslie's hand.

"Well, sometimes the science is ready long before the economy is. I think I've got the perfect guy to address your questions. Dr. Samuel Gilbert. Of course his work has nothing to do with nuclear weapons. That's not what we do here. But Dr. Gilbert is from New Zealand, not far from the mystery explosion. He's been a vocal opponent of nuclear proliferation."

Leslie led the way into the glass-enclosed elevator that zipped up through the lobby to the sixth floor.

"Great view, isn't it?" she said as Duke dawdled behind in the elevator, looking down at the lobby below. They walked across the shiny walkway toward the window wall overlooking the pastoral prairie landscape. When they stepped into Dr. Gilbert's small office, he was standing at his window looking out at the prairie. Duke thought it would be hard to get any work done here.

Gilbert was a small man, an aging nerd. Wisps of gray hair encircled a bald spot like a crown. A white plastic pocket protector packed with pens dominated his shirt, and thick tortoise shell–rimmed glasses obscured his face. His nose had an irritating twitch.

"I don't know how I can help you," Gilbert said, turning from the window and taking the chair behind the desk. As an afterthought, he waved toward the two chrome and leather chairs along the wall. "Have a seat."

Duke smiled at the scientist's accent. It was as if the little man had reversed his vowels and swallowed his final consonants He seemed to speak without opening his mouth.

"I'm really looking for some sort of explanation of this double flash they keep talking about," Duke said, taking one of the chairs.

"That's what Miss Gray told me, so I printed out this explanation of the forces in a nuclear explosion," the scientist said, handing over a six-page document stapled neatly along the left side to create a little book.

"Well, um, thanks, I, ah …" Duke paged through the document. He shook his head. "Glowing gopher golf balls! Could you just give it to me in a sentence or two? Dumb it down."

Dr. Gilbert raised his eyebrows in surprise, then looked down into his lap. Duke was afraid he wouldn't respond at all. But after a minute or so he looked up.

"It's like an explosion within an explosion," he said. "There's the fireball of the initial explosion." He used his hands to shape the upward thrust of an imaginary ball. "But then there's the shock wave." He formed a tight ball with his hands and then pulled them apart vertically. "It creates a double pulse of light that can be used to differentiate a nuclear explosion from some other explosive phenomenon."

Duke scratched the doctor's words on his pad, but regretted he couldn't capture the accent. When the doctor pronounced "nuclear," he said "nick-la." It sounded like some sort of Christmas treat.

"But how could a satellite notice that double flash? Isn't it awfully fast?" Duke asked.

Dr. Gilbert smiled. "This satellite was launched specifically to monitor nuclear weapons activity as part of the SALT II Treaty. It was programmed to look for the signs of a nuclear event."

"Couldn't it just be a volcano or something?"

"Could? Of course. It could be anything. It could be a malfunction on the satellite. But I suspect the US Air Force is flying over the area right now measuring the amount of radioactive dust."

"How far is this site from your homeland, New Zealand?"

"I'm not sure. About 2,500 kilometers … 1,500 miles."

"So that's a safe distance. There won't be any fallout in New Zealand."

Dr. Gilbert snorted a little laugh. "This is how Americans measure safety. Earlier this week the Americans set off a nuclear test in Nevada. That's roughly the same distance from Chicago as this mystery explosion was from Auckland. Do you feel safe from the Nevada explosion?"

Duke shrugged. "Well, yeah, I guess so. They wouldn't do it if it wasn't safe. Would they?"

Dr. Gilbert raised his eyebrows. "Tests at the Nevada test site are underground to reduce fallout. And by all indications, they are relatively safe. The United States hasn't done atmospheric tests since the 1960s. But the nuclear tests that were done in the '50s and '60s created fallout that has been measured all over the world. Even at the polar ice caps. They told us it was safe then. We believed them then. Should we believe them now?"

"I'm surprised at you, Dr. Gilbert. You work with nuclear physics every day, and here you are sounding like a conspiracy theorist."

"No conspiracy," the scientist said, closing his notebook and glancing at Leslie. "I have a great deal of respect for the energy inside the atom because I know what it can do. We work with relatively low-level radioactive isotopes here, and yet we follow every possible safety precaution. In this building, right over the middle of the accelerator, your exposure to radiation is no greater than from the cosmic rays and gamma rays bombarding the universe all the time. That is because of the strict protocol we follow. That is because of our respect for the energy with which we work."

"But you don't think these nuclear tests respect the power of the bomb?"

"Exactly. My country is a nuclear-free zone. We don't allow nuclear-powered ships or ships carrying nuclear weapons within twelve miles of our country. And that includes American ships. They are not allowed to dock in our harbors. That's been the policy for two years, and this year the legislature is enacting the policy into permanent law. If more countries would enact such policies, the world would be a much safer place. Nuclear energy is a gift to be respected."

Dr Gilbert rose to his feet. "If I have answered your questions, I would like to get back to work now."

"Sure." Duke followed the scientist out of his office. "So what kind of project are you doing here?"

"I am working with the collider, smashing protons into anti-protons. Millions of the little buggers," Gilbert said as he headed down the hall toward the elevator at a brisk pace. "We believe that's how the earth was formed. The Big Bang. I am measuring creative energy. Looking for new particles resulting from this activity. Quarks. The basis of everything."

Talking about his work, Dr. Gilbert became a different man. He glowed with excitement.

"That sounds really neat," Duke said. "Maybe I can come back sometime and see how you do it."

"I'm afraid it would take a lot of patience," Gilbert said as the three of them entered the elevator. "My measurements come from months of analyzing data. It's not a big showy explosion like a nuclear bomb."

At this point, Leslie jumped into the conversation. "Dr. Gilbert is too modest. His work is connecting quantum physics with astrophysics. From the smallest particles to the biggest star in the solar system. It's all related."

When they exited the elevator, Gilbert quickly crossed the hall. He joined a white-coated man who was twice his size.

"Oh, there you are," Leslie said. "This is Dr. Henri Baptista. He's from Samoa."

The big man looked down at Duke. His skin was dark tan, his large eyes like black coals. His hair was an unruly mane of black frizz, like an Einstein on steroids. Without saying a word or changing his blank expression, the big man held out a hand for Duke to shake. His hand was as wide as a Ping-Pong paddle. Duke wasn't sure how to grasp such a mitt. He felt like he was only circling the tips of the fingers.

"Nice to meet you," Duke said.

Baptista was young enough to be Gilbert's son. He looked more like a linebacker than a scientist. He didn't say a word, but his big black eyes burned into Duke's.

"Dr. Baptista's home is much closer to the site of the explosion," Gilbert said. "Islanders feel particularly threatened by the testing. Whole habitats have been lost, as I am sure you are aware. In Midway, your president is offering remuneration, but how do you repay a people for the homeland the gods have given them?"

"Samoans are peaceful people," Baptista said in a deep, quiet voice. "They believe they were chosen for these islands. The gods created them as one. The islands are members of the family."

"Like living people?" Duke asked.

"Definitely living creatures," Baptista said. "Islands are more complex than people or animals."

"The doctor and I have work to do," Gilbert said. He grabbed a small bright-blue plastic strip that hung from a fine chain around his neck. He stuck the plastic into a slot in the wall next to an elevator marked "Authorized Personnel Only." The doors opened, and the two scientists disappeared inside.

"Where are they going?"

"Down below," Leslie said with a shrug. "The accelerator. That's where the real work goes on. Did you get what you need?"

"Yeah, I have all I need for this story. But what would it take to go down into the hole? See all them little quarks and protons."

"You can't actually see them."

Duke chuckled. "It's hard to imagine working with something you can't see. I'm wondering if I may use your office. I need to call in a few comments to add to the wire story. We're on a deadline."

"A deadline is something you can't see, and yet it is very real in your work. Isn't that true?" Leslie said as she led Duke back to the public relations office.

☼

When Death Metal's Black and Purple tour bus pulled up outside the theater, the buzz inside became electric. Everyone seemed to be talking at once. Some rushed toward the wall of windows to get a peek at the star stepping down from the bus. Others jockeyed for position near the entrance to the lobby. Employees had set up a roped corridor for the star and her bodyguard, but the stands that held the rope were pushed and pulled by the anxious fans. Page, the *Daily News'* extra-tall photographer, had set up his tripod on a raised walkway that ran around one end of the room connecting the theater to the shopping mall next door.

Becky asked the clerk in the ticket booth to call the newspaper for her. She used the ticket booth phone earlier to call in her story, so the clerk was accommodating and fed the receiver through the ticket window.

"She's here," Becky said into the phone.

"OK," Nick replied. "It's a go." It was ten thirty-five. Becky could still make it back in time to write a short story for the final edition.

The shoving and excitement made Pete's job even easier. Sometimes he would grab two or three wallets before stopping to remove the cash and pitch the rest. It was so tempting to be greedy. His plan had been to leave when the star arrived because the security would increase. Until now there had been only two theater guards and four other employees trying to control the crowd. Now the mall security and a pair of city policemen were moving the crowd back, making way for the star. He should definitely leave.

But the crowd was so excited. It was so easy to snag another wallet or two. Squeals of excitement echoed through the room as the door opened and the star walked in. Anyone could tell she was a star. Normal people don't dress like that. She wore a huge white coat made of some long loopy fabric that looked like a shaggy rug. She had big silver hoops in her ears. Dangling from one shoulder was a huge purple purse with hot pink trim. Her dyed black hair was teased and sprayed into a shiny cloud that floated over her head like a dark halo.

"Hi-ee," she kept saying, turning a simple two-letter greeting into an elongated two-syllable word. The long shaggy arms of her coat waved over the crowd and reached into the confusion as she shook hands and signed autographs.

Pete had been working near the edge of the crowd, so he could slip out to a trash can regularly. But as Dee Licious came closer, the crowd surged. Pete was caught up with them. At the base of the steps leading up to the raised walkway, there was a podium. Someone official-looking in a suit with a Holiday Quad logo was leading the star toward the podium. Some dude in a black fedora followed. His black sport coat seemed too small for him. It flapped open, revealing his underarm holster. But it was the purse—the big purple and pink purse—that attracted Pete's attention. She was almost to the podium. Someone stopped her for an autograph. Someone else was crowding in. And the purple purse was right there. Easy reach.

Pete slipped his hand in. He'd long ago learned not to watch his hand. Keep his eye on the victim so he would know what she was about to do. Keep an eye out for anyone who might be watching. Anyone who could catch—

"Ow." Sharp pain startled Pete. He jerked his hand out of the purple purse so quickly that he yanked the strap off Dee's shoulder. At the same time he pulled his pistol out of his jacket. It was an automatic response to the pain, the threat of danger. But then he saw his hand. It was bloody. Why had he looked? The room was spinning. He clutched the pistol, as if snagging a life line to hold him up. But he felt himself falling away. And everything went black.

10:42 AM

A shot rang out, followed by two more in rapid succession. The room went ballistic. Horror fans were screaming and running in all directions. Some people—including Becky—fell to the floor to avoid being hit by stray bullets. Those who were running tripped over those who had taken refuge on the floor. They fell down in football-tackle piles, knocking others over in their wake. There were skinned knees and bloody noses everywhere. People were crying and screaming in pain. It was impossible to tell who, if anyone, had been hit by bullets.

Becky looked toward the podium where she had last seen Dee Licious. The shots had come from that direction. She saw the man with the black fedora, presumably the star's bodyguard. He was crouching with one knee raised and his gun drawn. Suddenly he fired toward the raised walkway. Becky gasped as Page fell backwards, and his camera flew over the railing.

She wanted to stand up, to run to Page, but something made her pull back farther into the floor. If the bodyguard shot Page, would he shoot her next? What was going on?

"Drop your weapon!" A uniformed police officer burst through the doorway. His gun was pointed at the startled guard.

"I'm a licensed bodyguard!" he shouted.

"I don't care if you're John Wayne, drop that weapon. Now."

The guard did as he was told. "I saw a sniper, up on the walkway."

"That wasn't a sniper, that was our photographer," Becky said, standing up. "He shot our photographer."

"Sit down and shut up," the officer said, glaring at Becky. "Everybody stay exactly where you are. Don't move a muscle."

Despite the bodyguard's protests, the officer slapped on handcuffs.

"I told you. I'm the bodyguard."

"He's heavy too," came a muffled voice. "Tell him to get off me."

The officer yanked the cuffed guard to his feet. The shaggy coat he had been kneeling on rustled.

"Miss Licious? Are you all right?" said the manager of the theater, who had been beside Dee when the shots started. He helped the star sit up. Dee's heavily sprayed hair had been squashed into a cockeyed trapezoid, which she vainly tried to straighten.

The police officer evidently recognized the manager and the star. "Take her to that office over there and sit tight," the policeman said, gesturing to the side of the lobby. "The rest of you people stay put until we can assess the injuries."

More police officers streamed into the room. An officer at the door directed one to the raised walkway. Another rushed to a bleeding woman who was sobbing in the center of the room. "She's been shot! My wife's been shot," the man beside her said. Another man with a bloody arm got up, took a step, and fell back down. One of the policemen went to him.

"Everyone stay where you are!" the policeman yelled, but his order was ignored. Ambulances were arriving. People were moving to accommodate stretchers. In the midst of this chaos, Dee Licious let out a scream that seemed horror-movie perfect.

"Spritzer's gone! My dog Spritzer! He's not in my purse!"

The manager coaxed and pushed the screaming star toward his office, assuring that the missing dog would be found. In the confusion, Becky snuck into the empty ticket office and snagged the phone to call the newsroom.

"There's been a shooting. I think Page has been hit."

"Page? What happened?" Nick asked. "I heard something about the shooting on the police scanner. How about Dee Licious? Is she OK?"

"Yeah, she's wailing about a missing dog. Her stupid bodyguard shot Page, mistook his long camera lens for a gun."

"Chee! How bad is he?"

"Don't know yet. One of the cops went to check him out. Ambulances are arriving. I can give you enough details for a rewrite, but I don't think they will let me leave for a while. We're all suspects."

Hidden on the floor of the ticket booth, Becky dictated her story. As she hung up, she heard a voice she recognized. She stood up in the ticket booth and saw Tom Cantrell.

"Baby, you're here!" she exclaimed.

Relief melted over his face. "There you are! Get a job selling tickets?"

"No, just trying to hide out."

Tom shook his head and reached his long fingers through the gap in the ticket window. "When I heard a *Daily News* photographer was hit, I was afraid—"

"You were afraid? I was terrified," Becky replied, clutching at his fingers. "I can still hear the gunshots echoing in my head."

"Well, get out here. Tell me what you saw."

Tom met Becky at the back of the ticket booth. Just as he was about to reach for her in the dark hall behind the booth, he stopped and lifted his foot.

"What the … shit! I stepped in dog shit!"

"It's my Spritzer! My baby. Have you seen my baby?" Dee Licious squealed, stepping out of the nearby office.

"No dog, just his poop," Tom snarled as he wiped his shoe with a napkin from the concession stand. "You stay right there, lady. I'll be in to talk to you as soon as I interview this reporter."

Tom pushed Becky back into the main lobby.

"This place is crazy," he said. "Some dog running around pooping everywhere. How are we supposed to secure this scene? It's like trying to put an insane asylum on lockdown. Look at these people," Tom said, indicating the collection of fans in horror makeup lining up along the wall. "They all look suspicious. Every one of them."

In addition to real bloody noses and fall-down injuries, several patrons were splattered with fake blood. One had a mock screwdriver protruding from his head. Another was wearing slasher fingers.

Becky tried to describe what had happened, pointing out where the star entered, how Dee and her bodyguard made their way through the crowd toward the podium at the base of the stairs. She told Tom about the three shots in rapid succession. She couldn't tell if they came from the same gun. She pointed out where Page had been standing and how she saw the guard shoot the fourth shot that struck the photographer. She mentioned the man who said his wife had been shot. She also mentioned the man who stood up and then passed out. Paramedics were tending to the injured at numerous locations around the room.

"So you didn't see the shooter? Nobody running away?"

"Oh, there were lots of people running. Some probably got out. It was bedlam."

"We surrounded the parking lot soon after the call went out. I don't think too many cars made it out before we got here."

As they talked, a pair of EMTs struggled down the stairs with a stretcher. The six-foot-seven photographer hung over on both ends.

"Oh, I need to make sure Page is OK," Becky said and scurried away from Tom. Page was pale. A huge blood stain covered his chest.

"It's just my shoulder," he said. In a whisper he added, "Get my camera."

Becky spotted the camera on the floor and headed in that direction.

"This area is being roped off," one of the officers said. "We're asking all the patrons to line up along the wall."

"But I need that camera. It belongs to the *Daily News*. We need those pictures for today's deadline."

"Sorry, the camera is evidence now."

Becky looked around and saw Tom in the office talking with the theater manager and Dee Licious. She burst into the office.

"Excuse me. I ... I ... I am Becky Judd, from the *Daily News*. I need to get a few comments for today's newspaper."

86

Tom looked peeved. "This is a police investigation. You'll have to wait outside."

"But I need the film from the camera. I need to get those pictures to the office now. It's a matter of life and deadline."

Tom's look didn't soften. "Close the door as you leave."

Becky backed out of the room. It was after eleven. If she had the film in her hands right now, she could just barely get back to the office in time to get it developed for the noon deadline. But if she had to wait, the pictures would never make today's paper. If she could just tell Tom how important it was. There wasn't time to mess around.

Becky marched directly back to the roped area and picked up the camera. She pushed the film release button and started rolling up the half-used film. The same police officer approached.

"What are you doing? That's evidence. You can't—"

"Detective Cantrell told me to remove the film," Becky said briskly, not even looking at the officer. "I just talked to him. He wants me to get these pictures in today's paper. It might help nab the shooter. If you don't believe me, ask him. I'm just following orders."

Becky heard the flap, flap, flap of the film releasing from the spool. She popped open the back of the camera, removed the cartridge, and dropped it into her purse. The police officer was talking to Tom on his handheld radio. Becky waved and smiled at Tom, who was watching her through the office window.

"Yes, sir," the police officer said into the radio. He snapped the radio back on his belt.

"Detective Cantrell said to escort you to your vehicle, ma'am," the officer said. "He's very concerned that those pictures make it into today's paper."

Becky smiled. "I'm sure he is."

☼

The phone in the newsroom had been ringing nonstop. Still, when Nick answered, he was surprised to hear Josie on the other end.

"What's going on?" she asked. "The deputies here at the school are acting funny. Have they found something they don't want to tell us?"

Nick wasn't sure how to answer. He hadn't heard from Mack and Rudy since they left for Bartlett Bridge Road. There hadn't been much chatter on the radio about the dive team. Nick didn't want to worry Josie about a submerged bus since he wasn't sure if that was a real possibility.

"It's probably the shooting at the theater," Nick said. "City cops probably alerted the county deputies about that."

"A shooting? At the Holiday Quad?" Josie exclaimed. "Did somebody shoot Dee Licious?"

"No, she's fine. But there was a shooting in the crowded lobby. Three injured, including Page."

"Page has been shot? I'm coming back to the office."

"No, no, don't do that," Nick stammered. "We need you at the school. Everything is under control here. Becky got the story. She even brought back Page's film. Dick is in the darkroom now. Did you know he was a photographer before he was a sports editor? Anyway, he should have a print by the noon deadline. Page has a shoulder wound. I talked to him on the phone in the emergency room. He's going to be OK."

"What about the other injuries?"

"A couple of people have minor wounds. Nothing sounds life threatening."

"What happened? Was anyone arrested?"

"Nope. Cops are baffled," Nick said. "Cantrell's in charge. After lunch Becky will go to his office. I'm sure he'll tell us whatever he can."

"That's one good break. I'd better come back in. There's nothing going on here. I feel like they're stonewalling us. Miller was supposed to come back at eleven and give us an update, but he didn't."

Ah, Miller must be at Bartlett Bridge Road, Nick thought.

"No news may be good," he said, chewing his lip. "Rudy is out working with the deputies on the rural roads, so I'm sure he'll call in as soon as they find the bus."

"Uh-oh, one of the deputies just came to get me," Josie said. "Looks like it's my turn to be interviewed. I'll come back to the office as soon as I finish."

"No, that's OK. Stay there," Nick said hurriedly. He was speaking to a dial tone.

Josie took a seat in the school psychologist's office, which was serving as the sheriff department's interview room. Stacks of children's board games filled a shelf behind the desk, reminding Josie of Kevin and Timmy and the other missing children. To her left she could see out the windows. It was lunchtime, and the playground was full of noisy children. She felt like she was going to explode.

The deputy noticed she was distracted by the playground.

"Sorry, it's a wee bit noisy," he said as he lowered the blinds.

"No! Please, I want to see them playing. I need to see them playing," Josie said. "Tell me some news. What have the patrols found?"

"I wish I had some news, Ms. Braun. This interview is not to give parents information. It's to find out what the parents may know that will help our investigation."

"And have any of the parents been helpful?" Josie said, trying to smile a little.

"Everyone is helpful, Ms. Braun." The deputy opened a folder on his desk.

A folder. He has a folder of information about me. They have been researching all the parents. What have they found? Divorces? Financial woes? Unexpected wealth?

"I can't discuss my interviews with the other parents, Ms. Braun. I'm sure you can appreciate that. We understand that you are the city editor at the *Daily News*. The paper prints stories that make people angry sometimes. Do you have any enemies, Ms. Braun?"

"Enemies? You mean somebody who would want to steal my kid to get back at me for a story we did? I don't think so."

"Take your time, Ms. Braun. Is there something you're working on now that someone might want to keep out of the paper?"

"You mean like the school referendum story?" Josie said. "A missing school bus can't possibly be good publicity for the school. But surely the opposition wouldn't do something like this to defeat a tax increase."

"Probably not," the deputy said. "Maybe a story about an individual, a powerful individual. Somebody powerful enough to pull this off."

Powerful? Josie thought. Zach Teasdale is powerful. He has the money and the connections to make a school bus disappear. But does he hate me that much? Surely not. Even if he was involved with drug smuggling as the DEA proposed, he wouldn't kidnap Kevin and two dozen other children just to keep the Daily News *from writing a story about it. I can't mention suspicions about Teasdale. He is the county coroner. To even suggest his name to a county deputy would be a political bombshell. I don't have any proof.*

"Have you thought of someone?" the deputy asked. "Any name you suggest will be kept confidential."

"No. I can't think of anyone. I'm sorry."

"We need your help, Ms. Braun. Even if you don't think it's important, it could be the answer."

Josie stood up. "No. You need to give us answers. The bus has been missing four hours. The deputies must have discovered something."

The deputy stood and gave a wan smile. Josie suspected he knew much more about the missing bus than he was saying.

"You think you have the right to withhold information from us," Josie said angrily. "You think you are protecting us. But these are our kids. We deserve to know everything. Where is Chief Deputy Miller? He was supposed to keep us updated. We're not going to sit around here waiting for information that never comes. If the sheriff's department can't find the bus, we'll do it ourselves. We'll gather our friends while it is still light and check out every barn in the county. Every place a bus could be hidden. I'm not going to sit around here any longer."

Josie headed for the door.

"I understand how frustrated you must be," the deputy said. "The sheriff's department isn't taking this lightly. We have been inspecting barns. We have a dive team at Bartlett Bridge Road searching the Jordan River. We have helicopters—"

"A dive team? You think the bus is in the river?"

"We are checking out all possibilities."

"Why didn't somebody tell us?"

"There's nothing to report."

Josie ran from the room. She didn't even go back to the library to pick up her coat. She ran outside through the closest door and headed for her car. All she found was one headlight. The mountain of snow at the end of the parking lot had tumbled over, burying her car. Crying hysterically, Josie pawed through the snow with her bare hands as if Kevin were buried there. She would dig the car out. She would drive to Bartlett Bridge Road. She would find her son.

☼

Rudy had arrived at Bartlett Bridge Road well before the county's dive team. The road was southwest of Jordan amid the expansive farm fields west of the interstate. The Bartlett farm was east of the river. The Russell farm was on the west. From either side, the road ended abruptly at the river. People in the area still called the dirt road by the old moniker even though the bridge had washed out a decade ago. By then, paved state roads offered several easy ways to cross the Jordan River. Only a few farmers used the old dirt roads, so there was no reason to replace the bridge.

Years of weeds and bushes had grown up along the river. The water wasn't even visible from the dirt road. On the Russell side, however, something had plowed through the snow-covered weeds and scrubby brush. Something had gone into the river.

Mack parked his black Jeep suburban near the Russell farmhouse. As Rudy tried the front door of the house, and then looked in the barn, Mack sat with his car door open, pulling on rubber boots. He wasn't about to ruin his shoes in mud and briars. Let the young reporters do that. Mack was the kind of photographer who believed in taking his time, setting up the shot, getting it right. He was never in a hurry.

No one seemed to be home at the Russell farm, so Mack and Rudy wandered over to the river where several squad cars had gathered, including Chief Deputy Miller.

"It's hard to say how old these tracks are," Miller told Rudy, examining the path running from the road into the river. "Sometime since the last snowfall, something large went down this road and right into the river."

90

The dive team was coming by boat, Miller explained. The department didn't get much call for the boat in the winter. They had to get it out of the garage, fuel it up, and run a safety check before launching. Then the boat had to travel several miles down the DesPlaines River to the mouth of the Jordan River. Then it would travel upstream to the site of the former bridge.

While they waited, Mack looked to the noonday sun to set up his shot, plan the right angle. Rudy stood on the bank watching the dark brown water. The river was broad and deep at this point, making a slow bend. The water level was a little higher than usual from the melting snow. The surface was smooth. No protrusions of a bright yellow bus. Not even a circling whirlpool indicating something just below the surface.

"So what do you think, Mack? Did the bus go into the river?" Rudy asked.

"I learned a long time ago, only think about things I can control," Mack replied. "I can't control where the sun is in the sky, but I can control where I put my camera. That's how I keep the dark shadows away. As for the bus, no sense worrying about whether it did or didn't go into the river. We'll know soon enough. We need to concentrate on what we can control. How we tell the story. That's all we can do."

"I don't know," Rudy mused, pawing the ground with his foot. "I'm used to seeing the bright side, the funny side, making light. It's the way I deal with stuff. But how do you joke about something like this? There's just nothing funny about this."

"You'll find a way," Mack said with a smile. "Like them Barletts on the other side of the river. They used to be neighbors. Now you gotta go five miles around if you want to borrow a cup a sugar from the house just across the stream. Doesn't that seem crazy? But the way the weeds are all grown up here, looks like they barely think about the neighbors just across the way."

"People don't borrow a cup of sugar anymore," Rudy said. "Even if they share a wall in an apartment building. People want their privacy."

"That's a fact."

The sound of a boat motor coming up the river grabbed everyone's attention. The boat, marked with "Cade County Sheriff's Department" in tall blue letters, stopped in the center of the river. The deputy on board exchanged shouts of greeting with the deputies waiting on shore.

Rudy was feeling a rising panic. His imagination was running wild. He'd known something was wrong ever since Gail said a bus was late. Until now, he'd managed to come up with reasonably easy explanations: a bus in a ditch or hidden in a barn. The passengers irritable and noisy, frightened maybe. But not injured. Not seriously. Now as he watched the divers in their black wet suits putting on their oxygen tanks, he imagined horrible things below the surface of the water. He could imagine a huge crane pulling the yellow bus out of the river, water gushing from the windows. Looking into the water, he imagined all those little faces looking back. All those children silenced. And this one child, Kevin. This special boy he had known since he was two years old. He thought of Kevin as a toddler with curly blond hair and a fist full of crayons. Kevin loved to draw. As he got older, he would draw a car from four different sides. Front view, back view, side view and bird's-eye view. He was brilliant, Rudy thought. Josie probably had no idea how brilliant her son was. And now no one might ever see the potential Rudy knew was there.

Farmer Bartlett and his wife came out of the farmhouse on the other side of the river and waded through the weeds to watch. Miller told Rudy that deputies had interviewed the Bartletts. They said they hadn't seen a bus this morning nor heard anything go into the river. Would it have made a loud splash or just a little plunk, Rudy wondered.

The divers sat on the side of the boat and fell backwards into the water. Rudy gasped to imagine what they might see.

Josie pulled in behind Mack's car. She didn't need a map to find Bartlett Bridge Road. She had been a young reporter when the bridge washed away in a flood. She had driven these country roads to write that story. That was so many years ago. Back when she was a young bride, pregnant with Kevin. How ironic that the river would call her back all these years later. She clutched her stomach now. It ached with an angry emptiness. Perhaps the river that took that bridge had claimed her baby too.

She spotted Rudy standing on a rise overlooking the river and ran to him. "Have they found anything?"

"Not yet. The divers just went down. What are you doing here?"

"What do you think? You should have come and gotten me."

"This is not a good place for you to be. Where's your coat? Your sweater is wet."

Josie looked down at the soggy pink sweater as if noticing it for the first time. "This isn't mine," she said, pulling off the wet garment. "It's Becky's. The one she loaned me when the gutter spilled."

"Looks like you got dunked again," Rudy said, taking off his coat.

"I had to dig the car out," Josie stammered.

"Here, put this on," Rudy said, draping his coat around Josie's shoulders. Any other time she would have shrugged it off, but she was so chilled she eagerly slipped her arms inside the coat and hugged them to her chest.

"I can't stand the waiting," Rudy said, looking at the water. "We've been waiting an hour for the divers to get here."

"An hour? Why didn't you just jump in and look under the water for yourself?"

Rudy smiled. "You would have done that, wouldn't you? You just can't get enough ice-cold water today."

92

Josie looked at him with the faintest trace of amusement. For a second, maybe half a second, they had thought of something other the missing bus.

One of the divers popped to the surface and swam toward the boat. As he climbed up the ladder, the second diver surfaced. Josie and Rudy rushed toward the cluster of deputies on the bank.

"Did they find it? Did they find the bus?" Josie yelled.

Chief Deputy Miller turned around. "Get her out of here," he said, gesturing to Rudy. "This is no place for a mother."

"What did they find? I want to know," Josie insisted.

The deputy on the boat keyed the mike on his radio and the unit in Miller's hand crackled to life.

"The divers found something," the voice said. "It's not the bus. It's an old tractor. Somebody's using the river as a trash dump."

Josie started laughing and cheering. She and Rudy clasped hands and twirled around in joyful release. The horror they had imagined was not to be. The bus had not gone into the river. At least not here. Their hopes for the children on the bus would live a little longer. But a minute later Josie's laughter crumbled into sobs. She was relieved that the bus wasn't in the river. Then fear took hold again. Rudy held her and she cried, unashamed.

He was trembling too. He was afraid this was a momentary reprieve. Once he had allowed himself to imagine the worst, a remnant of that vision continued to haunt him. Perhaps they had not found a bus full of drowned children, but somehow he couldn't shake the idea that the children could all be dead.

"I can't stand this," Josie said, pulling away. "I've got to do something before I explode."

"Let's go for a run," Rudy said, following after her. "It will clear your head, reduce the stress."

"I can't go running. What if they find them?"

"We can call Nick from the Y. He'll let us know if there's any news."

☼

Nick was glad to get Rudy's call. Glad the bus wasn't in the river. Glad that Josie and Rudy were taking a midday run. And glad the top story on the front page was finished. Duke had called in too, so Nick wasn't expecting any more changes to today's edition. He was hoping to grab a quick lunch when his phone rang again. It was Helen, the receptionist, announcing a man at her desk who wanted to speak to "the person in charge."

Nick walked up to the front desk with long, quick strides. It felt good to get away from the computer screen and ringing phone. The visitor was a distinguished black man dressed in a black suit. He was pacing the lobby when Nick welcomed him with a hearty handshake and his best dimpled smile.

The man identified himself as Robert Crawley. "Is there some place we can talk privately?" he asked.

Nick suggested the break room where they could enjoy a cup of coffee. He needed a shot of caffeine. Walking down the hall to the break room, Nick launched into friendly chatter about the weather and sports. Safe topics.

"Did you catch the Bulls game the other night? That was a great game. That Michael Jordan is unstoppable, isn't he?"

"I don't watch sports," Crawley said, his voice dripping with disdain.

Nick dropped the subject and started asking general questions about Crawley: hometown, occupation, family. By the time Nick had purchased two coffees from the machine, he knew Crawley had been born in Oak Park, lived in Jordan for ten years, and worked for a Chicago accounting firm.

They sat at an empty table in the break room, far from the only other occupant, a woman from advertising who was reading a book and nibbling at a sack lunch.

"How can I help you today?" Nick asked.

"I have a story for you. A big story," Crawley said. "A few months ago I started getting terrible headaches. The doctor found a tumor on my brain, and a neurosurgeon operated."

"Here at St. Mary's?" Nick asked.

"Yes. Right here at St. Mary's. Something went wrong, and I was in a coma for a week. The doctors said I was brain dead, and my wife almost pulled the plug. Then the next morning, I woke up. I felt great. Best I had felt in years."

"That's wonderful news," Nick said. "It's a miracle. That will make a great story if the doctor is willing to go on record with the tests that showed you were brain dead."

"It's not a miracle. It's hell, I tell you. My wife doesn't recognize me. No one does. I don't even recognize myself."

Crawley reached into his pocket and pulled out a wallet. He opened it to his driver's license and held it out for Nick to examine. The name on the license was Robert Crawley, but the photo was of a balding white man.

"I don't understand," Nick said.

"That's what I looked like ten days ago when I went in for the operation. When I woke up two days ago, I looked like this. One day I'm a 45-year-old white guy with a mortgage and two kids. I go under the knife, and when I wake up, my hands are black. My face is black. I don't have anything against black people, mind you. I am not a bigot. But it's quite a shock to look in the mirror and see this."

Nick chuckled. "Hey, man, that's a good one. Who put you up to this?"

"Nobody put me up to anything!" Crawley said, raising his voice enough to cause the woman from advertising to look over. He lowered his voice to a whisper.

"I'm telling you the truth. Why won't anyone believe me?"

"Like you said, it's a bit of a shock," Nick said.

"I went to an attorney this morning, and he didn't believe me either. I figured I had a malpractice suit at the very least."

"Malpractice?"

"I don't know what those doctors did to me. But I went into that hospital a white man. I come out totally different. Isn't that malpractice?"

"I ... ah ... well, it's hard to explain," Nick stammered.

"I went to the bank to cash a check. They just laughed at me when I showed my identification. I took a taxi to my house, but my wife won't let me in. She says her husband died a week ago in the operating room. She doesn't know me at all. She was crying and everything. Said she would call the police if I didn't leave. The paper has to do a story. I've been deprived of my family and my possessions. Everything I worked for."

Nick just shook his head. Even on a full moon Friday the 13th, this was too much.

"I'm afraid there isn't anything the newspaper can do for you, Mr. Crawley. This is a story that's a little hard to prove."

"Why should I have to prove anything? I know who I am."

After Duke called in Dr. Gilbert's comments on the explosion in the South Pacific, he chatted with Leslie Gray. Not on news, just conversation about her recent trip to Disney World with her husband and two kids. Then other subjects—car sickness, cat allergies, donating blood. A scattershot of topics that had nothing to do with their jobs and everything to do with getting to know each other better. Building a bond.

"Hey, when I was coming in here today, I saw a front-end loader picking up a buffalo carcass," Duke said with the same casual air of other random comments. "Those animals are huge."

"Like a small car," Leslie said with a big smile. "Most of them weigh more than 2,000 pounds."

"Do they graze all winter? It doesn't seem like they could find enough to eat."

"Oh, I believe the stable provides hay and grain," Leslie said. "Can I interest you in some lunch? Our café offers buffalo burgers. They're not just for decoration, you know. The bison provide delicious high-protein, low-fat meat."

"Tempting, but I'd better get back. We're having a busy news day. Did you hear that a school bus is missing?"

"A school bus? With kids on it? That's horrible. What do they think happened?"

Duke shrugged and stood up, gathering his coat and notebook. "Not sure. Maybe they've tracked it down by now. Say, I was wondering about that buffalo carcass. How many buffalo on your property?"

"Varies. Twenty to thirty."

"I happened to see a report from the sheriff's office this morning that a motorist spotted a dead buffalo off of Clark Road yesterday. Then I see another one this morning. Two deaths in two days. Isn't that a lot for such a small herd? Is winter hard on them? Or is it something else?"

Leslie placed her hands on her hips.

"Now don't start asking stupid questions about the buffalo dying from radiation poisoning. You know that's a silly rumor. Radiation levels are monitored daily using the latest high-tech equipment. We don't base our safety rating on how many bison die on any particular day."

Duke smiled. "I know it's a silly rumor, but I also know that the sheriff's department has asked for an autopsy of the animal they picked up last night."

"Good luck with that," Leslie said, following Duke out of her office. "The remains of both animals were covered by snow drifts for a month or more. They were discovered because the snow is melting. I suspect they are frozen."

"It just seems a little suspicious. Maybe I should get a comment from the executive director."

Leslie rolled her eyes. "You're serious? He's going to tell you the same things I've been telling you."

"I know," Duke said. "But the best way to combat silly rumors is with better facts."

"Look at this," Leslie said, extending her arms to indicate the expansive sixteen-story atrium. "Does this look like a place plagued with radioactive leaks? Everything about the National Atomic Particle Accelerator Laboratory is in top-notch condition. Have you ever seen such a beautiful, modern building?"

Duke looked around. Leslie was right. The black tile floor glistened. Shiny chrome banisters gleamed on the staircase and along the bridges connecting the office towers. Huge window walls in each office overlooked the atrium as well as the scenery beyond. And the glass walls at each end of the atrium embraced the prairie landscape that surrounded the building.

"Frozen frog farts," Duke exclaimed."I'm not saying you don't have a beautiful building. I'm saying you've got a couple of dead carcasses on the lawn. All I need is a little assurance from the big guy that it's not a problem.

The kingdom was lost for want of a nail, the poem says. Little things matter, if you can call a bison little."

"OK, let's see if Mr. Snyder is in his office. He may be out for a lunch appointment."

Duke and Leslie walked briskly across the atrium to the director's office. Duke noticed the hollow echo their steps made in the huge atrium. As big as the facility was, with a thousand scientists and other staff, the atrium was deserted.

Leslie paused at a counter in the director's office. In a matter of minutes, executive director Brad Snyder came through the door pulling on his suit coat. He was a stocky white-haired man with wire-rimmed glasses. The suit coat did wonders to hide the protruding beer belly that was more obvious in a white shirt and tie.

"Talked to Hammond this morning," Snyder said, holding out a hand to Duke "Thought you were all set up with Dr. Gilbert. Is there something I can add?"

"Oh, I just happened to see a bison carcass when I came in. I saw a sheriff's report about one last night. I was just wondering—"

"Oh, yeah, the radiation thing." Snyder chuckled. "Bet we'll get calls about that, especially since it's a full moon. My secretary keeps a kook file. What's in the file today, Martha?" He turned to the small dark-haired woman behind the counter.

"Oh, yes, we've received several calls about dead buffalo," the secretary responded, opening the file drawer in her desk. "And this morning we got calls about the glow in the fog. Some people swore it was from the electromagnetic field."

Snyder laughed. "Never a dull moment here, Mr. Dukakis."

Duke smiled. "I know it sounds like silly rumors to you people, but when folks call me, I like to be able to give them a straight answer."

"Of course," Snyder said, suddenly growing serious. "Give me the latest ATR report," he said, turning to Martha. "That's the daily measurement of radioactive emissions. Mostly tritium. That's a radioactive form of hydrogen. It occurs naturally in the environment, but it is also an expected by-product of the accelerator. Most of it is contained in our cooling operation. Some is released in the steam. Some will make its way into the wastewater. We monitor constantly. The typical atmospheric reading is a thousandth of a millirem. The EPA doesn't even require monitoring until it's above a tenth of a millirem. That's a hundred times higher than our usual ... see, here's yesterday's report."

Snyder took the paper his secretary offered and waved it in front of Duke.

"That's odd," Snyder mumbled, then continued more firmly. "It is up a little bit. But still well below the level that requires regular monitoring. And

97

the wastewater measure … hmmm. Well, that's also a very safe reading. A fraction of the Department of Energy standard of 9,500 picocuries per milliliter. You can tell your callers, without equivocation, those bison didn't die of radiation exposure. You'd get more radiation from a day in the sun. And wouldn't that feel good right about now?"

Duke laughed. "Can I have a copy of the report? So I get the numbers right?"

"Sure," Snyder said. "You can have this one. Just let me circle the final numbers. This is atmosphere, and this is the standard. And this is the wastewater figure. The standard is printed right here. Did Leslie offer you one of our bison burgers?"

"Sounds good, but I really need to get back. Full moon, you know," Duke said, tucking the report into his notebook.

"Oh, I'll bet you get some strange calls too. Was Dr. Gilbert able to help you with the nuclear explosion?"

"Perfect. Thanks for your help, Mr. Snyder."

The two shook hands. Snyder returned to his office. Leslie and Duke started across the atrium. Suddenly there was a breeze and a flash of white like a curtain flapping in front of them. Duke thought he saw a face as the curtain whipped by. Then there was a horrible thud. Right before their eyes, something had fallen and landed on the gleaming tiles. Duke stood paralyzed, unable to move or even close his mouth.

A young woman was sprawled at their feet.

12:01PM

Leslie screamed. Duke bent over to get a closer look. A pool of blood was forming around her brown hair. Another was seeping under her side, staining her starched white lab coat. Duke slowly reached out a hand to feel for a pulse at her wrist. He'd never actually done that sort of thing before. He'd seen his share of bodies, but never right at his feet like this. Never dangling on that thin thread between alive a second ago and maybe not anymore.

Snyder appeared at Duke's side.

"Is she—"

"I think so," Duke said, pulling his hand back abruptly.

Snyder moved in and felt the throat more authoritatively as Duke backed up a step. People were running from across the atrium. Duke looked up. People were standing on the bridges looking down.

"An ambulance is on its way," Martha said.

"I think it's too late," Snyder said, standing up. "Did you see where she fell from?"

Duke and Leslie exchanged glances.

"She was just there," Leslie said in a shaky voice. "One of the bridges, I assume."

They surveyed the bridges that crisscrossed at various intervals. The one directly over the body was too far up to see clearly. A crowd had gathered on the atrium floor. A middle-aged woman came running down the stairs. She pushed through the crowd around the body.

"Let the doctor through," somebody said.

Evidently a medical doctor in a room full of PhDs, the woman knelt beside the body, felt for a pulse, and quickly agreed with the amateur assessment. She gently brushed a strand of hair from the victim's face and stood up, shaking her head.

Duke glanced at his watch. It was a few minutes after noon. Probably too late for today's paper. But he'd let Nick decide. He slipped away from the crowd and made a call from Leslie's desk.

"You think it was an accident?" Nick asked as soon as Duke reported the death.

"Probably. Or a suicide. I guess somebody could have pushed her, but I was there. I didn't hear any struggle."

99

"We've got enough unknowns for one day's paper. We'll hold this one for Saturday," Nick said. "Still no word on the missing school bus and now we've got a crazy random shooting at the movie theater with three injuries. We don't even know who the shooter was."

"Shaking Shih Tzu sneezes! How's Josie holding up?"

"Rudy just called in. They're going to run through the park, try to work off a little stress."

"That's good. I'll probably be here for a while until the deputies and coroner get finished. You might want to send a photog."

"Oh, yeah. I forgot to mention we're down to one photog. Page is one of the three injured at the theater shooting."

"Page? Is he okay?"

"Took a bullet in the shoulder. Said he wants a caddy to carry his camera bag."

"That's good if he's making jokes. What's going on, Nick? This day is more than the usual full moon freak show."

"I know. Watch for Mack. I'll call him on the radio and tell him to head up there on his way back from the river."

☼

Rudy was right, Josie thought, as they ran through the winding streets of Murray Park. The sunshine and cool air filled her with hope and possibilities, two things she desperately needed for whatever news lay ahead.

During the past month, Josie had been running on the treadmill three to four times a week, an exercise so boring she could barely maintain her commitment to finish thirty minutes. But today the snow had melted off the roadways. Running outside was liberating.

At first, her green jogging suit and purple knit leg warmers were not enough to keep out the February chill. But as her heart beat faster, she warmed up and her mood lifted. She lengthened her stride, picked up her pace, and pulled ahead of Rudy.

Running always made her feel in control. Strong. She wasn't forgetting about Kevin and the missing bus, but she felt like she was running away from the mire of governmental bureaucracy that had been weighing her down all morning. She had to get away from it, had to run faster. She poured on the power. A little faster, a little farther, a little more. With each increase in effort, her body responded with an extra spurt of energy. Her body said, "You can. You can. You can."

As the Y came into view around the corner, she pushed herself to the limit. It was her goal. Her finish line. The end of the five-kilometer route Nick had mapped out. Usually at this point she would slow a little. The end was in sight. The cool-down was coming. But on this day, the sight of the familiar brown building only made her push harder. She was angry about the missing bus; she channeled all that anger into her legs.

Rudy was coming up behind her. He'd also increased his pace. His legs were longer and stronger. He caught up without too much trouble, and now the competition of being side by side urged each of them on. Faster. Harder. Usually it was Nick and Rudy competing for a photo finish. Josie was usually happy just to stay within sight of the men. But today she had to win. Had to because she could. She knew she could. As the road turned into the parking lot, she was several strides ahead of Rudy and threw her arms up in the racer's cheer of victory.

She stumbled into a walk and took big gulping breaths. She snagged her water bottle and guzzled long swallows. Rudy walked around the parking lot beside her.

"What about the driver?" Josie said as soon as her breathing slowed enough to talk.

"The bus driver?" Rudy responded, stopping to bend in half.

"Yeah. What did you find out about Mr. Joe?"

Rudy looked up and shook his head. "Nothing much. Deputies looked through his apartment and didn't find anything unusual."

"He's the answer," Josie said, her breaths coming more calmly. "We've got to find out everything about him. Talk to his neighbors, his pastor, his coworkers. Find his mother, for Pete's sake. He's the answer."

When Brittany pulled back the curtain, she was glad to see Claude Dixon was awake. "Well, there you are, Mr. Dixon. How are you feeling?"

"Where am I?" the man muttered.

"You're at St. Mary's Hospital. You have a gunshot wound in the arm. It isn't serious. The doctor removed the bullet. You had us worried there for a while. You kept passing out, and your blood pressure kept dropping. I need you to tell me what medications you are on. Are you on any heart medications?"

"Heart medications?" the man repeated. "I don't think so."

"We've finally contacted your wife. She was out shopping. Perhaps when she gets here we can get a list of medications. You were very lucky, Mr. Dixon."

"My wife?" the patient repeated.

"Do you remember what happened? There was a shooting at the movie theater. Three people were shot."

101

"Three shots?" the patient exclaimed, his eyes growing wide. "I don't remember any of this."

Brittany examined the bandage on his left arm, then she picked up his right hand, which boasted little pads of gauze on the first two fingers.

"You were shot in the left arm, but we're not sure what happened over here on your right hand. You had a couple of puncture wounds in your fingers like you were bitten by a vampire," Brittany said with a laugh.

"A vampire?" the man said, yanking his hand away from the nurse.

"Sorry. I'm just teasing. You were at a horror movie. I thought maybe you were into vampires and werewolves."

Brittany walked to the head of the bed to check the IV. The patient's eyes followed her to the bag of blood hanging just behind his head. "We're giving you a transfusion to replace the blood you lost. Mr. Dixon, are you OK?"

"Don't be alarmed," the patient muttered as his eyelids drooped. "I'm going to faint."

Brittany grabbed for his wrist and took his pulse.

"Mr. Dixon. Mr. Dixon," she repeated, slapping his cheeks.

Amy, the charge nurse, stepped into the cubicle.

"He passed out again," Brittany exclaimed. "He was awake and talking. Then all of a sudden, he said, 'I'm going to faint,' and he did."

"Hemophobia," Amy said. "Happens to some people. They can't stand the sight of blood. Even in a drip bag. If he knew he was going to faint, it must happen to him a lot. Just put a drape over the IV pole," she said, handing a sheet to Brittany. "If he doesn't see it, he'll be fine. His wife is at the front desk. I'll have them send her back."

As Brittany finished covering the IV pole, the patient came around.

"Well, you're back again," Brittany said. "Why didn't you tell us you had a phobia? We can deal with phobias."

"I'm sorry," the man said. "It's embarrassing."

"Oh, don't give it another thought," Brittany said cheerily. "How about some orange juice?"

As she left the cubicle, Brittany was stopped by a woman in the hallway.

"I'm looking for my husband, Claude Dixon. They told me he'd been shot."

"Just behind that curtain," Brittany said, pointing to the cubicle. "I'm on my way to get him some juice."

When Brittany returned, the woman was standing outside the curtain.

"I must have misunderstood," she said. "I thought you said my husband was in there."

"Isn't he? I just saw him a minute ago."

"Well, there's a man in there, but he's certainly not my husband. I never saw that man before in my life."

☼

"OK, let's go through this again," Tom Cantrell said, taking a seat across from Cord McCoy. As bodyguard for rock star Dee Licious, McCoy figured he was bulletproof. His posture showed it. He sprawled on his chair with one arm hooked over the back and his legs stretched under the table. Although police had confiscated his gun, his jaunty black leather fedora and holster were thrown casually on the table.

"I told you a dozen times. I saw a gun, I pulled mine. I heard a shot, I fired back a time or two. Then I heard somebody running above me. I looked up and saw the guy with a weapon. OK. It was a camera with an ungodly long lens, but in a quick glance it looked like a gun on a stand. You woulda shot him too, I bet."

"I'll take that bet and raise you one more," Cantrell said, leaning forward and resting an elbow on the table. "They've pulled slugs out of two of the injured parties: the photographer and a man named Dixon. Preliminary inspection says both slugs came from the same gun. Your nifty little 9mm Glock. That's two innocent bystanders shot by a supposedly well-trained marksman. One of the so-called good guys. "

"You know how it is in a crowd situation like that. You have to make choices."

"You'd better hope that third shooting victim doesn't turn out to be your slug too."

"If I hadn't shot when I did, the shooter might have hit Dee. It's my job to protect her, and I did that."

"By shooting two, possibly three, innocent people? Don't they teach you guys to confirm the target before you shoot? I'm sorry, but the choices you made were lousy."

"Who says the victims are innocent? When I saw the gun, I aimed for the gun."

"OK. Which one of the injured parties was holding the gun?"

"I couldn't tell for sure. There were too many people reaching out to touch Dee. But I aimed for the gun so one of the people hit must be the shooter. Didn't you say this Dixon guy was shot in the arm?"

"I'll give you that. You shot an arm. Sounds like the general vicinity of a weapon. What kind of gun did you see?"

"Oh, just some little revolver. A Saturday-night special. A .22 maybe."

"Well, we didn't find one of those on Mr. Dixon or on any of the other guests."

"So he stashed it. He got away in the confusion."

"Mr. Dixon didn't get away, and he didn't have much of an opportunity for stashing. He went into shock or something and was unconscious most of the time. You're just lucky he didn't have a heart attack and die. Michele Ames is still in surgery. If that slug belongs to you, then our mystery shooter is 0-3. You're the only one scoring hits."

"I'm sorry. It was just so crowded," McCoy said, looking down. His bluster was fizzling.

Cantrell fell back in his chair and heaved a sigh. "Listen, man, I'm trying to see your side of this. But I've got to charge you with assault with a deadly weapon and reckless discharge of a weapon."

"But I have a license."

"Not for long. Maybe you didn't start this, but you've got to think before you return fire. You've got to confirm your target. You know you didn't do that."

Cord slouched down into the chair and crossed his arms. "I guess I'd better get an attorney."

"I guess so."

When Cantrell returned after taking McCoy to booking, one of the other detectives was standing at his desk.

"They got the third slug from that Ames lady. Just like you suspected. It's the same as the rest."

Cantrell slapped his hand on the desk. "Damn. If we didn't have witnesses saying there were four shots, I'd swear McCoy was in this alone. Trigger happy. Or a publicity stunt. But there are only three shots missing from his clip. What happened to the other gun?"

"Got that for you too. They found it in one of the plants."

"So there was another shooter, and he hid it."

"Well, maybe not intentionally. They found it up in the branches of one of them potted trees. Ten feet off the ground. Not where somebody could reach easily. The lady who came in to tend the potted trees noticed it. She was looking for yellow leaves to trim."

"You mean somebody just threw it up there and it stuck? Dumb luck."

"And here's the clincher. It was loaded with blanks."

☼

Reuben Jetter pulled the little dog out of the sudsy water in the kitchen sink and sat him on the counter. The dog shivered under the long ropes of wet hair that dangled off his body and onto the counter.

"Hey, little fella, no wonder you're cold," Reuben said, wrapping a frayed bath towel over the pup and rubbing him dry.

"I don't know why anybody would let a little dog's hair grow this long," Reuben said, pulling out a strand that was taller than the dog. "You need a crew cut, boy." Reuben reached for the scissors.

"Nothing like a crew cut to make a man feel good about himself. We'll make do with scissors now. Maybe Monday I can take you to the barber shop with me. I'll bet Steve could zip you up in no time. You're such a docile dog. I've never seen a dog sit still like you do." Reuben started to snip.

"Your owner must have brushed that long hair all the time. Well, we're not going to worry about that old owner. She should never have taken you to a movie theater like that. And then the shooting. All those crazy people running around trying to get away. You could've been trampled. Good thing I found you and slipped out the back before the cops arrived. Cops don't pay no attention to me anyway. Look right past me. Yeah, Reuben Jetter is the invisible man. And you're the practically invisible dog. Look at you. Without all that hair, I can almost look right through you."

Besides changing the size of the little animal, cutting his hair made him appear more light tan in color. The dark gray hair on his back and head had been covering up the beige undercoat.

"With a good haircut, you are khaki-colored like an army private. You look like Elvis when he got drafted. Think I'll call you The King. Yep, that's what I'll call you."

Reuben picked up the tiny teacup-sized dog and held him out at arm's length for inspection. He immediately relieved himself on Reuben's shoes.

"Hell! What did you do that for?" Reuben squealed, dropping the dog.

The little animal gave a pitiful whine when it hit the floor and scampered under the recliner.

"Oh, gee, I'm sorry, fella," Reuben said, kneeling to look under the chair. "I didn't mean to hurt you. You just surprised me is all. Come out of there, and I'll take you outside. I'll show you where good doggies take a piss." Reuben stuck his arm under the chair and the frightened dog snapped at his fingers.

"Damn! Here we been such good friends and all. You're not going to go and get mean on me, are you?"

The little dog growled a high-pitched snarl that sounded like the ping of an old screen door.

"I hear ya, buddy. You don't know who to trust anymore. Well, I'm gonna try to win your trust. You like hotdogs? I got a fridge full of hotdogs. Not those cheap, skinny dogs neither. These are plump kosher franks. All beef. I'll get you one."

Reuben went to the fridge and returned with a long wiener almost as big as the dog. He reached it back as far as he could and the dog snapped at it. He pulled it out to find tiny teeth marks in the bright orange-red hide.

"This may be too big for your little mouth, but I'll let you get another taste," Reuben said, shoving the wiener to the back of the space again. The dog growled his little hoarse growl and snapped again at the red invader.

"That's good, now you've got a taste." Reuben went to the counter and pulled a paring knife out of the drawer. He cut a slice off the hotdog and proceeded to chop the slice into little pea-sized chunks. He rolled one under the chair and waited. After a few seconds the little dog crept forward, sniffed the piece of hotdog and ate it. Reuben rolled another piece barely under the chair. When it was gone, he laid a piece an inch in front of the brown flap of naugahyde that masked the opening under the chair. In less than a minute, the dog emerged, ate the piece of meat, and looked up to Reuben for more.

"See, I knew you would like hotdogs." Reuben dropped a handful of pieces in front of the dog. When those were eaten, the dog looked up at Reuben and sat still as the man reached over and picked him up.

"OK, King. This is the big test. It's kinda cold outside, but that's where you need to go pee. Come on, let's give it a try."

Reuben set his new friend onto the damp driveway in front of his house. The dog took slow, tiptoe steps as if he didn't want to get his feet wet. The soggy grass with the melting snow would be even colder, Reuben figured. King took a couple of steps and looked back at Reuben, whining.

"OK, we'll try newspapers in the bathroom for tonight. I'll let you use the shower stall. That should work," Reuben said, picking up the dog. As soon as he lifted the dog off the pavement and held him at arm's length, the dog tinkled again.

"Why that's the craziest thing I ever saw," Reuben exclaimed. "You don't want to pee on your own feet, you want to pee on mine. That will teach me to be careful how I pick you up. I'm not housebreaking you, you're housebreaking me."

The dog whimpered. Reuben pulled him close to his chest. "Are you done now? Is it safe?"

The dog snuggled under Reuben's arm, and the hefty man grinned. Then he looked up and noticed a light on in the large two-car garage behind his neighbor's house.

"Well, looks like the mad scientist is working in his lab today, King. We'd better keep an eye out for smoke going up the chimney. Did I tell you he tried to set the place on fire last summer doing some experiment? Crazy little guy."

106

1:00 PM

By one o'clock Josie was back in the office. She called a meeting of available staff.

Fridays were always busy because the *Daily News* put out two papers. The Friday afternoon edition would be delivered to homes about five in the evening, just as the weekend staff was arriving to work on the Saturday morning edition. Normally, a rotating weekend editor would be in charge of the copy desk and the reporter assigned to the Friday-night shift. But because of the full moon Friday the 13th, Hoss had double scheduled himself to work both shifts. He'd gone home just after the noon deadline with plans to get a nap and be back on duty by six.

Nick barely had time for a quick sandwich lunch. He and Becky joined Josie and Rudy in the conference room.

"I got a call from Duke," Nick reported. "They have identified the body at the A-Lab. Petra Oligivich, 24. A scientist from Moscow."

"A dead Russian scientist? This could become an international incident," Josie said. "Are the feds involved?"

"No doubt they will be," Nick responded. "Teasdale is there, but wasn't expected to give a statement on the cause of death for several hours. Duke's been talking to some of the other scientists, and they say the girl was a bit of a daredevil. Comes from a circus family. She would entertain coworkers during lunch hours by walking on the bridge railings in the atrium. The body was barefoot, Duke said, so it sounds possible. Maybe she was putting on a show and fell, but Duke said he hasn't found anyone who claims to have seen her fall."

"Let's be proactive on this one," Josie said. "Call AP. Alert them to the international element in this death. Let them do the heavy lifting with the State Department."

"You want to give AP this story?" Nick asked. "Sounds like it was just an accident."

"It won't make any difference from the international perspective. What if an American kid was killed at a Moscow research facility? We wouldn't believe it was an accident, would we? If world news takes the lead on this one, they can't scoop us. It will only drive more readers to the *Daily News* to read Duke's first-person details. What about the Dee Licious shooting?"

107

"All three of the injured people were shot by Dee's bodyguard," Becky said, flipping open her notebook."But they don't have any clue who fired the first shot and started the melee."

"The bodyguard did all the damage? That's terrible," Josie said, shaking her head. "Could this be a publicity stunt? What's the rock star saying?"

"They canceled all her other appearances for today and whisked her away for safekeeping," Becky responded. "They say her life is in danger. Whether that's true or not, they are getting all sorts of mileage out of the shooting. It's been on all the radio stations. I'll bet it's on the five o'clock news. She's supposed to do a press conference at four from her hotel in downtown Chicago."

"Ah, yes, serve up the tortured star on a silver platter," Nick said.

"I don't see any sense in covering the press conference all the way downtown. It will be all over television," Josie said. "Our story is here. What do the police say?"

"We'll see," Becky said, blushing a little. "I sorta stole Page's film from evidence, so I'm not sure Tom's even speaking to me. I'm going to take him a complete set of prints from the film as a peace offering. It just looks like a chaotic crowd to me, but maybe he'll see something I missed."

"Sounds good," Josie said. "While you're at the police station, can you check into whether the missing school bus driver, Joseph Wilson, has any sort of record? I know Miller told the parents he had no police record or complaints against him, but I'm wondering if there is something that was overlooked. Maybe trouble with a neighbor, or speeding tickets, whatever. The city doesn't have to release that information on an individual, but I'm hoping your peace offering buys us a little extra."

"I can try," Becky said, making a note on her pad. "Oh, yeah, I have this publicity shot of Dee Licious and her little pooch, Spritzer. The dog was in her purse. He must have gotten out of the purse when Dee was pushed to the ground. He got lost in the stampede. She's expected to offer some sort of reward at the press conference."

"That's local news," Nick said, reaching for the photo. "Everybody loves a dog story. And that pooch certainly didn't scamper all the way to Chicago. He's still around town."

"OK. Play the dog photo big," Josie said, looking at the print. "Check the dog shelters, Becky. Maybe somebody turned it in. I wonder if he's still got all his pretty purple bows."

"It was such a madhouse in that theater, he'll be lucky to have all four paws," Becky said. "He must be hiding under a desk somewhere in the theater."

"Good idea. Check there too," Josie said. "As for the missing bus, I've asked Rudy to concentrate on the bus driver. He'll be talking to the other drivers, Wilson's neighbors, his family. Even if we don't find anything remiss, there's interest in who he is. If he's not responsible for making the bus disappear, then he'll end up as the hero or the victim. Either way, readers will want to know more about him. And if I'm right, we might find something that will tell us why this bus disappeared."

"I had Sis pull the clips on everybody named Wilson," Rudy said. "That's a lot of clips. But she'll be reading through them to see if there's any reference to Joe or Joseph. We figured we might find him mentioned as a survivor in an obit and that would open the door to his family members."

"That's good," Josie said. "Are we missing anything here? Are we leaving a door unopened?"

"How about the notion that one of the parents is responsible for taking the bus? Are they still looking into that?" Nick asked.

"I'm sure they are," Josie said. "I'll stop by the school to talk to any parents who are there. I'll see if Miller has made any more announcements. If not, I'll go out to the sheriff's station and track him down. Let's get back together at four to see where we are."

After the reporters filed out of the conference room, Hammond walked in.

"Josie, I'm surprised to see you. Has there been some good news about the school bus?"

"I'm afraid not," Josie said. "I'm going to head back over to the school to see what I can find out."

"That's good," he said. "The newsroom is no place for you today. I don't think you are in any shape to be making news judgments."

"Excuse me? Not in any shape? You think because I'm a female I am falling to pieces?"

"Don't make an ugly scene, Josie. Just go home to your family."

"Family? Hammond, I appreciate your concern, but I am not going to go lie down and put a cold cloth on my head like a poor fainting female while the men of the world deal with the serious stuff. Do you realize the woman who died at A-Lab is a Russian scientist? There's probably going to be an international incident over this."

"Russian? Goodness, no, I had no idea."

"Nick will alert AP, but I suspect it's going to end up on all the Chicago television stations tonight. You might want to call your buddy Snyder at the A-Lab. Offer to help him deal with the media."

"Good idea."

"By the way, all the people injured in the shoot-out at the Holiday Quad Corral were shot by the licensed bodyguard. If that's not worth international outrage, it should be. The *Daily News* will be on top of every development in both those stories. As for the missing school bus, there's no way I'm going to sit around and wait for answers. I'm going to find out what happened to those kids, because that's what I do. I look for answers. I make news judgments. Any day. Every day. No matter what. Now if you'll excuse me, I'm going to visit the school."

Josie pushed past Hammond in the doorway. She had picked up a dry coat at her house, and it was waiting for her on the hall tree behind her desk. She grabbed her coat and purse, zipped past Nick's desk without stopping, and headed through the back door into the parking lot. Nick looked up at Hammond and shrugged his shoulders. Hammond smiled weakly and returned to his office.

Josie steamed into the parking lot so quickly that she almost didn't notice the familiar beige Mercury Sable circling the lot. It stopped as she stormed past, and a woman got out.

"Josie, honey, has there been any word? Have they found the bus?"

Josie was startled out of her determined course and jolted into the present moment.

"Mom, what are you doing here?"

"One of the reporters called us about Kevin. Has his bus been found?"

"No, Mom. No, it hasn't?"

"Oh, honey."

Josie melted into the welcoming arms of Sally Braun, a petite woman whose white curls were only a tad longer than Josie's blond pixie cut.

"Don't worry, it's going to be OK," Sally said, stroking Josie's back as she sobbed.

"Mom, I don't know if it is going to be OK this time. The bus has been missing too long. I never dreamed it would go on this long."

"I don't know how this will end, honey, but whatever happens, we'll be here. We'll get through it together. It will be OK," Sally repeated.

A burly, balding man joined them.

"How's my girl?"

"Oh, Daddy," Josie said, transferring from her mother's embrace to the beefy arms and expansive chest of Dan Braun.

"We went by the house first and no one was home," he said. "Surely they're not making you work during a family emergency like this."

"No, Daddy, the paper has been very supportive. It's just I can't sit around and do nothing."

"Let's go talk to the sheriff," Sally suggested. "That's where your father and I were going if we couldn't find you."

"I was on my way to the school," Josie said. "The parents are gathering there, waiting for word."

"Let's take my car," Dan said. "It's bigger than that little skateboard you drive."

"First, let's pray," Sally said, holding out her hands to her husband and her daughter. The three of them held hands, making a small prayer circle in the middle of the parking lot.

"Heavenly Father," Sally murmured, "be with our little Kevin at this terrible time. We don't know where he is, but you do. Wrap him in your loving arms. Protect him. Be with all the children. Be with Josie and all the parents. Calm their fears. Be with the deputies who are searching for the bus. We are trusting our children into your care, Lord. Bring them home safely."

When the prayer was over, Josie slipped into the backseat of her parents' car. After giving directions to the school, Josie told her parents the details of the foggy morning, the missing bus, the awful search of the Jordan River.

"I'm so glad to see you guys. I would have called, but I didn't know what to say. I thought it would be resolved before you could get here. I didn't want to bother you for nothing."

"Nothing? It's never nothing when my grandson is missing," Sally said, turning around to face her daughter.

"She bought one of those silly Transformer toys when we stopped at the gas station," Dan said over his shoulder. "She was that sure he'd be OK by the time we got here."

"Oh, Mom, I don't know what to think. It doesn't make sense. But it is so much easier to talk to you two about it, because he's your kid too. You know how special he is."

Josie dropped her head into her hands and sobbed. Her mother reached over the seat to rub her head.

"You're going to have to tell me where to turn," Dan said. "Is that school right here on Jackson?"

Josie snuffled her tears and leaned forward to tell her father where to turn for the school. After they parked and got out of the car, Josie walked into the school between them, an arm stretched around each of her parents.

"It's just so good to have you here. I've been trying to be strong for everybody else, but I feel like I can be myself with you. Thanks for coming."

☼

Brittany went directly to Amy, the charge nurse. She had never dealt with a misidentified patient before, especially one with a bullet in his arm and a mysterious blood phobia. Amy *tsked* and took charge. She grabbed a patient form on a clipboard and headed into the cubicle with Brittany at her heels.

"I'm so sorry, sir," Amy said as she handed the clipboard to the patient. "There's been some confusion We thought you were Mr. Dixon. It's really not unusual in trauma cases like this where the patient comes in unconscious. Sometimes the ambulance personnel pick up the wrong identification, especially at a mob scene like this one. Now, if you'll just fill out this form, we'll have all the information we need."

Pete Hampton looked at the paper and the pen the nurse handed him. It was a golden opportunity. They didn't know who he was. They didn't know anything about him. He expected he was about to be nabbed for pocketing Mr. Dixon's wallet, but these nurses assumed the paramedics made a mistake. Picked up the wrong wallet. It was all up to him.

"I ... I ... don't know," Pete stammered. "You said I was Mr. Dixon. You said I had a wife."

Amy and Brittany exchanged glances. "But Mimi Dixon doesn't recognize you," Brittany said.

"Oh, I was hoping," Pete said laying the clipboard beside him on the stretcher. "I'm all fuzzy in the head. I can't remember anything."

"You don't remember your name?" Amy asked.

"Dixon sounded familiar," Pete said with a smile. "Are you sure I'm not Mr. Dixon?"

Amy and Brittany exchanged glances.

"Are you saying you don't remember anything?" Amy asked.

"Not before I woke up an hour or so ago," Pete said, smiling. "You said I'd been shot. You said three people were shot. I don't remember any of that happening, but I remember you telling me. I don't remember anything before I woke up."

"You remembered you had a phobia to blood," Brittany exclaimed.

"I did?"

"Yes. You told me you were going to pass out, as if you recognized the feeling. And you said it was embarrassing."

"Did I?"

"Don't you remember? That's why I covered up the IV pole so you wouldn't see the blood running into your arm."

"There's blood running into my arm?" Pete jerked his arm up, spied the little red tube taped to his forearm and right on cue, passed out.

"Now you've done it," Amy said, reaching for the man's wrist.

"I don't believe him," Brittany said. "He's lying."

"Lying about amnesia or lying about fainting at the sight of blood?"

"Oh, I believe he has a blood phobia, all right," Brittany said. "But I don't believe the amnesia. He knows who he is, he just doesn't want us to know."

"I'm calling the police," Amy said, and the two nurses rushed out of the cubicle.

When the room was empty, Pete opened one eye. He was conscious enough to hear that Amy was calling the police. He had to get out of the hospital. He dropped his bare feet to the floor and started for the curtain. The IV pole still attached to his arm came crashing across the gurney. Pete turned around just in time to see the tube pull out of the bag of blood and drip bright red onto the white sheet.

He collapsed onto the floor.

☼

Tom Cantrell was on the phone when Becky arrived at the investigations office of the Jordan Police Department. Seeing her sparked an anger that had been simmering in Cantrell's chest all day. Across the room he could see her smiling and laughing, shaking hands with other officers who gathered around to ask her about the morning's shooting at the movie theater. That's the way Becky was, always the center of attention.

Look how they all fawn over her, like love-sick schoolboys. Even Mom is bowing to Princess Becky. Well, I'm not going to be one of them. She's not going to interfere with my investigation. I let her take the film from the camera. How stupid was that! And now she is here to weasel information from me. She probably doesn't love me at all. She's just using me as a source. A precious source.

"Excuse me, what did you say?"

Tom's thoughts were interrupted by the angry voice on the phone. It was Reuben Jetter, that lunatic. He'd been going on and on about the shooting at the movie theater. He was calling from the desk downstairs. He wanted to come upstairs, and the desk sergeant had wisely stopped him. He had some film. Shots he'd taken of the crowd. It might be valuable evidence, he said. He could bring it right up. But he didn't want to leave it with the desk sergeant. He didn't trust that man. He might lose this film. It was important.

"Yeah, sure. Bring it on up, Reuben, I'm here," Tom said to appease the crazy man and get him off the phone.

As he hung up, he looked back at Becky. How the other men adored her. She looked at Tom and smiled that toothy grin that seemed to explode right out of her face. *She was lovely. So lovely.* Cantrell turned his back to her and opened a file drawer. *I can't stand how she controls me. Get hold of yourself, man! Don't be her damn puppet.*

"You still angry?"

Becky's voice was soft, seductive. Right over his shoulder. He fiddled with a file to keep from looking at her.

"I'm not angry. I have more important things to do than waste my time being angry," he said as he slammed the file drawer and turned around.

"Good," Becky said. She held out a fist full of photographs. "I brought these. It's everything on Page's film. I thought maybe you would see something in the crowd."

"How's Page doing?" Tom asked as he took the photos and sat down at his desk.

"Good. They are supposed to release him this afternoon," Becky said as she slipped into the metal chair next to Tom's desk. "We need him. I suppose you heard about the lady who fell to her death up at A-Lab."

"I heard," Tom said, spreading out the photos.

"In this picture over here, I think that is the woman who got shot," Becky said, pointing to the photo. "She was right next to Dee Licious. And this guy over here. I think that's the one who got shot in the arm and went into shock or whatever. Mr. Dixon."

"That's not his name," Tom said, looking up at Becky. "Right after your paper came out, the real Mr. Dixon called. Said he was fine. Was having a liquid lunch with some pals. Said he must have dropped his wallet in the rush to get out of there. Evidently he reported it to one of the officers at the scene, but there was such confusion, it didn't make it into the report."

"Oh, so what is the name of the man who got shot?" Becky asked, pen poised. "I'll do a correction for tomorrow."

"Sorry, we don't have a name yet. The guy is claiming amnesia."

"Claiming?"

"Well, let's just say the hospital has its doubts. They're moving him to a private room with a guard. Did you see him act suspiciously?"

"Tommy, these are horror movie fans. They were all acting weird."

Cantrell sighed and leaned back in his chair. He wanted to open his heart to her, tell her everything he knew. It was so easy to talk to her. He'd said too much already, and she hadn't asked a question. He shook his head.

"What?" Becky smiled her electric smile.

His heart fluttered. She could have been shot today. There was that brief time when he first heard about a newspaper photographer being shot, that the thought occurred to him. He could have lost her for good.

"We gotta avoid career clashes," he said. "I know you need to get the story. But I've gotta sort out the truth, make a case."

"Sounds like a win-win to me," she said.

"Not necessarily. I thought we agreed it would be better if you didn't cover the cases I'm investigating. Then we wouldn't end up fighting about work."

"It's not my fault a movie star visit turned into a shoot-out."

"I know, it's just—"

Cantrell looked up and saw Reuben Jetter standing at the corner of his desk.

"Oh, you've already got some pictures," Reuben said, craning his neck to look at the display on Cantrell's desk. "Those must be from the newspaper." He glanced at Becky. "My pictures are better. I don't have a long lens, so I get up close and personal. I even got a close-up of Elvis. He was there, you know. Dee Licious is his daughter. He had me fooled at first. He was wearing a vampire disguise. I'm sure you'll recognize him. I did."

Reuben held out a film canister and let it drop into Tom's outstretched hand. When he lifted his arm a little dog's head poked out.

"Oh, my goodness. You've got a dog in your pocket," Becky exclaimed.

"Yep, that's King, my pocket pal," Reuben said, patting the tiny head that disappeared back inside his pocket. "I'll bet you hardly remember Elvis. You're too young. It will be ten years ago this summer that they reported his death. He just did that so he could get some privacy, you know. A man deserves a little privacy."

"Well, thanks for the film, Reuben," Tom said, standing up. "I'm in the middle of a newspaper interview here. I'm sure you understand."

"Oh, yeah, right," Reuben said, backing away. "You can just keep those prints. I've got lots of pictures of Elvis. And maybe those will help identify the shooter. I'm a pretty good photographer."

"I'm sure you are, Reuben. Thanks for your help," Tom said, sitting down again.

"Bye, Miss Judd," Reuben said as he backed away another step. "Good luck with your story. You can use any of my pictures, just credit me as the photographer. I won't charge you none. The paper's always treated me fairly."

"Bye, Mr. Jetter," Becky said, as the intruder reluctantly backed away another step. When Becky was sure Reuben was out of earshot, she resumed her conversation with Tom.

"I'll get Mack to develop those for you," she said. "I can have him put a rush on it."

"Oh, it's nothing," Tom said, fingering the canister as he watched Reuben exit through the office door.

"You never know," Becky said, taking the small canister. "Crazy Reuben might have caught the shooter in the act."

"We found the gun," Tom blurted. He hadn't planned to tell her, but somehow the words slipped out. "It was loaded with blanks. Probably some stage prop. Sounds more and more like a publicity stunt."

"A publicity stunt with three injuries? That's horrible. Won't there be a huge lawsuit?"

"Probably. A big-city lawyer showed up and whisked away the stupid bodyguard. He'll never see jail time. They'll pay the damage claims, reaping publicity for every day it's in court. At their fancy Hollywood parties they'll be laughing about those stupid rubes in Illinois. Sometimes I wonder why we try."

Becky wasn't taking notes. She knew Tom had wandered off the record even though he hadn't said so. "Do you know who the gun belongs to? Was there any registration?"

"We're checking that. And the fingerprints. I don't really have any more to give you."

"I know," Becky said. Her eyes locked onto Tom's.

"Oh, I almost forgot. The play. Mom's directing some play tonight at the college. Can you go?"

Becky smiled. "*Kiss Me, Kate*. Jennifer is in it. Duke's daughter. It's been on our calendar for months."

"It has?"

"Of course. There's no sense telling you what's on the social calendar since one of our jobs is bound to interfere. Which reminds me. The missing school bus. One of the kids on the bus is Josie's son."

"Oh, no!"

"She's wondering if there's anything in the police files about the bus driver, Joseph Wilson. Anything at all."

"I'm sure the sheriff's department has already checked, but I'll see what I can find out," Tom said, scratching a note on his pad.

"OK," Becky said and stood up. "I'll get Reuben's film developed and bring it by in an hour or so."

"Don't worry about it," Tom said with a wave of his hand. He smiled as he watched Becky's graceful stroll out of the office. He loved her so much it frightened him.

☼

From a perch high above, Duke watched as the ambulance staff loaded the body onto a stretcher and wheeled it away. Zach Teasdale, the coroner, was talking with Brad Snyder, the executive director of the National Atomic Particle Accelerator Laboratory. The center of the atrium was cordoned off with yellow crime-scene tape.

Duke was standing on the tenth-floor bridge. The real action at this point was two floors above him on the twelfth-floor bridge where more crime-scene tape was draped. The whole eleventh and twelfth floors had been closed so deputies could look for some trace that would tell them how Oligivich had died.

Fifteen bridges were staggered across the length of the atrium, one on each floor. Based on where the body landed, the deputies surmised she had fallen from the twelfth-floor bridge. She was barefoot. Where were her shoes? That would be a clue.

Employees had been standing along the railings watching the investigation on the atrium floor. Now that the body was gone, many headed back into their offices. Duke spotted a figure he recognized along the tenth-floor railing near where the bridge crossed. It was that huge man from Samoa. What was his name? Baptista. Henri Baptista. Duke wandered closer to speak to him.

"Hi, Dr. Baptista. This is sure a strange turn of events, isn't it?"

Dr. Baptista had been watching the deputies on the twelfth-floor bridge. He looked away suddenly like a child caught misbehaving.

"Can't get to my office," he mumbled, as he started to walk away.

"Is your office up there? On the twelfth floor?"

"Foolishness," the scientist said, continuing to walk away.

"I'd like to get a word with you, Dr. Baptista, especially if you're at loose ends right now, unable to get into your office.

He stopped, turned, and looked down at Duke. "What is it?"

"Were you in your office when she fell? Were you upstairs?"

"No. Below. The lab. You saw me go. Remember? With Dr. Gilbert."

"Inferno affirmo! You two are working together on a project."

"A couple of projects."

"Did you know the lady who fell? Miss Oligivich?"

Dr. Baptista's large dark eyes seemed to stare a hole right through Duke. "She was my assistant."

"Oh, my! I'm sorry."

"Foolishness," Baptista said, glancing over the railing at the atrium floor below.

"Some of the young people who work here told me she used to walk on the railings for fun. Did you ever see her do that?"

"Foolish," Baptista repeated, shaking his head. "Such a waste."

"You know, I'm sure this death is going to turn out to be an accident, but I have to ask if she was depressed. Do you think she killed herself on purpose?"

Baptista's eyes flared, and he looked away. He shook his head from side to side without saying a word.

"So she seemed to enjoy her work here?" Duke asked. "She wasn't lonesome for her homeland or mistreated by the others?"

"Mistreated?"

"You know, sometimes people aren't friendly to someone who's different—"

"Different? Mr. Dukakis, we are all different. More than a thousand scientists work here from twenty-four countries. We speak different languages. We have different complexions and hair color. But we are all the same carbon-based life. Sixty percent water. We understand science. Science is the language we all speak. She was one of us."

Duke struggled to write down Baptista's words. His accent wasn't as pronounced as Gilbert's, but he spoke with a melodic rhythm, like a rapper.

"Beaver logjam! That's pretty articulate for a scientist," Duke said. "So you are saying she fit in OK. Liked her work. Is there any reason somebody would want to kill her? Was she working on anything top secret? Could she have been a spy?"

Baptista smiled and shook his head. "A spy? How can you hide an accelerator? It's four miles around. And you don't have to hide quarks. Nobody can see them anyway. She fell. She died. Foolishness. That's all."

☼

As soon as they stepped inside the school building, Josie directed her parents to the restrooms. They'd been on the road more than four hours from their southern Illinois home. Josie was feeling relieved to have them here. It seemed childish to still need your parents when you were thirty-eight, but it felt good to be able to turn to them, no matter what happened. She wondered briefly who had called them. It must have been Nick. Or Hammond. Yes, it sounded like something meddling Hammond would do.

Josie was standing alone in the entry hall when Kurt stormed up.

"Where have you been? I've been looking everywhere. Nobody knew where you went."

"I had some errands, stopped by the office—"

"Oh, yeah? Our son could be dead, and you're out shopping and working like it's any other day."

"What are you talking about?"

"I thought I could count on you to be here. What do I have to do, hire somebody to stay here and wait for the updates?"

Josie shook her head in disbelief. "What's wrong with you? You could be waiting around here for updates. Why is that my job?"

"Because you said you would be here." Kurt poked Josie in the chest, and Josie noticed the school secretary was watching them.

"I was here all morning. Where were you?" she whispered. "And you'd better calm down before you get thrown out."

Kurt walked around with his hands on his hips. "I'll bet you don't even know what's going on. Did you know they dredged the Jordan River looking for the bus?"

"They didn't dredge it. They sent down a couple of divers. We had a reporter and photographer there."

"Divers. Oh, yeah. Well, excuse me, Miss Accuracy."

"Hello, Kurt."

Kurt spun around to see Dan Braun standing right behind him.

"Oh, hey, Dan. When did you get in?" In an instant, Kurt's tone changed. He held out his hand for shaking, but Dan didn't take it. Then Kurt saw Sally Braun coming up behind her husband. "Mother Braun. So glad you could come. Wish we had better news."

"Is there news?" Sally said, looking up at the men.

118

"No, nothing beyond what you've already heard," Kurt stammered. "The FBI is involved now, with helicopters. I saw to that. Called my congressman. My role at the development office carries a lot of weight."

Josie shook her head. She was surprised Kurt didn't take credit for the full moon too.

"Come on, Mom," Josie said, snagging her mother's elbow. Let's go to the library and talk to the other parents. You remember Polly."

As the women headed down the hall, Dan stayed behind with Kurt. Neither said anything for a long time.

"So, ah, you took Kevin camping yet?" Dan said in a folksy drawl. "Boy his age ought to go camping. And hunting. You go to his basketball games on Saturdays? Josie said he plays basketball at the Y right after his karate class. Ever shoot a few hoops with him? Boys like that, you know. What exactly are you doing with your son?"

"I'm here for him, Dan. I'm here," Kurt said with an affable smile.

Dan shook his head. "Sure you are," he said, and followed the women down the hall.

When she stepped into the library, Josie looked for Polly. She spotted her friend sitting at one of the child-size library tables looking at a book with her daughter, Aster, a preschooler who had been released from class at noon. Polly stood up as Josie approached, and the neighbors hugged.

"You remember my mom," Josie said, introducing Sally.

"Sure. It's so nice of you to come."

"So what's been happening since I left?" Josie asked. "I see Aster is finished with school for the day. What are you reading?"

"Loch Ness Monster," Aster said, lifting her book.

"Yeah, it's a little hard to talk right now," Polly said, smoothing Aster's blond hair. Polly's eyes were red and puffy. An errant tear ran down her cheek.

Sally snatched her opportunity. "Oh, I love the Loch Ness Monster. Can I read your book too?"

Sally slipped into the chair next to Aster and listened as the young girl summarized the story. Polly watched the two for a minute, then pulled Josie away from the table so they could talk without the little girl hearing.

"Oh, Josie, I think they've arrested Greg."

"What?"

"Yeah, he came here to the school about noon to find out what was going on, and they took him away. A couple of deputies. They just ushered him right out the door and put him in the squad car. Right in front of Aster and everything. Oh, my God, I don't believe it."

"What did you tell them about Greg?"

"Nothing special. Just what it says in the divorce complaint. And I told them about the order of protection after he hit me. I think that's what did it. Oh, what have I done? It's all my fault."

Josie hugged Polly.

"Don't be silly. It's not your fault. You didn't do anything wrong."

"But Greg wouldn't kidnap kids, I know he wouldn't. Why would he come here asking about the kids if he's the one who took them? Doesn't that prove it wasn't him? It can't be him."

Josie patted her friend's back and said soothing words, but silently she prayed that this was the answer. She couldn't imagine that Timmy's father would hurt the kids. He just took the bus because he was mad about losing custody. The bus was hidden in a barn somewhere. Greg would confess. He would tell the deputies where the bus was. The kids would all be home before supper. Safe. Oh, please, make it so, Lord.

2:05 PM

By two o'clock, the emergency room at St. Mary's Hospital looked like a Third World country or at least a war zone. There hadn't been an empty seat in the waiting room for hours. Those who were the least ill and had been waiting the longest were getting angry. They were yelling at the desk clerk, fighting among themselves, and pacing. Some had fallen asleep in their chairs. Others were crying.

Beyond the double doors in the treatment area, the scene was no better. Patients had long since overflowed the curtained treatment rooms. Gurneys lined the halls. Some patients who already had been seen by an emergency room physician were awaiting a specialist. Some were sick enough to be admitted, but the hospital admission process was backed up. A boy with pneumonia dozed on a gurney while his mother fretted at his side. A man who had been released after open-heart surgery earlier in the week had returned with coughing fits. He stood next to his gurney bare chested with his ugly red scar exposed. He clutched a pillow to his stitches every time he coughed. Down the hall, nurses set up a screen to afford privacy as a doctor gave a pelvic exam to a pregnant woman.

The call came in that an ambulance was transporting a whiplash patient from an auto accident. Although the actual injury might be minor, the claim needed to be treated seriously. Looking at the list of patients, the charge nurse realized Margaret Hinkle had been occupying an exam room for hours waiting for someone from social services. They couldn't wait any longer. The exam room was needed for the whiplash patient. Mrs. Hinkle could go out to the waiting room.

But when Brittany pulled back the curtain to inform Mrs. Hinkle, she found only a bowling bag on the floor in the center of the room. The patient was gone. The gurney was gone.

"I don't care what happened to her," the charge nurse said when Brittany reported the disappearance. "We've got too many people waiting in line to waste valuable time and space on people who don't want to be treated. That's what I told Mrs. Taylor this morning about her husband. He needs calcium carbonate for acid indigestion and heartburn. Not exactly life-threatening. If he runs off and hides, it's not our job to find him. I told her she'd have to find him herself."

121

The double doors of the emergency entrance burst open, and the charge nurse led the paramedics into the open exam room. She scooted the bowling bag under a chair to make room for the gurney carrying a woman with her head and shoulders encased in a bright orange plastic neck brace.

Following close behind the ambulance team was a man carrying a little boy by his feet.

"I don't have time to wait in the lobby!" the man yelled. "My kid got a peanut stuck in his throat. He can't breathe. You gotta help him now."

A doctor turned from the whiplash patient before Brittany could close the curtain.

"Here, lay the boy down," the doctor called to the father. The doctor moved to an open gurney and the father worked his way between the patients cramming the hall.

"When I lay him down, he chokes," the father said, dangling the crying toddler over the bed.

"Let me see," the doctor said, laying the boy down. The doctor used a tongue depressor to hold the boy's mouth open as he shined his light inside. As the father had predicted, the boy was unable to breathe when lying down and started turning blue. The doctor grabbed the boy's feet and yanked him up. Soon he was pink and wailing again.

"Call surgery and tell them I'm on my way," the doctor said as he and the father headed out of the emergency room with the boy held high by his feet.

"OK," the charge nurse said and headed for the phone. Under her breath, she added, "I think I'm the one with whiplash."

C hief Deputy Miller arrived at the school a little after two o'clock. Word spread quickly among the parents who had scattered around the school property: smokers in the parking lot, a couple of mothers in the music room entertaining toddlers, some fathers in the office talking to the principal. They rushed to the library to join the others, who were standing in a cluster in the front of the room.

"You can all sit down," Miller said, waving his hands above the podium. "I don't have any really big news for you. I know that's disappointing, but it's a good thing too. So just take your seats. Relax."

The tension in the room eased audibly as the parents sat in child-size chairs. After people began to quiet down, Miller said, "I'm sorry it's been so long since I've given you a report, but we've been very busy checking out a variety of possibilities—none of them good. I'm glad to tell you they've all been eliminated.

"Does that mean Greg has been released?" Polly whispered to Josie, who smiled back weakly.

"Several of the parents have expressed an interest in doing something productive, and I know the waiting is getting frustrating. A couple of the deputies are organizing some foot patrols to walk the farmland between the last stop and the first missed stop. It's only a couple of miles and the weather is mild. We have three hours before dusk, so it seems a good time to get as many people out there as possible. We'll be meeting at two different farmhouses along the route. I've got some maps here to pass out. Any of you who want to join this effort will be welcome, and if you have relatives or friends you want to call in, we'll be meeting there in a half hour."

"That sounds good," Dan Braun whispered to Josie. "I'm up for a walk. Sounds better than looking at these four walls."

"Me too," Sally said. "How about you, Josie?"

"Yeah, sure. I'll walk for a while."

"I don't know," Polly said, glancing over at Aster, who was snoozing on a blanket in the corner.

"Everybody doesn't need to go," Josie said. "I'm sure the other mothers of toddlers will stay here. And school will be getting out soon. Anyone who has other children in the system will stay behind."

The parents buzzed around making plans. Chief Deputy Miller chatted with a few fathers, including Kurt, then turned to Polly.

"Mrs. Garrett, I'm wondering if I might have a word with you … privately."

"Don't worry, I'll watch Aster," Josie said.

"Oh, we can just talk right over there beside your daughter," Miller said, taking a few steps toward the corner. "It's not bad news."

After the chief deputy finished talking to Polly, Josie and her mother wandered over.

"It's good, I guess," Polly said, pawing the tiled floor sheepishly. "Deputy Miller said they interviewed Greg, and he has a good alibi for the morning. He was at work. They checked it out. But Miller said it would be a violation of the order of protection for Greg to be here at the school with me, even though it's a public place. He said they told him it would be best for him to stay away from the school and the house. Greg is out there on the farm already, patrolling with the deputies. Chief Miller said it wouldn't be advisable for me to go out there right now. In fact, he told me I couldn't. But Greg's there. And he's OK."

Polly smiled a little, and Josie could see she was relieved to know her husband was not in jail for kidnapping.

☼

Looking over the prairie landscape from the tenth floor of the A-Lab atrium was fabulous. Duke could see the busy traffic on Clark Road running along the edge of the property. He could see a handful of small studio labs dotting the property, homes for scientists' individual projects. To the west was a field covered with solar panels which one scientist was studying. Then he noticed a pair of pickup trucks wrangling the buffalo toward the stable area. It must be feeding time.

"Bulging buffalo chips! I'll bet the Indians wish they'd had a couple pickup trucks," Duke said to himself, as he tapped the elevator button. He stopped on the sixth floor to see if Dr. Gilbert was in his office.

Big black notebooks, opened to charts of numbers, littered his desk. The doctor, wearing a checkered shirt with the sleeves rolled up, was copying numbers into his computer with his back to the door.

"Dr. Gilbert, I'm glad I caught you," Duke said, stepping through the open door.

"Can't talk now. I'm in the middle of something," the scientist said without looking up.

"Only take a minute."

The scientist ignored him and kept typing. Duke stood there. Finally the scientist turned around.

"Numbers are critical," the scientist said. He made an awkward twitch of his nose. "What exactly can I do for you? I'm running behind."

"I wanted to talk to you about Petra Oligivich, the woman who died today."

"Hardly knew her. We've got a thousand scientists and other employees here. Can't know everyone."

"Oh? Well, I understood she was an assistant to Dr. Baptista. Since you are working on a project together, I thought—"

"You thought wrong. She was an office assistant. An intern, if you will. She didn't work below. Computer models. Numbers. That was her work, I believe."

"Like this," Duke said, gesturing toward the notebooks.

"Yes, she helped Henri with data entry."

"I was surprised that his office was on the twelfth floor, and you're on the sixth. Since you are working on a project together, I would think it would be advantageous for you to have offices closer together."

"We come from different fields. We bring different expertise to the project."

"Dr. Baptista told me he was working below ground with you when she fell. Can you confirm that?"

"Confirm?" Gilbert said. "You mean like an alibi? Even the deputies didn't ask me that. They seemed to be satisfied that she fell. It was just an accident."

124

"Oh, that's true, but it's always my habit to try to confirm all the information I get," Duke said, shrugging his shoulders. "It's always better to have two sources."

"Well, yes, Henri and I were working on the project down below. I wasn't holding his hand every minute, but I have no reason to believe he left and went back upstairs. There wouldn't be any need. Our computers are connected. And there are phones. That's how we heard. We were together when the call came, first that there had been an accident. And then, maybe ten minutes later, Martha called and said it was Petra. He was shocked. We all were. Such a shame."

"I heard she used to put on shows, walking on the banisters. Did you ever see her do that?"

"I had heard that but I suspect it's more legend than truth. Maybe she did it once; the rest is apocryphal. When you deal with facts all the time as part of the job, sometimes people tend to exaggerate when it's just for fun. Especially the young people. Research is a slow, disappointing business, and young people are looking for a little more excitement."

"Could there be more excitement? Could she have been a spy? She was from Russia."

"And that's how people in your business make their jobs more exciting," Gilbert said, closing a notebook and placing it on a shelf. "It's too boring to accept that a foolish girl just fell to her death. You fantasize about spies and international intrigue."

"Foolish. That's the word Dr. Baptista used."

"What else would you call it?" Gilbert said, his nose twitching again. "Now I really must get back to work. Is that all?"

In the lobby, Duke ran into Zach Teasdale, the coroner.

"Great, you're still here. I won't have to track you down in your office," Duke said.

"I should be tracking you down," Teasdale replied. "I understand you saw the whole thing."

"Like I told the deputies, there wasn't much to see. All of a sudden, she was just there. It was so quick. I didn't even have time to get upset about it."

"Sounds like a senseless accident. I won't know for sure until the autopsy and toxicology results, but it appears from the people I've interviewed, she probably just fell. No suicide letter has been found. Her roommate said they were supposed to go to a movie tonight. She made a call this morning to schedule a haircut for next week. Doesn't sound like she was planning to check out. Left her shoes under her desk and evidently went for an invigorating stroll on a banister. It's what she did for fun."

"Her shoes were back in her office?" Duke said, making a note on his pad. "Doesn't that seem odd? Wouldn't you think she'd kick them off in the hall, right before she climbed up on the banister? I imagine these ceramic tile floors are pretty cold on bare feet."

"Well, evidently, that's what she did," Teasdale said, turning to walk away.

"But she didn't scream," Duke said, following the coroner outside. "If she slipped, wouldn't there be that moment of surprise? The terror? If she had screamed, Leslie and I would have looked up. But there wasn't a sound except the splat of her body on the tiles. And then Leslie screamed. That's what brought everybody out."

"Cultural differences," Teasdale said. "Russians are more stoic than Americans. Even the women. And circus people. Maybe it's a badge of honor. You don't scream when you fall."

Teasdale opened the door to his BMW and slipped inside.

"Oh, almost forgot," Duke said, leaning on the car. "What's this I hear about you bringing drugs back from Colombia? A new business?"

Teasdale shook his head.

"You people have such a limited view of the world. You hear Colombia, and you think drugs. Not coffee. Not lumber. Not cattle. I have all sorts of legal businesses in Colombia."

"You're not smuggling drugs?"

"A question like that doesn't deserve an answer. Next thing I know, you'll ask me if our unlucky aerialist was a Russian spy."

"Was she?"

Teasdale laughed and slammed his car door. He was still chuckling as he pulled away.

Duke purposely drove the side road to the buffalo barn. The animals were in a corral, and some were being loaded into a stock truck. Two more stock trucks were lined up. Duke got out of his car and walked up to a man in a heavy denim jacket, jeans, and muddy cowboy boots.

"Where are you taking the buffalo?"

"Farm. Downstate," the man said, barely glancing at Duke.

"Why?"

He turned and looked at Duke.

"How should I know? Got an order." He pulled a yellow sheet of paper out of his jacket pocket and handed it to Duke. Delivery was to a rural address near Centralia, Illinois, several hours south. Duke handed the paper back.

"Is this usual? Do you move livestock south because of the weather? Looking for greener pastures?"

"Pastures? Man, it's winter. You'd have to go a lot farther south to find green pastures," the man said, tucking the paper back into his pocket.

Duke stood there watching the huge hairy animals walk into the chute and plod up into the trailer. Once inside, they snorted and bellowed their displeasure. They certainly didn't look or sound sick.

As the last animal squeezed inside, the man pulled the gate closed. Duke thanked the man, got back into his car, and drove toward the exit from the A-Lab property. Two buffalo had died and the rest were headed south. How could that be related to the death of a Russian scientist? How could it not be?

☼

The two chubby women in the emergency room were mother and daughter, but they looked more like sisters. The same greasy hair pulled back in ponytails. The same baggy sweatshirts touting the Chicago Bears. The same blousy black pants… no doubt with elastic waist.

"I kept her home from school because of her stomach ache," the mother told Brittany. "But now I'm thinking it's her gall bladder. She keeps having these pains. And that's what the gall bladder is like. You ever had a gall bladder attack?"

"Oh, my God!" the daughter screamed, clutching her stomach.

"Here, lie back on the stretcher," Brittany said, assisting the girl. As she touched the girl's abdomen, she felt the hard muscle contraction and then an unmistakable movement underneath.

"Are you pregnant?" Brittany asked.

"No, she's only fifteen," the mother said. "She's just a sophomore in high school. She looks older because she's so tall."

"Mom, it hurts," the girl bellowed.

Brittany looked the girl in the eye.

"How far along are you?"

"What?" the girl said. "Can't you give me something for the pain?"

Brittany struggled to get a straight answer. "The baby. When is your baby due?"

"I'm not having a baby," the girl said. "I'm not married."

"She's having a gall bladder attack," the mother repeated. "Get the doctor in here. He'll tell you. I've had 'em, and they're hell."

"Take your slacks and panties off so the doctor can examine you," Brittany said, handing the girl a paper drape. "Put this over your legs."

Brittany stepped out of the cubicle and waved to Amy, the charge nurse.

"This girl's in labor and doesn't even admit she's pregnant."

"Why me, Lord?" Amy said and followed Brittany behind the curtain. The girl was lying on her side with one knee raised, screaming at the top of her lungs. The dark brown hair of the girl's crotch was visible under the drape. Brittany pushed her knee to one side to get a better look.

127

"The baby is crowning. I can see the baby," Brittany said, looking under the leg.

"We're not delivering that kid in the ER," Amy said, peeking under the drape. "You wheel her up to OB, and I'll call and tell them to expect you. She's fully dilated and ready to hatch."

"But it's just a gall bladder attack," the mother repeated as Brittany pushed the gurney into the hall. Wheeling the wailing girl away, Brittany almost ran over police detective Tom Cantrell, but kept going.

"I'm looking for the mystery man," Cantrell said, flashing his police badge to Amy at the desk. "The shooting victim who doesn't know his name."

"Sounds like the title of a country song," Amy said, hitching a thumb toward a cubicle with a security guard standing outside. "We're trying to get him moved upstairs, but it's been too chaotic."

Tom stuck his head into the cubicle and found the man sitting up on the gurney, leafing through a magazine. One sleeve of his dark gray shirt was rolled up, revealing bright white bandages on his left arm. The fingers of his right hand were also bandaged. The man seemed fairly nondescript. Short drab hair, ordinary features, tiny eyes.

Tom held up his badge. "Got a minute? I'd like to ask you a few questions about the shooting."

"I don't remember much," the man said, laying down the magazine. "I'd really like to get out of here."

"Sure, I can get you released from the hospital," Tom said, with a quick smile. "Just let me know your name and where you live."

Pete knew he couldn't keep up the amnesia charade. They'd never let him go. He didn't have a record, hadn't been arrested since he was a juvenile. Twenty years ago. He should just give them his name.

"It's still a little fuzzy but I remember now that my name is Peter Hampton. I would have told somebody, but the nurses never came back."

"Good, glad to hear you have a name, Pete. Can I call you Pete?"

"Sure, can I go home now?"

"Soon. The hospital is going to want you to fill out some paperwork."

"That's the problem," Pete whispered. "I'm sorta between jobs. I don't have any insurance. I don't know how I'm going to pay for this."

"You're a victim of a crime," Cantrell said. "And we've arrested the man who shot you. A bodyguard. I suspect your medical expenses will be paid."

"Oh?" Pete said, his eyebrows arching. For the first time, he was beginning to see the potential in his situation.

"Since your head is clearing, maybe you can tell me what happened at the theater," Tom said, pulling up a chair.

"It's not that clear," Pete said, sounding more feeble. "I don't even remember the name of the movie."

"Neither do I," Tom said with a laugh. "But then I didn't go to see it. You did."

"The nurse said it was a horror flick. I don't think I like horror flicks. Maybe I was just passing by."

"Maybe you came to see the movie star, Dee Licious."

"Dee who?"

Tom pulled out a revolver in a clear plastic bag.

"Recognize this gun?"

Pete's eyes grew wide. "Is that the gun that shot me?"

"Nope, this one was found in one of the potted trees," Tom said. "Any idea how it got there?"

"Potted tree?"

"Yep, it's registered to a factory worker. He said it was taken from the glove box in his car months ago, but he never reported it stolen."

"So he was the shooter," Pete said. "I thought you said I was shot by a bodyguard."

"Well, there were two shooters. The bodyguard saw somebody pull a gun and shot in the general direction. But the factory worker couldn't have been the one who pulled the gun. He was on the job, not at the theater. Somebody else brought this gun to the party."

"I don't like guns," Pete said, picking up the magazine again.

"I guess you don't," Tom said with a smile. "They tell me you faint at the sight of blood. How long has that been going on?"

"Ever since I was a kid."

Just then a nurse pulled back the curtain. "Somebody else to see you," she said.

"Oh, there you are, you poor darling," came the high-pitched squeal of a woman in a shaggy white coat. Her cloud of black hair was teased into gigantic proportions and sprayed as stiff as steel wool. "I'm Dee Licious. When I heard there were people still in the hospital from this morning's horrible shooting, I had to come and offer my condolences. You were so brave to try to step forward to protect me. You took a bullet for me. And I will be forever grateful. Just forever."

A man in a three-piece suit, who smelled like an attorney to Tom, was right behind the star.

"We're going to get you a private room, sir, right away," the suit said. "And the best specialists in amnesia. We'll make sure you get the best possible care."

"And I'm going to be right beside you, Poopsie," Dee said, snuggling against Pete's cheek. "You don't have anything to worry about."

"I don't think I have amnesia anymore," Pete said. "I don't remember the shooting, but I know my name now. It's Pete."

"Oh, Petey! Can I still call you Poopsie?" the star squealed.

Tom backed away as the star and the suit took over. If a little bullet in the arm was enough to send this unassuming man into a fit of forgetfulness, he was in for the shock of his life, Tom surmised. "Poopsie" was about to be buried by an avalanche snow job.

☼

Walking the fields seemed an exercise in futility. The land was flat. You could practically see all the way from the bus's last pickup point to the first missed stop. There wasn't a house or tree for three miles. Just farm fields. As far as the eye could see on either side of the road stretched the open fields. Some were lined with cut cornstalks, some were planted in winter wheat, some were plowed into neat rows waiting for spring. Little could be hidden here. Not even a tire track interrupted the even rows.

Josie walked beside her parents looking for a child's scarf or a book bag. Something. Anything out of place in the fields. As the volunteers tramped along, a yellow school bus appeared in the distance, traveling down the road. Was it a mirage? Or was it time for school buses to bring children home? The thought that all the other school buses would be returning to their neighborhoods over the next few hours made Josie gasp for air. How could they? How could the buses go on as if one wasn't missing?

When the yellow bus pulled into the farmhouse driveway, the rows of volunteers in the field seemed to turn as one and start running for the farmhouse. Could it be their bus?

Josie didn't dare believe it was, and yet she had to believe it could be. Their bus. Kevin. Just a few hundred yards away. Her mother was running behind her, her father too. Most of the volunteers had stopped walking the fields and were heading toward the farmhouse at various speeds. Josie was way in front of the rest. Although her footholds were unsteady in the soft ground, she surged ahead, riding on sheer adrenaline.

But then she slowed. The children disembarking from the bus were much too big to be Kevin and his friends. These were teens, big teens in school jackets. Josie stopped running and staggered on in slow, defeated steps. She wandered around for a minute, sucking in air. Some of the volunteers caught up to her.

"Who's on that bus?" a man asked.

"I don't know. Looks like high school kids. Athletes maybe," Josie replied between gulps for air.

More volunteers gathered nearby and looked at the teens. One mother burst into tears, and others tried to comfort her. Some returned to tramping the fields. Others had lost the desire and continued walking to the farmhouse.

Dan Braun came up beside Josie.

130

"So who's on the bus?"

"I don't know. Looks like the basketball team," Josie said, kicking at the dirt. "Their coach probably had them come out here to walk the fields instead of basketball practice. Sounds like something Kurt would have suggested. He probably called the coach."

Josie bent over, resting her hands on her knees. Her father laid a soothing hand on her back. Her mother joined them. Another school bus pulled into the farm driveway, but the volunteers barely noticed. The volunteers continued walking across the fields, searching for a solution that wasn't there. Trying somehow to conjure up an answer to the missing bus.

As Josie walked beside her parents, she seethed with anger at Kurt. He probably had talked to the coach or the high school principal. That was his idea of helping. Delegating. And he was good at it.

But some parts of parenting couldn't be delegated. Shouldn't be delegated. In her frustration, Josie's angry thoughts went beyond Kurt's arm's-length parenting. She was guilty of delegating too.

As a working mother, she had missed so many wonderful moments with Kevin. She wanted that time back. But would she do it differently? Could she? If Kevin was returned to her, she would make some changes. She would change her morning routine, fix a good breakfast for him, check his homework. Maybe even pack a nutritious lunch with all his favorites. And little love notes. She always liked that idea, and yet she'd never actually hidden love notes for Kevin. Why not? Why had she let all those opportunities pass by?

Josie stomped the ground more resolutely. *If Kevin comes back to me, I'll never send him to school on the bus again. I will drive him. I won't get to work until seven-thirty. Nick can handle the early rush. We can move the morning meeting back fifteen minutes. I'll have to be better organized, but I can do that. Weight lifting and working out will just have to fit into the lunch hour. Oh, Lord, if you just bring Kevin back.*

Josie looked up to see a familiar brown van pulling to the side of the road. Page, the *Daily News'* extra-tall, extra-quiet photographer, stepped out of the van and marched into the field. Although his right arm was in a sling, a large rectangular camera dangled from his neck. Josie ran to him.

"What are you doing here? You're all taped up. Shouldn't you be at home?"

"Why? It takes only a couple fingers to push the buttons, and my fingers are fine," Page said. "Can't lift my arm, so I dug out this old twin-reflex-lens camera. I used it in college. Shoots from the waist. I can look down from the top to focus."

Page shot a photo of the volunteers fanning across the field. Then another.

"Takes good pictures, large format. But the film's a little slow. Gotta have good light. Thought it was worth a try to see what I could do."

"I want you to go home. Rest," Josie insisted.

"I was getting stir-crazy in that hospital room," Page mumbled. "I had to get some fresh air."

"If you are headed back to the office, can you drop me off?" Josie asked. "I want to see what's going on."

Josie gave her mother a house key. They made plans to meet there by dark. Then she climbed into Page's van.

☼

Margaret Hinkle looked pretty in the pink quilted robe Neal had snatched from a hook in one of the rooms. They were seated in a corner of the cafeteria. Margaret was drinking a large Coke with lots of ice and nibbling a banana nut muffin. Neal was shoveling in large spoonfuls of beef stew and taking occasional sips from a glass of milk.

"Canteen isn't bad," he whispered to Margaret. "Good thing I figured out these ID badges work at the cash register. We could be set for years, darlin'. Just keep moving from room to room, robe to robe. No one will ever recognize us."

"You are such a clever fellow," Margaret said, looking down and batting her lashless eyelids.

"We need to find a room to catch a little shut-eye," Neal said, wiping away a milk mustache with the back of his hand. "We're better off sleeping during the day and prowling at night when the halls are quiet. Too many snoopy eyes during the day."

"We could sit in a waiting room and watch television. I haven't seen television in years," Margaret said, folding the paper cup that had wrapped the muffin.

"That's a good idea too. But we'll need to get some street clothes. People in the waiting rooms aren't dressed like patients and doctors. We passed a cloakroom back there, just outside the canteen. Let's go there and grab some coats."

Margaret giggled. "Oh, yes. This is such an adventure."

2:59 PM

"You got it," Duke called out to Nick as he hit the button on his computer to send his story into the system. Writing about a body falling at his feet was too easy to be considered work. The words had poured out.

Writing was the easy part of his job. Finding the truth was a lot harder.

Duke flipped through the file of business cards he had on his desk. He stopped at the one that said "Fred Wheeler, Department of Justice." This was one card he never expected to use. Wheeler had led the investigation of a sewer project in Jordan a few years back, and he had caused Duke lots of problems. But when the case was over, he had invited Duke to call him when he smelled a rat too big to catch in the local trap.

Duke dialed the number. A machine answered. He stammered. "This is Duke Dukakis at the *Jordan Daily News*. I was at the A-Lab today when that scientist fell to her death, and something smells wrong to me."

He left his phone number and went back to work at his computer. His phone rang in less than a minute.

"Wheeler," a gruff voice said.

"Wow, that was quick," Duke said, smiling. "I wasn't sure you'd call back."

"You said the magic word."

"Magic word?"

"A-Lab."

"Are the feds investigating the death at the A-Lab?"

"A Russian fell out of the sky. Of course, we're investigating. What you got?"

"Do you know about the buffalo?"

"Buffalo?"

"Yeah, a motorist reported one dead buffalo last night, and I saw another being hauled away this morning. Then after the woman died, I saw three trucks on the property loading up the whole herd and taking them downstate."

Wheeler chuckled. "Duke, Duke, Duke. Don't tell me you've been suckered in by all those superstitions about the buffalo being radiation indicators. A buffalo is huge. If the radiation was high enough to kill a buffalo, people would be falling by the hundreds."

133

"I realize that, but don't you think it's odd? I talked to Snyder about the two dead buffalo earlier in the day, and he didn't say anything about the truck coming to take the whole herd away."

"What's it got to do with the dead scientist?"

"I don't know. That's why I called you."

"OK. Duly noted."

"I was thinking maybe … Wheeler? Are you there?" The elusive federal agent had hung up.

Duke called the county to check the status of the autopsy on the buffalo from the night before, but it was still frozen. Then he saw Josie and Page coming in the back door. Duke and Nick both stood up to greet them.

"What's new with the bus?" Nick asked.

"Nothing," Josie said, shaking her head.

"A one-arm photographer is more useless than a one-arm paper hanger," Page mumbled as he headed into the darkroom. Josie watched him go and then turned to her coworkers.

"He's feeling a little awkward trying to shoot one-handed. He's using some old camera that focuses from the top, but he's unhappy with the film speed. He'll be the go-to man for running film through the processing machine."

"Sounds good. Anything from the volunteers walking the fields?" Nick asked.

"No. What's going on here?"

"Got a great story from Duke on the A-Lab death."

"A grade school kid couldn't mess that one up," Duke said, shaking his head. "I mean that story literally dropped at my feet."

"Well, it's great," Nick said. "You should read it."

"I will," Josie said. "First I need a Coke. Anyone want to join me?"

Nick made excuses about copy to read as Duke and Josie headed to the break room. Theirs was a rare relationship. Although they had had a brief affair several years earlier, the attraction between them was more mental than physical. They had an overwhelming respect for each other. No matter what happened, each sought the other's opinion. Duke would say Josie was too idealistic in her pursuit of truth, while he was more practical and realistic. But she would say he was even more stubborn and unrelenting than she was.

Josie couldn't wait to tell Duke about every minute of her roller-coaster day, from the horror of the divers at the Jordan River to the surprise visit of her parents.

"I don't know who called them. Maybe Nick."

"Polka-dotted poodle poo, of course it was him. He's a good manager, you know."

"I know."

Duke tried to distract Josie from the frustrations of the missing bus by giving an animated explanation of the A-Lab body whizzing by his face and almost landing on top of him. He actually had her laughing about the glow-in-the-dark buffalo being loaded into a stock truck.

"And after he closed the gate, I swear you could still see the green glow through the slats."

He slugged down the last of his Coke while Josie chuckled. Then he got serious.

"I talked to my buddy, Al Laepple."

"The county evidence tech."

"Yeah, he was there for the body, of course, but I asked him about the bus driver too. He led the team that inspected the bus driver's apartment."

"And …"

"Sounds like a straight arrow. No pornographic pictures or anything like that. Actually, he's a rah-rah patriot. Books about American history and some magazine called *American Liberty*. A deer rifle, but no hand guns. Peanut butter in the pantry. I mean, just a good guy."

"I know. That's what I thought too when I met him," Josie said, crushing her empty Coke can with the heel of her hand. "But he's the only clue we've got. I sent Rudy over to talk to his neighbors, find his family. It's the only thing I can figure."

"He sounds more like the hero type to me. Remember ten or eleven years ago when somebody kidnapped a school bus in California? They put the kids in a truck and buried it in a quarry."

Josie gasped.

"But the kids got away safely because the bus driver got them out. Remember that?" Duke patted Josie's hand. "That's the kind of driver Joe Wilson is. You wait and see. He'll be a hero."

Josie shook her head. "This is insane. Why would somebody kidnap a busload of kids?"

"For ransom. That's why they took the bus in California."

"Ransom? But we're just ordinary parents. We can't pay a ransom. And as far as I know, nobody has asked for money."

"Maybe the parents aren't the target. Maybe they're putting pressure on somebody else. Somebody rich."

"Rich? There isn't anybody rich in Cade County except Zach Teasdale."

"Uh-huh."

"Teasdale? You're kidding. Why would he pay a ransom to get our kids back?"

"Because he can afford it. And it certainly would guarantee him getting reelected as coroner."

"No, I won't believe it. That's too crazy."

"I agree, but all the logical options have come up dry."

135

"OK. Call him. See if he has received a ransom request. If you're right, he'll admit it because he'll want the publicity."

Duke smiled. "Now you're thinking."

Dottie, the lifestyle editor, and Helen, the receptionist, bought Cokes from the machine and joined Josie and Duke's table.

"Can we go home early? I never want to work another full moon," Helen said as she fell into the chair.

"Sorry, Josie. Our complaints are so minor compared to your situation," Dottie added as she sat down primly.

"Oh, that's OK, ladies. I'd love to hear about the silly phone calls you are getting. I need a good laugh," Josie said.

"Well, I just got off the phone with a woman who swears her family has been poisoned by a birthday cake," Helen said, sitting up and eagerly sharing her tale. "They ordered a cake shaped like a cat and had the bakery use black frosting because the family cat is black. Yesterday was the cat's fifth birthday. Well, this morning they found the cat dead in the basement, and everybody in the family is suffering from this greasy, black diarrhea. Black like tar, the lady says. I told her it was probably the food coloring in the icing that was making it black, but she swears they've been poisoned. Says we need to do a story about this murderous bakery."

"El gato negro! You mean the cat ate some of the birthday cake?" Duke asked.

"Evidently," Helen said, "and it killed him, the lady says. I told her if she really thinks the cake was poison, they should call their doctor. 'Oh, no,' she says. 'I wouldn't want to bother him.' Can you believe it? She wants us to do a story about how they've been poisoned, and she won't even call a doctor!"

"I've got a crazy food caller too," Dottie said. "Maybe they're sisters. My lady calls this morning saying she can't get her gelatin to set. I suggested she try using ice, use the speed-set directions on the box. She calls back a half-hour later. No luck. I suggest thirty minutes in the freezer. Thirty-two minutes later she's on the phone complaining that didn't work either. I told her to just leave it for a few hours in the fridge and don't open the door. You guessed it. She's calling me again. It still won't set. Finally, I said maybe she should come up with something else for the church potluck. Chee! She thinks I have nothing better to do all day?"

"Why would you?" Duke said. "She doesn't."

Josie chuckled. "Thanks, ladies. You cheered me up. Now, if you'll excuse me, I've got to get back and read some stories before our four o'clock meeting.

As Josie and Duke walked down the hall from the break room to the newsroom, they spotted police detective Tom Cantrell standing outside the locked back door. Duke hit the panic bar and opened the door.

"What are you doing standing out in the cold? Why didn't you go around to the front?"

"Oh, I figured it was three thirty and a crew would be heading home."

"Not today," Josie said. "Too much going on. You here to see Becky?"

"Yeah, I got an addition to the shooting story. One of the names changed."

Duke laughed. "Yeah, I heard about that. Paramedics picked up the wrong wallet or something and the guy's watching the noon news when he hears his name among the injured. That would be a real shocker."

Becky was typing away at her computer when Duke and Josie escorted Tom into the newsroom. He took the chair next to her desk. She looked up and flashed her electric grin. Tom smiled back.

"Got a name on the other guy who was shot in the arm. Peter Hampton, 36, from Jordan."

"His amnesia went away?"

"Aaaa, I think he was trying to avoid paperwork because he doesn't have insurance. But I told him Century Pictures was going to be footing the bill and then some. Before I left his room, that squealing movie star was hugging and slobbering all over him."

"Dee Licious was here? In town?"

"Yeah, I think that's her name. The one with hair out to there," Tom said, holding his hands six inches on either side of his head.

"She's supposed to be doing a press conference in Chicago in thirty minutes," Becky said, checking her watch.

"Well, you may want to double-check her agenda," Tom said. He was tickled to have given Becky a news nugget. "Looked to me like she and her attorney were planning to make all the mileage they could from injured people in a hospital setting. They were promising Pete a private room. Probably already had the cameras set up."

Becky stood up and called over to her editor.

"Josie! Sounds like the four o'clock press conference has been moved from the Chicago hotel to St. Mary's Hospital. Still think we should skip it?"

Josie turned around from the computer, where she was reading Duke's story. "It's here in town? Then I think we'd better be there."

"OK, I'll confirm," Becky said, grabbing her phone. "How can they change the press conference location and not call the local paper?"

"They probably only invited the television stations," Josie said. "Century Pictures doesn't read the *Jordan Daily News*."

"They're barely literate," Becky grumbled as she dialed. She quickly confirmed the four o'clock press conference had been moved to a hospital room on the sixth floor of St. Mary's. When she hung up her phone, Page was standing there.

"Where'd this film come from?" he said, tossing an empty canister onto her desk. "It had a note with your name."

"Oh, just some fan at the theater today," Becky said.

"Reuben," Tom added.

"Well, he's no photographer, I'll tell you that," Page said, pulling a stash of photos from inside the sling on his right arm. "Everything is dark, crooked, heads cut off. But he was in the middle of the fray. He got a pretty good picture of the gunman."

Page threw the prints on Becky's desk. The top one showed Pete Hampton grimacing in pain and pulling a small revolver out of his pocket.

Tom stood up and examined the photos. "Well, I'll be damned. That mousy little man packed a pistol."

Becky rifled through the photos with Tom. "I don't see Elvis in a vampire costume. Oh, no. Did Reuben mean this guy? He's really fat. Was Elvis that fat?"

"We're not supposed to be looking for Elvis. We're looking for the shooter," Tom said, holding out the incriminating photo.

"I know. You've already found him. I'm trying to find Elvis. Now that would be a story."

Tom shook his head. "Thanks, man, for developing this film." He patted Page's sling. "This photo is going to put that guy away. I just don't know if I should make the arrest before or after Century Pictures uses him as the star of their press conference."

"Oh, my God," Becky said, holding up one of the photos. "It's the dog. It's Dee's missing dog. Reuben got a picture of the dog."

Becky and Tom locked eyes. "The pocket pet," they said in unison.

Tom got back into his police car while Becky phoned Reuben. She rode to the press conference in Page's van. Tom needed to preserve his professional dignity. He could hardly make an arrest with a reporter and photographer in tow.

After Page and Becky left the office, Josie's phone rang. She was surprised to hear Duke's voice when she picked up. He was sitting at the adjoining desk.

"Teasdale insisted I transfer the call to you," Duke said.

Josie looked at Duke and rolled her eyes. She had forgotten Duke was even planning to call Zach about a possible ransom demand. She had avoided speaking to the county's wealthy, publicity-hungry coroner since their brief relationship ended badly two years ago. She certainly didn't want to speak to him now.

"OK. Put him through," she said. When the phone clicked, she gave a stiff, formal response. "*Daily News*, can I help you?"

"Josie, I had no idea Kevin was on that bus. I am so sorry. If there's anything—"

"Zach, it's nice of you to call."

"I didn't call. Your reporter called me, practically accused me of being responsible for this mess."

Josie rolled her eyes at Duke again and shook her head. "Now, I'm sure Duke never suggested you had anything to do with taking the bus. It did occur to us that if someone wanted a large ransom, they might approach you. That's all. We had to ask."

Zach snorted into the phone. "You didn't have to do anything. I can understand that you're grasping at straws with your only child among the missing. I know you suspect me of all manner of evil, but I hope you know I would never be part of anything so heinous as kidnapping."

"We're not suggesting any of this was your idea," Josie said, wheeling around in her chair so she could talk to Zach without Duke hearing every word. "But you must admit you have interests in South America where kidnapping and extortion are common business practice."

Zach paused. "If a bus was missing in Bogata instead of Jordan, then I would agree with you. But the Dons don't have much power in this country. I understand Duke was just checking to see what I knew. I expect you to have more faith in me. You know I would do anything in my power to ensure the safe return of Kevin and those other children."

Josie didn't doubt that Zach was telling the truth. But that was the problem, wasn't it? She always believed Zach, even when his lies were gigantic. When she didn't respond, Zach continued.

"You may be suspicious of my family background and my motives, but you know I believe wealth carries responsibilities. What good is money if it can't work miracles? If there is anything I can do, at any price, you will let me know, won't you?"

Josie smiled. Zach had the kind of power that was frightening, but she did believe he wanted to help.

"Yes, thank you."

As Josie hung up the phone, Rudy bounced into the office. He was closer to this horrible story than any other reporter besides her, and yet his optimism kept shining through. She had seen him at his lowest, when he was accused of abusing a child in his care two years ago, and even then he was more concerned about the child than his crumbling career. Now he approached her desk with a tentative smile, trying to be encouraging.

"How are you holding up?" he asked. "Ready for the four o'clock meeting?"

"Yes. Let's go."

Josie let the strength of her staff carry her along when it seemed like she could barely walk forward anymore. She took her seat at the table in the conference room with Duke, Nick, and Rudy. The goal was to figure out placement for the stories they'd collected, but all anyone wanted to discuss was the missing bus.

"I found some good stuff on the driver," Rudy told the group. "Landlady said he goes to St. Alphonse on Sundays. I talked to the priest there. He says he's a regular guy. Helps out with K of C fish fry. Lady across the hall said he helped her when she couldn't get her car started last week. Nobody said anything bad about him."

"I'm not trying to find something bad," Josie said, with a sigh. "I'm just trying to find something useful."

They discussed the other stories briefly. Becky had told Nick on her way out the door that she felt the gunman who started the Holiday Quad shootout was about to be arrested. Duke explained the body at the A-Lab appeared to be an accidental fall. He reported his concern about the two buffalo that died and his conversation with Fred Wheeler at the Department of Justice, but said he doubted anything would come of that story before Monday at the earliest.

Sis, who managed the "morgue" of newspaper clips, approached the table.

"I might have something. I found an obit for a Lillian Wilson who died three years ago. Joseph Wilson is listed as one of her sons. That could be the bus driver. There's a Catherine listed as a daughter, and the obit lists Michael Dudley as her spouse. When I looked up Michael Dudley, I found a story about D & D Storage."

"Kickin' kangaroo crap! I did that story," Duke said, jumping to his feet. "The old gypsum mine. Dudley bought that property and uses the mine as a warehouse to store food for area grocery stores. It's dry and basically temperature controlled year round."

"I remember that story," Josie said, shaking her head, "but I don't think—"

"The mine. Don't you see?" Duke was practically jumping up and down. "It's not a deep shaft like some old coal mine. It's this huge drive-in facility. A labyrinth of tunnels. A million places to stash a bus."

3:52 PM

Duke pulled his turquoise Pontiac into D & D Storage on Button Road.

"No, not in front," Josie said. "Take the drive that goes behind the building. The one marked for trucks. That's where the bus will be."

Duke complied and bypassed the small parking lot in front of the one-story frame building that served as the office for the business and living quarters for the owner.

"Shouldn't we go to the office first?" Rudy asked from the backseat.

"If they are hiding the bus, they aren't going to admit it," Duke said. He drove down the gravel lane that spiraled into the ground behind the building.

"But Nick was calling the sheriff's department," Rudy continued calmly. "Shouldn't we wait until a squad car gets here?"

"Go, go, go!" Josie shouted, pointing straight ahead. "Drive right into the mine. Don't stop."

Duke pulled into the wide opening of a darkened tunnel. His headlights bounced off a pair of taillights reflecting just ahead. As he pulled closer, they could see the unmistakable bright yellow of a school bus. As soon as Duke stopped his car, Josie leaped out and ran toward the bus.

"Kevin, Kevin, are you here?" The door was open and she ran up the stairs. Row after row of black leather seats sat empty with only the beam from Duke's headlights for illumination. Josie walked down the aisle, her steps echoing through the vacant bus. All the coats and backpacks were gone. A silver foil gum wrapper crinkled under her shoe. Josie knelt to pick it up.

"Duke gave me a flashlight," Rudy said as he came up behind Josie. He played the beam across each empty seat. "They're not here."

"They're here. Somewhere in this mine," Josie said, running back to the front of the bus. Mr. Joe's winter coat still hung behind the driver's seat, dangling over the rubber boots and toolbox. "They haven't gone far. He didn't even take his coat."

"I'm going back up to the office," Duke said as Josie and Rudy stepped down from the bus. "You wait here. There are all kinds of tunnels going every which way. I'll see if they will give me the map."

"Give you a map!" Josie exclaimed. "These people kidnapped our kids. You expect them to give you a map to where they stashed them?"

"Wait here for the police," Duke repeated, as he marched out of the tunnel. "We need more lights and a map. The police will be able to convince them."

"These tunnels are wired for electricity," Rudy said, gesturing toward the small lights every fifty feet or so that marked the path of the tunnel ahead.

"Give me that," Josie said, grabbing the flashlight. She played the beam across the ground. The light glistened off something shiny. Josie went to it. Another gum wrapper. "Kevin!" she called as she started farther down the tunnel.

"Wait," Rudy said. "Wait for help to come."

"I think I can see footprints in the dirt. Yes, I'm sure I see footprints. Kevin!" Josie ran ahead.

"Wait!" Rudy called after her. "You can't go in there alone."

"He's here. I know he's here," Josie called back. "Kevin!"

She ran ahead, pausing only slightly when another tunnel branched off to the left. Which way? The dirt was undisturbed to the left; she continued down the main tunnel. She heard a sound. A faint sound. Laughing? Crying? To the right. There were footprints down a narrower tunnel on the right. She ran quietly now, listening for the sound. She came to a huge metal door under one of the small tunnel lights. The door was marked with a faded sign. Three yellow triangles on a black circle. It was an old fallout shelter. Shining her light to the ground below, Josie could see the half circle in the dirt. The door had been opened.

"Kevin!" she bellowed, pulling on the handle with both hands. The door moved an inch or two and stopped. It was dragging against the ground. She put her ear to the crack. Yes, definitely she could hear voices. She needed something to pry the door open. A stick? Something. She tried to wedge her fingers into the crack. If she could just budge it a little more. Rudy's hands joined hers on the metal handle.

"I thought you were going to wait for the police," she said.

"I couldn't let you come in here alone."

Rudy paused and kicked the bottom of the door. "It's digging into the ground. We gotta clear the path."

Josie shined a light at the base of the door. Rudy got down on his knees, scraping his hands across the ground. He stood up, and both of them grabbed the handle. They pulled again. It budged another inch, enough to fit their fingers into the crack.

"I knew we shouldn't skip weight lifting," Rudy groaned.

"This isn't funny," Josie said, pulling next to him.

"Wait. We need to concentrate our efforts," Rudy said. "On three. One, two, three."

They pulled together. The door budged several more inches, enough that tiny Josie squeezed through the crack. She started down the hall toward the light, the voices. Then she paused, realizing Rudy was too big to squeeze through the opening. She returned to the door.

"I'll push and you pull," she said, leaning against the door. "On three. One, two, three."

Again the door moved several inches, and Rudy squeezed through the opening.

"Gotta give up ice cream," he said. Josie ignored the quip. She was heading down the hall. Light was coming from a room ahead. And voices.

When she reached the doorway, she saw a large open room like a small gymnasium. A woman was seated at a table near the door reading a magazine. Beyond children were playing. Some building with blocks, some bouncing balls, some seated at tables coloring. Others were chasing each other around, laughing. Then she saw Kevin as though a heavenly beam had singled him out. He was laughing, playing a table game. Foosball. He and Timmy were playing foosball.

"Kevin!" Josie shouted and ran toward her son. "Kevin, you're all right." Josie grabbed the boy and hugged him to her. Oh, he felt so good.

"Mom?" Kevin squirmed out of her grasp. "What are you doing here? Do we have to go home already? Mr. Joe said we could spend the night."

"Oh, Kevin," Josie repeated, pulling the squirming boy to her chest again.

The woman who had been seated by the door was now standing at Josie's side. "Excuse me! What are you doing here? How did you get in?"

Josie put her body between Kevin and the woman. "I'm his mother. Who are you?"

"I'm Cathy Dudley. This is our shelter," the woman said, pulling at Josie's arm. "I must insist that you not touch the children. Go back to playing, boys. I'll talk with your mother in the kitchen."

Cathy pulled at Josie, who yanked her arm free.

"I don't want to alarm the children, but your clothes are probably contaminated," Cathy whispered, tugging Josie away. This time Josie followed. Contaminated? What was this woman talking about?

"We'll have to get them off right away," Cathy said. "How did you manage to escape? We're all anxious for news. Our radio isn't working. No reception down here. Mike didn't think of that. Here we have six transistor radios and a box of extra batteries, and none of it works."

Rudy was standing in the doorway.

"Oh, another one. You must be the boy's father," Cathy said. "How did you find us? I hope we don't get inundated with people. We have quite a bit of food down here, but we can't accommodate everybody. I told Joe not to spread the word, but obviously he's told you two. My brother is always trying to save the world."

"Where is Mr. Joe?" Josie asked.

"Mr. Joe. Isn't that a cute nickname? He and Mike are in the workshop building some extra beds. That's where we're headed. That's where the Geiger counter is. I'm sure you're bringing in radiation on your garments. By now it's in the air everywhere."

"Radiation?" Rudy and Josie echoed.

"Yeah, that's the dangerous part. People think, if you escape the fire, you'll be OK. But that's not the half of it." Cathy led to a door in the hall. She opened it into a large room stacked with used lumber. Assorted tools lined a long wooden table. Joe and another man were on the floor hammering a wooden frame.

"They're starting to arrive," Cathy said. "I told you not to invite people, Joseph, but you didn't listen to me. Where's the wand? I want to check their clothes. We can't have people bringing in radioactive dust."

"Whoa, I didn't tell anybody. I swear," Joe said, rising to his feet. "How did you find us?"

"It took a little detective work," Josie said. "What in the world were you thinking bringing the kids here and not telling anybody?"

Joe grinned. "When I saw the explosion this morning, I knew what it was. We've been expecting it. We're all prepared. I hurried right over here and told Mike and Cathy."

"We didn't see the explosion, but we heard the talk on the radio," Mike said. "We knew it was just a matter of time before a Russian missile hit Chicago. A big city in the middle of the country. Anybody could have told you that would be the primary target."

"I figured it might happen when Joe was driving the bus," Cathy added, as she waved a big black paddle over Josie. "We were prepared to take a busload of kids if necessary. They're the future, you know. Not old people like us. It's important that the children survive."

"I knew if I called the school, they would want to send all the buses here," Joe said. "We couldn't manage hundreds of kids, so I just turned off my radio. It was a tough decision, but necessary, if you know what I mean."

"No radiation on either one of them," Cathy said, fiddling with the dial on her instrument. "Are you sure this Geiger counter is working?"

Rudy stepped forward. "OK, if I understand you correctly, you saw the glow over the state forest this morning and thought it was a nuclear explosion."

"It was a nuclear explosion," Mike said. "It was all over the radio."

"Are you saying there was no explosion?" Joe asked. "But I saw the mushroom cloud and everything. Just like they said on the radio."

"It was fog and the new vapor streetlights," Josie said.

"No explosion?" Cathy repeated. "Oh, my!"

They heard a noise in the hall and looked out to see deputies rushing in, weapons drawn.

"Halt," a deputy shouted.

"I don't want the children frightened," Cathy said, stepping into the hall with her hands raised. "Please don't scare the kids."

Joe also stepped into the hall with his hands up. "The kids are safe. It was a misunderstanding."

While deputies cuffed Joe and the Dudleys, Josie and Rudy led the rest of them down the hall to the room where the children were playing. They explained what they knew about the misunderstanding, as the investigators walked through a well-stocked kitchen, a dormitory filled with bunk beds and a utility room with a generator, huge tanks of water, and a ventilation system.

"Looks like they know everything about science and nothing about common sense," one of the deputies said.

While the investigation continued, Josie stayed close to Kevin. She couldn't take her eyes off of him. He was getting so big. He seemed to have grown a foot since breakfast.

"Hey, Rudy, I'll beat you at foosball," Kevin shouted across the room.

"I'll play a game of foosball with you," Josie said, tapping his shoulder.

"Naaa," Kevin said. "You're a girl. I could beat you easy. I'd rather play Rudy, show him the new moves I've learned."

Rudy smiled. "Sure, I'll play if you think you're up to 'man' competition. But I warn you, I majored in foosball in college."

Josie stepped back and let the "men" play. Maybe Rudy had been right. Maybe Kevin was hungry for male companionship, a role that Kurt was failing to provide and that a mother, no matter how loving, could never fill.

"Ms. Braun?" The low gruff voice of Chief Deputy Miller interrupted Josie's thoughts. "We're going to take the kids back to the school. We've announced to the parents that they've been found safe. Everyone is anxious to see their kids."

Josie looked at Timmy and the others playing. The kids were so full of life and energy. That's what had been drained from the parents. They all needed their kids back as soon as possible.

"The school transportation department has a driver here," Miller continued. "They've checked the bus, and it seems in good shape. We plan to load the students back on the bus now and take them to the school."

"The bus?" Josie shuddered. She couldn't imagine putting Kevin back on the bus. "I'll take my son with me, if that's OK."

Then she remembered. Duke had driven them to the mine because he was familiar with the location. Where was Duke now? She hadn't seen him since they arrived.

"I passed Dukakis on my way in," Miller said as if reading Josie's thoughts. "He was in a hurry to meet his daughter somewhere. He asked me to offer you and the reporter a ride back to the newspaper. You're welcome to ride back on the bus with the kids. I plan to have some deputies on the bus too. We want to talk to the kids in familiar surroundings. See if there was any abuse."

"That's good," Josie said. "It's hard to believe, after all the horrors I imagined, that the kids are just fine. Better than fine. They seem so happy."

☼

By the time Becky entered the sixth floor hospital room where the press conference was to be held, it already was filled with television cameras and reporters. It was a large room, easily big enough to accommodate two beds, but instead there was one bed in the center of the room surrounded by people. Evidently the room had been set up for just such an occasion.

Becky carried a folded tripod for Page and set it up in an opening by the wall. She helped attach his camera to the stand. Their spot was a good one for capturing the chaos in the room, the backs of television personalities and video cameras. Getting a clean shot of Dee and the patient, Peter Hampton, was going to be a little more difficult.

"You should ask for special privileges," Becky whispered to Page. "After all, you're as much a part of this story as that guy in the bed. You're just as injured as he is. They should put you right up front."

Page responded with an accusing look that warned Becky not to mention it again. He was a big bruiser of a guy, but he was shy. He certainly didn't want any attention.

Becky leaned against the wall and let Page finish setting up his camera with his one free hand. His right hand could steady the tripod, but the shoulder sling kept him from lifting it very high.

Becky looked across the room at Tom and another police officer who were nestled in the dark shadows of the room, far from the windows and cameras. Tom smiled at her, and she smiled back. She knew he loved her just as much as she loved him. She was sure of it. But he was difficult. He saw more clash between their jobs than she did. To her their careers were the perfect complement. They both wanted truth and justice. She knew he was afraid too much publicity could interfere with an investigation. But she'd never revealed any of his secrets, not that he usually shared secrets. She needed him to trust her more. She needed him to know she would never print anything that would hurt a case. If she ever faced a conflict between what her job demanded and what Tom needed, there was no question in her mind which she would choose. She just needed Tom to believe that.

Like today. She knew Peter Hampton was the one who brought the gun that started the whole shooting match. Reuben Jetter's film had proven that.

146

But she had no idea when Tom was planning to make an arrest. The fact that he had not interrupted the press conference implied he was waiting for something. So she would wait. She would prefer he didn't do it in the middle of the press conference with all the television cameras rolling, but she would deal with it if necessary. It was Tom's move to make.

Dee was standing next to Hampton, posing for the cameras.

"Let me kiss your booboo," she giggled, taking his hand in hers and making a big show of kissing the bandage on his arm. "Peter was so brave. I want everyone to know. If he hadn't been there to take a bullet for me, why it could have been tragic. Just tragic."

"Oh, I don't know," Hampton stammered. "It was really nothing. It happened so fast."

"I thought Mr. Hampton and the other injured people were shot by the bodyguard," one of the television reporters said. "At least that's what it said in the newspaper."

"Gracious me, bullets were flying so fast I don't think anybody knows who shot who," Dee said with her infectious giggle. "All we can say for sure is someone pulled a gun and tried to shoot me. Cord, my bodyguard, shot back, and three unfortunate people were caught in the cross fire."

"Century Pictures is doing everything in its power to make sure Mr. Hampton and the other two injured parties are receiving the best in medical care," interjected a man in a blue suit. He wasn't identified, but Becky assumed the suit was an attorney. "We have provided this private room for Mr. Hampton and another like it for Michele Ames. She's recovering from surgery this afternoon and not able to join us on camera. The third gentleman, Stanley Pajenewski, asked to be released from the hospital. And in fact, I believe that's him back there, taking pictures for the *Jordan Daily News*. Can we have a round of applause for Mr. Pajenewski?"

The television cameras turned on Page. Hampton, Dee, and the suit applauded. The television reporters joined in.

"Mr. Pajenewski, do you have a few words?" one of the television personalities said, shoving a microphone in Page's face.

Page looked woefully at Becky and then back at the microphone.

"Come on. You must have something to say about getting shot on the job this morning. That must have been quite a shock. Is there anything you'd like to tell us?"

"Yeah," Page said in his usual low-key manner. "Could you get out of the way so I can get a picture of the star and the patient?"

The television reporter stepped back a bit and then burst out laughing. The other reporters and cameramen stepped to the side so Page could shoot Dee, who mugged for the camera, kissing the top of Pete's head. Then she scampered forward and threw an arm around Page so all the television cameras could get some footage of the sling-wearing photographer. Becky hurried away so she wouldn't be captured on film as well. She ended up retreating to the corner where Tom was standing. He leaned over and said in a conspiratorial whisper, "They're getting carried away."

"I wish somebody would carry them all away," Becky said.

When the room had settled down, and the reporters and cameras were once again clustered around Dee at Pete's bedside, the reporter's questions turned to the movie *Dieday the 13th*. Dee told about her short murder scene. She was at the peak of excitement, describing a dagger raised over her head, when the door to the hospital room opened quietly and Reuben Jetter snuck in. He slipped in next to Becky.

"Has she talked about the reward yet?" Reuben asked in a whisper.

"Not yet," Becky replied.

The reporters were peppering the star with questions. Someone brought up the morning's shooting and asked the status of the investigation. "Did they ever find the guy who tried to shoot you?"

The suit stepped in front of Dee and placed a hand on her shoulder to signal she should remain quiet.

"I think that question is best answered by the police," he said, gesturing toward Tom. "I think I see Detective Tom Cantrell back there. So, what about it, Mr. Cantrell? Can you tell these people the status of your investigation?"

As the cameras turned toward the back of the room, Becky slipped as far away from Tom as possible, crossing back to Page. She could see Tom was caught off-guard. He hadn't planned to speak to the television cameras. Was he ready to show the photographs tucked under his arm? He could be the hero. He could make a dramatic arrest right on television. He seemed to be considering the possibility.

"At this point, I think it's best to say the investigation is ongoing," Tom said quietly. "I should have something to report in a day or two."

Becky glanced back at Peter Hampton. His smile had faded, and he eyed Tom warily.

"While we're talking about that terrible shooting," Dee said, snatching the attention back to the front of the room, "I want to remind you all that Spritzer, my beautiful little puppy, was grabbed out of my hands during the chaos. He's lost and I must have him back. If anyone has seen my little Yorkie—here, you can show that picture I gave you of Spritzer. He's a show dog. A beautiful specimen. Century Pictures is offering a thousand-dollar reward for the safe return of my baby."

Reuben looked to Becky and mouthed the word "now"? Becky shook her head side to side.

The suit took control, thanked the television stations for coming, and asked everyone to leave so the patient could rest. As cameramen unplugged lights and television personalities snapped each other's photos with Dee, Becky pulled Reuben over to Page.

"Wait until all the television stations leave," she whispered to Reuben. "You want to have her to yourself."

"Huh? Oh yeah, I guess so," Reuben said, watching the cameras packing up.

Becky folded up Page's tripod and tucked it under her arm. She helped him stash his camera into its canvas bag. He pulled it up over his good shoulder and joined the television cameramen who were heading out the door.

As the suit bid farewell to the final television reporter, Peter Hampton threw off the blanket that had been covering his legs and jumped out of the bed.

"I need to get out of here," he said. "I need to go home. I promised to stay for the press conference, but the doctors said I could be released. I don't like hospitals. I want to go home."

"Wait," Tom said, stepping forward. "I have a few more questions. As soon as everybody else leaves." Tom glanced at Becky and Reuben with the same dismissive look he gave Dee and the suit.

"I'm ready to go," Dee said, heading for the door. "I need a drink. It's been a long day."

The suit seemed offended that Tom dared to take charge of the room and send them away, but he quickly picked up his briefcase and headed out the door. "I need to make some phone calls," he said and buzzed past Dee. Becky nudged Reuben and they followed closely behind the star.

"Now," Becky whispered in Reuben's ear.

The two of them followed Dee toward the elevator.

"Miss Licious?" Reuben said, as they stopped at the elevator door. "I know where your dog is."

"Spritzer?" Dee exclaimed. "You have my Spritzer?"

Reuben reached into his pocket and pulled out the shivering, closely clipped little dog.

"Ewww," Dee exclaimed, backing away. "That's not my Spritzer. That's some ugly, flea-bitten mongrel. He doesn't have any hair at all!"

"He's not ugly," Reuben said, cuddling the pup close to his chest. "I cut his hair off. It was matted with blood and popcorn and stuff. He didn't need all that hair hanging off him. I think he looks better this way."

"That is not my beloved Spritzer," Dee exclaimed haughtily. "Yoo hoo, Robert," she called to the suit who was talking into a phone attached to the wall nearby. "This awful man is trying to scam me out of the reward money with this horrible little mutt. Make him go away." She turned back to Reuben. "I won't give you any money. That isn't my dog."

"But it is," Becky said, stepping forward. "Mr. Jetter took a photo of your dog at the theater this morning." Becky held out Jetter's picture of the little dog scampering away from the stampeding crowd.

"That's what King looked like when I picked him up this morning," Jetter said, playfully rubbing the tiny dog's nose. "I cleaned him up, cut his hair. I didn't know he was yours."

"That is not my dog. I don't care about some silly photograph," Dee said, waving a dismissive hand at Becky. "My Spritzer is a show dog. An award winner. Robert, get over here."

The suit quickly appeared and tried to take control of the situation. He told Reuben to "take that mutt and leave." When the elevator door opened, he started to shuffle Dee inside.

"Wait, I can prove it," Reuben said, holding the little dog out at arm's length, blocking the elevator door. The dog promptly squirted a stream of urine on Robert's fine blue suit and shiny black shoes. Dee giggled and covered her mouth.

"You taught him to do that. I know you did," Reuben said.

"So what if I did," Dee said, trying to cover her laughter. "I live on a bus most of the time. I can't go walking a dog. I just hold him out the window."

Robert turned up his nose and gave Dee a look of pure revulsion. Then he held a hand up to Reuben and the tiny dog. "Kindly step back and allow that door to close before I report you to security."

"I changed my mind," Reuben shouted as the door was closing. "You can't be the daughter of Elvis. You're not anything like him!"

The elevator door closed and Dee disappeared.

"Wait, wait," Becky said, banging on the elevator button. "Come back."

But the elevator was gone. "Oh, I'm sorry. You didn't get your reward money," she said to Reuben.

"I'm not sorry," Reuben said, hugging the little dog to his chest. "She doesn't deserve a sweet dog like King."

The neighboring elevator opened. A man wearing the light blue scrubs of the hospital's transportation team backed out of the elevator, pulling a wheelchair. He was humming the "Marine's Hymn." As he turned around, he almost bumped into Becky.

"Sorry," he mumbled.

Becky looked down at his passenger, an elderly woman in a pink quilted robe. The woman giggled when she saw Becky. As the transport man wheeled her away, the woman raised her hand and wiggled her frail fingers in a small wave.

☼

Inside his hospital room, Pete Hampton sat on the edge of the bed tying his shoes. "It's just a little wound in the arm. The doctor said I was free to go home. I only stayed to please Century Pictures."

"So they would pay your medical bills?" Tom said, taking a seat in a chair next to the bed.

"Yeah, they're paying the bills. That's not a crime is it, detective?"

"Are they paying you for anything else? Did Century Pictures hire you to create a fake shooting scene at the Holiday Quad Theater?"

"Fake shooting scene?" Pete's eyes were wide. "You think somebody staged this? As a publicity stunt? Whoa! Then Century Pictures would owe a lot of money to the people who got shot."

"Yes, I think they would."

Pete chuckled. "That would be something, wouldn't it? How much you think they would pay for something like that? In a court settlement, I mean."

"That would be up to the attorneys if they settle out of court. Do you have an attorney?"

"Nah, where would I get the money for an attorney?"

"Well, you're going to need one," Tom said, tossing a photo onto the bed. It was a scene of chaos, everyone crowding in to get closer to Dee Licious. But in the lower right corner, Pete was easily identifiable, pulling a gun out of his coat pocket.

"So who paid you to bring a gun to the party?"

"Paid me? I don't know what you're talking about."

"It's clear from this picture that you have a gun in your pocket."

"Oh, that. I can explain that. It was part of somebody's costume. I found it on the floor. I told you I don't like guns."

"Uh-huh. So why did you pick it up? And why didn't you recognize it when I showed it to you earlier?"

"I forgot about it. Yeah, that's it. Just like I forgot my name at first. I didn't remember it until you showed me this picture."

"Uh-huh," Tom rubbed his chin. "So you just found this gun on the floor, loaded with blanks, and put it in your pocket? And the bodyguard saw it in your hand and started shooting. Is that your story?"

"Yeah, I guess so. Yeah, that sounds like what happened." Pete laughed nervously. "All a big mistake."

"Uh-huh," Tom said, crossing his arms. "But the bodyguard said you fired first. Why did you shoot the gun?"

"Shoot the gun? I don't remember shooting any gun. I don't even know how to shoot a gun. It must have been an accident. I picked up the gun, and it just went off. Yeah, that must have been what happened."

"Peter, Peter, Peter. This isn't adding up."

"Well, I can't help it," Pete said, rising to his feet and grabbing a coat out of a locker in the corner. "None of this is my fault. I'm going home. I need some rest."

The police officer who had been leaning against the wall by the door, walked over and opened the drawer in the table next to the bed. "Hmmm, quite a wad of cash here. Is this yours?"

"Oh, yeah. I forgot," Pete said, snatching the bills by handfuls and stuffing them into his coat pockets. "The nurse said they emptied my pockets when they brought me in."

"Yeah, and they counted the cash and put it on the inventory so you could be sure it was all there. Three hundred and forty-seven dollars. That's quite a wad to take to a movie, don't you think?" Tom said.

"I don't carry charge cards," Pete said, grabbing the inventory slip from Tom. "It's not a crime to carry money."

"Not if it's your money. But the picture is getting a little clearer for me, Pete. Several people reported having their wallets lifted at the theater, and then we found them in the trash. Minus the cash. You wouldn't know anything about that, would you?"

"Why would I know anything about their wallets?" Pete said, zipping up his coat. "I gotta go."

"Wait a minute. You have a pocket full of cash but no wallet. No personal identification. Except the wallet of Claude Dixon that the paramedics found on you. Did you lift Mr. Dixon's wallet? Are you a pickpocket, Peter?"

"I don't have to stand here and listen to you accusing me of a crime. I'm a victim. An innocent victim," Pete said, heading toward the door.

"I'm afraid you do have to listen to me," Tom said, grabbing Pete's right arm. "The way I figure it, you dipped this hand into the movie star's big purple purse. Couldn't resist, could you? And instead of cash, you found a dog. A dog that bit you and caused these puncture wounds."

Tom lifted up Pete's hand with bandaged fingers.

"And because you got some crazy blood phobia, you panicked when you saw the blood on your fingers. You started to pass out, and you got scared. You grabbed the gun in your left pocket. That's the picture here."

Tom whipped the photo into Pete's face as he pushed him against the wall.

"And you pulled the trigger because you were scared. It was loaded with blanks, maybe because you didn't want to take a chance on shooting someone and causing a bloody wound that would make you pass out. Or maybe because it was part of a costume, and you just found it on the floor. It doesn't matter. What matters is you pulled a gun in a crowd. You shot that gun. And an overzealous bodyguard did all the rest."

"But I didn't shoot anybody," Pete squealed, withering away from Tom's rampage. "I would never shoot anybody. I can't stand blood!"

"But you pick pockets, don't you Pete? You took Mr. Dixon's wallet and those other ones we found in the trash. We're going to find your fingerprints all over them, aren't we, Pete? You might as well admit it."

"I want to call an attorney. I got rights."

"You sure do," Tom said, backing away from Pete and leaving him huddled next to the wall. "Read him his rights, Charlie."

☼

The waitress topped off Jennifer's coffee for the second time. "Your Dad late again?" she asked.

Jennifer smiled. She hated that this waitress presumed to know her, but that's the way it was in Jordan. It seemed like everyone knew her father, Duke Dukakis, the newspaper columnist. By association, they knew her.

Duke always was late picking her up from the junior college. That's why he had told her to wait in the coffee shop so she wouldn't be cold. And sometimes he would even call the shop if he was going to be an hour late. But sometimes he'd be out covering a story, a car accident or robbery, and he wouldn't have access to a phone to call her. Of course, every filling station had a phone, and there was a station on almost every corner, so there wasn't any excuse. Still Jennifer wished he had one of those mobile phones she had read about. Phones you could carry in a little black briefcase with their own batteries and everything. So people could call you anywhere. It was real 007 James Bond sort of stuff. Then Jennifer wouldn't have to wait for her Dad to call her. She could call him, and right in the middle of interviewing somebody, he would stop and answer the phone and tell her when he would arrive.

Jennifer checked her watch. Four thirty. If he didn't hurry, they wouldn't catch the bridge tender who thought he was a band leader. Dumb idea. Jennifer didn't want to go see him anyway. Hadn't she done enough penance? She'd made the court appearance. She would pay the fine out of the money she was saving to buy a car. She'd even gone down with her Dad to visit the broken bridge. It had been kinda fun to tour the bridge tender's station and actually try out the controls to close the bridge. But why did she have to go to the community center to track down the bridge tender who had been working last night? The guy her Dad keeps saying saved her life.

Jennifer saw her father's turquoise Pontiac pull into the parking lot. She grabbed her stack of books off the counter and headed for the door.

"Sorry, I'm so late," he said when she opened the car door. "It has been an amazing day."

"They're all amazing days," Jennifer said, tossing her books into the backseat.

"Yes, they are," Duke said. "But this was extra amazing. Did you hear about the missing school bus?"

"Yeah, I heard something on the radio."

"Well, Kevin was one of the kids on that bus."

"Kevin Walsh?"

"Yep. Josie's son. Anyway, we just found the bus at an underground storage facility. Kids are OK. It was a huge relief. We should celebrate."

"You want to skip the community center?" Jennifer suggested.

"No, we're not skipping the community center," Duke said, patting his daughter's knee. "You have a unique opportunity here to meet the man who saved your life. You can see him in his element. See who he really is. And you can apologize. If you miss this opportunity, you're going to regret it the rest of your life. You owe him big-time."

"It's almost five o'clock. I don't know how long he's in this band practice thing. And I have to be back at the college at seven to get into my makeup for the play," Jennifer explained.

"Makeup? Are you going to be a clown or a monster or something?"

Jennifer shook her head. "No, Dad. I told you. I play Lois Lane."

"Lois Lane? Are you doing *Superman*?"

"Daaaaaad! I told you a hundred times. We're doing *Kiss Me, Kate*.'"

"OK. So you're playing Lois, not Kate, so you don't get kissed."

Jennifer blushed.

"Wait a minute," Duke said, glancing back and forth between the road and his daughter's flaming face. "Does some guy kiss you in this play?"

"You'll just have to come tonight and see," Jennifer said, smiling.

"I wouldn't miss it for the world," Duke said, returning her smile.

After they pulled in and parked in the community center parking lot, it wasn't hard to find Stan Barrows. They could hear the band playing from the parking lot. They followed the reverberations into a gymnasium. At one end, three boys were shooting baskets. At the other end the band members were seated in three rows of folding chairs. This was a marching band, not an orchestra. There were a few woodwinds—flutes, clarinets, and a sax—but mostly big brass horns—trumpets, trombones, and tubas. In the back, a big girl beat a big bass drum in a stand. The sound was deafening.

Duke and Jennifer took seats in the bleachers that ran along one wall. It wasn't hard to pick out Stan Barrows as he jumped up and down from the conductor's box. He would wave his hands over the band or tap his stick on the black metal music stand and tell them to start over. Often he walked among the students, correcting sitting positions or holding a hand behind his ear to encourage a musician to play louder.

Even when the band finished playing and the musicians started packing away their instruments in worn black cases, the conductor was busy joking with one, correcting another. Finally, as the young band members dispersed, Duke pulled Jennifer toward the rows of empty chairs.

"Mr. Barrows," Duke called, as he crossed the gym with his right hand extended. The conductor paused a moment and then extended his hand as though trying to recall who Duke was.

"I'm Ormand Dukakis, from the *Daily News*," Duke said, shaking Barrows' hand. "And this is my daughter, Jennifer. I believe you two met last night. She was on your bridge."

"Oh, yes. You look different when you're not hysterical," Barrows said, offering his hand.

"I'm so sorry," Jennifer said. "I didn't mean to cause you so much trouble."

"Nobody ever does," Barrows said with a sigh. "Learn your lesson?"

"Oh, yes. I'll never go out on the bridge again when the gate is down. Never."

"Good. And tell your friends. You gotta respect those big old bridges."

"Yes, sir."

One of the young musicians was folding up the chairs and stacking them on a wheeled cart. Duke joined in behind the boy, folding and stacking.

"You don't have to do that, Mr. Dukakis," Barrows called after him.

"Oh, that's OK. It needs to be done," Duke said. Jennifer followed her father's lead and soon all the chairs were stacked on the cart.

"I admire what you're trying to do here with this band," Duke said. "Do you have concerts?"

"No," Barrows said with a chuckle. "We'll be in some parades in the summer and maybe a drill competition. In the winter, we just practice for fun."

"Well, you're doing good work with the kids in this neighborhood," Duke said. "We stopped by the bridge earlier today. I'm impressed with that too. Looks like a high-tech airplane control center in there."

"Oh, yeah. We get all of NASA's leftovers," Barrows joked.

"I think Jennifer was impressed," Duke said, throwing an arm around his daughter.

"Yeah, it was cool," Jennifer said. "I got these tickets for you, Mr. Barrows. I'm going to be in a play this weekend at the Junior College. I would love for you to be my guest. I want you to know I'm not always causing trouble. Sometimes I can sing and dance pretty well."

"Oh, I heard the college was doing *Kiss Me, Kate*," Barrows said, taking the tickets Jennifer offered. "I love that show."

"I know you work nights on the bridge, but we've got a matinee performance on Sunday," Jennifer said.

"That should work out well," Barrows said, sticking the tickets into his shirt pocket. "Funny how this turned out. You getting stuck on my bridge and all. When I saw you kids out there, I certainly wasn't thinking, 'There's my ticket to *Kiss Me, Kate*."

Jennifer giggled. Duke slapped Stan Barrows on the back.

"That's why people should get to know each other," Duke said. "We've got more in common than you think."

5:00 PM

Fridays were never ending. The work on one day's paper just blurred into the next. This Friday had been worse than normal. But Nick had been expecting it. After all, it was a full moon Friday the 13th. It had been hectic, but as the newsroom clock struck five, all the day's stories were wrapping up fairly well.

When Rudy returned from D & D Storage, he was so excited he did a cartwheel in the middle of the newsroom and knocked over a trash can. Nick was glad Hammond had left for the day. He would never abide such foolishness. But who could blame Rudy for being excited? They all loved Josie and her son, Kevin. Who would have guessed the horrors they imagined just hours ago would melt away so easily? The children were all fine and had been returned to their homes.

As Rudy typed his story, he kept talking out loud, unable to contain his enthusiasm.

"You should have seen this place. It was all fixed up like a playroom. It was like Pleasure Island in *Pinnochio*. Remember that? Except the kids didn't turn into donkeys in the end. It's just so perfect. And you should have seen the school when that bus arrived. The parents were lined up outside. They were so excited. I know it made the kids feel special to have their folks cheering them like heroes. They were proud. Like they were the winning team. Oh, it was just so wonderful to see."

Becky was trying to write her own story and asked Rudy to keep quiet more than once.

"Save it for the paper," she said. "The rest of us have work to do too."

Becky's story also had a happy ending. A pick pocket had been arrested. Jetter's photo proved that Pete Hampton had been armed, giving bodyguard Cord McCoy a little more credibility for firing three shots and injuring two innocent people. The injured were on the mend. *Dieday the 13th* was opening to packed theaters across the country. And Spritzer, the poor little missing pooch of Dee Licious, had found a new home and a new identity as King, the pocket pet of Reuben Jetter. Best of all, Reuben finally was featured in a photo in the newspaper. Becky laughed to herself, thinking how proud he would be. It was the kind of recognition he had hungered for all his life. But she knew fifteen minutes of fame would never be enough for Reuben Jetter.

157

He would be back at the police station Monday morning reporting another sighting of Elvis.

Hoss came in with a small cooler packed with a six-pack of Cokes to get him through the evening. During the day, when Hammond was there, the newsroom observed the professional standards their managing editor preferred. Reporters didn't eat or drink at their desks; they used a break room. But in the evenings, writing and relaxing merged into a single passion. Putting out the paper was their life. The evening shift was intense with less staff. No one had time to leave the phones and go to the break room. They ate at their desks, answered the phone with food in their mouths, dropped crumbs on their keyboards, and worked frantically to squeeze all the news and sports scores into the paper before the midnight deadline.

The arrival of Phil, the evening's copy editor, and Donna, the intern working the weekend cop beat, signaled the evening shift was officially under way. The day shift needed to wrap up their stories and leave. Nick wandered over to be sure Hoss knew about all the stories planned for Saturday's paper. Hoss still teased him about one of his first shifts as assistant city editor when he failed to list a story on the budget about a shooting victim.

"Lost any bodies lately, Tricky Nick?" Hoss said.

"Nope, all the bodies are accounted for," Nick replied. He explained that Becky and Rudy were still writing their stories, but should finish soon.

"You've got Duke's piece on the lady who fell to her death at the A-Lab. It doesn't have a report from the coroner's office. We probably won't get results of the autopsy until tomorrow at the earliest. Maybe not until Monday. Sounds like an accident. Keep an eye out for anything from the Associated Press on the international implications of the death. With all the stories we were covering, Josie thought it would be better to let the AP deal with the State Department."

"Probably so," Hoss said. "Glad to hear little Kevin's back safe and sound."

"Yeah, Josie called. She's having a party at her house tonight. Everyone's invited."

"Now, why did you go and tell me that? You know I have to work."

Nick smiled. "I know, but she said she would have a couple of pizzas delivered here, so the Friday night shift could join the celebration. She's walking on air. I've never heard her sound so happy."

"Guess you have to glimpse the worst to appreciate how good you have it," Hoss said.

Nick had his coat on and was about to head out when his phone rang. He thought about ignoring it, but figured it probably was Brittany wondering why he was so late. When he picked up the phone, he heard the sobbing voice of Deluded Debbie.

"Calm down," he said. "I can't understand what you're saying."

158

"It's getting dark, and I'm getting scared. The moon will come out. I'm scared. Ooooooo. It hurts."

"What hurts?"

"The moon."

Nick shook his head. "You're afraid of the moon?"

"Yes, very afraid."

"Is there anyone you can call to come stay with you? A neighbor, maybe?"

Debbie screamed. "Oooooo … it hurts so much."

"Debbie, I can't help you if you won't give me your address. I could ask a policeman to check on you."

"No, no police. No doctors. They scare me."

"OK. Just give me your address, and I will come by to make sure you are all right. You trust me, don't you, Debbie?"

"Just you?"

"Just me."

Debbie recited an address not far from downtown. It amazed Nick that she could sound so isolated in the middle of town. When he left the office, he drove to the hospital to pick up Brittany.

"Sorry, I'm late," he said when she came out of the double doors next to the emergency room. "It's been one of those days."

"I know. Step on the gas and get out of here before somebody calls me back in," Brittany said, slouching into the passenger seat. "It's like a war zone in there. And most of it is stupid stuff. Not life or death, but it all takes time. And energy. I don't have enough energy left to turn on the TV."

"Good thing because you're not going to have a chance to watch TV. Josie is having a party to celebrate her son coming home safely. And tonight's the night that Duke's daughter is in the play at the junior college."

"Oh, yeah. I forgot. Well, at least I need to go home and take a shower. I feel like I've been marinating in grime all day." Brittany chuckled. "Almost forgot. They gave me the Florence Nightingale award this morning."

"An award?" Nick said. "For what?"

"Oh, it's just a joke." Brittany pulled a long white goose feather out of her purse. "They said it was for going beyond the call. But they are just making fun. Some drunk shit all over me this morning. I was covered, head to toe. You had to be there. I showered and changed, but I still feel dirty." Brittany sighed and closed her eyes.

Nick smiled. "Wish I could have seen that. Before we go home, I want to stop by and see a weird lady. She's called the office six or seven times today. I finally got her to give me an address. I just want to be sure she's not in immediate danger."

"What makes you think she might be in danger?"

"She's afraid of the moon."

"That makes sense."

"And this morning she told me her DNA went down the drain."

"Sounds like most of the patients who came in today."

"I know. I just want to check on her. Then we'll clean up, have a drink, and decide whether to visit Josie or go to the play."

"I vote for the play. I don't feel like making small talk at a party. I'd rather sit and listen."

"Josie will have plenty of guests. She won't need us."

"So the kids on the bus weren't traumatized at all?"

"Not at all," Nick said with a big smile. "Josie said they were happy campers. Had no idea they were considered missing."

"What will they do with the bus driver?"

"He'll be charged with kidnapping or unlawfully detaining the children. At the very least, he'll lose his job. The whole school district is in turmoil. Rudy said the Parent Teacher Association is calling an emergency meeting tomorrow. They want to put a parent volunteer on every bus with a radio to call in if there are any problems."

"Sounds like a good idea."

"One thing's for sure. They can't expect parents to put their kids on the bus the same as always. They will have to come up with some assurances."

Nick turned down a street with old frame houses from the early 1900s. It was getting dark, and the full moon was low on the horizon at the end of the street. The huge yellow ball was hypnotic, drawing them farther down the street.

Some of the houses were painted bright colors and well kept up. Others were in disrepair. Some had been divided into apartments. Nick spotted 2639, the number Debbie had given him. The faded white clapboard house was hidden by overgrown cedars. The front porch was hanging off the house at an odd angle. A board was nailed across the front steps, which appeared broken.

"She lives here?" Brittany asked. "Walking out the front door could be dangerous in this house."

"Looks like this place should be condemned," Nick said. "Why is anybody still living here?"

A light in the kitchen window suggested someone was home. Nick pulled into the driveway.

"Come to the door with me," he said to Brittany. "I don't want to scare her. Maybe she'll trust you. You have a nice face."

"Thanks. You're pretty cute yourself," Brittany quipped.

They walked to the side door hand in hand. Two metal trash cans stood next to the door, which opened onto the driveway. There was no doorbell, so Nick opened the storm door and knocked on the glass pane in the door. When there was no response after a minute or so, he knocked again.

"I don't think she's home," Brittany said. "Or she doesn't want company. We should go."

Knocking a third time, Nick called out to her. "Debbie, it's me, Nick, from the newspaper."

They heard a scream coming from inside the house.

"She sounds like she's in pain," Brittany said, suddenly concerned.

"You should be on the other end of a phone when she does that," Nick replied.

"Why didn't you call an ambulance?"

"She doesn't want one."

A second scream sounded even more desperate.

"We've got to get in there," Brittany said, trying the doorknob unsuccessfully.

"Stand back," Nick said. He kicked the door near the knob and the door frame easily gave way. Inside, a few steps led up into the lighted kitchen.

"Debbie, where are you?"

"In here. The moon is coming out," a voice called.

Nick and Brittany walked through an old but neat kitchen. A faucet dripped into a yellowed, porcelain sink. Next to the sink, a clean saucepan was overturned on a drain board. A large serving spoon was propped against the pan. A small wooden table was set for three, but only the place setting in the middle, arranged on a bright orange paper placemat, seemed to be in use. The place settings at either end of the table, set on faded green mats, were dingy with dust and cobwebs. In the darkened room beyond, Nick and Brittany could see a woman of about thirty or forty lying on a frayed sofa.

"Help me, the moon is coming," she wailed.

Brittany ran to the woman and knelt beside her while Nick fumbled to turn on a table lamp.

"She's having a baby," Brittany exclaimed.

"It's the moon," Debbie corrected, clutching her huge stomach. "It's the full moon."

"It's a baby," Brittany repeated looking into the woman's face. "Have you seen a doctor?"

"She doesn't trust doctors. She thinks they killed her father," Nick said, taking Debbie's hand. Although he was meeting Debbie for the first time, he felt like he knew her well. She seemed like a distant cousin or some other relative he hadn't seen in years.

"Don't worry, everything is going to be fine," he said.

"It's going to be soon," Brittany said. "Call an ambulance."

"No, no," Debbie said, squeezing Nick's hand.

"I won't let anyone hurt you," Nick said, looking into Debbie's eyes.

Brittany headed back into the kitchen, called 911 from the phone hanging on the wall, and quietly requested an ambulance. She opened drawers and cabinets, collecting a paring knife, a large mixing bowl and an arm full of clean dish towels. She scrubbed her hands at the sink with the minty green bar of soap she found sitting there. Then she returned to the sofa.

Nick was talking to the woman in soft, consoling tones. He really was a sweet man, Brittany thought. She had never seen him like this before. Usually she thought of him as a tough competitor on the Media Moguls softball team or trying to run past the other joggers. He was a tender lover, but this was the first she had seen his compassion and coolness in an emergency. She was so proud of him.

She lifted Debbie's knees and placed two dish towels under her bottom. She draped an afghan over Debbie's knees, tenting it. During Debbie's next scream, Brittany quickly pulled off the woman's slacks.

"Just keep her calm," Brittany said. "Talk about the weather or the moon. She likes the moon."

"My moon," Debbie said again, holding her stomach. "I swallowed the moon."

"Do you have a boyfriend, Debbie?" Nick asked. "Where is he?"

"Mr. Matlock on TV," Debbie said proudly. "I like him a lot. Mr. Matlock is my boyfriend."

Nick and Brittany shared a smile before Debbie was screaming in pain again.

"Here it comes," Brittany said. "She's fully dilated."

"I didn't know you delivered babies," Nick said.

"I play catcher in this game," Brittany said as she reached under the afghan. "Debbie's the pitcher, and she's winding up right now. You're doing great Debbie. Go ahead and push."

Debbie yelled and cursed and grabbed at Nick's arms.

"It's OK," Nick said. "Everything's OK."

Debbie growled and sputtered and gasped for breath. She grunted. Nick soothed. She lurched forward with the loudest scream yet, then fell back into the sofa, exhausted. Nick was afraid at first that she was dead. She lay still with her eyes closed and sweat wetting ringlets of hair on her forehead.

Then they heard it. The faint, high-pitched cry of the baby.

Debbie's eyes popped open at the sound.

"It's a boy," Brittany exclaimed, lifting the bloody bundle over the afghan.

"Oh, the man in the moon," Debbie squealed, reaching out her arms for the crying baby.

With the cord still attached, Brittany laid the baby on Debbie's chest. Before she could cut the cord, she needed something to tie it off. A shoestring, a clamp. Just then the ambulance pulled into the driveway and paramedics were soon storming through the kitchen. Brittany backed away. She'd let them cut the cord and clamp it.

Nick remained at Debbie's side, whispering assurances. Brittany offered one of the dishtowels for wrapping the baby when the cord was cut. Then she handed them a bowl to hold the placenta. Soon mother and baby were wheeled into the ambulance. Brittany and Nick stood in the driveway waving goodbye.

"That was really cool," Nick said, hugging Brittany.

She laughed. "Yeah, I guess it was, in a full moon Friday sort of way."

☼

Josie's neighborhood was like a summer block party. Although it was dark before six o'clock and cold enough for people gathering outside to see their breath, there was a warm, friendly atmosphere that spilled out of the houses and into the street. Many of the missing children on the bus were from this block. Friends came to bring food and balloons and cakes and beer. Cars lined both sides of the street, and porch lights were on.

Dan Braun looked out Josie's picture window at the crowd gathering outside. "It's like Jesus said about the lost sheep. 'Come and rejoice with me. That which was lost has been found.'"

Josie looked at her father and smiled. Then she wrapped her arms around Kevin. "I want to climb up on the roof and shout: He's back! My boy is back!"

Kevin squirmed away to play on the floor with Timmy and the new Transformer his grandmother had bought. Timmy's parents, Polly and Greg, were in the kitchen visiting with other neighbors and nibbling the pizzas that had been delivered. Some of the reporters and copy editors from the *Daily News* were also in the kitchen, but Josie couldn't bear to have Kevin out of her sight for a second. When the doorbell rang, Sally Braun opened it to Tom and Becky bringing a case of beer and a cake decorated with the words "Welcome Home." A few minutes later, Sally opened the door to a strange sight: a clown wearing white makeup, a metal colander on his head, and a huge red suit that dragged on the floor when he stepped in. He wore large black-framed glasses and fake buck teeth that made him speak with a lisp.

"Hold this," he said, handing Sally a droopy flower.

She giggled with embarrassment.

"Mr. Baggy Pants!" Kevin squealed and jumped up from the floor. He ran and hugged the clown.

"Welcome home, Mr. Droopy Drawers," the clown said, swatting Kevin's backside with a Ping-Pong paddle shaped like an enlarged Mickey Mouse cartoon hand. "I've got something for you. Let's see, it's in one of my pockets."

The clown opened his red suit coat and a silver helium balloon escaped and headed for the ceiling.

163

"That's not it. It's in here somewhere. Hold this," he said handing another droopy flower to Kevin.

"What am I supposed to do with this?" Kevin asked.

"Just hold it, while I look for your surprise," the clown said. He pulled dozens of brightly colored scarves out of his pockets and dropped them on the floor. Children and parents came from the kitchen and family room to see the clown in the living room. Josie stood back behind the crowd and smiled. She remembered Rudy's clown character from the days he ran the Ranch Rudy day care center.

When Mr. Baggy Pants came across another droopy flower, he handed it to Timmy, who was crowding in to be close to the clown.

"What is it with you people? You're killing my flowers," Mr. Baggy Pants said. He snatched the droopy flower from Sally. He held it by the tip of the stem gave it a shake. It stood erect like a fresh blossom.

"Oh, I see," Kevin said, holding his flower by the tip of the stem and giving it a good whip. It too stood up tall. Timmy tried unsuccessfully to make his stand up.

"Trade ja," Kevin said, handing Timmy the tall flower and taking the droopy one. He tried several times to shake it straight without luck.

"Goes to show you, smarty pants. Not all flowers are alike," Mr. Baggy Pants said, taking the droopy flower from Kevin. "Sometimes you need to give it a kiss first." The clown kissed the blossom, then whipped the stem from the tip. It stood tall and straight. Kevin, Timmy, and the other kids gasped in amazement.

"Here, Mom," the clown said, handing the flower to Sally. "You hold the flowers so the kids can help me with the surprise. Here's what I've been looking for."

Mr. Baggy Pants pulled a pink polka-dotted cylinder out of a deep pocket in his suit leg.

"OK, kids. I want you to help me by picking up all the scarves that I dropped on the floor. Put them in this cylinder. Don't miss any or the surprise won't work."

The children, and some of the adults, gathered the rainbow of scarves from the floor and stuffed them into the cylinder. Then Mr. Baggy Pants walked over to Josie.

"I want you to hold this for me. Can you do that?" He handed the cylinder to Josie with a wink. "Hold it nice and high."

Josie lifted the cylinder over her head.

"Not too high. Kevin needs to be able to reach the bottom of the cylinder," Mr. Baggy Pants said. "Now I need to say the magic words."

Mr. Baggy Pants placed both hands on the cylinder. "Presto, change-o gone away; Presto, change-o come back again."

Mr. Baggy Pants pulled the corner of a white scarf out of the bottom of the cylinder and handed it to Kevin. "OK, Kevin, take 'er away."

Kevin pulled and pulled, but the scarf kept coming.

"Keep pulling. Walk over there and keep pulling the scarf. Hold it high."

Kevin pulled out a long white banner with multi-colored letters spelling "Welcom Home." Several in the crowd applauded.

"Hey, Mr. Baggy Pants. You can't spell," one of the copy editors from the *Daily News* shouted.

"Oh, my," Mr. Baggy Pants said, standing back to look at the banner. "One of the scarves must not have been picked up. Hmmm. Let's see. Must be a purple one. We're missing a purple one."

"There it is," one of the children squealed, pointing to a purple scarf hanging out of the back pocket of Mr. Baggy Pants. When the child pulled the scarf out of his pocket, a purple letter "E" dangled from the other end.

"There's our missing letter," Mr. Baggy Pants said. He discretely removed the clear paper backing and stuck the purple letter in the proper spot on the sign. "Now where should we hang our banner surprise?"

"How about over the picture window," Dan Braun suggested. "Here, let me help."

The clown gave Dan some sticky strips from one of his pockets, and together they hung the banner.

"How did he do that?" Josie heard Timmy ask.

"It's magic," Kevin replied.

Josie placed the polka-dotted cylinder on a high book shelf where she hoped it would be forgotten until Rudy wanted to pack up his props. She didn't want the kids to notice that the multicolored scarves were still there.

Children and parents were gathered around Rudy, who was quick to tell a funny story or pull another droopy flower out of a pocket. Josie knew he had to have been working at the office until five o'clock at least. How had he transformed into a clown so quickly? Did he keep a stocked clown kit in his trunk, complete with a "Welcome Home" banner?

"When did you have time to hire a clown?" Sally whispered to Josie. "He's wonderful."

"I didn't hire him. He's a friend," Josie replied. "You've met him before. That's Rudy. The guy who used to run the day care center. He works at the paper now. He's my education reporter."

"Rudy Randolph. That's where I heard the name before. He's the young man who called me this morning. He said he was one of your reporters, but I couldn't remember meeting a reporter. Now it makes sense. I met him at the day care center."

"Rudy called you?"

"Yes, he's the one. I remember now."

"I wish he hadn't done that."

165

"Are you kidding?" Sally said, beaming. "I wouldn't have missed this for the world."

Sally joined the others gathered around the clown, who continued to entertain parents and kids alike with the many discoveries in his pocket. Josie stood back and watched as her parents and the other guests delighted in Mr. Baggy Pants. What was wrong with her? Everyone else loved Rudy. Why did she feel like he was manipulating the situation to his benefit? Trying to win her love by winning her son and pleasing her parents.

I was delighted when my parents showed up this afternoon, just when I was at my lowest. Now, I discover Rudy is the one who called them. Four hours before they could arrive, he is the one who took a risk and called them. I was unwilling to make that decision. My parents could easily have made the drive for nothing. The bus could have showed up with a flat tire an hour after the phone call, and my parents would have been worried for no reason. Rudy had no right to overrule my decision to postpone calling them. Yet, I am glad they came. They are glad to have been included in this important day. Am I angry with Rudy because I made the wrong decision in choosing not to call them? And he made the right decision? Am I jealous that Rudy seems to know how to win Kevin's attention at a time when my son is outgrowing his need for mothering?

6:15 PM

Showering together was the high point of every day since Brittany and Nick had married three months ago. No matter what was going on in the outside world, the shower door closed everything out. Those five minutes were concentrated on worshiping each other. As they slowly stroked arms and legs and backs with soapy sponges, they admired every crevice. They smiled watching suds skitter over nipples and belly buttons. Usually they adored in silence, speaking only with soft caresses. Comments were as intimate as a touch.

"I love this little birthmark under your arm," Brittany said.

"That's not a birthmark. That's where my mother kissed me on the day I was born," Nick replied, carefully sponging Brittany's back.

"Oh, she must have been wearing that long-lasting lipstick," Brittany quipped.

Inevitably, showers led to sex. Sometimes it was fast and furious, greedily gulping each other over the bathroom counter or pushed up against the wall still dripping wet. These times were so potent and passionate that Nick and Brittany would often return to the shower to rinse off and cool down.

But sometimes, as on that full moon Friday, the stroking in the shower led to more patient stroking on the bed, fingers confirming every muscle and bone was as delightful to the touch as it was to the eye. This lingering carnal worship service would crescendo into a hallelujah chorus of praise and ecstasy. They ended wrapped in each other, listening to every breath and heartbeat.

"What do you think will happen to Debbie? Will they let her keep the baby?" Brittany asked.

"I don't know. There will have to be a competency hearing." Nick replied, kissing Brittany's forehead. "She keeps the kitchen neat, so I think she is capable of taking care of herself and the baby even if some of her ideas are a little ... childish."

"It will be so hard on her if they take the baby away."

"I know. We'll have to find out if she has any relatives who could help. And what about the father? Somebody took advantage of her because she is so simple. Maybe that's why she's so afraid. She's been abused."

"But when she saw that baby, the delight in her eyes. Anybody can understand that. It doesn't take a high IQ to love a baby."

"Do you think that love is automatic?" Nick asked, pulling back a little to look into Brittany's face.

"Automatic? I guess. Don't you think so?"

"I never thought about having a baby until tonight. That was so amazing, hearing that faint baby cry."

"The cries get louder real fast," Brittany said. "And pretty irritating at two in the morning. But it was amazing to see, wasn't it?"

"Do you want to have kids?"

"Of course. Don't you?"

"I never imagined myself as a father. I don't know how."

"Nobody knows how. But the way you were with that lady tonight. So compassionate. You'll make a great Dad someday."

Nick chuckled. "And you'd be a great Mom."

Brittany sighed and curled tighter into Nick's chest. "Right now, I want to go to sleep. It's been a long day."

"We can't do that," Nick said. "We've got to go see Duke's daughter in the play. I promised."

"The play continues all weekend," Brittany mumbled as she closed her eyes.

"We really should stay awake," Nick said, shaking Brittany slightly. "This full moon Friday the 13th isn't over. Anything could happen between now and midnight."

"Anything can happen every night," Brittany mumbled without opening her eyes.

"But this is different. You saw how it was at the hospital today. We need to stay alert. We may be needed to deal with a crisis again."

"You don't really believe in that silly superstition."

"It's not just a superstition," Nick said. "It's some kind of phenomenon I don't understand, but it's real. Like us walking in just as Debbie was about to deliver. What do you think would have happened to her if we hadn't come by?"

"She would have called somebody else. It's just a stupid superstition."

Nick looked down at Brittany. Her eyes were closed, her breathing steady and shallow. She was falling asleep. He didn't dare tell her that the last time there was a full moon Friday the 13th was the night Scott was killed. That wasn't some silly superstition. He brushed a hand over Brittany's long blond hair, still damp from the shower.

"Yes, you're right," he whispered. "It's just a silly superstition. Sleep now."

Nick lay beside her. Weird things happened every day. Women got pregnant; some of them delivered babies alone at home. It could happen any day, not just on a full moon. Murders happened during the new moon or a little crescent moon. They happened on Tuesday the tenth as well as Friday

168

the thirteenth. The logical part of him knew it was nonsense to expect things to go wrong on Friday the thirteenth.

Lying there in the dark, Nick replayed the day. It had been full of strange events from the mistaken forest fire, to the body guard shoot out and the bus driver hiding his students from a non-existent nuclear explosion. Any one of those could happen any day of the week, any phase of the moon. But all of them together? That had to be a full moon. Had to be.

Nick's stomach growled in the silence, and he remembered he hadn't eaten since that quick sandwich from the vending machine. He slipped out of the bed and padded into the kitchen.

☼

Josie wandered into her kitchen to visit with her guests. The table was covered with food: the pizzas she had ordered, the cakes and chips that people had brought. The cooler in the corner was filled with ice and beverages. Through the sliding glass door she could see more boxes of beer keeping cool on the patio. Beyond, the full moon was rising high, lighting up the backyard, much as it had the night before. Chippie's muddy paw prints still decorated the glass. Oh, that seemed a lifetime ago.

A couple of smokers were clustered outside on the patio. Was that Greg, Polly's husband? And Tom, the police detective? Oh, no. This gathering violated Polly's order of protection. Were Tom and Greg talking guy stuff or was Tom arresting him?

Polly came up beside Josie at the window.

"The missing bus had an amazing effect on Greg," Polly said. "It made it real for him. He knows he could lose Timmy and Aster forever. He said he will get some counseling and stop drinking. He's violent only when he drinks."

"Is he in trouble for being here at the party?" Josie asked without taking her eyes off the pair on the patio. "It's a violation of the protection order."

"I know, but I don't think that police detective cares. He knows this is a special situation. I really want Greg to come home again. We're going to talk to a lawyer on Monday, see what we can work out."

Josie hugged her neighbor. So many times horrible experiences can have good effects.

"Did the boys eat?" Josie asked.

"I saw Timmy and Kevin get slices of cheese pizza when we first opened the box," Polly said.

"Kevin should eat some fruit," Josie said, picking up a fruit tray and heading into the living room. "Kevin?"

Josie looked around at the people crowded into her living room. Rudy had removed his oversized red suit coat and pants. He was wearing black

169

sweats. He'd removed the buck teeth and glasses too, but he still had white clown makeup on his face and that ridiculous metal colander on his head. He seemed so silly drinking a Coke and joking with Josie's neighbors.

"Where's Kevin?" Josie asked as she glanced around the room.

"Haven't seen him in a while," Rudy replied.

"Kevin?" Josie called a little louder.

"I think I saw them go upstairs," Dan whispered to his daughter.

"Kevin?" Josie called from the bottom of the stairs. Her son peeked out of his bedroom at the end of the hall.

"What?"

"What are you doing up there?" Josie said, heading up the stairs. "I couldn't find you."

She found Timmy and Kevin on the bedroom floor with another boy from the neighborhood. They had Transformers lined up on bed, desk, and chair.

"It's too crowded downstairs," Kevin complained, returning to his friends.

"I brought you some fruit," Josie said, holding out the fruit tray. Two of the boys took a piece and promptly gobbled it down, but Kevin didn't look up from his toy.

"No, thanks," he mumbled.

."I'll leave it up here in case you get hungry," Josie said, laying the fruit plate on the desk. She backed out of the room slowly. She bumped into her mother in the hall.

"Are you OK?" Sally asked.

"Yeah, sure. Just bringing the kids some food."

"He's going to be OK, you know."

"I know."

"Don't smother him."

"Mom! I was just checking on them."

Sally gave her daughter a critical look that didn't need words. Josie rushed past her mother and back to the kitchen.

"We need to get going pretty soon for the play at the college," Becky was saying. "Are you planning to go, Josie?"

"Maybe tomorrow night," Josie said, pulling a Diet Coke out of the cooler and popping the top.

"I don't think my mother would forgive me if we missed this play," Tom said, giving Becky a hug. "Mom's the theater director at the college, and this is a big musical. She's been working on it for a year."

"Duke's been bragging about Jennifer having a role since before Christmas," Becky added. "He's a proud Papa all right."

SUE MERRELL

Just then the doorbell rang. Dan opened the door. Josie was surprised to see Zach Teasdale standing in her entry hall. She pushed through the kitchen crowd and walked to the front door.

"Zach, what are you doing here?"

The coroner was wearing a camel-hair topcoat, unbuttoned, over a dark blue suit. He looked like a television evangelist making a house call.

"I heard there was a celebration," Zach said with his usual sales-pitch enthusiasm. "I want to do my part. I'm so glad everyone is home safe and sound. Especially Kevin. Where is the little tyke?"

"He's playing with friends," Josie said warily.

"I brought a little welcome home surprise," he said, gesturing toward the door. Bill, one of Zach's football-player-sized assistants, stood outside the glass storm door. He was holding a wrapped package almost as big as he was. Zach leaned toward the storm door with one hand and welcomed Bill into the house.

"Hi, Miss Braun," Bill said, with a nod of his head. "Should I take this to the family room?" Without waiting for an answer, Bill headed through the entry hall toward the kitchen and the stairs that led down to the family room area.

"I ... ah ... you really shouldn't have," Josie stammered. "Kevin doesn't need presents. He has plenty of toys already."

"I know, but us guys can never have enough toys," Zach said. "Isn't that right?" he added, patting Dan heartily on the back. "You must be Josie's father. I heard you were in town. Zach Teasdale. Glad to meet you."

"You heard my parents were in town?" Josie asked.

"Newspaper reporters aren't the only ones who pay attention," Zach said, pumping Dan's hand. "I've got my spies, you know. And I'm glad to hear the kids are all safe and sound, having a good time. Hell of a good result, I'd say. Better than any of us could have imagined. I know how concerned you were. I want to show my full support. Why there he is!"

Kevin stuck his head around the corner at the bottom of the bedroom stairs. "I thought I heard you, Mr. Zach. I haven't seen you for a long time."

"That's right, pardner. We need to make up for lost time. Bill's got a little gift for you."

Kevin's eyes lit up when he saw the huge package. "For me?"

"Go ahead, open it," Zach said.

Josie shuddered. The guests had stopped their visiting. Everyone seemed to be standing around watching as Kevin tore into the blue and red striped wrapping paper.

"Is this what I think it is?" Kevin asked when he had uncovered the illustration on the front of the box. "Is this a real foosball table?"

"The very same," Zach said. "Every boy should have his own foosball table."

171

"Oh, wow!" Timmy said, descending the stairs and helping Kevin rip away the paper.

"I heard how much he enjoyed the one at the fallout shelter," Zach said. "Bill here will set it up for you. The family room, I assume, would be the best place."

"I don't know—" Josie stammered.

"The kid's going to love it," Zach continued.

"Down here," Kevin said, leading the way down the short flight to the family room. Bill carried the box down the stairs, following Kevin.

"Zach, you really shouldn't have."

"I wanted to. It's a small thing. Do I smell pizza?"

"Sure, come in," Josie said, leading the way to the kitchen. Zach took off his coat and handed it to Josie. "I think everyone probably knows Zach Teasdale," she said, introducing him to the kitchen crowd.

"Puts a bit of a damper on a party when the coroner shows up," Greg said, offering his hand and introducing himself.

"I can be a fun guy if I'm not here on business," Zach quipped.

As Josie hung the coat in the closet, her father came up next to her.

"I don't like that guy," he said. "He's too smooth. I think he's a crook."

"I think you're right, Dad, but we haven't had much luck proving it," Josie whispered.

A slice of pizza later, Zach took a seat next to Josie on the living room sofa.

"I'm just glad to find out some Colombian cartel didn't steal that bus," Zach said as he sipped a glass of red wine. "That could have been a real problem. You guys had me scared."

"We did not," Josie said, smiling slightly.

"I know you can't wait to nail me on something," Zach continued. "I rather enjoy your interest."

"You have a strange sense of fun."

"Say, if you see Dukakis, tell him to check his messages on his phone at the office."

"What's up? Something to do with that death at the A-Lab?"

"Yeah. Won't have a full autopsy until tomorrow, but the medical examiner says it's suspicious. There's a blow to the head that isn't consistent with the line of impact. Looks like she was knocked out before she fell."

Josie sat up, suddenly interested. "Oh, God, that could be an international incident."

"It could," Zach said, nodding. "A Russian spy story is even bigger than a Colombian cartel. You reporters will have a blast with that. And you think I have a strange sense of fun."

☼

Brittany padded into the kitchen, rubbing her eyes. Nick was stirring a big pot on the stove.

"What's for dinner?" she asked.

"Oh, hi, Sweetie. I thought you were going to sleep through. I made a big batch of refrigerator stew. The last of the roast beef, some vegetables, a little spaghetti sauce. Whatever was left in the fridge. It was my specialty during my bachelor days."

"Sounds good," Brittany said, opening the refrigerator and snagging a half-gallon of skim milk. As she poured two glasses, she looked up at the clock. "Almost seven. We'll have to hurry to make the play."

"That's OK. We can go tomorrow night if you're too tired."

"No, tomorrow night is Valentine's Day. I want to have a nice dinner in one of those restaurants with a real tablecloth and a band playing so we can dance."

"Dance?"

"It's Valentine's Day. The only night married women get to dance."

"Oh, I see," Nick said, hugging his wife.

Brittany stroked the cleft in Nick's chin. "Besides, I figure if we go to the play tonight, it will get over about ten. Plenty of time to check by the office before the final deadline. Make sure they have all the full moon disasters under control."

"You're making fun of me."

"Not at all. It's important to you, so that's what we'll do."

7:10 PM

After the foosball table was put together, Zach and his trusty assistant left the party. Most of the neighbors returned home as well to get children ready for bed. Josie slipped into her bedroom to call Hoss with an update on the A-Lab death.

"Add that Coroner Zach Teasdale termed the death 'suspicious.' His office is investigating the possibility that the woman might have been unconscious before she fell from the atrium bridge," Josie explained. "They should have more after the autopsy. I'll have Duke follow up tomorrow for the Sunday paper. Call AP and be sure they have the addition. That's going to open a whole can of worms."

As Josie came down from her bedroom, she bumped into Rudy sitting on the stairs.

"The kids are loving that foosball table. The adults too," he said. "How can us ordinary guys compete with big bucks like Teasdale?"

"Compete? You mean in the race to impress Kevin?"

"And his mom."

"No competition there," Josie said, sitting down next to Rudy. "Zach and I have an uneasy truce. I suspect he's involved in all manner of evil, and his money is dirty. But I can't prove it. He gets a kick out of my struggle. He likes appearing to be the hero when I know he's not."

Rudy shook his head. "You have an uncanny degree of acceptance. You don't approve of the man, and yet you allow him in your house, accept a gift. Why didn't you throw him out? Your dad and I would have helped."

Josie chuckled. "You? In clown makeup? I wouldn't invite Zach into my home, but since he showed up, I didn't think it was worth causing a scene in front of the neighbors. He's the county coroner. What if he tells a television station that the editor of the local newspaper kicked him out of her home when he was being a good guy bearing gifts? It would seem to the public that the newspaper is prejudiced against him. Besides, we need him. He gave me a tip for tomorrow's paper. That A-Lab death is looking suspicious. He didn't have to tell me that. He could have told the TV stations first."

"Wow, do you think that scientist was a Russian spy?"

Josie shrugged. "Probably not. It will turn out to be a lover's quarrel or something routine. But it was a pretty dramatic death. I can imagine the movie version already. Right out of James Bond."

174

Josie looked at Rudy. With his black shirt and white face, he looked like a mime. It was hard to have a serious discussion, but she would try.

"Mom says you're the one I should thank for alerting them."

Rudy shrugged. "I was afraid you might be mad."

"I am," Josie said. "I don't like being wrong. But you made the right decision. How did you know?"

"When I lost Theresa and Sarah I couldn't get home to my parents fast enough. They got me through it. You never outgrow that bond."

Becky came into the entry hall pulling Tom behind her. She paused in front of Josie and Rudy on the stairs.

"Now we really do need to get over to the college," she said. "It's almost seven thirty and the play begins at eight. Thanks for having us. It's a great way to end an awful day."

Josie stood up and hugged Becky. Standing on the bottom stair put tiny Josie within reasonable reach of Becky's shoulders. "I was so busy worrying about Kevin that I didn't say a word to comfort you. You must have been scared to death when shots were fired into a crowd like that. It must have been horrible."

"Yeah, it's not a situation I ever want to face again," Becky said, glancing at Tom. "But it turned out OK. That's what matters. I'm so glad Kevin and the other kids are OK."

"This has been a classic full moon fiasco," Tom said, shaking Josie's hand.

"And Friday the 13th, don't forget that," Rudy said, offering his hand to Tom.

"I'm not going to hug you," Becky said, holding up her hands to block Rudy. "You'll get that white makeup all over me."

Josie was so busy chatting with her remaining guests, she didn't hear the phone ring. Suddenly Sally was standing in front of her, dangling the white curly wire of the kitchen phone receiver.

"It's somebody named Sharon, and she sounds upset."

Josie grabbed the receiver. "Hi, Sharon. You must be excited about seeing Jennifer onstage tonight."

"Is Duke there?" Sharon asked.

"Duke? Here? No. Maybe he's still at the office."

"I'm at the office. Hoss said he hasn't been here tonight. He took Jennifer to the college at seven for makeup. He was going to stop by the office to make some calls. He suggested I swing by and pick him up here at seven thirty. It was his idea, but he isn't here!"

Sharon's voice was panicky.

"Now, don't worry," Josie said in a low, calming tone. "I'm sure he's just been delayed somewhere. Why don't you go on over to the theater. I'll have some of the reporters call around. We'll find him and make sure he gets there."

"No. Something's wrong. Duke wouldn't miss this play. He knows how much it means to Jennifer."

Josie looked from Rudy to Becky and Tom. Everyone was hanging on her conversation.

"OK. I'll be right over. We'll make some calls. We'll find him. Becky is on her way to the theater anyway. She can look for him there and call us at the office when he shows up. I'm sure it's just a misunderstanding."

"No," Sharon insisted. "Something horrible has happened."

When Josie hung up the phone, Becky raised her hands in submission.

"Got my orders, Peter Pan. I go to the theater, look for Duke, and call the office."

Tom whispered in Josie's ear, "I'll call the police station and make sure he wasn't involved in an accident."

Becky and Tom headed out the door. Rudy was standing in the kitchen doorway rubbing off his white makeup with a damp cloth.

"If I'm going to go back to the office, I'd better look a little more professional," he said.

"I hate to leave with some guests still here, but Sharon sounded desperate," Josie told her mother. "I want to be supportive."

"I can clean up," Sally said. "You go on."

"I'll only be gone a half hour," Josie said. She ran down the stairs to the family room.

"I need to run to the office for a little while," she told Kevin. "You OK?"

"Sure. Whatever," her son replied, not taking his eyes off of his game.

Josie stood at the base of the stairs and watched him.

"Are you sure you want to do this?" Rudy asked, coming up behind her.

Josie turned and headed up the stairs. "I don't know. What do you think?"

"You're asking me? You're the boss."

"I don't mean about work. I mean about Kevin. You understand this child psychology stuff. Will it be OK for me to leave him so soon after a trauma?"

"Kevin's fine. He didn't have a trauma, you did. Sharon can't fault you if you need to be with your son and your parents tonight. I can help her find Duke. You don't need to go."

Josie shook her head. "Sharon doesn't ask me for help very often. When she does, I think I need to be there for her."

"And you're worried about Duke."

"Yup."

Josie had forgotten that her car was still at work, so she rode back to the office with Rudy.

"You concentrate on finding Brad Snyder, the executive director of the A-Lab," she said as they drove the few miles. "That's the story Duke was working on today, so that must be where he went. Maybe he called in and got the message from Zach that the death looks suspicious. He may have tried to track down Snyder for a comment. Or he went out there. See if the security department can verify whether he's been there. I wish we had a couple of those new mobile phones. Then Duke could carry one with him when he heads off someplace."

"Yeah, those are pretty cool. Expensive though. The bag phones aren't too bad, but if you want to get something smaller, it costs a fortune."

"I'm not sure it would work all the way out at the A-Lab. Those things only work in town."

"One of these days," Rudy said wistfully as they pulled into the parking lot.

"Duke told me he talked to a guy in the Justice Department who was interested in the A-Lab death," Josie said, as they walked toward the back entrance of the building. "I have his number, so I'll try him. Maybe he called Duke because something came up. You'd think Duke would have called Sharon before he ran off somewhere."

"He must have thought it would only take a few minutes," Rudy said as he opened the back door. "Or maybe he got kidnapped."

Josie stared at Rudy, who shrugged and smiled mischievously.

Sharon ran to meet them. "You're here. Thank you."

"Are you sure you don't want to go on to the theater?" Josie asked. "You don't want to miss your daughter's opening night."

"I wouldn't be able to keep my mind on the play," Sharon said. She wrapped her arms around herself as if she were chilled. "Something's terribly wrong. I can feel it in my gut. Duke told me that the buffalo are dying at the A-Lab. Maybe he passed out somewhere from radiation poisoning."

Josie and Rudy exchanged glances. Josie put an arm around Sharon and urged her back into the newsroom.

"Listen, Sharon, don't go ballistic on us. That rumor about the bison being used to indicate a radiation leak is a joke. A big joke."

"I know that, but … but Duke was concerned about it. He said they were loading up the animals on trucks and taking them away. It's got to mean something."

"I'll call out to the A-Lab," Rudy said and headed to his desk. "We'll find out if he's there."

"And I'll call the Justice Department," Josie said. "Duke's got a friend there. Maybe he's talked to him. Why don't you go get a Coke?"

"I don't need a Coke," Sharon said, dropping into Duke's chair. "I tried to call the bridge tender. Duke and Jennifer went to visit him today to clear up that mess from last night."

"What mess last night?" Josie asked as she spun her Rolodex looking for Fred Wheeler's card.

"Oh, I thought Duke would have told you. Jennifer got arrested for bridge riding."

"Jennifer?"

"Yes. I guess Duke didn't want to tell anybody that our precious daughter can make some whopper mistakes."

Josie dialed the number on the card. After three rings, Wheeler's answering machine picked up.

"Mr. Wheeler? This is Josie Braun. I work with Duke Dukakis at the *Jordan Daily News*. He told me he talked to you today about the A-Lab story. Now he's missing. I thought you might know where he is."

Josie left her phone number. Then she walked over to see how Hoss was doing on the Saturday edition.

"Well, Peter Pan, that nuclear explosion in the South Pacific has become a political hot potato. Reagan says it's the Soviets. Says it's a perfect example of why he chose to defy the SALT II Treaty last year. He says the Soviets are constantly growing their arsenal. Gorbachev denies they are doing any nuclear testing in the South Pacific. Never been their testing ground. Always been the testing ground of the US, Britain, and France, so one of those three must be testing a new weapon. The USSR has no choice but to expand its self-defense."

"They sound like a couple of kids fighting on the playground," Josie said as she glanced at the wire copy. "How will you play this, with all we have going on locally?"

"Actually, it ties in fairly well with the death at the A-Lab because of the Russian factor," Hoss said. With a few clicks on his keyboard, he called up the story on his computer screen. "I'm playing the A-Lab death across the top with two refers, one to a wire story on page 2 about the Reagan/Gorbachev blame game. The second refers to a demonstration at the UN where protestors claimed the scientist who died was a Russian spy."

"Oh, wow, the death at the A-Lab has sparked a demonstration at the UN?"

"Yep. And it came up in Congress too. Some of those radical-right conservatives are claiming she was a spy 'caught in the act.' They're calling for action against all working professionals holding Soviet passports. They claim there's an effort by the academic community to undermine our government from inside our borders."

"Good grief, she died only a few hours ago and word has spread to Congress already?"

"They need only one word—Russian."

"So if the A-Lab death is played across the top of the page, what will you do with the busload of kids being returned safely?"

"That's the main art on the page." Hoss rolled his chair over to a second desk covered with paper dummies. He grabbed a photograph out of a vertical file and tossed it on top of the dummies. "Page got a great picture of the bus arriving at the school. Not bad for a one-arm photographer."

Josie picked up the photo and smiled. Kevin wasn't in the picture. He must still have been on the bus. But she recognized the happy kids coming down the steps of the bus and the even happier parents greeting them.

"You know, the missing bus story connects to the top story too," Josie mused. "The kids were hidden in a fallout shelter because the bus driver thought there had been a nuclear explosion in the Chicago area. The whole page is about the tensions of the arms race."

"Sign of the times," Hoss said.

"Josie, your phone is ringing," Sharon called.

Josie punched a couple of buttons on the phone at Hoss's desk to pick up the incoming call across the room. "Newsroom. Can I help you?"

"Nope. I can help you," responded the brusque voice of Fred Wheeler. "What do you mean Dukakis is missing?"

Josie figured her dramatic description of Duke's status would grab Wheeler's attention.

"He failed to show up for an important appointment," Josie said. "We're concerned."

"Have you tried the bars?"

"Duke doesn't drink anymore," Josie said, glancing at Sharon.

Wheeler chuckled. "The bars are full of people who don't drink anymore. Something must have knocked him off the wagon. Maybe he found out that teenage daughter of his isn't a virgin anymore. That can drive a daddy crazy."

"I'm not interested in your personal problems," Josie responded snippily. "I'm making a professional inquiry. Is Duke working with you on the A-Lab murder case?"

"Murder? Who told you it was a murder?"

"We have sources, Wheeler. We know the young woman was unconscious before her body was thrown off the bridge."

"Then ask your sources where Dukakis is. Maybe he wised up and went home to his wife."

"Sharon is the one who reported him missing."

"Ah, yes, Sharon. I remember Mrs. Dukakis. A tough cookie, that one. Believe me, if I knew where Dukakis was, I would send him home just to keep his wife out of my hair. How long has he been AWOL?"

"He dropped his daughter off at the college at seven."

"What? It's not even eight o'clock. You're sounding the alarm when a guy's been on his own for less than an hour?"

"What about the bison? Has your investigation shown any connection between the bison being removed from the A-Lab and the death of the scientist?"

"I'm not answering questions about our investigation. I only offered to help you locate a lost reporter. If I see him, I'll tell him to call you."

With that, Wheeler was gone.

"I don't see why Duke even bothers to talk to Wheeler," Josie said, slamming down the receiver. "The man's an arrogant idiot."

Sharon released a huge sigh of disappointment. "He hasn't seen him, has he?"

"He didn't admit it, but that doesn't mean he doesn't know where Duke is. At least now he knows we're looking for him."

Rudy joined Josie at the copy desk. "I left messages for Snyder," he said. "The county has closed down the whole A-Lab property as a crime scene. The death has officially been termed 'suspicious.' Most of the workers had gone home by the time they made that decision. The collider is not something they can turn on and off, so an underground night team is monitoring that. I suspect Snyder's busy making lists of necessary staff who can have access even during the lockdown. County squad car is at the main entrance. I told the dispatcher we were looking for Duke, and she said she would ask the patrol team to call if they see him."

☼

D uke tried to open his eyes, but it hardly seemed worth the effort.

His head hurt. Bad. His thoughts were muddled. His left cheek and jaw throbbed, but when he tried to touch them, he discovered his arms were secured to his sides. He opened his left eye, but it was too dark to discern much beyond the fact that he was in a confined space.

And that space was moving.

The right side of his head was pressing against the floor of a truck or van. He could hear the whir of tires underneath him. He wasn't bouncing much. The truck was traveling a smooth road, maybe an interstate highway.

Duke tried to remember how he got here. He recalled picking up Reuben Jetter just after he dropped off Jennifer at the college. Jetter was standing alongside the road with his thumb out. His car had broken down. He needed a ride home.

Jetter told some ridiculous story about a werewolf and the full moon. Duke's head throbbed remembering it. After Duke dropped Jetter off at his place, Duke saw it. The werewolf. Or at least something big and hairy, something Jetter probably had mistaken for a werewolf.

Duke saw the shadowy creature in the open area behind the house next door to Jetter's house. There was something about the shape that seemed familiar. Duke had parked along the street and walked back to where he had seen the huge shadowy form. But it was gone.

At least he thought it was gone. Until he was hit over the head, punched in the gut, and slugged in the jaw. Those are just the jabs Duke could recall. The ones before he passed out. Now his shoulder and side hurt too, evidently from blows he couldn't recall. And he'd been stuffed into a vehicle.

Who knew werewolves drove trucks?

8:07 PM

Becky and Tom buzzed into the back door of the *Jordan Daily News* a few minutes after eight.

"I thought you were going to the play," Josie said.

"We'll go tomorrow night," Becky said as she hung her coat on the hall tree at the back of the room. "Besides, Nick and Brittany are there. If Duke shows up, they'll call us."

"You didn't see him?" Sharon said, with only the faintest questioning inflection.

"No, but Tom has a good lead," Becky said, throwing an arm around the police detective perched on a corner of her desk.

Tom smiled. "Yeah, while Miss Reporter here was running all over the theater trying to find somebody who might have seen Dukakis, I went to the coffee shop on the corner. I had quite a few beers tonight, so I figured I'd better sober up a bit. Got to talking to the waitress, Gracie. Soon as I mentioned Dukakis, she said he often picks up his daughter there after class. Said he had been in about four thirty this afternoon. Then she saw him again about seven."

"When he dropped Jennifer off at school," Sharon interjected.

"That's not what Gracie saw," Tom said, his eyes twinkling. "Gracie saw his turquoise Pontiac stopped along the road by the coffee shop. He was picking up a hitchhiker."

"A hitchhiker!" Josie and Sharon exclaimed.

Tom smiled. "Yep. That's when it hit me. I had just seen a tow truck getting ready to load a car alongside the road. I ran out there as he was about to pull away. Showed him my badge and got the owner's name just like that."

"Reuben Jetter," Becky said. "The town crazy man."

"A crazy man!" Sharon exclaimed. "Why would Duke pick up a crazy person?"

"Reuben's not dangerous crazy," Tom said with a shrug. "Not unless you are afraid of Elvis sightings."

"Reuben was at the Holiday Quad today because he thinks Dee Licious is the daughter of Elvis," Becky explained.

"Wasn't it his photo that incriminated the shooter?" Josie asked.

"Yep," Tom said. "He gets a lucky photo once in a while."

"And he picked up the dog that belonged to Dee Licious," Becky added. "He gave the dog a crew cut, so now the star won't have anything to do with it. But he'd rather have the dog than a reward anyway. He's just a goofy guy. His picture with the dog will be in tomorrow morning's paper."

"But where's Duke?" Josie asked.

"I'm on it, Peter Pan," Becky said, moving around her desk and plopping into the chair. "I tried calling Reuben from the theater, but his line was busy. We decided to skip the play and try him again from here."

As Becky dialed her phone, Tom confirmed the code for an outside line so he could use the phone on Nick's desk. "I'll have a patrol check out the area around Jetter's address. See if they spot Duke's car."

Soon Becky was talking to Reuben. Sharon and Josie leaned on Becky's desk following every word.

"I heard that Duke gave you a ride home tonight," Becky said. "Is he still at your place?"

Becky listened for a minute and then shook her head side to side for the benefit of her eavesdroppers. "So how long ago did he drop you off? Did he say where he was headed? A werewolf? Are you sure about that Reuben?"

Josie sighed and walked away from Becky's desk. "This isn't going to get us anywhere. The man is batty."

"Maybe he is more dangerous than you think," Sharon said, following Josie. "He's the last person to see Duke."

Becky hung up and headed to Josie's desk. Tom and Rudy moved in to hear.

"You'll never guess!" Becky exclaimed.

"Reuben saw a werewolf," Josie said without looking up.

"How'd you know?"

"Elvis sightings. Werewolf sightings. Not a lot of difference. What does he say happened to Duke?"

"He said he gave him a ride home about an hour ago. Didn't stop. Said he was going to a play and drove away."

"What about the werewolf?" Sharon asked.

"Well, Reuben said he saw this big hairy monster in the open area behind his neighbor's house. He thinks there might be a werewolf living in the woods there. I told him we might come over and look around his neighborhood tonight. He said to ring the bell three times so he'll know it's us. He's afraid to open the door with a werewolf on the loose."

"Oh, goody. A costume party," Rudy exclaimed. "I've still got the Mr. Baggy Pants suit in my car and a box of grease paint."

"I always wanted to be Count Blackula," Tom said in a Transylvannia accent. He drew one arm over his face to pantomime a cape as he attacked Becky's neck.

Becky giggled and pushed him away. "Get away from me. That was a terrible movie."

Sharon wasn't laughing. "This isn't funny. We've got to go over there, talk to this Reuben person. Maybe he attacked Duke."

Nick's phone rang and Tom grabbed it. All ears turned to the one-sided conversation.

"OK. Anything look suspicious? ... Just leave it. We'll be right there. Thanks a lot."

Tom hung up the phone and slipped his leather coat off the chair. "The patrol says Duke's Pontiac is parked on the street about a block from Jetter's address. Locked. No sign of any problems."

Tom headed toward the door. Becky, Josie, Sharon, and Rudy were at his heels.

He stopped. "I don't think we all need to go," he said. "I'll take Sharon. The rest of you wait here."

"I'm going," Becky said. "Reuben is expecting me."

"I'm not staying behind," Josie said. "It's starting to get interesting."

"And I'm the one with the greasepaint," Rudy said with a mischievous grin.

☼

Duke felt the truck slow down, stop. He opened one eye. A man in the front of the truck was talking to someone. He couldn't hear what they were saying, but the deep voice jogged at his memory. The familiar form in the shadows. The hairy monster Reuben had called a werewolf. Duke didn't get a good look at him, but his gut told him it was Henri Baptista, the Samoan scientist. Not many people are that big. And Baptista had a wild, curly mane of dark hair. The shape he saw near Reuben's house reminded him of Dr. Baptista. And now the voice. The same lilting South Pacific accent. It's Baptista!

Then he remembered the box he had seen, the two men. Just before he got hit. A big box. The memory jolted Duke. Behind one of Reuben's neighbors. Two men loading a huge metal trunk into the back of a van. The big one—the one he now believed to be Baptista—was backing toward the van, holding his end of a box about waist high. But the other one, much smaller, could barely keep the box from dragging on the ground. Too heavy for a body, Duke remembered thinking. That was when he decided to park his car down the street and walk back to investigate. He should have kept driving. He should be at Jennifer's play, not all beat up in the back of some werewolf's van.

The smaller man could have been Samuel Gilbert, Duke thought. It had been the contrast in the size of the two figures that had made Duke stop.

184

They reminded him of the two scientists he had interviewed that morning. Now he could hear them. Gilbert's clipped New Zealand accent with no final consonants, Baptista's sing-song rhythm. And a third voice. Someone formal, asking questions. Like a cop. Like a roadblock.

"I'm sorry, your name isn't on the list," Deputy Edwards said, shining his flashlight on the crisp typewritten sheet attached to his clipboard.

"But we work here," complained the driver. He offered two employee identification badges: Dr. Henri Baptista and Dr. Samuel Gilbert. "There must be some mistake. We have work to do."

"Sorry, only essential services," Edwards said, shining his flashlight into the cab of the van. A solid wall behind the driver's seat blocked any view into the back.

"The National Atomic Particle Accelerator Laboratory has been closed as part of a federal investigation," Edwards explained.

"Federal investigation?" said the passenger who had identified himself as Dr. Gilbert. "Is this about the woman who fell in the atrium?"

"The Russian woman," Edwards said.

Duke mustered all his strength. He had to make a noise. Alert the cop. His arms were bound to his sides. Tape covered his mouth. He tried to move his legs. He was wedged in between boxes, the heavy cargo he had seen them loading. But his feet had a little more space. He kicked the back of one boot against the side of the van. Once, twice, three times.

"What you got in the truck?" Edwards asked, his light bouncing off the partition behind the seats.

"It's part of our study," Baptista said, glancing over his shoulder as another tap sounded against the side of the van.

"Sounds like you got somebody back there," Edwards said. "I'm going to have to ask you to open it up."

Baptista and Gilbert exchanged glances. "It's the monkey," Baptista said. "He's part of our study."

"I like monkeys. Open it up," Edwards said.

Baptista turned off the ignition to the van and held out his key.

"You are welcome to look, if you like, but I must inform you that we are carrying a shipment of radioactive isotopes for our study. The back of the van is specially lined with lead to reduce unnecessary exposure. Personally, I wouldn't open that door without the protection of a hazard suit. I have a great deal of respect for radioactive isotopes."

Edwards looked at the key Baptista offered as though it were glowing in the dark.

"What about the monkey? Isn't he being exposed?"

"The animal has been exposed, yes. It's part of the study."

A Cade County Sheriff's Department car pulled up next to the truck, and Deputy Chet Sanders jumped out.

"Got a problem?" Sanders asked, approaching his partner.

"These two aren't on the list," Edwards said. "They say they've got radioactive cargo they need to deliver."

Sanders peeked into the cab of the van.

"Oh, yeah. I saw your picture in the paper today. You're those scientists from New Zealand," Sanders said. "Glad to meet you. Sorry about this formality. Feds want to control the number of people who go in and out."

"I'm sure there's been some mistake," Baptista said. "If I could just talk to your superiors."

"I think we can take a little leeway here, don't you, Ted?" Sanders said as he took the clipboard from Edwards and handed it to Baptista. "Just add your names to the list. It was pulled together in a hurry. The executive director said he might have forgotten a few folks. As long as we've got the names of everyone who has access, that should satisfy the feds."

Sanders gave his partner a pat on the back and headed into the guard shack. Edwards remained at the truck window to accept the clipboard as Baptista finished signing.

"If anything goes wrong tonight, you two can expect those federal agents to come raining down on you and your monkey, hazards suits and all," Edwards said. "You may have respect for radioactive icicles—"

"Isotopes," Baptista said, starting the engine.

"Yeah, whatever. Personally, I put my respect in the feds. I don't know how it is in New Zealand or wherever you guys are from, but in this country, our federal agents are the best cops anywhere. You better believe nobody messes with the feds and gets away with it. Understand?"

☼

Tom pulled his city-issue beige Taurus into a parking place behind Duke's turquoise Pontiac. Rudy parked his blue Honda Accord across the street. All five members of the unofficial Duke Dukakis search team descended on the Pontiac.

"You got the key?" Tom said to Sharon as he shone his extra-large flashlight into the driver's side window. Sharon unlocked the car. Tom bent down and stuck his head and his flashlight into the car. The faded leather bucket seats were worn at the edges and starting to fray. There were a couple of pens on the floor. Two spiral-bound reporter's notebooks had been tossed on the bench seat in the back with a blue denim backpack.

"That's Jennifer's," Sharon said, opening the back door and reaching for the backpack.

Rudy picked up the reporter's notebooks and started flipping pages. He spotted the word "Snyder" and assumed these were the notes from Duke's interview with the A-Lab director.

"We're about a block from Jetter's address," Tom said, shining his flashlight toward the small frame bungalows that lined the street. "Wonder why he parked all the way down here? Did he visit one of these houses?"

"That's an excellent question," Josie said. "Let's fan out and go door-to-door between here and Jetter's house."

Without waiting to see if her suggestion would be followed, Josie started down the sidewalk toward the bungalow closest to Duke's car. She rapped on the door. When the door opened, she was enveloped in a hospitable glow of light. Tom, Becky, Rudy, and Sharon stood beside Duke's car watching Josie. They couldn't hear her questions, but the conversation seemed friendly enough.

After a few minutes, Rudy started walking up the sidewalk to the next house. He looked back over his shoulder. "You want to come with me, Sharon?"

"Tom and I will get the ones across the street and meet you at Reuben's house," Becky said. "He lives in that little brick one with all the lights on at the end of the block."

The team worked their way down the street asking if anyone had seen Duke. Most people were familiar with the popular newspaper column. Some wanted to chat about their favorite story or a time they met Duke. But no one had seen the missing reporter. Several had comments about "Crazy Jetter." No one had seen a werewolf or anything remotely like a werewolf.

"Werewolves don't really exist," a small white-haired woman confided to Josie.

"I know," Josie replied. "We're just checking out a rumor. Asking if anyone saw anything unusual. Keeping an open mind."

Josie, Sharon, and Rudy finished their side of the street and crossed to the small dark frame building next to Jetter's house. Tom and Becky were up on the porch, knocking on the door, but all the windows were dark. It appeared no one was home. There was no vehicle in the driveway that curved around the side of the building. Josie, Sharon and Rudy wandered up the driveway toward a large detached garage in the rear.

"There's a flickering light back there. Like a welding machine or something," Rudy said.

"You can hardly see that garage from the street because of those cedar trees," Josie said.

Rudy knocked on the side door to the garage. He put his ear to the door. "Sounds like a bad fluorescent bulb. Flickering on and off."

"What's this?" Josie bent over to pick up something her foot had kicked in the gravel driveway. "It's a notebook. It looks like one of Duke's notebooks."

Sharon grabbed the notebook out of Josie's hand. "He was here. Duke was at this house."

Tom and Becky came down the steps from the front porch and walked around to join the others.

"Nobody's home," Becky said. "Let's go talk to Reuben."

"Duke was here. He was in this driveway," Sharon said, waving the notebook.

"Where did you find that?" Tom asked, shining his flashlight down the dark driveway.

Josie pointed out the spot where she kicked the notebook. Tom examined the ground with his flashlight. It was hard to see much in the pattern of the thin layer of gravel. Some tire marks. Some footprints. A few dark splotches that might be flecks of blood, but not enough to be alarming. Sharon shook the doorknob on the garage.

"He could be in here. They could be holding him captive. We need to break in," she announced.

Tom shone his flashlight on the door.

"Not exactly a high-security lock," he said. "Wouldn't keep out a determined high school kid, let alone a well-equiped crook."

"Can't you break in to save him? You're a cop," Sharon said, shaking the knob again.

"There's not enough cause to justify breaking the door down," Tom said, pulling Sharon away from the door. "Let's go talk to this Jetter dude. He's the last one who saw Duke."

"I don't think so," Josie said. "That notebook means Duke came down this driveway after he dropped off Jetter."

"And the way the trees are, he might not have been able to see down the driveway from Jetter's house," Rudy added, pointing to the row of cedars. "But once he drove past the driveway entrance, past the trees, he would be able to see better between the houses. That's why he parked and walked back. Something caught his eye as he was driving away. Maybe the dreaded werewolf."

Tom shook his head and chuckled.

"There's not a good cause to break into this garage," he said. "All we have is a notebook dropped outside. If you break in, that's a crime. If I break in, it ruins any case I try to make. I can't allow it."

Tom started walking away. "If you want clues, go back and look through Duke's car. You have legal access to that vehicle, Sharon. You'll probably find everything you need. In the meantime, I'll be talking to Reuben. He's such a storyteller, I'll probably be tied up a half-hour or more. Coming with me, Becky?"

Becky looked at Tom and smiled. "No, I think I'll help Sharon go through Duke's car. Come on, guys."

Becky led the way down the street. The others hurried to catch up.

"We've already looked through Duke's car. There wasn't anything," Sharon said, fishing her keys out of her purse.

"I really think we need to look in that garage," Josie said. "That's where the answers are."

"Shh," Becky said, linking arms with Sharon and Josie. "We'll break into the garage after we get the tools out of Duke's car," she whispered. "You have to learn to read between the lines when Tom starts talking legal stuff. He's giving us time to break into the garage while he interviews Reuben."

"The toolbox," Sharon exclaimed. "Duke has a toolbox in the trunk. There's probably something in there we could use to pick the lock."

"Or pry open a window," Rudy added.

"Let's just drive Duke's car back into the driveway," Sharon said.

"No, park it on the street, blocking the driveway," Josie said. "Then if the owner comes back home, we'll have a little warning."

Josie volunteered to stay with the car and watch for the resident to return. The others headed to the garage with a selection of screwdrivers for door or window opening. Josie said she would honk the horn if someone came and wanted to get into the driveway. That would give enough warning to evacuate the garage while Josie moved the car.

A little patient jiggling of a small screwdriver and Becky opened the door.

"There are benefits to growing up in the 'hood," she said as she held the door open for the others. Rudy flicked on the light switch. The room was scary neat. Two long counters were bare except for a glass cage of some sort. Cabinets overhead were marked with a jumble of letters and numbers. A code perhaps.

"Reminds me of chemistry class," Rudy said, looking around.

"Yeah, but where are all the beakers and chemicals?" Sharon said.

"No wonder they don't need a good lock on the door. These boxes are locked with some sort of number combination," Becky said.

"Ah, now I feel more at home," Rudy said, standing over an old wooden desk piled with papers. "Looks like math problems." He picked up one of the sheets of paper, then looked through the papers while Becky and Sharon opened the cabinets that weren't locked.

"Oh, my God," Sharon said, looking in one of the lower cabinets. "These containers say flammable. This looks like enough explosive to make a bunch of bombs."

Becky came to inspect.

"Now I remember. Reuben told me a story once about a mad scientist who started a fire in his garage last summer. Maybe this is where the mad scientist lives."

"Ya think?" Sharon exclaimed. "It worries me that somebody known as 'Crazy Jetter' is calling a scientist 'mad.' This neighbor must be super looney."

"Look at this," Rudy said, waving a large detailed drawing. "It looks like plans to build some sort of device."

"But there isn't a single clue that says Duke was here," Sharon said. "I guess we were wrong."

"Yeah, we need to remember what we're looking for," Becky said. "We need something that will tell us where Duke went."

"Let's get out of here," Rudy said, folding the drawing up and sticking it in his pocket. "I've seen enough." He slipped out of the door and headed for the car, leaving Sharon and Becky to turn off the lights and close up.

"Whoa, is that a space suit?" Sharon said, pointing to a white coverall with hood hanging behind the door.

Becky examined it closer. "Looks like a klansman on steroids

Rudy found Josie standing beside the car.

"Here, take this," Josie said handing Rudy a gun. "We might need it before the night is over."

"Where did you get this?" Rudy said, turning the weapon over in his hand with two fingers, as if examining a dead bird.

"It's Duke's. He told me he had one under the seat."

"I don't know anything about guns," Rudy said, handing the weapon back to Josie. "You want a gun; you carry it."

"I don't know anything about guns either," she said, pushing the weapon back toward Rudy. "You carry it. You're the guy."

"That's the most sexist thing I've ever heard," Rudy said, refusing to touch the gun. "Put it back under the seat."

"Give me that before somebody gets hurt," Sharon said, grabbing the gun. "Becky went to get Tom. I don't think a cop is going to appreciate any of us being armed."

"Did Duke teach you how to shoot?" Josie asked.

"No, but how hard can it be?" Sharon said, stuffing the gun inside her cloth shoulder bag. "We played cowboys and Indians when I was a kid. Guns haven't changed much."

Tom joined them. "I don't see Duke, so I guess it's safe to assume he hasn't turned up."

"No, and we didn't find any clues, either," Josie said.

"Well, Jetter tells me the guy who rents this house is one of the scientists out at the A-Lab. Duke must have gone out there with him. It may be something to do with that girl who died." Tom looked over his shoulder toward Jetter's house. Becky was standing on the porch talking with him. Her high-pitched laugh could be heard every now and then.

"I need to go out to the A-Lab to look for Duke. But with the added security, they're not going to let the rest of you in," Tom said. He pulled his shoulders back and his voice took on a commanding air. "Sharon, you take Becky with you in Duke's car. Go back to the newspaper office. I will have Duke call you there when I find him. Rudy, you might as well take Josie home. She's got company."

He put a hand on Josie's shoulder. "We'll track Duke down. He just can't let the story go. You know how he is. Like a dog with a bone. If I find him in the jaws of a werewolf, I'll call you. Otherwise, you can sleep peacefully. It's under control."

Tom gave a quick glance toward Becky, who was still talking to Jetter, and then headed swiftly down the sidewalk toward his car. Josie glanced at Sharon.

"Go on," Sharon said with a half smile. "Tom's right. Duke got sucked into a story. I didn't think he would dare disappoint that darling daughter of his, but I guess he's missed her recitals and birthdays before. This is really nothing new. I'll drop Becky off at the newspaper office and go see the end of the play."

"Come on, Josie," Rudy said, jerking his head in the direction of his car. "We're spinning our wheels here. I can take you home or drop you at the office to get your car."

Sharon headed toward Jetter's house. "I want to meet this crazy man," she said. Josie released a deep sigh. She looked at Sharon and Becky and the lights of Jetter's house on one side and the shadows of Tom and Rudy walking in the opposite direction down the sidewalk. Nothing about this felt right. They were missing something obvious. She looked up. The round full moon was high now, swimming in a sea of clouds. A cool wind was blowing. Josie pulled her collar around her neck. This was no time for indecision. In her heart, she knew what she wanted: to go home and watch Kevin sleep. Safe and warm.

"Thank you, Lord," she whispered and headed down the sidewalk to catch up with Rudy.

Sharon squeezed next to Becky on the small front stoop of Reuben Jetter's brick bungalow. Her jaw was set, her eyes narrowed, as if she was dealing with a junior high con artist.

"Oh, hi," Becky said. "Reuben, I want you to meet Sharon, Duke's wife."

"I want to know what happened to him," Sharon blurted. "You were the last person to see him."

191

"Me?" Jetter squealed. "Like I told Miss Judd, he dropped me off. Gee, must be two hours ago. He drove away. I watched his lights go."

"Tell her about the werewolf," Becky said. "Listen to this, Sharon. Tell her what you told me."

"You ladies want to come inside? Have some hot chocolate?"

"Oh, we can't," Becky said. "Tom is waiting."

She glanced toward the street and realized that the others had left.

"Na, Tom's gone," Sharon said. "Sure, we'll come in for a minute, Mr. Jetter. It's cold out here."

"Tom left me?" Becky said, following Sharon and Reuben into a cluttered living room.

"Yep. He turned into a cop and left us civilians behind," Sharon replied. "I'm in charge of taking you back to the office."

Sharon surveyed the dirty clothes, empty coffee cups, and newspapers strewn around the room. It was messy but not as bad as a teenager's room. She was hoping to spot something of Duke's, something to prove he didn't just drop off this man and drive a block away. Sharon craned her neck to look down the hall. She could see an unmade bed at the end. Every space seemed to have a light on.

Reuben was chattering about the moon's gravitational pull and the tides as he gathered a jacket off the back of a chair and an armload of papers off the seat.

"Sit down. Sit down. I don't get much company," he interjected between his confident explanations of lunar effects.

Sharon smiled to herself while keeping a wary eye on her fast-talking host. Why did people think the moon was bigger when it was full? The moon doesn't change size. The increase in tides during a full moon or new moon is because the sun, moon, and earth are aligned. The combined pull of the sun and the moon affect the tides. Any seventh-grade science student knows that.

Sharon knew the same side of the moon always is illuminated by the sun. When the moon is full, the earth sees all of this illuminated circle. But as the moon makes its monthly orbit around the earth, less and less of this illuminated side faces the earth, creating the half moon and crescent shapes. The moon doesn't really get smaller and larger; the earth views smaller and larger portions of the illuminated side. The phases of the moon are all a matter of perspective.

But Sharon didn't correct Reuben's assumption that the "big moon" exerted greater pull on "blood flow," which somehow explained the transformation of a werewolf. She was listening for some clue in his nonstop rant, some indication of what really happened to Duke.

Becky stood by the window, looking down the quiet street. Clouds were covering the moon now, and the street seemed to be getting darker and more foreboding every minute. Becky couldn't believe Tom had left her behind.

What worried her the most is that he hadn't trusted her enough to tell her his plans. This wasn't the kind of openness she expected from Tom. But he knew she would read between the lines. If he didn't want Sharon and the reporters tagging along, it must mean he was beginning to suspect danger. He was afraid something had happened to Duke. He didn't want Sharon along if he discovered Duke had been hurt.

But why hadn't he been honest with her? Why didn't he just ask her to distract Sharon? Because Tom knew Becky and her cohorts wouldn't walk away from a developing story. Especially one that involved Duke. He was on the trail of something.

Becky turned to see Reuben pouring hot water into three mismatched mugs clustered on his small green Formica table. Sharon was seated at the table. She pulled one of the mugs closer and stirred the hot cocoa mix in the cup while Reuben continued talking nonstop.

"Reuben," Becky said as she approached the table, "your neighbor. The scientist. Does he live there alone?"

"Oh, no. He has a wife and two daughters," Reuben replied as he handed Becky one of the mugs and a spoon. "But that's just the thing. They left last Saturday."

"Left?" Becky repeated.

"Yeah. Early in the morning. A taxi came. I think she was leaving him."

"What makes you say that?" Becky asked as she stirred her cocoa.

"They took a lot of luggage. And it's the middle of the school year. They had to take the girls out of school. And Dr. Gilbert cried. He didn't want the girls to see it. He hugged them and smiled and waved goodbye. Then after the taxi was gone, he cried. He went right back inside, but I saw he was crying. Wiped his eyes with the back of his hand."

Becky sipped her cocoa. If the scientist's wife left him, maybe he was distraught. Maybe he would go on a rampage. Maybe he was planning to blow himself up. Or blow up the A-Lab. Or maybe the wife left because he was having an affair. Maybe he was involved with someone at work. The girl who died?

Sharon asked permission to use the bathroom, and Reuben directed her down the hall. King, the little dog that had been curled up on one of the coats thrown over the sofa, jumped down and followed her. When Sharon was sure no one was looking but the snoopy dog, she continued past the bathroom and inspected the bedroom for any sign of Duke. She also looked into the spare bedroom—Reuben's shrine to Elvis. The room was lit up like Vegas with neon signs flashing and posters of the King covering three walls. The fourth was a timeline of snapshots—the early ones cut from magazines, followed by fading Polaroids and square Instamatic prints. Photos from the funeral and the Graceland grave were in the center of the timeline. After the funeral, the timeline continued as flush as before with "sightings" tacked up with push pins winding back and forth on the wall. The display stopped with a picture from this morning's event at Holiday Quad.

In the corner, an Elvis mannequin modeled a glittery white costume with flowing cape. Scattered on tables were scrapbooks of tickets, posters, autographed photos, and various other mementoes.

Back in the kitchen, Becky listened to Reuben's theories about werewolves. She took a long sip of cocoa and set down her cup. "So this werewolf. You said you saw it through the trees. Could it have been Dr. Gilbert you saw? Maybe with a furry coat?"

"Dr. Gilbert? Oh, no. Dr. Gilbert is a small man. Smaller than me. He doesn't even have enough hair to cover his head. No, the werewolf is huge. Bigger than any man. And wild looking. Scary."

Becky shook her head. "Listen, Reuben, we talked to your neighbors. Nobody remembered seeing a big hairy monster. Could it have been an animal? A bear perhaps?"

"Bears hibernate in the winter," Reuben said, gathering the mugs from the table and taking them to the sink. "I know everybody in town thinks I am seeing things. I didn't expect to see a hairy monster, as you put it. I've never reported seeing a werewolf before. It's not like my sightings of Elvis. I've been following him for years. But this was different. It was just there. In the moonlight. I didn't go looking for a werewolf. I took the dog out in the driveway to tinkle, and there he was. Standing in the trees, like I said."

"Did the dog bark at him?"

"Yeah, sure. But I quickly brought King back into the house. I didn't call the police. I wasn't going to mention it to anyone because I didn't believe it myself. But then I went out to get some dog food and stuff for little King, and the stupid car just died. Deader than a doornail. I called a tow truck, but it was cold out there waiting. Then Mr. Dukakis pulls up and offers me a ride. One thing led to another, and I told him about the werewolf."

"What was his reaction?"

"Oh, you know. He didn't believe it, but he didn't tell me I was crazy. He just nods and smiles and listens. You know how he is. You can talk to Mr. Dukakis about anything."

Sharon returned, carrying the dog.

"This sure is a friendly little fellow," she said. "He was right at my heels every step of the way."

Sharon set the dog on the couch and picked up her coat. "Appreciate your hospitality, Mr. Jetter, but I want to get back to the college and catch the end of the show. You ready to go, Beck?"

"Sure," Becky replied as she took the coat Sharon handed her. "One more thing, Reuben. Was Dr. Gilbert at home when you saw the werewolf?"

"I told you. It wasn't Dr. Gilbert. What I saw wasn't anything like Dr. Gilbert."

"I know. But was Dr Gilbert home? Was a light on or his car in the driveway?"

"Come to think of it, there was a blue van in the driveway. One of the trucks from the A-Lab. You know, the kind that have the hazard sign on the back. Transporting Radioactive Material."

Becky and Sharon walked back to Duke's car, which was still parked across the driveway to Dr. Gilbert's house.

"If you are expecting a fast trip back to the office and your car, you might as well get out now and start hitchhiking," Sharon announced as she put the key in the ignition and started the engine.

"Why? Where are you headed?" Becky asked. She barely had time to yank the passenger door closed before Sharon pulled out of the parking spot.

"The A-Lab, of course. That's where they've taken Duke. If radioactive materials are involved, we may be too late already."

"Oh, don't worry about the label on the back of a truck," Becky said, fastening her seat belt. "That's just a precaution. Doesn't mean the truck actually was carrying anything radioactive. And if Duke left with Dr. Gilbert, it doesn't mean he was kidnapped. Maybe he's just following the story. Too busy to get to a phone to call you."

Sharon shot Becky a knowing glance. "You don't actually believe that poppycock, do you?"

"No," Becky admitted. "I'm just trying to be a supportive friend."

"Speaking of friends, do you realize how looney that Jetter is? He's got a shrine to Elvis, with a life-size model and everything."

"I'm not surprised," Becky said with a shrug.

The women rode along quietly, the interior of the car illuminated in quick flashes by the cars they met on the two-lane highway. A stormy sky had swallowed the moon. Tiny snowflakes littered the windshield. Sharon looked straight ahead. Intent. Determined.

Becky hesitated, but she wanted to be sure. "Sharon, if we go out to the A-Lab, you've got to be prepared for the worst. There, I said it. If Duke has been hurt and you get all hysterical, we're going to end up in as much danger as he is. You've got to keep your head."

Sharon shot Becky a quick look in the dark.

"Listen, you skinny child. I've been through a lot worse with Duke. A lot worse. Get a few years under your belt before you start telling me about hysterical women. Wives and mothers have a toughness you little girls can only begin to imagine."

"Oh, I know," Becky said, retreating a little from Sharon's fierce snarl. "I'd rather go into battle with an angry mother at my side than any marine in boots. But I want you to know we don't need to do this. The cops are on it. If

Duke is in danger, they are his best bet. We can go back to the college. Pick up Jennifer after the play. She needs you."

"Jennifer's not a baby. She's grown up tough. I need to get out to the A-Lab and find Duke. I know how cops are. They are more interested in the greater good than rescuing some curious reporter who stuck his nose where it shouldn't be."

"OK," Becky said with a satisfied sigh. "Turn right at the next road."

"What? The A-Lab is up ahead, on Clark Road."

"I know. But the place is on lockdown. They'll have guards at the main gate. We're going in the back way."

Sharon looked at her passenger. "Won't this back way be blocked as well?"

"Could be. But you've got to understand the politics between the feds and the county cops. The feds are calling the shots, but the locals are doing the work. They aren't going to volunteer information about a back entrance, because then they'd have to come up with another squad to man it. And they figure this federal lockdown is overkill anyway. There are a couple of roads back here that service the barn where the buffalo supplies are kept."

"Duke said the buffalo were shipped out."

"All the more reason the feds won't think about this entrance."

9:10 PM

Tom showed his police ID to Deputy Edwards at the A-Lab entrance. "I'm looking for one of the scientists who works here. A guy named Dr. Gilbert. Has he been here tonight?"

The name didn't ring a bell instantly with Edwards, so he grabbed the clipboard off the hook. Even in the bright light of the guard shack, the handwritten scrawls at the bottom of the sheet were hard to decipher. But he noticed the flowery "G" at the beginning of the last name and something clicked.

"Yeah, he's here. Came in at eight-fourteen with a really big dude named Baptista. British sounding but wild hair like Einstein. They were in a blue A-Lab panel van. Said they were delivering some radioactive ice."

"Yeah, that would be them. Was another guy with them? Dark wavy hair, gray at the temples, and a bushy mustache?"

As Tom described his friend's face, his hand automatically went to his own thin mustache. Duke often teased him about the "razor cut" under his nose. "When you gonna grow some facial hair?" Duke would say. But Tom could never understand how Duke could put up with so much hair on his lip. Didn't it get in his food? And ice. Tom remembered how Duke's mustache would get icy on a cold day just from the moisture in his breath. If Duke was outside right now, his mustache would look like Jack Frost.

Tom realized he hadn't heard the deputy's response.

"Sorry, what did you say about the third man? The one with the mustache?"

"Nah, there were just two of them. And a monkey. They said they had a monkey in the back of the van."

"A monkey?"

"I never actually saw the animal. Could have been your mustache man back there for all I know. He was making noise. Trying to get attention. I was suspicious and wanted to see for myself. That's when they said they were carrying radioactive cargo. They are up to something, aren't they? I told my partner those guys were trouble."

"Good instincts," Tom said. "So any idea where they were headed on the A-Lab property?"

Edwards surveyed the dark landscape. One well-lit winding road led to a glowing pot of gold: the striking A-shaped building at the center of the campus. Even in the distance, it shone like a space-age palace.

"The headquarters, I assume," Edwards said with a poke of his thumb. "It's the only place with lights on."

"How about the federal agents and the executive director, Snyder? Are they here?"

"Yes, sir. Snyder is in the main building. But I'm not sure about the location and number of federal agents. They've been coming and going all night. You want me to get Snyder on the line? Tell him you're headed that way?"

"Yeah. That would be good. And we might need backup. You have squads stationed at the back gates?"

Edwards' jaw dropped. "No, actually, sir, the traffic is too light out here. My partner has been driving the perimeter and interior roads checking for anything unusual."

"Shit. So we know Gilbert drove in fifty-five minutes ago, but we don't know if he drove out the back way. We don't know where in the hell he is."

King jumped down from his perch on the back of the sofa, where he enjoyed looking out the window. Reuben was in his recliner, drinking a beer and nodding off during commercials. He awoke to hear King whining and pawing at the front door.

"What's up, pal? Someone coming up the walk?"

Reuben turned on the porch light and peered through the window. He didn't see anyone, but King pawed at the door and barked in short, high yips.

"OK. If you need to go out, I'll take you. Let me grab a coat. It looks really cold out there, and it's snowing again."

As soon as Reuben opened the door, King ran down the steps, across the driveway and into the row of cedars.

"Damn it, dog," Reuben said, running after the little pooch. He paused at the edge of the trees. "Come out of there, King. Come on, boy. No telling what you'll find in there. Come out."

Reuben was afraid to venture into the cluster of trees, so he walked along the perimeter. Without a flashlight, he couldn't see where the dog had gone.

"Here, boy. Come get a treat," Reuben called weakly. At the end of the cluster of trees, Reuben could see Dr. Gilbert's house. There was a light on in one of the downstairs rooms toward the back of the house. The kitchen? And a flash of light in an upstairs room. An eerie ghost-like light flitting from one window to the next. Reuben shuddered.

"Come on King, get back in the house." Reuben ventured down the driveway until he was almost at the back door of Gilbert's place. Yes, the light was on in the kitchen. Dr. Gilbert must be home. But there was no car in the driveway. King was standing at the base of the steps leading to the back door, yapping frantically.

"Come on, King," Reuben said, grabbing the pooch. "Leave Dr. Gilbert alone." Suddenly the kitchen light went out, and the house was dark again. Reuben held the dog close to his chest, standing as still as he could with his knees shaking. A finger pulled the kitchen curtain to one side. Reuben held his breath. King gave a low growl. The kitchen curtain fell back into place.

Reuben backed up slowly, stepping along the side of the garage until he reached the dark wall of cedars at the property line. He ducked between two trees and ran back to his place as fast as he could.

The kitchen door opened. Josie stuck her head out. The garage and the driveway were dark and still. She pulled her head back inside. A beam from a flashlight found her face.

"What are you doing? Leaving me here alone?" Rudy asked.

"I thought I heard someone outside," Josie said. "But it looks quiet. Did you find anything upstairs?"

"Three bedrooms. One was too hard, one was too soft, and one was just right," Rudy said as he turned on the kitchen light and turned off the flashlight. "But I didn't find Goldilocks or Duke, for that matter. Looks like a typical family home. Gilbert must have a couple of kids, girls, from the look of frilly pink bedspreads. Closets are a little bare though. Suspect the family may have returned to New Zealand."

"That's not good," Josie said. "I looked down in the basement. Just a washer and dryer. Not even much in the way of toys or storage stuff. No sign of a struggle. No Duke."

"That's probably a good sign," Rudy said, opening the refrigerator. "I just didn't want to leave with this stone unturned. Seemed like we had to look under it."

"I agree," Josie said, surveying the contents of the refrigerator: mostly condiments, a few cans of Coke, and a jug of milk. She reached for the milk, sniffed, and put it back. Rudy looked at her, shook his head, and reached for a can of Coke.

"You can't steal something out of Gilbert's refrigerator," Josie said as Rudy popped the top.

"We can't pick the lock on the back door either, but we did," Rudy said, taking a long swig of Coke. "Man, I was getting withdrawal. Ever since I stopped drinking booze, I've been addicted to Coke. Guess it's the lesser of the evils."

"You were a drinker?"

"Of course, I was a drinker. How did you think I got to be a sponsor in AA? You knew I was Duke's sponsor. Remember a couple of years ago when you and Sharon found Duke and me having a late-night coffee at Denny's? He told you right then and there that I was his sponsor in AA."

"Yes, I remember. But I just never thought of you as a drinker."

"It was the only thing that made sense after my wife died. Lost two years. Then a friend pointed me to AA. Been sober twelve years. Never even think about it anymore. But don't deny me a six-pack of Coke every day. Did you call your house?"

"Yeah. Mom was still up but Dad and Kevin were asleep. I told her to go to bed. I told her I'd explain in the morning. She didn't say much, but I could tell she was angry with me. I'll get the lecture tomorrow. A mother's place, and all that."

"What did Hoss have to say?"

"Donna's the reporter tonight. She added a couple of quotes to Duke's story about the lockdown at the A-Lab. She put a call in to Wheeler's office, but no one has called back. And they haven't heard a word from Duke."

"I was afraid of that," Rudy said. He reached into his pocket and pulled out a handful of coins.

"I don't know much about chemistry, but from what I remember, 'Co' means Cobalt, a metal," Rudy said as he dropped the coins into the change jar he spied on the windowsill behind the sink. That would cover the Coke he was taking.

"Cobalt? Isn't that the pretty blue dye?"

"Yeah, they make dyes from cobalt salts," Rudy said, pulling a folded paper out of his pocket. "But according to this drawing, Gilbert designed some device. It's inside a case made out of cobalt. I found a receipt from a local metal fabricating shop. He had them make a case out of cobalt."

"So what difference does that make?"

"This isn't a fancy rich man's house. Why is he spending all that money on making a device with a fancy cobalt case? It sounds a little scary."

"Yeah, isn't cobalt radioactive? Isn't that the stuff they use for radiation treatments for cancer?" Josie asked.

"That's one isotope of cobalt," Rudy said. "But I think I remember some sort of recipe for an atomic bomb that used cobalt. When the bomb goes off, it turns the cobalt into this really bad radioactive isotope that poisons the area for years."

"Why are you talking about an atomic bomb?" Josie asked, studying the drawing. "You're not saying the device described in this plan is a bomb, are you? An atomic bomb?"

"I think it's possible," Rudy said.

Josie picked up the receiver of the phone hanging on the kitchen wall, dug out a small address book from her purse, and started dialing.

"Who are you calling now?" Rudy asked.

"Fred Wheeler. He's not my favorite fellow, but if you are talking nuclear bomb, we've got to tell the feds."

"I'm not saying he's building a nuclear bomb. That would be pretty advanced even for a nuclear physicist. But maybe a traditional bomb with some radioactive components."

"Whatever. This is way out of our league."

"I could be wrong."

"You could be right."

Wheeler's answering machine kicked in.

"Mr. Wheeler, Josie Braun. I thought you might want to know about a possible nuclear bomb threat. In our search for Duke, we've come across some plans for an explosive device using cobalt. We believe Samuel Gilbert, one of the scientists at the National Atomic Particle Accelerator Laboratory, might be building such a device."

Josie hung up and stared at the phone on the wall.

"Unless I miss my guess, that's one call Wheeler will return."

Rudy and Josie stared at the phone, but it didn't ring.

"You didn't give him this phone number," Rudy said. "He's probably calling the office."

"No, those federal agents have a caller ID gizmo on their phones."

"You think that gizmo tells him we're calling from the Gilbert residence?"

Josie stared at Rudy with wide-eyed alarm. Rudy rolled his eyes and grinned. Josie broke into a laugh.

"We'd better get out of here," she said, opening the back door.

"Right behind you, Peter Pan," Rudy said, turning off the light.

A giant white-clad figure burst through the doorway with Duke's squirming body thrown over one shoulder. It took slow, heavy steps to the center of the room, bent over, and laid Duke on the floor.

Duke was a duct tape mummy. Several bands were wrapped around his arms and torso, several more around his legs. A final band covered his mouth.

Looking up from the floor, Duke could hear the whoosh of a noisy backpack evidently pumping cooling oxygen into the heavy vinyl hazard suit that stood over him.

"I thought we were going to leave him in the van," Dr. Gilbert said.

Duke turned his head and saw Gilbert standing in front of a control panel of lights and switches. Gilbert wasn't wearing his lab coat. He looked relaxed in jeans and a sweatshirt, like someone who might ask you if you wanted a beer.

The noisy motor stopped and Henri Baptista lifted his hood off and laid it on a table. Baptista's hair was pulled back into a ponytail, but unruly ringlets were plastered to the sweat that rimmed his forehead.

"Little bastard somehow managed to open the van door and get to the floor. He was inch-worming his way out of the building," Baptista said.

Gilbert laughed. "Gotta give the man credit for trying. I'm afraid we haven't been too accommodating to our guest. Can't we take that tape off his mouth now? We're a mile from the nearest building. No one would hear him if he yelled."

"Why should we? You planning to serve tea?"

"No, but he's a reporter. He's bound to have questions. What's the point if we don't tell people why this needs to be done?"

"The consortium in Auckland will read the announcement. That was the plan. It won't do any good to tell this guy."

Duke rolled on the floor so he could get a better look at Gilbert and Baptista. Their banter was confrontational, but their body language was friendly. These two were definitely in this thing together, whatever this thing was.

"You about set in here?" Baptista asked, looking over the wiring Gilbert was connecting.

"Should be ready for the midnight deadline, just as we planned."

"Yeah, but we didn't plan on him," Baptista said, hooking a thumb in Duke's direction. "Or a body in the lobby. With all the extra attention, I think we should go for ignition as soon as possible. They'll catch up in Auckland."

Gilbert look flustered. "We have a plan. When you start changing the plan, that's when errors occur."

"We've got time to double-check everything. All the rods have been pulled."

"You're sure?"

"I'm sure. I'm getting out of this sauna suit," Baptista said as he ripped the Velcro closure and dropped the top half of the suit. Then he leaned one hand against the table as he stepped out of the bottom half. "That's one thing I won't miss. Hazard suits."

Gilbert looked up from the control board. "Well, I suppose, strictly speaking, it is pretty much optional at this point."

Baptista grunted. "I like to keep my options open. Just in case."

"Always a good idea," Gilbert agreed.

Duke rolled as forcefully as he could, running into the table leg next to Baptista. He didn't like being ignored.

"What's your problem, man?" Baptista shouted and kicked Duke in the side.

"That was unnecessary," Gilbert said, running to Duke's aid. "The man just wants some recognition. It's the least we can do."

Gilbert lifted Duke by the shoulders and propped him against a support beam in the middle of the room. Duke got his first good look at his surroundings: a metal pole barn with concrete floor. He didn't see any windows, just a door on his right that stood ajar. It must lead into the garage area where the van was parked. Several wooden tables were scattered around the large room. One held the control panel Gilbert was wiring. Another had a couple of computers with the familiar green MS-DOS numbers glowing on black screens. Baptista dropped into a comfortable-looking rolling desk chair in front of the computers.

Gilbert grabbed hold of a corner of the tape on Duke's cheek and gave a quick yank. Duke gasped involuntarily at the sting and the rip of several mustache hairs. His arms jerked but were bound firmly to his sides.

"Perhaps a drink of water will help," Gilbert said, reaching for a clear plastic bottle in a box under the control table. He twisted off the top and tipped the bottle against Duke's stinging lips. Duke swallowed a few gulps as the excess poured over his chin and onto the collar of his leather jacket.

"Where are we?" Duke said softly.

"This is technically Lab 67. The office of a solar panel project," Gilbert said, rising to his feet and looking around the room. "It's in the wopwops."

"That's New Zealand–speak for the sticks," Baptista said, looking over his shoulder.

"Yes, we are quite a ways from the main building, surrounded by a sea of solar panels," Gilbert continued. "You can scream as loud as you like. No one will hear."

"Solar panels?" Duke said. "What are you doing, running an illegal power grid?"

Gilbert chuckled. "That's a good idea, don't you think, Henri?"

The big man in the chair grunted and swiveled to face his computer screens.

"You must be breaking some enormous elephant excrement law, else your big bad buddy here wouldn't have tied me up like a bundle of twigs," Duke said, regaining some of his normal spunk.

"Actually, we're just borrowing Lab 67 because of the remote location," Gilbert said, glancing around the room. "It allows us time to complete our project uninterrupted."

"And reduce casualties," Baptista mumbled without turning around to face Duke. *Reduce casualties?* Had Duke heard that right? What kind of experiment were these scientists conducting?

"Yes, there's that," Gilbert said, squatting to look into Duke's face. "We are not bad people, Mr. Dukakis. Though I am sure at first America will brand us as the worst criminals ever. But in the long run, this will save lives and make the world a safer place."

"Like Baptisa made the world a safer place for Petra Oligivich?" Duke said.

"No, that was just a fall. An accident. It had nothing to do with us," Gilbert said, standing up and turning around to face his partner.

"That right, Dr. Baptista?" Duke shot back.

"Some sacrifices are necessary," Baptista mumbled without looking up from his computer.

"Don't tease him, Henri." Gilbert said with a chuckle. "Tell him that the girl just fell."

"She didn't just fall, did she, Baptista?" Duke said.

"Henri?" Gilbert asked, looking at his partner.

"What difference does it make, now? The bomb would have killed her anyway in a few hours."

"Bomb?" Duke exclaimed.

"But you didn't kill her, did you? That would be murder," Gilbert said, looking confused.

"She found out about the weapons-grade plutonium. Sent me an email," Baptista said, continuing to look at his computer screen. "I couldn't take a risk she might ruin the project. I hit her over the head. She was unconscious when I dropped her from the bridge. She never felt a thing."

"I had no idea," Gilbert said, shaking his head.

"Bomb?" Duke repeated. "Are you guys going to bomb something?"

"Just tell him, why don't you?" Baptista said, spinning around in his chair. "We are detonating a nuclear bomb. A bomb that will make this spot uninhabitable for years. We're doing to America what they've been doing to the rest of the world."

"Henri! You make us sound like monsters," Gilbert said, shaking his head. "How do you expect to be understood when you are so vitriolic?"

"Nuclear bomb?" Duke exclaimed. "You must be kidding. This morning you both said you were pacifists. Opposed to nuclear proliferation."

"And we are. We are!" Gilbert exclaimed. "The United States says their nuclear arms are a deterrent to war. And yet they keep building bigger bombs, testing new weapon systems. And more and more countries are obligated to develop nuclear weapons in self-defense. Like that unclaimed explosion today. These countries think it is OK to pollute the South Pacific, destroy the fishery, and make islands uninhabitable because it only affects a few people. Islanders. They don't count. They can't fight back."

Gilbert paced as he talked, looking at the ceiling. He paused and shook his head.

"I'm sorry. I suppose I sound angry too. And I am. But I want you to know this response has been well considered by many intelligent minds. This is not a knee-jerk reaction."

Gilbert ran a finger under his eye, and Duke realized he was crying.

"Many intelligent minds?" Duke said. "There are more people involved in addition to you two?"

"A consortium," Gilbert said, regaining his composure. "There are ten of us, representing eight countries. The rest have flown to New Zealand, which we expect will offer asylum. Henri and I have volunteered to stay behind and detonate."

"Volunteered our lives," Baptista said as he stood up. "That's how important this is to us."

"Let's not dwell on our personal sacrifice," Gilbert said, walking back to his control panel. "So many lives will need to be sacrificed to make a point."

Duke wanted to explode out of his bonds, throw himself across the control table. He had to do something.

"You guys are crazy!" he yelled. He lurched forward with all his power, landing face first on the concrete floor. He flapped around frantically like a fish in the bottom of the boat, yelling, "Hyena haystacks! Cuckoo cocoa! Dodo bird dingdong crazy!"

Baptista stood by observing, as if Duke were in the clutches of an epileptic seizure. "Look who is calling us crazy."

Gilbert shrugged. "I have work to do if you want to move up detonation."

"Hush," Baptista whispered. "I think I heard a car stopping."

"Help!" Duke yelled before Baptista could fall on him and clamp a huge hand over his mouth.

9:58 PM

Dozing in his recliner, Reuben was jostled awake by King's yapping and a commotion of cars outside.

Reuben pulled back the curtain and saw two police cars parked in the neighbor's driveway. A third pulled right up into the front yard. Two shiny black cars were stopped in the middle of the street. Policemen and men in dark clothes with white FBI lettering on the back jumped out of the vehicles and ran toward the house, like a swarm of black flies covering a carcass.

Spotlight beams lit up the porch, and two men pushed through the front door as though it wasn't there.

Reuben hurriedly put on his heavy corduroy coat and knit sock cap. Before he headed out the front door, he tucked King into his pocket. It was snowing harder, and the dark cedars were outlined in white. Warily Reuben walked down his driveway toward the street to get a better view of Gilbert's house. The neighbors across the street were on their porch, and lights were coming on down the street. One by one, the lights in Dr. Gilbert's house came on. Then the lights in the garage popped on.

Two more police cars arrived. The policeman exiting the most recent car came directly toward Reuben with his arms spread.

"I'm going to ask you to go back inside, sir," he said. "We may need to evacuate the area. For now, we need everyone to stay inside their homes."

"But I'm the one who saw it. I guess I should have called the police."

"You saw something suspicious at the Gilbert residence?"

"Yes, I could describe it for you."

The policeman turned Reuben, steering him toward his house.

"I need you to go inside and wait for a police officer. Keep your door locked and only open it for the police. Do you understand?"

"Oh, yes, sir. Right away."

Reuben scurried up his driveway and into his house. As he slammed the door and locked it, he realized he had left the door open when he ventured outside. What if the werewolf had come inside while he was out? He tiptoed down the hall. He went to his Elvis room first. Reuben paused and smiled. He enjoyed this room so much that for an instant, he forgot the werewolf.

He stuck his head cautiously into the hall, looked both ways, and continued to the bedroom. He threw back the closet door and stepped to one side as if he expected a life-size jack-in-the-box to pop out. He got down on his knees and looked under the bed. King took this opportunity to climb out of the coat pocket and run down the hall.

"Come back, boy," Reuben called, but the dog scampered away without slowing down.

Reuben looked into the bathroom and pulled back the shower curtain as apprehensively as a guest at the Bates Motel in *Psycho*.

When he returned to the living room, the dog was on his favorite perch on the back of the sofa, yapping at the commotion outside. It was a good sign. If the werewolf had been in the house, King would know. King was tiny and had only been Reuben's for a few hours, but already Reuben felt like this dog was a buddy he could trust.

Reuben checked the back door. It was locked. He glanced down the dark basement stairs. Could the werewolf be down there? He slammed the door at the top of the stairs and pushed the bolt lock just to be safe.

Just then King's yapping intensified. Reuben hurried to the window and looked out. There were two men in suits standing on his front porch. One looked toward the window and flashed a badge. FBI. Of course. Reuben should have known a werewolf required more than local police. He threw open the door.

"Yes, sir. I should have guessed they would send the best. Come in. Come in. Can I make you some cocoa?"

The two men glanced at each other and shook their heads.

"I'm Fred Wheeler, DOJ. This is agent Samuel Kent. One of the police officers said you had something to report."

"Yes sir, I saw it with my own eyes earlier tonight. At dusk. I should have called you right away."

"What exactly did you see?"

"The thing!" Reuben waved his arms as words failed him.

"Where was this 'thing'?" Wheeler asked, pulling a small notebook out of his pocket. His partner wandered around the room, looking at pictures and magazines.

"In the cedars. I had to look twice. I didn't believe it."

"How big was it?" Bigger than a bread box?"

Reuben chuckled. "That's a good one, sir. It was huge." Reuben held a hand over his head. "Seven feet tall, at least."

"Seven foot?" Was it on a trailer behind a truck?"

"No, it was just standing there. There was a truck in the driveway though. One of those trucks from the A-Lab. The ones that say radioactive. You think that has something to do with how big it is? The radioactivity?"

"No doubt."

Reuben was so intent on his story that he didn't notice when agent Kent wandered down the hall.

"I told the other policeman about the radioactive truck, and he seemed really interested. I should have figured that out myself."

"Another cop was here? When was that?"

"A couple of hours ago. I have his card over here on the fridge. That's where I keep all the important stuff," Reuben said, stepping into the kitchen to retrieve the card. Reuben handed the card to Wheeler, who made a note of the name on his pad and handed it back.

"Did you call the Jordan police?"

"No, sir. He just showed up at my door. He said it wasn't an official visit. He was just looking for a friend of his. Mr. Dukakis from the newspaper. Dukakis gave me a lift home tonight."

"Dukakis was here?"

"Yeah, we've had a busy day," Reuben said, smiling as he picked up the still-yapping dog. "Started out at the movie theater this morning. You heard about the shooting there. And then I brought home this little fella, and turns out he belonged to the movie star Dee Licious. But after I gave him a haircut, she wouldn't have nothing to do with him anymore. Well, that's fine with me. I love you, little King."

Reuben nuzzled the dog against his cheek. "I'd rather have you any day than a thousand dollars. Spoiled little movie star doesn't know a good thing when she has it."

Kent emerged from the hallway shaking his head and making a circular "crazy man" motion beside one ear.

"I was taking little King outside to tinkle when I saw the werewolf. Wouldn't have seen it if it hadn't been for the dog. It's amazing how that worked out, isn't it?"

"Werewolf? You saw a werewolf?"

"Yeah, didn't believe it at first or I would have called you. But I mentioned it to Dukakis and then Detective Cantrell and now the FBI. Guess I really stumbled into something major this time, eh?"

"Let me get this straight. You saw a werewolf standing over by the cedars. A big werewolf. At least seven-foot tall."

"Yeah. It was right after dusk. The full moon was just coming out. You think the television stations will want to talk to me since it's such a big story?"

"No doubt," Wheeler said.

☼

Sharon pulled Duke's car to the side of the dark road, scraping the huge solar panel next to the roadway.

"Shit! I didn't even see that thing there. Don't you think they should put reflectors on them or something?"

"They're solar panels. They're for a sunny day, not a moon-lit night," Becky quipped. "Why did you stop?"

"I thought I heard something coming from that building," Sharon said, opening her car door.

Becky tried her door. It wouldn't budge. It was jammed up against the huge panel. Becky crawled over the seat and emerged from the driver's door.

"I don't hear anything. Wait. There's a sort of hum. Is that the sound of the accelerator running down below? I'll bet that's what that is."

"No, that's something to do with the solar panels," Sharon whispered. "This was different. It was a man yelling. A deep voice. It sounded like Duke."

Becky shook her head. "You remember what I said about getting hysterical?"

"Shhhhh," Sharon said and motioned for Becky to follow her toward the metal building.

It was so dark that no doors or windows were apparent. Becky pulled a small penlight out of her purse, but the beam was too small to illuminate more than a few inches at a time. Sharon pressed an ear against the metal and shrugged. Becky continued her inch-by-inch survey down the side of the building and around the corner. She found a door, the same dark gray of the building. She reached for the knob. It turned.

They were in an open garage. The blue van Reuben had described was parked there. The back doors were open. Sharon peeked inside and shook her head. Becky looked into the passenger compartment and shrugged.

Sharon spied a door across the room and pointed in that direction. The women went to the door, both placing an ear against it. Silence. Becky placed her long, slender fingers over the knob and turned it ever so slightly. She pressed the door open just a crack, and both women peered into the well-lit room beyond. At first they could see only the computers and the control panel beyond. They didn't see anyone there. Then someone stood up from behind the control panel. He had a satisfied smile.

"That should do it," he said. "Just need to run a few checks."

He must have been talking to someone, but they couldn't see who. Becky pushed the door a little farther to expand their view. They couldn't see anyone else, but they could hear a sound in the room, a moaning. Sharon could wait no longer. She threw the door open.

"Where's my husband?"

In an instant, Sharon had the answer to her question. Duke's silver-mummy figure flapped across the floor as if dancing The Worm.

"Duke! Oh, my God! What have they done to you?"

Sharon ran to Duke. Becky rushed in behind Sharon, grabbing Gilbert. She was a head taller than he was and she was determined to hold tight.

There was so much duct tape wrapped around Duke, and he was flopping so furiously, Sharon wasn't sure what to hug. She managed to get him to hold still for an instant, wrapped her arms around him, and started to sob.

"I've been so worried. We couldn't figure out what happened to you."

Sharon found his eyes—those deep amber eyes she loved so much—peeking over a strip of duct tape. His look showed some relief, but there was a fear there greater than any Sharon had ever seen.

"What is it? What's happening?"

Duke moaned. Sharon pulled at the tape wrapped around his head and stuck in his hair.

"I need something to cut this stuff," she said, heading toward the table with the computers. "Hey, you. Got some scissors?"

"Scissors or a knife," Becky said, shaking Gilbert without loosening her hold.

"It won't do any good," Gilbert said. "The process has begun. Nothing can stop it now."

"What process?" Becky asked.

Duke was moaning and flopping on the floor again. Sharon reached into her cloth shoulder bag and pulled out a small manicure set. She returned to Duke with tiny cuticle scissors.

"I'll get you out of that stuff, honey. Just hold still."

Sharon was cutting the strip across Duke's face when his eyes opened wide with alarm. Sharon turned just in time to see a huge hairy man yanking Becky away from Gilbert and throwing her across the floor. Becky was not easily dissuaded. She bounced up and ran back at the man. He growled like a bear as Becky clawed his face.

"Stupid bitch," he said, knocking Becky to the floor and pulling back a hand to hit her again.

"Please, no violence," Gilbert said, his nose twitching.

"Leave her alone, you big oaf!" Sharon yelled. She grabbed her shoulder bag by its long straps and swung it over her head like a whip. Baptista turned to look at her, and the purse caught him on the side of the head. He staggered. Sharon kept swinging the purse, hitting the huge man until he fell backwards against the computer table. He slid to the ground and melted under the table, unconscious and bloody.

Becky sat up. "Wow. What do you have in your purse?"

"Duke's gun," Sharon said, pulling the weapon out with two fingers. "I may not know how to shoot it, but I can swing it."

Gilbert knelt beside his friend. "His nose is broken, and he may have a concussion."

Becky grabbed the gun and pointed it at Gilbert. "What's this process you were talking about?"

"The bomb will detonate in eighteen minutes, twenty-two seconds," Gilbert said, smiling proudly at his control panel. A digital timer in the center of the display counted down the seconds.

"Well, turn it off," Becky said, jabbing the gun into Gilbert's chest.

"I'm afraid that's impossible," the scientist said, smiling more broadly. "I've installed override security and an ignition backup. If this countdown is interrupted, it will trigger another relay. The bomb cannot be stopped."

By this time, Sharon had snipped enough of the duct tape to get a good hold on the strip across Duke's face.

"Sorry, sweetie," she said and gave a quick yank. Duke yelped as the tape once again ripped across his lips and mustache. Sharon touched his lips tenderly and kissed them. They paused just a second to look at each other.

"Nuclear bomb," Duke said. "They've created some nuclear device."

"Nuclear!" Becky exclaimed. She jammed the gun into Gilbert's chest. "You can stop it. I know you can. Do it now!"

Gilbert only smiled.

"Weren't you the one screaming 'no violence' a couple of minutes ago?" Becky shouted, bending down to get her face right next to Gilbert's.

"They've got some fool notion about world justice," Duke announced, wiggling an arm free as Sharon snipped. Together they pulled off his leg bonds.

"We are trying to be responsible and conserve life," Gilbert said with a twitch of his nose. "We could detonate this bomb in downtown Chicago and kill half a million people easily. But out here in the rural area, at night, we expect much lower casualties. Probably only a hundred thousand."

Finally free, Duke strode to the control panel and confronted Gilbert.

"Tell me again what you expect to gain with so *few* casualties," he asked.

"Respect for radiation. The United States has no respect for the long-term effects of the bombs they are building. Now they will know," Gilbert said. "By using ordinary cobalt to make the case of the bomb, we have created a device that will release vaporized cobalt-60 radiation. This will make the area around Chicago uninhabitable for dozens of years. And it will make the US government face up to the responsibilities of dealing with radiation."

"Well, I'll tell you what, Dr. Gilbert," Duke said, glancing over the control panel. "I am not going to stand by and watch your 'process' reach its inevitable conclusion."

Duke emphasized his words by yanking a wire loose.

"No," Gilbert screamed, lunging forward to stop Duke.

"What are you doing?" Sharon squealed, holding her hands over her ears. "You might set it off."

"If I do, we die eighteen minutes sooner," Duke said, pulling another wire loose. Gilbert grabbed Duke's shoulder, but Duke shrugged him off.

"Hold on to him," Duke said to Becky, who wrapped an arm around Gilbert.

"Shouldn't we wait for the bomb squad?" Sharon said, wincing.

"What bomb squad?" Duke said, pulling another wire.

"Please, you don't understand what you are doing," Gilbert protested, trying to wiggle free of Becky's hold.

"Isn't there a phone? Can't we call for help?" Sharon continued. "These computers. They must be on the network. There must be some way to send an email to the main facility."

Sharon rolled the desk chair aside and peered into the computer screen. She pushed a few buttons on the keyboard trying to find the mail program. Suddenly Baptista grabbed her legs from under the table and pulled her to her knees.

"Stop what you are doing or I will break her neck," Baptista said. His hefty arms were wrapped around Sharon. His nose was twisted to one side from Sharon's purse attack, and blood had run down over his lips.

Duke stopped and stared at his wife, held under the table in the clutches of this bloodied madman.

"Let her go or I will blow his head off," Becky said, cocking the revolver as she pressed it against Gilbert's temple.

"Stop it, all of you," Gilbert shouted. "The process is begun. It cannot be stopped. When you pull the wires, you only stop the digital display and data transfer. The relay has kicked in. The bomb will detonate. You are only destroying my scientific record which was being transferred to New Zealand."

Duke stood back and lifted his hands in surrender. "Let her go," he said.

Baptista released his hold, and Sharon scrambled into Duke's arms. Becky released Gilbert but continued to point the gun at the scientists.

"We're leaving," Becky announced. We're going to the headquarters, and no one is going to stop us. Understand?"

The three ran outside, got into their car, and drove a away.

Baptista rose to his feet and put a hand on his buddy's shoulder. "Can you save it?"he said, mopping blood from his lips.

"I think so. He only pulled out a few wires."

"I'll go outside and hold them off as long as I can," Baptista said, heading for the door.

"Henri. You're a scientist. You don't have to become a battering ram."

Baptista stopped and looked at his partner. "No matter how fancy you make the bomb, it's basically just a big fist," he said, raising his immense primal weapon.

Gilbert went to Baptista's side. "I know you. You are a soft, caring man. It must be eating you alive what you did to that Russian girl. All for the project."

Baptista sighed. "It will be over soon."

212

☼

Nick inserted a small plastic card into the slot at the back door of the *Daily News*. At the sound of the buzzer, he opened the door.

It was after ten, and the sports department was in full swing. Stringers as young as high school kids and as old as graying veterans were crowded around terminals and phones, typing, talking loudly, and laughing a lot. "Did you see" and "could you believe" were repeated at every desk, peppered with so many curse words that Nick was embarrassed to walk his wife through the melee.

Nick and Brittany headed to his desk in the center of the newsroom cluster. Brittany sat in Josie's chair at the command center. Nick threw his coat over his chair, glanced at a couple of phone messages that had been left on his desk, and headed toward Hoss on the copy desk.

"How's it going?""

"Don't tell the bosses, but we're hauling in that big 'L' from the Hollywood sign," Hoss said, barely looking up from his computer. "Both of them. Put this one in the big-loss column. Too much going on. We'll never catch up. One of the former mayors went missing, and just a little while ago, an army of cop cars descended on some home in the west end. Haven't figured out what's going on there."

"Can I help?" Nick asked as Brittany joined them.

"Well, maybe your wife would have better luck with the hospital than we did," Hoss said, rolling to his dummy desk and grabbing a sheet of paper where he had scratched some notes. "They've been looking everywhere for Neal Taylor, a former mayor."

"Mr. Taylor used to be the mayor?" Brittany exclaimed.

"From 1956 to '60. He was a war hero back when people prized that kind of stuff," Hoss said, consulting his notes.

"Do you know Taylor?" Nick asked.

"Know of him," Brittany said, shrugging her shoulders. "His wife brought him into the emergency room this morning. You know I can't talk about a patient."

"Well, according to his wife, Kitty Taylor, big society dame, hubby was spitting up blood and the emergency docs were treating him for a bleeding ulcer," Hoss read from his notes. "But he disappeared from the emergency room. Wife holds a press conference. Cops put an APB out on him. Volunteer society dames are putting up posters. And guess what? They find him where missing hubbies are usually found. In the arms of another woman."

"No kidding? Go, Taylor," Nick said.

"Heard it on the police scanner that a man matching the description was found in one of the hospital rooms with an unidentified female," Hoss said, throwing his notes on the desk. "But when Donna called the hospital, they wouldn't tell her bupkis. PR office closed. Patient confidentiality. You know the routine."

"OK. Between Brittany and me, we'll piece together a story for you on the missing mayor. Where's Donna?"

"She just left. Trying to track down that cop convention on the Westside. I sent Page too. He was finishing up in the photo lab. Should have gone home to bed, but hey, this could turn into a page 1 hostage situation or something. No telling what's going on."

"Have you heard from Josie or any of the people looking for Duke?"

"That's another conundrum," Hoss said, rolling back to his computer. "Josie called. Said they found Duke's car and one of his notebooks at some scientist's house. They figured the pair of them had gone out to the A-Lab. That detective Cantrell from the Jordan police called in for Becky. When I said she wasn't here, he asked for Josie or Rudy or Sharon. When I told him none of them had returned, he started cussing like Ditka in the locker room."

☼

Going around a curve, just inside the back entrance to the A-Lab, Rudy's blue Honda Accord slid across the frozen pavement and then returned to the right side of the road.

"Maybe we should call this off tonight," Rudy said. "It's getting too slick to be out here. Let the police find Duke."

"I'm more worried about Becky and Sharon than I am about Duke," Josie said, leaning forward in the passenger seat to get a better view of the road. It was snowing harder now, big lacey flakes that looked too pretty to be dangerous. Off to the right she could easily see the towering headquarters of the A-Lab. Above it the full moon played peek-a-boo with the clouds. Full and bright, then half covered, then gone.

"I know Sharon didn't take Becky back to the office as Tom suggested," Josie continued. "Hoss hadn't heard from them. They are out here someplace, looking for Duke. And then there's your theory that Gilbert is building a bomb. A big bad nuclear bomb. I'm worried about that too."

"Even if I'm right about that, it's probably in the planning stages. It takes months to build something like that, I'll bet."

Josie chuckled.

"What?" Rudy asked.

"I was just thinking how funny it is that we ended up spending the whole day together. This morning, I was planning to avoid you."

"Sorry. Must be the skunk-scented deodorant. I got it on sale."

Josie laughed. "No. I felt embarassed about your call last night. I was afraid I might have hurt your feelings by laughing. I'm terrible about getting the joke sometimes."

"That's my fault. I'm always joking, so people don't know when I'm serious."

"Well, I want to apologize if I seemed rude."

"Forget it."

"I was just surprised. We've known each other so many years and never talked about dating."

"I wanted to ask you out, but it never seemed like the right time," Rudy said, looking straight ahead at the road. "You seemed so vulnerable after your divorce. I didn't want to take advantage. And then you were going through that thing with Duke."

"You know more about me than most people," Josie said, admiring Rudy's profile in the shadows. He was really a nice-looking man. "You've been a good friend to me through so much. And you're a good reporter too."

"Why do I think there's a 'but' coming?"

"It's just that I'm not very good at relationships," Josie said. "I wouldn't want to ruin our friendship by dating."

"That's not true. Relationships are your strong suit. Just because some guy—who will remain nameless—broke your heart and convinced you it was your fault doesn't mean you don't relate well with people. Nothing could be further from the truth."

Rudy took his eyes off the road and looked at Josie a second too long. The car hit a patch of ice and slid sideways.

"That's it! We're going home," Rudy said. "There's no excuse to be out driving on a night like this."

Without waiting for Josie's agreement, he pulled across the road and backed up a little to complete his U-turn.

"What are all these metal boxes in the fields?" Josie asked as the headlights illuminated the unusual crop.

"Solar panels, I think."

As Rudy returned to the roadway, heading home, he continued his thought. "I've watched how you've grown since the divorce. You've accepted the responsibilities of being a single mother and leading the newsroom. You've taken charge. You've encouraged Duke in his sobriety and helped him rebuild his marriage. You've pushed Hoss to give up smoking and accept more responsibility in the newsroom. You spotted Nick's management potential hidden behind those pretty-boy dimples. You don't let Hammond run over you anymore. You've even come up with a way to keep Teasdale under control. You're just amazing. And if I haven't said that before, I should have. I think you are—"

"Stop!" Josie blurted.

215

"No, I mean it," Rudy continued. "You're one of the most fantastic—"

"I mean, stop the car."

Rudy complied as quickly as he dared on the icy pavement.

"I saw the werewolf," Josie said. "Back there by the solar panels."

"Great. A werewolf that feeds on renewable energy sources. That's so much better than being limited to the monthly cycle of the full moon."

"There. That man by the metal building."

"What about him?"

"He's so big. That's the man Mr. Jetter saw. Back up."

"He may be big, but that doesn't make him a werewolf," Rudy said as he backed up toward the building. The man moved toward the car when Rudy stopped. Josie jumped out, hand extended.

"Hi. I'm Josie Braun from the Daily News."

She would stride into a lion's den, smiling and shaking hands, Rudy thought. He walked around the car toward the building. He stayed a good distance away from Josie and the huge man. The man's unruly hair was frosted with snow, making him seem like a mythical creature in *Dungeons and Dragons*. His face was bruised and bloodied like he'd been in a fistfight.

"This is private property," the man said in the curt, official tone a security guard might use.

"I realize that," Josie said. "But I think you might be able to help us. We're looking for one of our reporters. Ormand Dukakis. Have you seen him?"

The man paused, noting Rudy's position on his right, but not taking his eyes off Josie.

"He left twenty minutes ago with a couple of lady friends."

"Which way did he go?"

The man pointed toward the shining headquarters. "You must have just passed him."

"Oh? May I use your phone?" Josie headed toward the light and warmth seeping out of the cracked doorway into the building.

"Just a minute, lady." The man lunged forward, grabbed Josie at the waist with one arm and lifted her off the ground.

"Put me down!" she said as the man deposited her next to the car.

"You'd better go," he said.

Rudy had made it to the door of the building. He pushed it open and shouted, "Duke, are you in here?"

This time the monster man didn't hesitate. He tucked Josie under one arm like a squirming toddler and yanked Rudy into the building.

"More reporters," he announced as he arrived in the control center.

"Good grief," Gilbert said, looking over his panel at them. "How many are assigned to this story?"

"Put me down!" Josie wailed.

Baptista did so, shoving Josie against the support beam in the center of the room. He tried to yank Rudy toward the post too, but Rudy slipped away. Baptista's long arm caught him and pulled him back.

"Sit. Now," Baptista commanded, pushing Rudy to the ground. Rudy sat against the beam, back to back with Josie. Baptista used his knees to press the two in place as he pulled a roll of duct tape out of his coat pocket and started wrapping it around them.

"You'll have to excuse Dr. Baptista," Gilbert said. "He's just discovered duct tape, and he gets a little carried away."

"I recognize you from the paper. You're Dr. Gilbert," Rudy said. "You're the one building a nuclear bomb. That's what Duke figured out, isn't it?"

Gilbert chuckled. "Smart, but a little late. The bomb is built and will detonate in less than five minutes."

Josie gasped. "Duke wouldn't have left if he knew you were planning to detonate a bomb. Where is he? What have you done to him?"

This time Baptista chuckled as he stood up, satisfied the reporters were securely bound to the post. "You think your Duke friend is such a hero, but he's getting as far away as he can. Running for cover. He's not trying to save the world."

"Now, Henri, you don't know that," Gilbert said. "I am surprised he hasn't returned with security agents by now. I expect he alerted people at the headquarters, but they didn't believe him. Or they decided to go underground. That would be a quick and safe choice. Yes, if Snyder is there, he would definitely choose to go underground."

"Did you really make a nuclear bomb?" Rudy asked. "In the paper you were quoted as being opposed to nuclear weapons."

"Let's just say it takes one to stop many. Detonating a nuclear weapon is the only way to convince the United States they must stop the arms race." Gilbert pulled a chair up to the control panel. "I can't answer any more questions now. I don't want to miss any of the readings. This is the critical point."

"How did you get access to the uranium to build a bomb?" Rudy persisted.

Baptista took the rolling chair facing the computer screen. "Plutonium, if you must know. We have our sources"

"The timing seems to be a little behind," Gilbert said, watching his panel. "Must be the circuits that Dukakis unplugged. The control panel is not in sync with the computer.

"Still showing red on the ignition cycle," Baptista said as he studied his computer screen.

"Dear God, protect us," Josie mumbled. "I always wondered what I would do if there was a nuclear attack. Would I go home to be with my family or go to the office to cover the story?"

"Bet you didn't think you'd be tied to a post," Rudy said.

"If I had just left Kevin and those children in the gypsum mine, they would probably be OK. But no, I had to mess with destiny."

"Don't blame yourself. If Gilbert is using a cobalt casing for his bomb, the radiation will last longer than the food in the fallout shelter."

Gilbert smiled. "It sounds like one of our reporters was paying attention in chemistry class."

"Naaa. I just watched *Dr. Strangelove* about a hundred times."

"If only I could be there for Kevin," Josie sobbed. "If only I could hold him. I know the answer to the question now. I would go home."

"Don't spend your final minutes fretting," Rudy whispered in a soothing tone. "You can't control the madness others create. The only thing you can control is what you think."

"I believe in prayer," Josie said. "I know God is in charge. I try to give him all my worries and regrets. But even after I pray, I can't stop worrying about Kevin."

"Prayer is a good beginning," Rudy agreed. "Worry is wasted energy. Spend your final moments thinking happy thoughts. Memories of good times. Dreams of what could be."

"Ignition cycle shows green," Baptista announced.

"One minute," Gilbert echoed.

"Are you thinking happy thoughts?" Rudy whispered.

"I am thinking about us," Josie replied.

"Us?"

"I've been thinking about us all day," she continued. "Ever since you suggested it last night. You and me. Married. Raising Kevin together. Maybe a little girl too."

"I've been thinking about us too," Rudy said, desperately stretching his fingers against the duct tape to stroke Josie's hand. "I've been thinking how much fun it would be to build a life together."

"We should have done that a long time ago. I don't know why I didn't understand that before."

"No regrets. Only positive thoughts. Like playing foosball with Kevin."

"Reading bedtime stories."

"Going to museums together."

"Thanksgiving dinner. Christmas morning."

"You and me at his high school graduation."

"His wedding. His babies. Our grandchildren."

"Just the two of us slow dancing in the kitchen."

Josie smiled. "Thank you, Rudy, for giving me happy thoughts."

"I'm sorry I waited so long to ask you out."

"No regrets, remember?"

"All green!" Baptista shouted.

Gilbert smiled at his partner. "Ignition in five, four, three—"

Rudy clutched Josie's hand. "I love you," they said in unison and smiled in opposite directions.

11:01 PM

"Something's wrong," Baptisa said, clicking keys on his computer.

"The panel shows ignition complete, countdown over," Gilbert said. His nose was twitching.

"Maybe it's the relay program."

"If it failed, another backup would have taken over."

Gilbert and Baptista fiddled frantically with computer keys and electric switches. One minute passed, then another.

"Shit! Not knowing is worse than knowing," Rudy said finally.

"Please, God. We know you're in charge. Protect us," Josie said.

"There must be a design flaw in the ignition system," Gilbert mumbled. His nose twitched continuously like an inquisitive bunny.

Baptista turned to his partner. "No, it was a beautiful design. Everyone said so. Perfect. The error must be in the monitoring program."

"I've failed!" Gilbert exclaimed, throwing his hands up. "Something this important, and I failed."

"Nonsense," Baptista said, patting his friend on the back. "This is why they do nuclear tests. Computer models are not 100 percent accurate. Consider this the first test of your design."

"First test?" Gilbert said, jumping to his feet. "We won't get a second chance. I gave up my family for this, Henri."

"We'll leave the country," Baptista said. "I booked two tickets for us on the morning flight out of O'Hare just in case something went wrong."

"You suspected something was wrong with the design, didn't you? You knew it was going to be a failure!"

"No, of course not. It was a perfect design, Sam. But it is good science to keep your options open."

"How will we get out of here? The van will attract too much attention. Police are bound to set up a roadblock."

"Lucky for us this nice young couple brought us a snappy little Honda. And I just happened to snag these keys from his pocket," Baptista said, holding up a silver key with a Mickey Mouse fob.

"Hey, what's going to happen to us?" Rudy said, pulling against the tape.

"Don't worry. Your hero, Dukakis, probably is on the way," Baptista said. Gilbert and Baptista took their coats off hooks on the wall and disappeared out the door.

"I don't understand," Josie said. "Is there going to be an explosion or not?"

"It looks like we have a fission fizzle," Rudy said.

"Or is it fusion confusion?" Josie shot back.

☼

The parking lot along the riverfront was empty when Eric Thomas pulled his old rusted Chevy into a parking spot. It was after eleven at night, and downtown Jordan didn't have much nightlife. Jennifer Dukakis and three other college girls jumped out of the car. Three more cars pulled into the lot, each one filled with students laughing and chattering.

Carolyn Cantrell corralled the group.

"Now we are agreed that we will all behave like ladies and gentlemen. The point is to thank Mr. Barrows for saving two of our lead characters from their own foolish judgment."

Some in the group ribbed Jennifer and Eric, but they didn't seem to mind. Singing for Barrows had been Jennifer's idea. Cantrell recognized the suggestion as an ideal bonding experience for her cast. Theater is all about bonding. The relationship between the cast members creates the fourth wall. It wraps them in a fantasy world and makes that world come to life. It protects them from the disappointment of half-empty theaters and lackluster applause.

And Cantrell knew of Barrows' work at the community center. Several of her theater students over the years had been introduced to music through Barrows' community band. Singing a song to thank him was a good idea. Besides, if anyone saw their public performance, it would be good advertisement for the show.

The young people filed out onto the bridge, lining up opposite the tender's station so he would be able to see them easily through his windows. Eric banged on the tender's door and called out his name. Then Cantrell turned on the boom box at top volume. Snow was falling in big lacey flakes. A winter tune might have seemed appropriate, but they had decided to sing the first song in *Kiss Me, Kate*.

One boy stepped forward and sang, "Another opening, another show."

A second boy joined in with "In Philly, Boston, or Baltimo'."

"A chance for stage folks to say hello," one of the girls sang.

"Another opening of another show," the three sang together.

Soon the others joined in until sixteen young people raised their voices. Stan was watching them from the window. Despite the winter chill and snow flurries, he opened the window, stuck his head out, and waved.

They sang out, shuffling back and forth along the sidewalk in a modified version of their dance routine. Barrows smiled, recognizing Jennifer and Eric among his serenaders. An occasional car came by, crossing the bridge slowly, trying to hear what the crowd of kids was up to.

By the time the song ended, Barrows was at the door applauding. The students filed by to shake his hand and invite him to the show. Some walked out onto the bridge to enjoy the moonlit view. They promised to leave the bridge immediately if they heard the warning bell and swore they would never try "bridge riding."

☼

Minutes after Gilbert and Baptista left, Rudy and Josie heard the commotion of cars arriving, doors slamming and several voices talking at once. Police officers with guns drawn burst into the room. They fanned out, crouching, prodding, searching as if the bare furnishings hid something heinous. No one paid any attention to the elephant—Josie and Rudy—in the middle of the room.

Fred Wheeler—without gun drawn—followed the armed intruders with Duke, Tom Cantrell, and A-Lab director Brad Snyder close behind.

"Josie! Rudy! What are you doing here?" Duke exclaimed.

"We came to rescue you," Josie announced proudly.

Duke and Wheeler exchanged glances and shook their heads.

"Gee, thanks," Duke said, kneeling to cut the tape with his handy pocket knife.

"Don't let him fool ya," Sharon said as she and Becky walked in. "He was a lot more thankful an hour ago."

"I thought I told you to stay in the car," Duke said to his wife without looking up.

"I told all of you to stay out of it," Wheeler added. "What happened to Baptista and Gilbert?"

"They escaped in my car," Rudy said, standing free of his bonds. He reached a hand down to assist Josie. When their eyes met, everyone else in the room disappeared. Josie leaped into his arms, and they kissed passionately.

The rest of the people in the room stared in stunned silence.

"Whoa! I think we missed something," Becky said.

"Purple polka-dotted peacock piddle!" Duke added.

Rudy threw his hands up in the air. "We're alive!"

Josie threw hers up as well: "And we're in love!"

Rudy spun her around. Then they turned to see everyone staring at them.

"We never thought we would see any of you again!" Rudy exclaimed.

Josie began hugging everyone in sight. "Sharon! Becky! I was so worried about you. Duke! I was afraid you'd been killed. Mr. Wheeler. Thanks for your help!"

Wheeler seemed taken aback by Josie's enthusiastic embrace.

"Enough of this smaltzy stuff," he said, pulling away. "Everyone out! We've got a bomb to dismantle. Everyone out. Go home. Now."

"But they took my car," Rudy said, his arm firmly around Josie.

"You two can ride with us," Sharon said. "Duke will want to go back to the office to finish his story."

"Is there time?" Josie asked, looking at her watch. It was only a quarter past eleven. The last twenty minutes had seemed like hours. It would be tight to make a midnight deadline, but Duke could do it. She looked over her shoulder. He had his pen and notebook in hand and was talking with Wheeler.

"I don't think you can honestly say it was a nuclear weapon," Wheeler said. "Just say they were attempting to set off a bomb on the A-Lab property. The nuclear capability was an exaggeration. Ego. A couple of rogue scientists couldn't pull off that kind device."

"They were pretty convincing," Duke said. "They said the bomb could kill a hundred thousand."

"Do you really want to start that kind of panic with the public?" Wheeler asked. "It was a dud. Leave it at that."

"Especially since they will be in jail by morning," Cantrell added. "We've put out an APB for Rudy's Honda. They won't get far."

Two figures in hazard suits entered the room.

"Come on, clear the area," Wheeler said and started pushing everyone toward the door. "These guys have work to do."

On the way out, Duke stopped Snyder.

"I still don't understand about the buffalo," he said. "Were they dying because of the increased radiation?"

Snyder laughed. "Radiation? Gilbert and Baptista brought in some weapons-grade plutonium that caused a minor increase in the radiation level of the area. This increase was noted by our daily monitoring and set off red flags for me. Before Petra Oligivich died, she sent me an email about the plutonium shipment she had discovered. I didn't find the email until after she was dead. You should give her the credit. She's the real heroine. She was just a kid. A Russian kid at that. But she spotted something that seemed wrong. Her email led me to call in federal agents. But at no time was the radiation anywhere near a dangerous level. Certainly not enough to kill a buffalo."

"So why were they dying?"

"Old age? The cold? Everything dies, Mr. Dukakis." Snyder tried to walk away, but Duke grabbed his elbow.

"Sorry. I'm not buying," Duke said. "You shipped the buffalo south for some reason."

Snyder glanced around to be sure he wasn't overheard. "It was just a precaution, totally unrelated to the radiation issue. There's a situation developing in England right now. One of the scientists alerted me last week. Some illness among the cattle. Possibly contagious. It may affect the meat. British tabloids are calling it "Mad Cow" disease. When you became concerned over two dead buffalo, I removed the animals to a private farm just in case our herd was found to have this bovine malady."

Becky followed Cantrell to his city-issued beige Taurus.

"You should have seen Becky with a gun," Sharon told Tom. "She was a force to be reckoned with. 'Let her go or I'll blow his head off.' She was tough!"

"Yeah, she was just lucky those scientists don't know much about guns," Duke added with a laugh. "She didn't even have a clip in it. She was threatening everybody with an empty gun."

Tom pulled Becky close and kissed her cheek. "Maybe we'll have a few gun-safety lessons," he said.

"Sharon is the one who needs safety lessons," Becky said. "You should see her swing a purse."

"Learned it from the girls in junior high. They can clear a room."

"So, you going to go chase those scientists and rescue Rudy's car?" Duke asked Tom.

He was still snuggling with Becky. "No, I'm off duty. Let the county cops chase mad scientists. We're heading home."

"To our place," Becky added.

Rudy and Josie had skipped outside ahead of the rest. They were dancing in the street, tasting snowflakes like they had never seen them before.

"They really are in love," Sharon said to Duke. "Reminds me of the way we were in college, hyper-aware of every sensation."

Duke hugged his wife. "Should we tell them it only gets better with time?"

Sharon squeezed him back. "They'd never believe us."

As the cars left, Wheeler and Snyder walked toward the black Lincoln assigned to the federal agents.

"So, do you think Gilbert and Baptista could have pulled it off? A real atomic bomb?" Wheeler asked.

"If Gilbert hadn't programmed the ignition system into a network computer, we would have never been able to stop them," Snyder said. "Thank goodness computer brains way beyond my understanding were able to program a way to fool the computer. Convince it the ignition had been successful. If we'd tried to stop it any other way, the backup systems would have taken over. We'd all be an inkblot in history by now."

Wheeler chuckled. "Guess these new-fangled computers might come in handy after all."

☼

Duke and Sharon went directly to the office. It would be tight to get anything written in time for the midnight deadline. Duke rewrote the lead story about Petra Oligivich, with Snyder calling her a heroine. He added that police were looking for two A-Lab scientists who in had attempted to detonate a bomb at the facility and were suspected of killing Oligivich..

While Duke typed, Josie worked with Hoss to figure out how to accommodate the additional copy.

Sharon called home to see if Jennifer was there. When there was no answer, she sat with Brittany discussing the opening performance. Nick went to the back shop to help Hoss clear the pages as they were pasted up. Rudy camped out by the police scanner, listening to the APB on his car.

"Is this going on my record?" he asked, turning up the radio to listen. "When I get my car back, will my license number be in some 'suspicious vehicle' file?"

Deputies Edwards and Sanders were listening to the APB in their car. The lockdown of the A-Lab had ended as abruptly as it had begun. Edwards and Sanders were relieved of guard duty and returned to their usual patrol.

"Did they say Dr. Baptista and Dr. Gilbert?" Sanders asked after the radio announcement.

"Yep," Edwards said, making a note of the license number on his pad. "The same two suspicious characters that showed up at the A-Lab tonight. The van with the monkey in the back. I knew they were up to something. Especially when a Jordan cop came by looking for them. Now the whole state is after them."

"Wonder what they did?" Sanders asked.

"Can't trust those foreign scientists," Edwards said. "Way too many foreign scientists working at that Accelerator Lab. Just looking for trouble."

Sanders smiled. His partner wasn't a bad sort. He was a good cop. Alert. Dependable. But a little distrustful of folks.

"I'm ready for a break," Sanders said. "Starting at seven is going to make for a long night. How 'bout we stop by the Pilot and see Lizzie a little early tonight?"

When they pulled into station, a large camper was fueling up, and the deputies didn't see beyond it. Sanders headed inside, intent on sweet black coffee and powdered sugar donuts. Edwards patrolled the exterior of the station on foot before going inside, as was his habit. That's when he saw the 1985 blue Honda at the far pump. He didn't recognize the little man in the flap-eared hunting cap who was manning the nozzle on the passenger's side. But behind the wheel he could see the expansive shoulders of a long-haired figure much too big for such a small car. The license plate rang a bell. He was certain that was the number he had jotted down.

"Halt, police," he shouted as he drew his gun.

The little man looked up, dropped the gas nozzle and jumped into the car. The Honda pulled out in such a hurry, it almost struck a woman returning to the camper with a poodle on a leash.

Edwards dropped to one knee and shot at the Honda, breaking the rear window. Sanders dropped his coffee and tore out the door.

"It's them! The mad scientists! They're getting away!" Edwards yelled as he ran for the cruiser.

Sanders jumped behind the wheel and peeled onto County Road 17 heading east. Edwards radioed into dispatch with the Honda's location. They were in farm country, west of Jordan. It was so flat, they could see the taillights of the Honda even though it was quite a distance ahead.

"He's probably heading for the interstate," Edwards said into his radio.

"Roger that."

Soon the radio was buzzing with cars calling in their locations, roadblock plans being coordinated.

Tom Cantrell was also on County Road 17, not far away, about to turn onto the unpaved road that led to Becky's farm. If he had been alone in the car, he wouldn't have hesitated to join the chase, but he looked over at Becky.

"That's not far from us," he said.

She paused only a second. "I've had enough adrenaline for one day," she said. "Let them catch the crooks without you tonight. I don't want to chase stories anymore. I want to chase you."

"I'm already caught," Tom said as he turned onto the gravel road.

Rudy also heard the chatter on the police scanner.

"The chase is on," he announced to the newsroom. "Deputies are chasing my poor little car on County Road 17 heading toward the interstate."

"I left my purse in that car," Josie said, joining others gathered around the scanner. "I hope the chase doesn't end in a fiery crash."

"Me too," Rudy exclaimed. "My car's worth a whole lot more than your purse."

"But your car is insured," Josie teased.

Two state police cars blocked the entrance ramp to the interstate, so Baptista veered onto Lincoln Road, heading into Jordan. City traffic proved to be an asset for the low-profile Honda, which could slip out of sight behind a truck or van. The Honda weaved in and out of traffic on the busy Lincoln Road lined with fast-food restaurants and too many Friday night partiers.

"Damn! I've lost them," Sanders said, slowing down. Although he was running with lights and siren, he kept a close eye on other motorists. There were just too many people on the road. You couldn't trust that everyone would yield the right-of-way.

Two more city squads had joined the chase, and soon someone spotted the Honda on Jackson.

"He's headed right downtown," Edwards said.

"His best bet to shake us. He could slip into a parking garage. Change cars. We'd never find him," Sanders said, turning onto a cross street, trying to catch up to the others.

"How does a nuclear physicist learn to drive like that?"

"Video games."

Five police cars were converging on Baptista. He could see the red lights flashing in his rearview mirror, up ahead, and off to his left. He charged through a red light at a busy intersection, causing two other cars to collide and block two of the police cars. Then he turned to the right, going east on the westbound Rose Street. Oncoming traffic parted like the Red Sea, running up onto sidewalks and hitting parked cars. But Baptista didn't sway. He continued heading downtown the wrong way on a one-way street.

"Oh, my poor baby car!" Rudy exclaimed when the police scanner reported the Honda was threading through wrong-way traffic.

Stan Barrows was listening to the police chase on his scanner. When the bridge tenders realized the chase was headed in their direction, they knew exactly what they must do. It wouldn't be the first time the tenders had coordinated a bridge raising for something other than river traffic.

The bridge bells clanged a warning. The red-striped gates came down. Almost in unison, the five bridges started going up, making an impenetrable wall along the river. All roads into Jordan were effectively closed.

Baptista saw the gate coming down. He saw the bridge going up.

"Go for it," Gilbert said. "What have we got to lose?"

Baptista floored the accelerator. The little Honda gave as much power as it had. It burst through the gate and onto the rising bridge.

Barrows saw the wrong-way car land on the bridge. In any other situation he would have released his grip on the control. Stopped the bridge's ascent. It might make it possible for the car to leap the bridge and get away. But the car might also fall into the river, blocking barge traffic. Barrows didn't have to consider his options. He held on to the control and the bridge floor continued to move up.

The little Honda's wheels spun forward, losing speed as the incline increased. It hung suspended for a second, the wheels spinning forward, gravity pulling backward. Then, with the bridge fully erect, gravity won. The little car slid backwards into the base of the bridge. The car hit the gap in the bridge floor with a thundering crash. It flipped over onto its top, smashing into the concrete supports. Flattened, it slid down under the bridge, the rear wheels in the river, the squashed passenger compartment leaning against the concrete base of the bridge.

"Oh, my baby car," Rudy moaned when the Honda's fate was reported on the police scanner.

"Oh, my purse," Josie wailed.

"Oh, my story!" Duke complained. "I just finished, and now I'll have to rewrite it again!"

Valentine's Day
Saturday
February 14
1987

12:01AM

Instead of news or a police scanner, the radio on Becky's bedside table played Smokey Robinson's "Being With You." For Tom and Becky, the world didn't reach beyond the walls of that room.

After the hectic day, they wanted nothing more than complete immersion. First Becky rubbed Tom's muscled back. Her long black fingers kneaded his soft honey brown flesh, pressing deep, squeezing out the tension. Then she lay across her bed on her belly as he relaxed her long, lean legs, starting with tender foot massage. When her toes were tingly, he extended long, rhythmic strokes up her calves, wandering higher and higher over her thighs.

Soon neither of them could contain their desires. They intertwined in hot, sweaty lovemaking. When he was spent, Tom rolled out of the bed and headed for the kitchen. He returned with two cold beers. But the bed was empty. Becky had already slipped into the shower. It was becoming their pattern. *Lovers always develop patterns*, Tom thought as he set one of the beers on the table next to the radio. DeBarge's "Rhythm of the Night" was playing.

He took long, greedy pulls from the bottle as he stood looking out the window. The snow had stopped, but the wind still whipped across the flat fields. Gusts of white floated across the landscape like strokes of an artist's brush. Becky came up behind him silently, surprising him with a kiss on the back of his neck. She wrapped her arms around his chest and pressed her body into the hollow of his back. He shivered.

"It's beautiful, isn't it?" she said, resting her chin on his shoulder and looking out at the winter scene.

"Gorgeous," Tom said, slipping around so he faced Becky. They kissed again and then embraced for a long minute before Becky reached for the beer on the nightstand. She upended the bottle and took a big gulp. Drips dribbled over her lips. She brushed the back of her hand across her mouth and then giggled at the unladylike gesture. She handed the beer to Tom, and he took a swig. His was already empty. Sharing the second beer was another part of their pattern.

"So, are you moving in this weekend?" Becky said, looking at Tom. Their dark brown eyes were so similar, it was like looking into a mirror.

"Moving? ... I don't know," Tom replied in a throaty whisper.

"Come on. Maybe just a suitcase or two at first. I'll clear out some drawers for you. We can get you settled in. Then maybe have your mom and Linda over for dinner on Sunday. I make a mean chili."

"Mom!" Tom exclaimed. "We have to go to the play tomorrow. She's going to be so pissed that we didn't see it tonight."

"We can all go together to the Sunday afternoon performance. Wouldn't it be wonderful to see the show with your mom? She could tell us all the backstage stories. Brag a little. And then we'll come here afterwards for chili. I want your mom to see the place. She needs to imagine you living here. With me. Can't you imagine it, Tom?"

"Of course, I can," Tom said, then released a big sigh. "It's just—"

Becky placed a finger on his lips. "Shut up and kiss me."

☼

Duke was typing away on another rewrite of the A-Lab story. Hoss would be making over the paper anyway at 1:00 a.m. to get in some late sports scores. He could accommodate a new version of the lead story, but Duke would have to squeeze it into the same length.

Police had been able to rescue Baptista and Gilbert from the crushed car, but both were in critical condition. Duke was hoping he would be able to get an interview with one of the scientists sometime Saturday for the Sunday paper. They would be angry that the Saturday story used Wheeler's description of their bomb as a "dud." Duke wanted to include some of the scientists' comments about teaching the United States about the dangers of nuclear weapons. None of that fit into the story for Saturday's paper.

Sharon sat nearby reading an early copy of the Saturday paper. When Duke's phone rang, she grabbed it.

"Mom? What are you doing at the newspaper office? Is Dad there?"

"Naturally your father is here," Sharon replied. "Where are you?"

"I came home at midnight and the house was dark. I was worried sick about you. When you didn't come backstage after the play, I couldn't figure out where you went."

"You know your dad. He got pulled into a story." Sharon smiled at her husband who was so engrossed in his writing that he didn't even look up. "But we'll be at tomorrow's performance. I promise."

"You mean you didn't even see the play?"

"It's complicated. But where were you? I called the house a half hour ago and no one answered."

"We were downtown. We went to serenade Mr. Barrows, one of the bridge tenders. The whole cast practically. And Mom, the most amazing thing happened. There was this car chase, and this car rammed the gate and went out onto the bridge when it was halfway up. Then it slid back down into a heap. It was awesome!"

"I know. That's part of the story your dad is working on."

"Were you there?"

"No, we followed it on the police scanner."

"Oh, Daddy never gets to do anything really exciting. He gets everything secondhand."

"Not everything."

☼

Nick and Brittany chattered all the way home. So much had happened on this day, so much they hadn't had time to tell each other before. Brittany told about the strange power outage in the trauma room that morning. Nick described the optical illusion created by the vapor lights in the fog, how the phones started ringing with people calling in who imagined everything from the second coming to a nuclear holocaust.

The tales continued as they went up the stairs to their second-floor apartment. Nick poured two glasses of orange juice as Brittany told about the confusion over the identity of Peter Hampton, and then got into details of former Mayor Neal Taylor.

"Police said he went home with his wife," Nick said as they went into the bedroom and got ready for bed.

"That must be hard for a wife to accept," Brittany said.

"Yeah. Finding your husband in the arms of another woman. And the whole world knowing."

"Not that. But watching the man you've loved and lived with for so many years losing his mind."

"Too many more days like this one, and I might go over the edge," Nick said, slipping into bed.

Brittany crawled in beside him, resting her head on his shoulder. Nick turned off the bedside lamp. They just lay there, saying nothing, comfy together in the dark. All the stories of the day seemed to fade away like sandcastles washed away by the surf.

Brittany broke the silence. "You know, I realized there was a full moon that Friday the 13th when Scotty died."

"Yeah, I figured that out too," Nick said, squeezing his wife's shoulder

"You don't have to try to protect me," Brittany continued. "I think about Scotty every now and then. Less since we got married. Our marriage is different. You're not just a stand-in for another softball player. The pinch hitter. You and I have our own relationship. And it's good."

"Very good," Nick said, smiling.

"But Scotty didn't die because the full moon happened to converge with some date on the calendar," Brittany said, sitting up to get a good look at her husband. "That's ridiculous. You're too smart to believe in such nonsense."

"It's nonsense, I agree," Nick said, reaching for Brittany and pulling her down for a kiss. "There's a lot of nonsense we accept every day. Like now that it's after midnight, it's Valentine's Day. A day for lovers. It's just part of the game."

"OK. As long as you realize the difference."

"If it matters that much to you, I'll never mention the full moon or Friday the 13th again."

"That sounds like your promise to always put the lid down on the toilet."

"I put it down—sometimes."

"I know I sound like a nag, but I don't want you teaching our kids silly superstitions."

"Our kids?"

"It's time we started thinking about the kind of parents we will be. The kind of kids we'll raise. It's important."

"Yes, it's important," Nick said, nestling against Brittany's head on his shoulder. "I want to be the kind of dad who teaches his son to put the lid down on the toilet and to load the dishwasher after dinner. I want to teach my daughter to fish. And I want to take their mother dancing, even when it's not Valentine's Day."

Brittany snuggled closer. "You're such a smooth talker."

"I try."

☼

It was snowing, but Rudy and Josie dawdled along the walkway beside the Des Plaines River. A tow truck was on the bridge trying to haul up Rudy's car. They knew the car had been totaled, but they hoped the tow truck driver could retrieve Josie's purse from the wreckage.

Although snow was sticking to the pavement, they were walking on air. Neither one could imagine sleeping or even going back to their separate lives. A whole new world had opened up. The world of them as a couple.

They had made out in the backseat of Duke's Pontiac all the way back to the office, like teenagers who had just discovered French kissing. Yet neither seemed ready to rush to the next step. So they walked along the river, hand in hand, just trying to get used to this new excitement they felt.

"It's like a fantasy world," Josie said. "It's like a fairy godmother waved her magic wand, and now I'm Cinderella."

"Maybe it was Cupid's arrow," Rudy said. "It's Valentine's Day, you know. I have this pain in the pit of my stomach. Must be love."

233

Josie shoved his shoulder. "You're making fun of me!"

"Maybe a little."

They walked on down the pathway, lit by old-fashioned streetlights. A ribbon of moonlight danced on the river.

"Do you think we are going to wake up in the morning the same grouchy, selfish people we were yesterday?" Josie asked.

"You weren't that grouchy," Rudy said, pulling Josie into his arms for a kiss. During the embrace, Josie let her fingers explore Rudy's thick, auburn hair. She giggled. "Your hair is longer than mine."

"You just noticed that?"

"I knew what it looked like, but I never imagined how it felt. It's so thick and luxurious."

They were kissing again when they heard the crunch and pop of steel scraping concrete. They bent over the railing to watch as the tow truck pulled the wreckage free from its resting place. The remnants of Rudy's car dangled from a hook.

"I'm sorry about your car," Josie said, rubbing Rudy's back.

Rudy shook his head. "It doesn't matter. When I think what we almost lost yesterday. First Kevin. And then the world as we know it. Losing a car is nothing."

"It does reorder your priorities."

"Yeah. I've been thinking. If our relationship is going to be a problem at work, I'll look for another job."

"We'll talk to Hammond on Monday," Josie said. "See what he thinks. The fantasy world might return to rotten reality pretty quickly."

"No, not now," Rudy said, wrapping his arms around Josie. "We've imagined our future together. Nothing can take that away from us."

"Imagined. That's the operative word. It's like the way I imagined the world when I was in fifth grade. I used to write 'Mrs. Raymond Selfridge' on line after line of my notebook paper."

"Raymond Selfridge?"

"He sat behind me in fifth grade. We were going to have six kids. Of course, I never told him that. But in my mind I imagined we'd live happily ever after. Somewhere along the line, I lost the ability to believe in happily ever after. Until a few hours ago. Now I believe again."

"Facing death can be a life-changing experience."

"No, you are the life-changing experience," Josie exclaimed. "We could have spent our last minutes consumed with mushroom clouds and burnt flesh and Armageddon. Instead, you filled my mind with fabulous fantasies of forever."

Rudy pulled Josie closer. "And you shall have it. Every minute of it. To the very best of my ability."

Discussion Questions

1. More than 400 years before Christ, Aristotle identified the lunar effect. He believed certain mental problems were aggravated by the full moon. The words "lunatic" and "lunacy" come from "luna," the Latin word for moon. Do you agree with Aristotle that the moon causes crazy behavior? Can you cite examples from your experience?

2. Fear of Friday the 13th is called friggatriskaidekaphobia. It is one of the most common superstitions. It is said to cost hundreds of thousands of dollars each year in lost business, even though there is little reputable documentation for that claim. Have you had any experiences with bad luck on Friday the 13th?

3. Although Hoss doesn't believe in superstitions, he believes human nature leads to more incidents in superstitious situations, such as the full moon or Friday the 13th. (Page 23) Things go wrong because people expect it. Would you agree?

4. *Full Moon Friday* is dedicated to "All the lonely people." Several of the unusual characters in the book are also alone for one reason or another. Do you think there is a connection between loneliness and crazy behavior?

5. Duke tells Jennifer that people who go against the rules not only put themselves at risk, but cost the whole community. (Page 7) Do you think that's true? In another lesson (Page 156) he says if people get to know each other better, they will discover common ground. Do you agree?

6. Josie often has idealistic expectations. She wants romantic love. She wants her son to eat his cereal with a spoon and a bowl of milk and wear the hood on his coat. Should she settle for less?

7. Becky is a risk taker. She wants a strong relationship with Tom and risks calling his mother in the middle of the night. (Page 17) She also steals the film from a camera in evidence. (Page 87) Her ploys are successful, but such chances could backfire. Does she go too far?

8. Tom is conflicted about his feelings for Becky. He wants her desperately but he is afraid to lose control. Did you ever want something so badly it scared you? Josie has a similar conflict over Rudy. She admires him as a friend, but committing to love would open her to pain. Can such fears ever be overcome?

9. Rudy deals with problems by making jokes. How does he cope when the situation is too serious for laughter? Is his positive attitude a healthy approach or just another means of escape?

10. Baptista and Gilbert propose an extreme solution to what they perceive as an international problem. Are they "mad scientists" or simply expressing a different political point of view?

About the Author

After more than 30 years working for newspapers in four states, Sue Merrell retired in 2009 to write books. The Jordan Daily News series is inspired by her career. She is the mother of one (very talented) grown son and lives on a lake in Michigan with her psycho cat. She spends her winters in the Florida Keys with an even crazier fisherman.

You can follow her blog at suemerrellbooks.com

Made in the USA
Charleston, SC
07 June 2014